Slave to Fashion

Slave to Fashion

A NOVEL

REBECCA CAMPBELL

BALLANTINE BOOKS • NEW YORK

Slave to Fashion is a work of fiction, and all of the events, situations, incidents, and dialogues contained in it are products of the author's imagination. Other than those well-known persons to whom references are made that are incidental to the plot, the characters in the work are creations of the author, and any resemblance to actual persons, living or dead, is entirely coincidental. Where the names of actual persons are mentioned, the situations, occurrences, and descriptions relating to them, and any statements and dialogues that may be attributed to them, are completely fictional and are not to be construed as real.

2005 Ballantine Books Mass Market Edition

Copyright © 2002 by Rebecca Campbell

Published in the United States by Ballantine Books, an imprint of The Random House Publishing Group, a division of Random House, Inc., New York, and simultaneously in Canada by Random House of Canada Limited, Toronto.

Ballantine and colophon are registered trademarks of Random House, Inc.

Originally published in hardcover in 2002 by Random House, an imprint of the Random House Publishing Group, a division of Random House, Inc., and in the United Kingdom by HarperCollins Ltd., London, as *The Favours and Fortunes of Katie Castle*.

ISBN 0-345-47818-5

Printed in the United States of America

Ballantine Books website address: www.ballantinebooks.com

OPM   9   8   7   6   5   4   3   2   1

To my husband, Anthony,
who provided much of the philosophy,
many of the jokes, and all of the semicolons.

Thanks also to Stephanie Cabot and Tim Farrell
for their expert help and guidance.

The last and best Cure of Love Melancholy,
is, to let them have their Desire.

—ROBERT BURTON, The Anatomy of Melancholy

But I'm always true to you, darlin', in my fashion,
Yes I'm always true to you, darlin', in my way.

—COLE PORTER, Kiss Me, Kate

PART ONE

The Razing
of Katie Castle

CHAPTER 1

The Way We Were

At five past six, every day, the same question:

"Katie, what have you *done*?"

For some people that might have been a question filled with foreboding. You know, what have you done with your *life;* or look what you've screwed up *now*. But from me, at this time, it always got the same answer, a smart answer:

"Made coffee, chatted to the girls, tried (and failed) to make the printer print, had my nails done next door at the N.Y. Nail Bar, went for a latte at Gino's (flashed my second-best smile at the divine boy Dante, but I wouldn't tell *Penny* that), chatted some more to the girls, thought about the collection, phoned the factory (why *can't* they learn to speak English?), got a sandwich from Cranks, puked it up in the bog, had a spat with the French, sent reminders to Harvey Nicks and the new shop in Harrogate. Just the usual."

And Penny, breathing exasperation into the phone, always came back with, "You know exactly what I mean. What did you *do*?"

And so I'd give up. "Three and a half."

"Not bad for a Tuesday."

"Bloody good for a Tuesday. But today's Wednesday."

"Well, not bad for a Wednesday, either. What did you say you did?"

"*Three and a half.*"

"And what about Beeching Place?"

"Just one and a half."

"Oh. Still, that's . . . six thousand for the two shops."

"Five."

"You know I'm no good at fractions. What did you say you did?"

The miracle is that I managed to stay sane for so long.

I suppose when I first went to work for Penny she was pretty good. After all, she'd built up Penny Moss from not much more than a market stall into a perfectly respectable business, a business that people had almost heard of, even if they sometimes got us mixed up with Ronit Zilkha, or Caroline Charles, or, heaven forfend, Paul Costelloe. Two shops and a wholesale side that had taken off and was cruising at a comfortable altitude. People had worn our clothes on daytime telly. Penny, conspicuously *without* Hugh, had been in *Hello!*. Well, okay, *OK!* But, as Penny pointed out to anyone who'd listen, it's got a bigger circulation anyway. A cabinet minister wore one of our suits at the party conference (a coffee-tussah-silk affair, like a funked-up Chanel) and, for the first time, looked more feminine than her male colleagues. Professional women who want to look chic and chic women who want to look professional wear our clothes. The next time you're at a wedding, look around you. There, among the neuralgic pink and monkey-puke yellow, you'll see our clothes: subtle, perfectly tailored, elegant.

Where were we? Yes, just as we were beginning to

make some real money, Penny started to get battier. She'd always had tendencies. Odd flights of fancy, a fondness for viscose. But now she was forgetting things. Losing things. The usual signposts in the foothills of senility. If I sound callous, it's because she's not *my* mum. She's Ludo's. Oh, God! It's all getting complicated already. I'll have to set it out straight, or you'll never catch up.

My name is Katie Castle, and this is the story of how I had everything, lost it all, and then found it again, but not quite all of it, and not in the same form, and, if I'm perfectly frank (which, I have to confess, doesn't come naturally), not, in every single particular, *quite* so good. The story's mainly about me, but it also involves, in no special order:

- Penny, my employer, the wife of Hugh;
- Hugh, the husband of Penny;
- Liam, my Big Mistake;
- Jonah, who was nearly an even bigger mistake, but who turned out to be a Good Thing;
- Veronica, my loyal and faithful servant, up to a point; and
- Ludo, who *is* the adored child of Penny and Hugh and who *was,* at the very beginning, the point at which you came in, my beloved, my betrothed.

There're lots of other people as well, friends and hangers-on, but you'll meet them when you meet them. I've decided to be honest, so you might find yourself thinking me a madam or a minx, but even if I do some bad things, and some silly things, you must try to stay on my side, because in the end I turn out to be quite good, I promise.

*   *   *

In the beginning. Like everybody else, I live in London. Like almost everybody else, I live in Primrose Hill, the bit of London where Camden stops being horrid and Regents Park stops being boring. Like not quite everybody else, but like an awful-lot-of-body-else, I work in fashion. So I'm not really a designer, but anyone who works in fashion will tell you that the most important person in any fashion company is the production manager. We *all* know that. What's a designer, anyway? A tricky East End nonce who knows what to steal and who to screw. Or who to be screwed by. Not even an original thief, but a parasite on parasites. A magpie collecting bits of tinsel other magpies have thieved. Art school losers too good at drawing to make it as artists, too vain to be teachers, too thick to be anything else. I love them, but I wouldn't want to *be* one. And anyway, we don't really have designers in our company. We have Penny. And Penny has me.

I started in the shop. There was a card in the window: "Help Wanted. Experience preferred." Well, I had *experience*. Penny and Hugh interviewed me. I did my trick of being girlie and grown-up at the same time: girlie to Hugh and grown-up to Penny. The shop's on a little lane just off Regent Street. It looks quite small from the front, but it goes on up forever, stairs winding into the sky. I should say that it starts out as a shop, and then it becomes a studio, where the samples are made, and then at the top it turns into an office. I spend most of my time at the top, with Penny, who goes home at four o'clock every day except Friday, when she goes home at three. That's why she always phones me at five past six to find out how we've done.

The girls in the shop don't like me very much. We all

chatter away whenever I drop down to see how things are going, but I know they bitch about me when I'm gone. That's just the way shops are—there's nothing else to do. If it's not the fat bums and flabby tits of the customers, then it's the stupidity and cruelty of the bosses, and that sort of includes me. They don't like the way that I skipped upstairs, leaving them behind. They think *I* think I'm too good for them now, which I do, and I am. But our warfare is cold, and mainly takes the form of sulks and obstinacy over rotas.

Things are different with the studio. The problem there is that I have to tell them when things go wrong. I have to make them do things they don't want to do, and then I have to make them do them again. I have to tell them off. Penny is too grand to concern herself with such matters as stretched necks, lumpy zips, badly distributed ease on the sleeve head, sloppy felling, and wavering seams. And that means, of course, that it's me who has to stand there as Tony, our unreliable, temperamental, irascible, but entirely essential sample machinist, throws one of his tantrums, spitting out curses in Maltese and rending pieces of calico to frayed white ribbon. It's me that has to endure the open enmity of Mandy, with her leopardskin pants and tongue to match.

But I didn't care. And why didn't I care? Because my life was perfect.

A poet died in my square. I read her poems once, but they were all *me me me*. The flat isn't mine, of course. It's Ludo's. But it felt like mine. I'd *made* it mine. Everything apart from the brick and slate had been chosen by me. Out had gone Ludo's schoolboy clutter—his saggy old armchair, his disgusting family heirloom curtains;

pictures of dead people. So now we had clean lines, a gleaming wood floor, blinds that seemed to make the rooms lighter rather than darker when they were down. There were always flowers. Ludo hates flowers. "I'd see the point if you could eat them," he'd say. His horrible old books were confined to his study—the Smelly Room, I called it.

Ludo. Everybody loved Ludo. He was so helpless. He looked like a completely random pile of clothes, hair, shoes, and beer bottles somehow come to life. I tried to do for him what I'd done for the flat, but it didn't take. It was like trying to polish suede. At least I managed to get him to cut his hair, which was something, even if he resented it in that slow-burning way of his.

The really funny thing about Ludo is that he was a teacher. And he didn't even have to be. He could have done all sorts of things, he was so clever. But instead of all sorts of things, he taught English at a school in Lambeth—the kind of school where even the teachers carry knives. I suppose it was some kind of reaction against his parents. Or rather against Penny. He'd spend all night marking in the Smelly Room. He had views about the National Curriculum, but none of our friends ever listened.

Seducing Ludo was easy. I could tell that he liked me because he blushed the first time he met me. I was still in the shop then, and he came in to see Penny. Although it was August, he wore a hairy tweed jacket, like a cowpat with arms.

"Mum in?" he said to Zuleika, the Lebanese girl who'd been there for years without doing very much, unless you count having lovely skin as doing something. Before she had the chance to answer, I carpe diemed.

"She's lunching with *Vogue*. You must be the genius.

I'm Katie Castle." Before he knew what was happening, I had him out of there and into Slackers wine bar. During the first bottle of Pouilly-Fumé we did, in a slow spiral downward, his favorite books, his favorite films, his job, his loves, his hates, his inner despair, his aching loneliness, his family. I sighed and nodded, eyes moistening in sympathy. And then, in a textbook maneuver, I led him from that dark place and showed him that life could be fun. I joked, I flirted, I sparkled, and we spiraled up through the second bottle, like pearl fishers. I made it seem as though he were doing the entertaining: I laughed at his first jokes, moved closer, bent toward him, touched his arm.

And, you know, it really wasn't all pretend. Underneath all that hair and cobwebs and mustiness, I found a perfectly nice-looking man, with a lovely, shy smile and really quite kissable eyes. Even if he hadn't been my big chance, I still might have fallen in love with him.

We made it back just before Penny—I was always a good judge of a lunchtime. Zuleika was fuming, but that didn't matter. Penny made her entrance and enveloped Ludo in her customary critical embrace. And instantly, with that famous low cunning of hers, she knew.

"Darling, have you been getting in the way of the girls?" she declaimed, and without pause swept Ludo up the stairs to write the check. But on his way out, a long, long half hour later, he asked for my number, and his fate was sealed.

Of course, Penny tried to fight it. Penny understood me very well. Because, I suppose, we're really quite alike. Or could it just be that she always thinks the worst of people and the worst, on this one occasion, just happened to be true? I always had an ally in Hugh. Hugh loves women, and the prettier they are, the more he

loves them. And whatever they might say in the shop, or
the studio, or anywhere else, I *am* pretty. Hugh always
thought I was good for Ludo. "You're good for Ludo,"
he'd say. "You bring him out of himself. Stop him from
brooding and sulking all the time like a wolf in its lair."
It became clear that Ludo was a disappointment to
him. Hugh was big and bold and successful and confident. He'd sent Ludo to his old school, hoping it would
turn him into a copy of himself. Instead poor Ludo
emerged broken and resentful. To Hugh and Penny's despair, and despite insanely good grades, he refused even
to *apply* to Oxford, but went instead to some college in
Wales. "Not even a wretched redbrick," as Hugh be-
moaned. "Looks like a Bulgarian nuclear power station."

It was always hard working out Hugh and Penny as a
couple. Hugh was posh, you couldn't escape that. He
had that faint sheen that only posh people seem to carry
with them, even into late middle age. Not like my parents. Not, I suspect, like Penny's. Penny had been an actress. She would rattle off titles from TV series in the
sixties I'd never heard of. She talked about a play. There
had been a couple of films. Sean Connery was mentioned, but I never worked out in what connection. She
said that she had given it all up for Hugh and Ludo.
Penny Moss—her maiden name—began as a hobby. She
made her own clothes in the sixties—tie-dyed head
scarves, crocheted ponchos with matching berets, that
sort of thing, I imagine. People liked them. She began to
sell them to friends. The next thing she knew, she had a
Saturday stall in Portobello, just a bit of fun, really. And
then the first shop.

All this time Hugh's enterprises—things in the City,
investments, speculations—were starting to "go a little
stale," as he put it. And then, sometime in the early

1980s, there came a point when Penny Moss began to bring in more than he did. Rather than pick up the gauntlet, he capitulated. Drew up the drawbridge and took to golf. Penny used to drag him into the office occasionally, to help with hiring and firing, but it was more symbolic than anything. He didn't seem too bothered about it. He'd bought the fabulous house in Kensington. He still had a few investments, and Penny Moss was doing nicely. Why work when, again in his words, he could simply "live off his hump"?

But this had all led to a power shift in the relationship. And Penny was never one to miss an opportunity. As Hugh retreated, so she advanced. She'd been attractive (I'd seen—who hadn't?—the photographs) as a young woman, but as a woman of a certain age, she was a stunner. She went every year to Cannes during the festival, and there were rumors of affairs with the most surprising people. Could Peter Sellers *really* have proposed one moonlit night on a yacht chartered by the French minister of culture? She claimed she kept the ring as a memento when he refused to take it back. Did Marcello Mastroianni *really* suggest a spot of troilism with a Scandawegian starlet? Penny used to talk about these things in a wistful sort of way, as though it were something she'd desired rather than achieved, but Ludo's grumpy silence on the subject offered some kind of authentication. I got the feeling that he'd been teased about her at school. I found it hard not to laugh whether or not the stories were true.

But that's all ancient history. I'll cut to the chase. Ludo was mine, whatever Penny thought about it. We lived together in the Primrose Hill flat, and we were engaged, although Ludo could never quite remember when or how he had asked me to marry him. When it became clear that she could not maneuver me out of Ludo's life (she'd tried both blackmail and bribery), Penny had the good sense to draw me up to the office, to avoid the shame of her sweet boy consorting with a shop girl. I was made an assistant to Carol, the previous production manager. But Carol must have known the writing was on the wall, and after a week, to everyone's relief, she left to do volunteer work in Egypt and was never heard of again. I used to like to think that she'd been eaten by a crocodile. I know that might suggest that I'm a bit lacking in the generosity of spirit department, but I used to be much preoccupied by the question of whether it would be better to be eaten by a crocodile or a shark. Crocodile always seemed more likely, because of Tarzan. You see, I could always imagine myself as Jane, whereas sharks mainly seem to eat Australians, and imagining oneself as an Australian is out of the question.

With my new job I soon found that I had new friends. The London fashion world is a small one. There are six people you have to know. Enter that blessed circle and you will never miss a party and never brunch alone. If I hadn't quite made it into that circle, I was at least a satellite of a moon orbiting a planet that was part of the circle, and for now, that would do.

And then—could it really be just nine months ago?— came that phone call from Penny and my usual smart reply. But it was not to end there.

"Katie darling . . ." A bad sign, that "darling."

"Yes, Penny?"

"There's some trouble at the depot. Cavafy says he can't find the right interlining. I know it's there, some- where. You couldn't go out there tomorrow morning

and check for me, could you? There's really no one else
I can ask. You can do it on your way in to work."

I pulled my Jean Muir face and hissed out three shits
and a fuck. The depot was the worst thing about my job.
A hideous warehouse in outer Mile End, full of toiling
women whose lives were simply too awful to contem-
plate. Cavafy was the old Greek who ran the place, with
his idiot son, Angel. And the "on your way in to work"
was typical Penny. Mile End was no more on my way in
to work than my ass is on the way to my elbow.

"Don't look like that, Katie," said Penny, which was
clever of her given the miles of phone line between her
and my grimace. "You've got Paris the day after tomorrow to look forward to, and Mile End won't kill you."

Paris meant Première Vision—the world's biggest fab-
ric fair. For the past two years I'd gone along with
Penny, as her girl Friday. It was the polar opposite of
Mile End, the good to its bad.

"Anyway," she added with her characteristic contempt for logic, "aren't you going to a party tonight? *I*
haven't been to a party for months and *I* don't complain."

"What about cocktails at the Peruvian embassy last
Thursday to push vicuna yarn?"

"Darling, that was business and not pleasure. And I
still don't know what a vicuna is, which was the main
reason I went."

"But didn't you get legless and have to be escorted out
for biting a general's gold braid to see if it was real?"

"I was only being playful. And he wasn't a proper
general. But he did have such a virile . . . mustache." The
line paused as Penny drifted off into a romantic Latin
American reverie involving, or so I imagined, an abduction by the besotted colonel, adventures with wild

gauchos, a palace coup, a forced wedding, the adoring crowds, the assassin's bullet, a coronation . . . "Anyway," continued the queen presumptive of Peru, "that wasn't a *real* party. What I want is a party with paparazzi and people I've heard of. It's not for me, you understand: it's for the good of the company. We need a . . . one of those things, you know, a *higher profile.*"

"Well, why not come tonight, then?" I only said it because I knew she wouldn't.

"Don't be ridiculous, Katie. I wouldn't dream of gate-crashing. And I don't even know where it is." I was a little concerned about the relish with which she pronounced *"gate-crashing,"* which suggested that the idea had a wicked appeal.

"Look, Penny," I said, "come or don't come, it's entirely up to you. But now I have to get home: I haven't a clue yet what I'm going to wear."

"Oh. Okay. And Mile End—you will remember to kiss Cavafy for me, won't you?" she said.

"Of course, Penny," I said, suppressing with an effort that made my eyes water, a jostling crowd of curses and expletives.

CHAPTER 2

In Matching Knickerbockers

The party to which Penny alluded was a launch at Momo's. I can't remember what was being launched—chocolate-flavored vodka or something—it never really matters. Milo, naturally, was doing the PR, and the place was packed with B- and C-list celebs. Not all fashion, of course, but given that it was one of Milo's, there was bound to be a fashiony feel. There were models, a smattering of out-of-favor designers, and a few vaguely familiar telly people from daytime soaps or early evening quizzes. Milo had clearly been coasting: this really wasn't his best work. The one real catch was Jude Law, who'd promised to make an appearance in return for the indefinite loan of a Gucci lizardskin jacket.

I was in my element. I have, you see, the sort of face that people think they know: people are always convinced that they've seen me on something. And best of all, I knew people in several of the discrete clusters that had formed. That meant I could island-hop, moving from one to another as soon as the conversation dulled, which in the PR fashion cosmos took on average four and a half minutes.

First, there was Milo's lot by the bar: that's Milo himself, PR Queen of London, sleek and wondrously handsome in black neoprene suit and a pair of piebald ponyskin shoes. Next to him, close as a gun in a holster, there pressed Xerxes, Milo's Persian Boy. Xerxes was an exquisite miniature, eyes dark and lustrous. Milo said he was a Zoroastrian, a fire worshiper, and that he'd never let him blow out a match but would make him wait until the flame had eaten all the wood and licked at his fingers. No one had ever heard him speak. Some said he was dumb. Others disputed his origins. I'd heard, of course, the story about Xerxes being a Bangladeshi waiter, but who knew the truth in this world of rumor, fantasy, and Fendi handbags?

Pippin, Milo's ex, a perpetually resting actor, hovered close by, although it was hard to work out if his interest was in his old lover, or the Persian Boy, or the barman, or the bar. Pippin was a hard one to like. Pretty, of course, in a high-cheekboned, floppy-haired, pastiche Eton kind of way—he would never otherwise have kept Milo's attention for eighteen months. But there was something fetid and creepy about him, as if he'd just pulled himself away from an act of gross indecency with a minor.

Two of Milo's PR girls fluttered among them. I called them Kookai and Kleavage. Although I always thought of them as essentially the same person, and indeed often mixed them up, there *were* some differences. Physically they weren't alike at all. Kookai was a pretty little thing, soooo Asian babe that I could never understand why she wasn't reading the news on Channel 4. Sadly, she was also too dumb to realize that all she had to do was ask and she could drape herself from head to toe in the

Prada and Paul Smith samples that lined the office walls back at Smack! PR. Hence Kookai.

Not a mistake that Kleavage was to make. Less naturally attractive than Kookai, with a jawline perhaps a little too well defined, she was nearly always the best-dressed girl in the room. Best-dressed and least-dressed, showing off her miraculous tits and supermodel midriff. Where Kookai was sheer gush, Kleavage was always more calculating: you could see her working out the angles, searching with those violet eyes for openings . . . weaknesses. So different from the broadband PR love-beam that was Kookai.

I slipped in beside Milo, who was whispering something obscene into the ear of the Persian Boy. He looked at me, frowned for a nanosecond, and then kissed me on the lips, sliding in his tongue just long enough to make his point.

"You look amazing," he said with that luscious, creamy voice of his. The voice had been his making; telesales his first arena; cold-calling his métier. "Yes," you'd have said to the double glazing, "Yes, yes," to the encyclopedias, "Oh, God! Please, yes," to the financial services, and only ever, perhaps, "No," to the dog shampoo. So that fifty-thousand stake was his, and Smack! PR born.

The tongue trick worked on most people, throwing them off their stride, giving him an instant advantage.

"Put your tongue in my mouth again, you fucking old queen, and I'll bite it off," I replied. It's what I always said.

"Less of the 'old,' " he said, looking around with theatrical paranoia, "there are *clients* about."

We bantered for a little while, with Kookai and Kleavage giggling and trying to join in, Pippin smoking and self-consciously ignoring us, and the Persian Boy lost in his private world of fire, or chicken tikka masala.

"Where's your handsome rustic?" said Milo after a while, miming a telescope. "Haven't left him back at the flat with an individual pork pie and a work of improving literature, have we?"

Pippin giggled like a girl showing her knickers to the boys for the first time.

I didn't like Milo sneering at Ludo—that was my job, and it's different when you love someone—but I couldn't object without slithering down a snake to the bottom of the board.

"Really, Milo," I replied quickly, "surely you know that it's *after* we get married that I start to leave him at home. He's looking for the cloakroom. Could be hours."

"*After* you're married?" Milo said slyly. "Have you set a date, then? Or are we still in the realms of whim and fancy?"

I wasn't sure if Milo had deliberately passed from teasing into malice, but he had found his way unfailingly to the nerve.

"Milo, I know you're bitter about never having the chance to be the glorious center of attention of everyone you know for a whole day, and never getting to wear white, and never having troops of pretty choir boys sing *your* praise, and never having literally hundreds of presents *forced* upon you, and never having a cake with a tiny statue of you on it, but you have to rise above all that."

Had I gone too far? Milo was famous for his grudges, which could lie dormant for years before bursting into

poisonous fruit. But no, the operatic look of spite he
threw my way was reassuring.

"You can keep the juicer," he said through pursed
lips, "and just how many Gucci ashtrays do you need? A
wedding is a tiny rent in the straight universe that gives
you a glimpse of the infinite glory of the camp beyond.
I'm there already."

"Ain't *that* the truth," said Pippin from the bar.

As soon as I felt Milo's eyes begin to flicker over my
shoulder, I moved on—talk to any PR for more than five
minutes and it'll happen to you. The core of the next
group was formed by three models, one posher than
princesses, one of the middling sort, and the last born
under the chemical cloud that covers Canvey Island, in
deepest Essex. Despite spanning the entire range of the
English class structure, there were few differences between them discernible to the naked eye: they all smoked
the same cigarettes, they all had the same hair, the same
black-ringed eyes, the same magnificent bones, and here,
unshielded by the doting camera's veil, the same tired
skin.

I knew Canvey Island quite well: she'd modeled for us
more than once. She had a little more conversation than
the other two, but even so it was limited to accounts of
her appalling sexual experiences. I always liked her
story about losing her virginity at thirteen to a guy with
a tight curly perm and pencil mustache, who'd picked
her up at a nightclub in Billericay. He started dancing
next to her, expertly separating her from her friends, his
white slip-on shoes moving like two maggots on a hook.
He bought her three sweet martini-and-lemonades and
then led her outside to a Ford Escort van in the car park.
He exclaimed, "Ta-da!" and threw open the back doors
to reveal a flowery mattress, with a stain the size and

color of a dead dog in its precise center. He bundled her
into the back, fumbling at his stone-washed jeans. Her
skirt was up and her knickers off before she knew
what was happening. His cock was smaller than a mini-
tampon, so she felt little pain. After four weasily thrusts
he came, yelping out an excited, "Fuckfuckfuck." With
a smirk of satisfaction he tied a knot in his condom and
chucked it down the side of the mattress, where it joined
dozens more. He locked up the van and went back to the
club. She went for some chips and ate them as she
walked home.

She was telling the story again to four men strutting
and preening around the models. Two were tall and
good-looking, two squat and ugly: a footballer and the
footballer's agent, an actor and the actor's agent. The
actor had made his name playing East End villains in
low-budget British gangster films, but a public school
drawl kept breaking through the studied Cockney. The
footballer was famous for biting the testicles of a more
talented opponent, and this singular act of brutality had
mysteriously given him access to the world of celebrity.
I sensed that my presence was desired and realized at
once why—I'd round out the numbers nicely. But I knew
I'd be stuck with one of the uglies. Life, like these agents,
was too short. And Ludo, of course, was out there,
somewhere. I smiled and moved on. Still, the footballer
had been rather good-looking, decked out by some tame
stylist in an Oswald Boateng suit, conventionally, almost boringly, tailored, but showing, when he moved,
flashes of brilliant electric blue lining, like a fish turning
on a coral reef.

There were, naturally, endless scrounging journos. I
knew most of the fashion writers, "the clittorati," as

Milo called them, as bitchy in the flesh as they are fawning on paper. They were never quite sure what to make of me. They knew that I was oily rag, a production pleb. But they also knew that I was heir presumptive to the Penny Moss throne. And, okay, it's Ruritania, and not the Holy fucking Roman Empire, but royalty's royalty, after all.

"Hi, Katie. So what are we all going to be wearing next year?" said one, but with a flickering eye that added silently, *As if you'd know.*

"Oh, you're in luck,"—I smiled back—"it's kaftans, kaftans, kaftans." I pirouetted away without waiting to see if it detonated.

I preferred the nonfashion hacks, honest cynics, eyes peeled for the goody bags and the drinks tray, even if, as one of them slurred into my ear: "Christ, Katie, we stand out in this crowd like white clots of fat in a black pudding."

Who else? Ah, the nervous group of execs from the Norwegian vodka company, terrified in case they'd made some dreadful mistake, but completely unaware of what a mistake, or a triumph, would look like. I thought about being nice and talking to them, telling them how well it was going, but life, like a Norwegian winter's day, is just too short.

In truth, it wasn't going that well. Jude Law had still not appeared. I wondered if Momo had perhaps borrowed the security people from *Voyage* and they hadn't let him in—"sorry, darling, this really is more of a *snakeskin* party." The free drinks had run out and the journos were quick to follow. I went to find Ludo.

As I'd figure-of-eighted around the room, Ludo had waited patiently in a corner, moving only to reach for the trays of chocolate-flavored vodka, or vodka-flavored chocolate, or whatever, as they floated by. He was hammered and had turned melancholic.

"Fucking hell, Katie," he began, the language harmless in his gentle voice, "you've left me standing here like a cunt all evening." He'd taken to using the dreaded c-word. He claimed he wasn't trying to shock, but that it was an attempt to reclaim it, like rap artists calling each other nigger. I didn't quite see how that worked, with him being a man and not a woman, and therefore not having one to reclaim, but I usually let it pass.

"Ludo, you're a grown-up; there are plenty of people here that you know. Why didn't you talk to them?"

"I tried a couple of times. But you know how it is: there's nothing I have to say that would interest them."

I pictured Ludo explaining some innovative use of a scientific metaphor in the poetry of John Donne to a ditzy *Marie Claire* stylist, and I felt one of my waves of affection. Perhaps I should have talked to him, or introduced him, or something. But I'd been trying that for eons, and it never worked. I'd introduce him to someone nice in fashion, or a Channel 5 TV director, and he'd bark into their ear about sea eagles and that would be that. And I had to be strict: every couple needs at least one set of teeth between them.

"Oh, come on, Ludo. It's not my fault that you've got about as much small talk as a cactus. And you hate fashion people, and anyone trying to sell things, or make money, or enjoy themselves."

"Then why do you make me come to these bloody things?" The tone was half whine, half grump. *Not* attractive.

"No one made you come, and you know you'd only sulk if I didn't invite you."

"I should have been marking," he slurred on. "I

mean, look at these people. What have they got to offer the world? How would the world be a worse place if they were all burnt to death in a tragic airship disaster?"

"But who would organize parties if Milo wasn't around? And who would people take pictures of if there weren't models? Really, Ludo, you *are* silly."

It was then that I noticed it arrive. I've no idea how it managed to pass through the security cordon: perhaps the heavies were shocked into torpor. The "it" was a beige safari suit, fastened at the front with a mathematically ingenious system of leather laces and eyelets. And at the bottom, omigod, there they were in all their obscene glory: the matching knickerbockers, laced with wanton exuberance under the knee. This wasn't seventies revival, oh no. This was seventies pure and simple, served straight up, as she comes, rayon in tooth and claw. It was prawn cocktail, and steak tartar, and bird's angel delight; it was Demis Roussos backed by the Swingle Singers. It was Penny.

The conversation came back to me. Days before in the office, Penny had described the suit.

"That's so *in*," I'd said. "You *have* to wear it."

It's the kind of thing you always say when people tell you about the old stuff in their wardrobes.

"Really? Perhaps I will," she replied, and I tuned-out to concentrate on the dancing lines of figures in the costings book.

The problem—the mistake, if you like—was the gap between the seventies in the seventies and the seventies now. You see, whenever there is a revival there are always touches, not *necessarily* subtle, that distinguish it from the real thing. Miss those touches and you look

like a children's entertainer. Penny was certainly provid-
ing entertainment. Her progress through the party was
followed with rapt attention, the very intensity of which
somehow drove out the wholly natural laughter reflex.
Penny's actressy poise, her wonderfully controlled refusal to glance around her, gave the whole thing something of the flavor of a visit by an aloof Hapsburg
dowager to a small town in Montenegro.

Ludo saw her, too. "Mum . . . oh, Mum," he
mouthed, and shrank back into the shadows like a
schoolboy who knows he's about to be kissed in front of
his mates. I was caught between admiration and horror.
How I'd love to have a tungsten ego like that, such a fla-
grant assumption that my whims were a sure guide to
glory. But for now it was good to be on the outside
laughing in.

Bloodhound keen, her nose led her to the bar and, co-
incidentally, into the middle of Milo and his courtiers. I
winced in anticipation of the rebuff she must surely re-
ceive: would she perish by fire or by ice? Milo, abetted
by his jackals, was adept at both.

Penny began a conversation. I heard the odd phrase—
"Warren Beatty and I . . . Prince Rainier . . . often at San-
dringham"—above the renewed party hubbub. And
miraculously, I saw that Penny was dappled with laughter. Milo smiled indulgently on her; Pippin had turned
from the bar and was whinnying appreciatively; Kookai
and Kleavage coiled themselves like cats around her
legs.

The explanation was simple: Penny had found her
way by chance or instinct to the one place in the party
where she would find a receptive audience. You see, as
had suddenly become clear to me, Penny was a fag hag

waiting to happen; and her moment had come. Here the absurd miscalculation of her attire was transformed into a camp triumph. Here her curiously masculine femininity could be seen as the playful challenge of the drag queen.

I thought about rejoining the group but decided that the moment was too perfect to risk spoiling. And anyway, it wasn't fair on Ludo. He looked pleadingly at me and said: "Please please please, we have to go *now*, before she sees us."

I kissed my way to the door with Ludo clinging to my hand, and we went to find a taxi. As always, the taxi worked its aphrodisiacal magic on him, but I really couldn't be bothered with it.

And *that* isn't like me at all.

So that's the immediate background to my trip to the depot. It isn't quite true to say that I was in two minds over marrying Ludo. I loved him, by which I mean that whenever I said it or even thought it, it rang true to me, and I never felt that I was pretending. I never thought for a moment of dumping Ludo. Apart from the love thing, there were practicalities: life would be impossible without him. Where would I live? What would I do? My life was built, not around him, exactly, but directly above him. It assumed his continued existence, as a city assumes the continued existence of good drains. Sorry if that sounds unkind, but I'm trying to be honest.

But despite the love, and despite the need, I was still tingling with that faint, unpleasant dissatisfaction that comes when you know you have to do something, and you know that it is for the best, but it means not being able to do lots of other things that you'd really rather like to do. Yes, I was desperate to get married and frustrated about his dallying over the date. But equally, if I was going to do something naughty, and on balance I thought I probably was, then time was running out.

CHAPTER 3

Cavafy, Angel, and the Loading Bay of Doom

The tube was full of the usual freaks, psychopaths, and mutants. It really annoyed me that Penny would never pay for a taxi out to Mile End. She always said, "But Katie darling, the tube's so much quicker. And think of the environment, you know, the hole in the rain forest, and whatever it is that's wrong with the ozone layer. Save the whale, and the pandas and things." She hasn't set foot on public transport since they put the electronic gates in the tube stations, the operation of which proved to be completely beyond her mechanical capabilities.

I say the usual freaks and psychos, but there were actually two rather good ones. One was a woman, normal looking, prim even, but about once a minute her face would convulse and contort into a hideous grimace, as though she'd just found half a worm in her apple. The awful thing is that she obviously knew it was going to happen, and she would try to cover her face with a newspaper, but she was always a split second too late. It was impossible not to stare, not to wait, breath held, trembling with expectancy, for the next fit.

Because of the convulsion lady, I didn't notice

Rasputin until a few moments before my stop. Everything about him was long and filthy: his hair, his nails, his smock, his teeth. He had a big rubber torch in his hand that he kept switching on and off. And he was staring at me. He'd been staring, I guessed, for the whole journey. I felt myself blushing. Please God, let him not speak to me, I prayed. You see, nutters on the tube are bearable until they speak to you. If they speak to you, you enter a whole new world of pain.

"He's dead. We've killed him."

That was enough. I got up and walked down to the other end of the carriage. Mercifully we were just coming into the station. I'd never been so pleased to reach Mile End. As I hurried along the platform, I glanced back. Rasputin was staring at me through the window, his face pressed to the glass. Over his shoulder I saw, for one last time, the woman's face contort.

It's only a ten-minute walk up the Mile End Road to the depot, but it always manages to get me down. People outside fashion think it's all about Milan and catwalks and supermodels. It's only when you find yourself on the inside that you see the sweatshops, and the depots, and the dodgy deals, and Mile End.

I hate Mile End. I hate its dreary streets, its horrid little houses, its crappy shops. I hate the people with their cheap clothes and bad hair. I hate the buses in the high street, and the fish-and-chip shops offering special deals for pensioners. I hate the way it always rains. I hate it because it reminds me of home. I hate it because I know it wants me back.

It's okay—I've stopped now. I promise no more whining about Mile End, which I don't doubt is a fine and noble place, beloved of its denizens, admired by urban historians for its fascinatingly derelict music halls and art-deco cinemas, and seen as Mecca by those who worship the Great White Transit Van. The Mile End I rage against is a Mile End of the mind, a metaphor, a symbol. And what is it a symbol for? Well, you'll know when we get to East Grinstead in, oh, I don't know, about another hundred pages.

Back to the depot. The depot is where we store our cloth. "Depot," believe it or not, is actually too grand a word for what we have. Who would have thought that depot could be too grand a word for *anything*? And what we have is a room, about the size of your average two-bedroom London flat, stuck onto the side of Cavafy's Couture. Cavafy's is a big shed, in which toil four rows of six machinists: middle-aged women with fat ankles and furious fingers. I always make a point of chatting to the machinists as I walk through to our depot. They make jokes about me being a princess, and I suppose I must look like some exotic bird of paradise dropped down into a suburban back garden. I always pause by the woman who sits nearest the door that leads off into our depot. She's probably the last woman in the country to have been called Doris. She must have been born right on the boundary between "Doris" signifying something sophisticated and classy, cigarette holders and champagne flutes, and it meaning "Look at me, I clean other people's houses for a living, and I wear special stockings to support my varicose veins, and my hair will always smell of chip fat, and I will never be happy, or fulfilled, or loved."

"How's that chap of yours, then, my love?" she said, her fingers never pausing as she worked her way along a seam.

"Oh, you know men," I replied, smiling and shrugging.

Doris shrieked with laughter, as if I'd just come out with the joke of the century. As she laughed, her fibrous hair, the texture of asbestos, moved as a piece. Her dress, a gray white polyester, sprayed with pink flowers of no particular species, picked up I guessed from the local market, having failed C&A quality control, would have looked almost fashionable draped over a girl half her age and weight.

"Men! Oooo, men!" she cooed, as if she'd sampled them all, from lord to serf, and not just the abusive, hunchbacked railway engineer who'd stolen away her, in truth, rather easy virtue twenty-six long years ago and left her with the baby and no teeth. "But you've a good-un there, you know. And I says when you've a good-un, you 'ang on in there."

I blushed a little and looked around. Cavafy was in his office—a glass-fronted lean-to affair at the other end of the factory. Angel was there, too. Angel was, is, Cavafy's son. He loves me.

Everybody loved Cavafy. He's one of those tiny old men you just want to hug. I'd never seen him without his brown lab coat, with at least six pens crammed into the breast pocket. I think he rather hoped something would happen between Angel and me. He'd invite me into the office for a coffee and embarrass the poor boy by listing his many accomplishments: ". . . and the high jump . . . only a small one, but the jumping, the jumping he could do. . . . And the running. And the GCSEs, look, we have them all on the wall, see, in frames: geographia, historia, mathematica, only a D, but a D is a pass."

But Angel, Angel. Years ago, when I was still in the shop, I'd come up here to the depot to help schlep stuff around. Angel had just started working for his father. He'd trained as an accountant, without quite passing his exams. I shouldn't really have called him Cavafy's idiot son. That was ungracious and unnecessary. In fact we used to have a bit of a laugh together: he'd make fun of Cavafy, and I'd make fun of Penny. Tight curly hair, fleshy lips, really rather good-looking, except for the height thing. Angel, you see, was a good three inches shorter than me. And that really wouldn't do.

It all came to a head one afternoon when I was sorting through some rolls of linen for a remake on that season's best-selling outfit: an oyster duster coat that would fall open to reveal a tight sheath in a pale pearly gray to match the coat's luscious silk satin lining. Even doughy-fleshed, big-boned country girls became simpering Audrey Hepburns (such was the Penny Moss magic recipe). Suddenly I felt a presence. I turned round and Angel was close enough for me to smell the oil in his hair and pick out individual flecks of dandruff. He didn't say anything: he just had a look of utter determination in his eyes, and I could see his jaw was rigid with fear or anxiety or lust.

"Angel!" I said breezily, determined to avoid a confrontation. "How about a hand with this stuff. It weighs a ton."

But Angel still stood there, straining forward, apparently unable to move his feet.

"Angel, you're being silly," I said, beginning to feel uncomfortable. And then he reached out and put his hairy hand on my bottom, where it stuck clammily to the pale silk. Somehow I knew that this wasn't intended as a gross sexual assault, and I never felt my virtue was at stake: Angel simply couldn't get the right, or indeed any, words out and his mute gesture was his only way of expressing his feelings. Had his pass been verbal, I would have been happy to parry verbally. But it wasn't, so I felt that there was only one way to bring the incident to an end. Anyway, I suspected that Angel's hand would leave the damp print of his palm and fingers on the skirt, and that annoyed me. So I slapped him.

I'd never slapped anyone before: it always seemed like such a pointlessly feminine gesture, an admission that you haven't the wit to inflict a more serious injury. Almost as soon as I'd done it, I regretted the act (and I certainly had cause to regret it later). Angel took his hand off my bottom and put it slowly to his cheek. A fat, oily tear built in the corner of his eye and rolled down his face until its way was blocked by the broad fingers, whereupon it found some subterranean passage and disappeared. Still without saying a word, Angel turned and walked away.

Boys don't understand how hard it is to break a heart. They think we have it easy, dispensing joy or misery with a nod or shake of the head, as they cavort around us, offering themselves for humiliation. But you really have to be a complete bitch to derive any pleasure out of kicking some hapless youth in the teeth. In fact, the only thing worse than having to reject a boy is having no boy to reject at all.

Anyway, after a few minutes I went out to apologize to Angel. I liked him, and I didn't want things to be awkward. I saw that he was in the office. Cavafy had his arm around him. He looked at me blankly and made a slight shooing gesture when I began to walk toward them.

It was shortly after the Angel incident that it all began with Ludo, and for one reason or another it was a couple of months before I went back to the depot. On that first post-Ludo visit, Angel was nowhere to be seen, and Cavafy stood silent and stony-faced in his office, staring coldly through the plate glass. Even Doris sat aloof and barely returned my smile. Penny must have told Cavafy. The two of them had known each other for decades. The old Greek had made her first collection. Now that Penny had moved on to bigger and better things, she would still send him the dockets for fifty or so skirts or a couple of dozen jackets, for old times' sake. I can imagine what kind of spin Penny put on it: Katie the golddigger, Katie the counter jumper, Katie who thinks she's too good for your son, Katie servant of Beelzebub, Katie mistress of the secret arts, Katie who suckles her cat familiar with her third teat. That sort of thing.

But I toughed it out (and in truth it wasn't *that* tough, bearing in mind that everything else in my life was starting to go so well), and it seemed that things had blown over. After a couple of months you'd hardly have known about the crisis, except for the sullen yearning you sometimes saw in Angel's eyes and, if I'd been more perceptive, something colder in Cavafy's.

I sensed the sullen yearning thing as I slipped by Doris and through the door into the depot. It didn't take me long to sort out the interlining: it was hiding under a roll of wool crepe. The depot has an exit out to the loading bay, and I didn't fancy going back through the factory with Angel moping at me. The exit leads onto a ramp, and, as you know, heels hate ramps, so I usually sat at the top with my legs dangling over the edge and let myself down the few extra inches. I was just doing that when something emerged from the shadows.

"Give you a hand there, Katie," came a voice, the type of gorgeous Irish voice that just cries out to be called "lilting," and bugger the clichés. I managed to feel both startled and soothed at the same time. A face followed the hand out of the shadows. It was vaguely familiar.

"Do I know you?" I asked harshly, trying hard to mask the fact that I had been caught by surprise.

"Sure you do. I'm Liam . . . Liam Callaghan. I drove for you last year at the London Designer Show."

Thaaaat was it. Normally I'd go with the clothes, helping to set up the stand, arranging the stories—a story, by the way, for you fashion know-nothings out there, means that part of a collection made out of the same cloth—and all that, but last season I went in the car with Hugh, and he insisted on stopping off at his club for a G'n'T, which turned into about seven, and by the time we got to the stand all the work had been done. Penny was furious but didn't say much because it was all Hugh's fault. I just managed to catch Liam as he was leaving, an empty clothes rail balanced on each shoulder. As he'd passed me, he'd half turned and thrown me a wink, which was naughty.

"Oh, hello, yes, Liam. Of course. What are you doing skulking back here?"

"Skulking's a little harsh now, isn't it? What could be a more natural habitat for your common or garden van driver than a factory loading bay?"

He had a point, although the "common or garden" bit was fooling nobody, as he well knew. Although I'd only come across him that one time, I knew that Liam Callaghan drove for almost every designer fashion company in London. He was reliable, hardworking, relatively honest, and heterosexual. In the fash biz, any one of those would have set him apart; taken together, it meant you had to book him weeks in advance. And yes, Liam was something of a looker, in an almost caricatured Irish rogue kind of way: dark curly hair, blue eyes, a long face that had a suggestion of melancholy about it, you know, as if he'd just finished playing a piano concerto, until he wheeled out his smile. And that was some smile: a smile that could stop trains. And hearts. It was a smile he must have worked on in front of the mirror. It began, like all the great smiles, with the eyes: a barely perceptible widening, followed by an irresistible crinkling. And then the lips would purse for a moment before collapsing exuberantly into a lovely white roller coaster.

"Well, are you going to give me a hand down or will I have to leap and sprain my ankle?"

He gave me a smile for that: not an all-guns-blazing, blow-your-knickers-off special—perhaps just a 7.5 on the Richter scale of smiles. But it made me want to bite him, for all that.

He was strong and lithe: not a pumped-up gym-fairy strong, but a lifting, shifting, working strong. His hand stayed in mine for a second or two after I landed.

"Are you going back into town?" I asked.

"I am that. Do you need a ride?"

"Mmm. Anything's better than the tube. Even a smelly old van cab, with fag ends on the floor and porno mags under the seat. I know what you drivers are like."

"Well, you know, you could always give it a wee tidy for me, if you've a mind."

The van, of course, was spotless. He opened the door for me and again offered me his hand, saying, "This is habit-forming."

Despite the traffic, the drive back into town was fun. We joked about all the appalling old dragons he had to work for: the cranky, tight-fisted Elland sisters, who'd always make him show his hands were clean before he was allowed to touch any of their precious hats; Emelia

Edwards, who'd once actually *pinched* him for eating an orange, for which fruit she had a notorious aversion; Kathryn Trotter, who wouldn't let any of her actual employees carry Kathryn Trotter bags, as they simply could not convey the right image.

"And Penny Moss?" I asked.

"Wouldn't say a word against the lady. Fierce as two ferrets in a bag, but never rude unless provoked. And always pays her bills on time. And I'd hardly say otherwise when you're set to marry the precious boy, now, would I?"

"I wouldn't tell."

"Well, maybe you would and maybe you wouldn't. And how do you feel about getting wed? All a-tingle?"

"I'm slightly past the tingle stage."

"Second thoughts?"

"I can't quite see how that's any of your business."

"I'm only making polite conversation, am I not?"

"Of course I haven't got second thoughts. Everybody loves Ludo. He's a honey."

"And you're the bee."

When you thought about it, that was really rather a horrid thing to say. But he said it with such a charming twinkle that I didn't mind.

"Won't you miss all the parties and suchlike, when you're wed?" he continued.

"What do you mean, miss them? Why should I stop going to parties?"

"Ah, there's no reason under the sun. But when did you last meet a married couple at a fashion shindig? Isn't it all single people, or boyfriends and girlfriends? There's something about the married state that leads you on to quiet nights by the telly and Ovaltine before bed. And that's before we even start talking about the kids. No, let's give you a couple of quiet years first, then the time of chaos with the children—let's say you have two, a couple of years apart, and they stay like millstones round your neck till they're eighteen and they go off to college. Well, that's twenty-two years before you're clear of the last of them. And then you might be in the mood for a party, but who the hell's going to invite you then?"

I laughed, but it sounded hollow even to me.

"If you knew me better, you'd realize that nothing could stop *me* going to parties. Anyway, it's my job. How else could I know who was wearing what, or who was wearing who? How could I keep up with the scandal and gossip? My life isn't going to end when I get married."

"But some things will have to stop now, won't they, Katie?" He unfurled a smile. It was simply impossible not to smile back.

There was no way he could have known about my one or two little flirtations. And you're not going to like this, but I had, it's true, been thinking about one last, final, meaningless, harmless little fling before settling down in utter and complete faithfulness with Ludo. The idea had half formed itself in my mind. I knew it was there. It nudged and winked at me. And without explicitly acknowledging its presence, it became part of me, and I knew that I was going to do it.

But who with? No one in my circle. The best-looking men were, naturally, gay. The sexiest men were married—and I may be naughty, but I'm not *bad*. No, it had to be an outsider. There was the aforementioned divine Dante, who always put chocolate on my morning latte (which I always spooned off with a shudder back in the office). Handsome, in that baby Vespa way that Italians have.

But really, no. I thought about Max from Turbo Sports next door but one. I once saw him, glistening with sweat, at the gym. Body hard as a pit bull terrier. He had the cold eyes of a serial cat strangler, which I rather liked. So different from lovely, helpless Ludo. But again, no: his head was too small, and he conversed principally in grunts and lewd gestures. There was always the queer little man who came in to fix our Mac whenever it crashed. He once gave me a big, embarrassing sunflower. But beware geeks bearing gifts, as I always say.

So it went with all of the men I met: too old, too silly, too ugly, too gay, too small, too close, too far.

"What does your girlfriend think about you working with all these glamorous fashion women?" I asked shamelessly.

"And what makes you think I've got a girlfriend? Could I not be a sad, melancholy soul, drifting forlorn and loveless through life?"

"No," I said.

"As it happens, I am between girlfriends at the moment, which is saving me a fortune in roses, but costing me one in Guinness."

"I hate Guinness," I said. "Tastes like old man's bile to me."

"Well, you see, it all depends on where you drink it, and—"

"Who you drink it with?"

"I was going to say how it's poured. But now you mention it . . ."

"There's a rather good Irish word I've heard occasionally," I said sweetly. "Gobshite." For the first time he laughed. The laugh was less studied than the fabulous smile, but lovelier for it.

"Gobshite, is it? Will you look at the tongue on her! She'll be calling me an auld bollix soon."

"So where should I be drinking Guinness?"

"The only place for a pint of slow-poured black stuff, amid convivial company, with your ears caressed by the finest fiddle playing, is the Black Lamb in Kilburn."

"Kilburn. Is that where you live, then?"

"Not every Irishman lives in Kilburn, you know."

I did know. About half the people you meet at parties are Irish: Emerald Tiger types, fresh out of Harvard Business School or journalism college, sleek, clever, ambitious. The girls are all beautiful, if a touch wholesome and buttery, and the boys are all puppy-faced and eager. They'd no more live in Kilburn than I would. Of course, I'd been to the Tricycle Theatre a couple of times, dragged by Ludo. Once we saw a version of some Brecht play performed by Eskimos. The second time was less commercial. The whole show consisted of a man buried up to his neck in a heap of broken watches, screaming, "It's later than you think! It's later than you think!" Even Ludo agreed we shouldn't go back after the interval.

I looked out of the window and caught a glimpse of myself in the wing mirror. I'd just had my highlights done at Daniel Galvin's. I always think I look better in bad mirrors, caught in movement or glanced at an angle. Unless you're obviously at one end or the other of the spectrum, it's impossible to really know how attractive you are. Models know they're gorgeous. They might pretend to be riddled with doubt, but that's just them trying to seem more clever than they are. And people with harelips and things. I suppose they must know that they're ugly. Sorry, sorry—beautiful on the inside, I'm sure, but, whatever you might say, ugly on the outside.

Actually, in my experience ugliness does something horrid to the soul. Knowing that whoever you're talking to can only think, God, but she's ugly, must burn into you like acid. Unless you're especially stupid. Which makes it all the sadder that pretty people are so often dim, and ugly ones clever. (I know it's a cliché, but clichés get to be clichés because they're true. Sometimes, anyway.) Hugh once gave me a very good piece of advice. I don't know where he got it from. "Katie," he said, "always tell pretty girls that they're clever, and clever girls that they're pretty. They'll love you forever."

"And what do you say if they're pretty and clever?" I asked.

He smiled and patted me on the bottom. "You say yes, Katie. You say yes." Naughty man.

But I'm drifting off my point. Which was, unless you're at the extremes, you really don't know where you are. And I thought, as I looked at myself in that wing mirror, Are you pretty, Katie? Or are you plain? If you're pretty, how pretty? If plain, how plain? I'd always had boyfriends and men to tell me that I was pretty, or better than pretty. But men lie. And even the ones who didn't lie, who believed it, did they *know,* were they *right*? If you get the devotion of some poor simpleton who thinks that because you don't buy your clothes from a shop with two letters with an "&" in the middle you must be pure class, does that count? Any man will say he loves you, any man will say you're beautiful, when he has a fistful of your knickers and his nose in your Wonderbra. Girls know, of course. We can cast our cold eyes over one another. But knowing that girls think you're pretty is like drinking alcohol-free wine or decaffeinated coffee: it just doesn't hit the spot. No, what we want—or at least what I want—is for men to find us, me, beautiful, and for them to be *right*.

But after all that, I think I know what the truth is. The truth is that I am *quite* (a lovely word that can mean "really quite a lot" or "not really very much at all") pretty. I'm not very tall, perhaps about five six. I'm slim, but not, by anyone's reckoning, skinny. My hair is naturally a dark browny yellow, the color, as Ludo once said, not *meaning* to be horrid, of a nicotine-stained finger. Hence the highlights. My eyes are gray, which is good. I have no eyebrows, which is sometimes good and sometimes bad. My eyelashes are too pale to be of any use, so I have them dyed. The second time we slept together, Ludo lay gazing into my face. "Your eyelashes," he said, his breath heavy with wine and cigarettes, "they're amazing. They're so dark and long! I love them, and your eyelids and your eyes and your face and your head and your everything." I didn't have the heart to tell him. I still haven't. It's one of the things Penny thinks she has over me. My breasts are small enough not to embarrass me in the world of fashion and big enough not to embarrass me in the world of men. And all the bits in between? Oh, God! Who knows?

My point is, and I know I've come the long way round, that I'm a good-looking girl, but not good-looking enough to be blasé, not good-looking enough not to need the glances, the praises, the presents, the adulation, the worship, the flattery, the fawning, of men. You see, what makes me interesting is that I'm close enough to be able to reach out and grab these things, these meaningless, gaudy, pointless baubles, but too far away for them to drop into my lap.

And now I was reaching, foolish, foolish, girl, for the

bauble that was Liam Callaghan, van driver, Irish blarney merchant, borderline beautiful boy.

"Your Black Lamb doesn't sound like the kind of place a girl could just wander into on her own."

"Ah, Jesus, there's plenty of girls come into the Lamb, but it's true enough none at all like you. A good-looking lady by herself might attract a bit of attention, but then you wouldn't have to be by yourself." It was coming. "You know, if ever you wanted a taste of the dark stuff—the real thing, mind you—then I could show you the place. It might be the making of you."

I have no idea how serious he was up to this point. Was he just playing the Irish rogue to pass the time on our way into town, his mind in neutral? Was this just a diversion? The bluff, if bluff it was, was about to be called.

"Okay."

"Okay what?" I noted with pleasure that he was a little taken aback.

"Okay, why don't you show me what a good pint of Guinness looks like."

Now there was no smile at all.

"When can you come?"

"Today's Wednesday, isn't it? I'm in Paris from Thursday through till Sunday. How about a week tomorrow?"

That "I'm in Paris" was precious. Thank heavens for Première Vision.

"Thursday week it is, then. What if I meet you in the pub at, say, eight o'clock?"

I suddenly felt giddy. Was I in control? I thought I had been. But here I was, agreeing to meet an almost complete stranger, in a desperate pub in Kilburn, a part of

London I knew about as well as I knew the courtship rituals of the white-tailed sea eagle.

"Jesus, look, it's Regent Street," said Liam. "Why don't you leap out here?"

"Thanks for the lift," I said.

He said nothing, but looked at me and smiled. It was like being overwhelmed by a warm Caribbean wave: giddy, intoxicating, engulfing, fatal.

CHAPTER 4

A Technical Interlude, Concerning Leases, and the Provenance of Penny

I cannot say that my endeavors that afternoon represented the triumph of the production manager's art. Whatever Penny might think about me, she knows that I work hard and efficiently. Being good at anything is all about focus, filtering out the white noise. Ludo told me once that some scientists had done an experiment where they monitored the eye movements of different types of chess players, you know, grand masters or whatever they're called, and ordinary chess club hopefuls, with tank tops and dirty cuffs. The really great players, it turned out, spent all of their time scrutinizing just a couple of squares—the ones that really mattered. The eager amateurs, on the other hand, roamed busily over the whole board, eyes darting feverishly from square to square, in search of the secret, the code that they would never crack.

Ludo, of course, was useless at chess. He was too softhearted; he could never bear to lose a piece and could no more sacrifice a pawn than he could drown a puppy in a sack. Not that I used to play him. His chum Tom would come round, and they'd disappear into the Smelly Room with the board and a bottle of whiskey.

No, that afternoon I couldn't focus at all. My eyes were all over the board. Or off it altogether. I oscillated wildly between the fear of what I was getting myself into and a bubbling, uncontrollable excitement. Sitting at my desk, I found myself, amazingly, turned on. I crossed my legs and thought of Ireland.

I could tell Penny was getting annoyed: she kept making a little noise that began as a *tut* and ended in a grunt. Her mind was turning slowly as she tried to find something to throw at me. I pictured an ox tied to one of those big grindy things they have in biblical epics.

"Katie," she called slyly from her place under the skylight, "have you spoken to Liberty yet about the reorder? We have to let them know today."

"You know I haven't. Couldn't you have done it while I was at the depot?" I didn't normally bite back at Penny, but as I say, I was elsewhere.

"No, Katie, you dear thing." Ouch! One of the things I remember from "A" level English was that in Restoration comedies whenever the level of explicit courtesy rises, you know a sword is being drawn somewhere beneath a frock coat. Penny was like that. "Lady Frottager came in drunk and peed on the ottoman."

"What, *again*?"

"Yes, *again*."

"Someone," I said in a half-conscious echo of Penny's own grande dame manner, "ought to tell that woman our ottoman is not a public convenience."

"Well, anyway, she was terribly distressed, and I had to comfort her until the taxi came."

"Did she buy anything?"

"I coaxed her into one of the pashminas, but that's hardly the point. And then that ugly brute Kuyper came a-calling."

"Still banging on about the rent rise?"

"Without a . . . a . . . bazooka, there is simply no stopping that man."

Kuyper, a South African who'd learned his social skills as a torturer under apartheid (well, he might have), really was a brute. His company, Kuyper and Furtz, had bought the freehold on our shop and three other units in the lane, one of which was empty and officially cursed after a string of businesses had tried, and failed, to sell, in order, posh bras, camping equipment, cameras, and, inevitably, candles.

The first thing Kuyper and Furtz did was to invite the utterly pointless Anita Zither, who was currently between retail outlets, into the empty unit. Pointless, because despite being the press's darling, and the Establishment's pet English designer, she's never managed to put together a collection anyone would want to wear or buy, and every two years she goes bust, owing her suppliers tens of thousands. The day after she'd signed her lease, Kuyper came to us claiming that she was paying three times the rent we were. And there it was, in black and white. As it was time for our rent review, this spelled serious trouble. Kuyper ranted on about market rates, his bullet head and fat neck glowing red with greed, his fat finger pointing away, like a school bully bursting balloons. We couldn't afford anything like what he was asking, nor, surely, could Anita Zither.

The next day we got at the truth. One of Anita's girls was an old bitching partner of Nester, our rather stately manageress. They went off for a coffee, and word came back of the dastardly scheme. The enormous rent existed only on paper. The Anita Zither shop was to be given a two-year rent holiday. After that she could renegotiate something more realistic or just do her usual evaporating trick. The bogus agreement was the perfect stick for beating the rest of us into submission.

Penny, tough cookie that she is, stonewalled, and Kuyper became more and more aggressive, issuing all kinds of threats, legal and physical, and cursing in Afrikaans.

(Sorry if that was all a bit drab and technical, what with leases and freeholds and things, but it wasn't completely irrelevant, as you'll see later. Look on it as being like the half-talky bits in operas that fill in between the nice songs, the recitative, I think it's called. Ludo took me to see *The Marriage of Figaro* when we were first seeing each other. I read the program, which went on for pages. Too many notes.)

Back to Penny and her mood.

"Sorry I wasn't here to help." Conciliation seemed a good idea. "I'll call Liberty's now."

"No need to apologize, I *am* one-third American, after all," she said, as if that explained everything.

There was a pause as I did a quick calculation.

"Can you be a third *anything*? Doesn't it have to go in halves and quarters and eighths, and things?"

"Of course you can. I'm one of three children. My mother was an American. And everyone knows that American flows through the female line."

"Isn't that Jewishness?"

"Ah, no, you see, *I'm* two-sevenths Jewish as well."

And so the afternoon passed.

Paris meant an early start, so I was *quite* pleased that nothing was happening that night: not a dinner party, not a launch, not a soiree, not drinks, not clubbing, not anything. Ludo always loves it when there's nothing to do: he bumbles about making silly remarks, giving me pointless, spontaneous cuddles. He'll find a way of nuzzling the back of my neck, and unless I'm *very* discouraging, he'll end up carrying me to the bedroom. No, at home I really couldn't ask for a sweeter boy. It's the social world he can't cope with; my world.

But Ludo's lack of engagement with my world wasn't why I was contemplating the mad, bad thing. You're probably wondering what reason there *could* be. Here I was with a good man; not perfect, but good. Perhaps even very good. Kind, handsome(ish), and just about rich enough. Yet I was setting out on a course that could lead only to disaster. You despair of me, I know. I suppose I'd better try to explain.

It's all to do with the trouble with people, the fact that all of the different bits of them are connected up. I don't just mean the knee bone connected to the thigh bone and all that. I mean the different bits of their personality. If you try to get rid of one bit, a bad bit—say, Penny's towering self-regard—you find that it's attached to a piece of string, and you pull and pull at the piece of string and then out pops some other bit, a good bit, that you don't want to get rid of at all, like Penny's drive. People come all jumbled together, and you know you're supposed to accept them or walk away, although of course there's always the fashion option of smiling to their faces while deftly sinking a stiletto between their shoulder blades.

So, you see, Ludo's good bits—all the loveliness stuff— were joined up with the bad bits. And one particular bad bit buzzed away in my mind, like a bluebottle at the window. It *really* wasn't the social misfit business. It wasn't the mess. It wasn't the obsessions with things that nobody else cared about—the plight of the white-tailed sea eagle or the rights of reindeer-herding nomads in the wastes of Finland. It wasn't the brooding or the sulking whenever I did anything a teeny-weeny bit naughty, like putting a CD back in the wrong case or the case back on the shelf—sin of sins—*out of alphabetical order*. It wasn't the way he sometimes licked his plate before putting it in the dishwasher. It wasn't his habit of tweaking distractedly at his crotch whenever he was nervous, although we *are* getting a little warmer.

No, the problem was that Ludo, lovely, helpless, hapless Ludo, just didn't have the sexiness gene.

And now you want me to define my terms. Ludo's always telling me to do that—it's another of his annoying habits. The only way to shut him up is to say, "Well, define 'define,' then," a trick I learned at school for dealing with clever boys. But sexiness is strange, and you really do have to say what you mean. Or at least say what you like.

For me, being sexy isn't just about being good-looking, although it is, whatever anyone else might tell you, at least *partly* that. Sorry, nine-tenths of the boys out there. And it certainly hasn't got anything at all to do with being *nice*. Sorry, Ludo. Or buying you presents. And I think you know what's coming here. Anyone who's ever read a romantic novel from Jane Austen to Judith Krantz knows what I'm about to say. So get ready for a splash-down in the wide and welcoming sea of cliché—originality is not my aim, but that odd fish, truth. Yes, what we're looking for is our old friend the "element of danger." Not "take you down an alleyway and slap you silly" danger. More the knowledge that the object of your interest could go off with someone else more or less whenever he felt like it. More that you see the shape of a sneer behind a smile. More that you don't know what you'd find if you went through his pockets.

I knew exactly what I'd find if I went through Ludo's pockets, not that I bothered to anymore: two handkerchiefs, both as crunchy as Quavers; a tube ticket from a month ago; the chewed top of a cheap pen; a used plaster, screwed up into a ball; a poem, scrawled on a tissue; and a paperback by someone you've never heard of, with a name like Zbignio Chzeznishkiov.

There. I'm a stock character from fiction: the silly girl who, not content with the respectable young man she can have, wants to inject a bit of risk in her life. But fiction makes us what we are; we live in worlds densely populated by characters dreamed up by writers or film directors or magazine editors, characters more real than the insubstantial ghosts that swarm past us in the street, or drive by in cars, or hang like carcasses in the tube. Often when we think we are being most ourselves, it turns out that our words, our actions, even our thoughts, have been given to us. Sorry, I'm raving.

Anyway, on that evening, however, something like contentment reigned in our household. We had a lovely time tutting over the soaps and wincing at *ER* (it was the one where Doug Ross saves a boy from drowning in a land drain, surely the best ever).

At about eleven I made some remarks about having to pack. Ludo said something stupid about that not taking long. Boys just don't have a clue about girls and packing. There are things that we need that they don't even know *exist*. It takes Ludo from thirty to forty-five seconds to pack, depending on how long it takes him to extract his socks from yesterday's trouser legs. We didn't make love, but we kissed, properly kissed, and I went to sleep thinking about all the wonderful things there are in the world to buy and how most of them were waiting for me in Paris.

CHAPTER 5

Visceral Couture

The Eurostar left at nine-thirty. That meant up at six-thirty, tea in bed till seven, bath till seven-thirty, dress and tarting till eight-fifteen, quarter of an hour to collect myself, leave at eight-thirty, tube down to Waterloo, get there by five past nine, just late enough to send Penny into fits, but leaving, in the real world, plenty of time to check in and board by quarter past nine.

I dressed comfortably for traveling, in a Clements Ribeiro, and my second favorite pair of J. P. Todds. There was the inevitable quick panic before I left, and I had to run to the station, wrestling with my smart new Burberry. Even worse, I was forced to finish my makeup on the tube, which always makes me feel like a slut.

I met Penny by the Eurostar check-in. As usual, she was sowing chaos around her, pushing where she should be pulling, gesticulating at strangers, and snapping at Hugh, who'd come along to see her off—with, I don't doubt, a heavy sigh of relief.

As ever, her look hovered somewhere between magnificence and absurdity, generally keeping just on the right side of the border. This time she was doing her "film star traveling incognito" number, in dark glasses and a mad Pucci scarf, which helped to draw the eye away from the truly magnificent full-length sable coat. She had somehow inherited or otherwise acquired the coat from Hugh's side of the family, and such was its luxuriance that nobody ever suspected it was real. The overall effect was very Sophia Loren.

Hugh kissed me hello, then quickly again for good-bye. Penny managed a condescending peck on the cheek, acknowledging that our Paris trips were not quite work and not quite play.

The drama reached something of a peak on the way up to the platform. There was the usual choice between squishy lift and jostly escalator. As the lift queue seemed to be full of Belgians, Penny decided to go for the esca-lator, a device she habitually shunned. Big mistake. She clung to the rail as though the escalator were a tiny ship caught in a tempest.

"My feet, Katie," she cried, "my feet! What do I do with them? Where do they go?"

"Just close your eyes and pretend it's a normal stair," I said, coloring at the attention we were attracting. "Oh, God, let me . . . hang on . . . just put that . . . and that one there."

People were looking round. The Belgians in the lift queue pulled Magritte faces and pointed with umbrellas.

And then it stopped.

Stuttered.

And then stopped.

"We'll asphyxiate!" yelled Penny, illogically. "Come on, we must go back."

By this stage we were halfway up, and there must have been fifty people crammed in behind.

"Penny, we can't!" I tried feebly.

But Penny had switched from helpless panic mode to

all-action hero. She swept around, through, or over the hapless travelers, who were all waiting patiently for the wretched machine to get going again. She was like one of those ships that smash through the arctic pack ice on the way to pointless expeditions. "First Woman to Reach the North Pole without Sanitary Protection" sort of thing. I followed, shamefaced but, as so often with the indefatigable Penny, not a little admiring.

The lift doors opened just as we reached the foot of the escalator. Penny hesitated not one second but barged straight in, past the bemused Belgians, waving an arm, and saying, in a tone that forbade any argument: "Excuse me, this is an emergency. We are designers. I am Penny Moss."

A Eurostar lackey bowed. Honestly, he did. He may, of course, have been drunk.

Things settled down a little once we found our seats, and within twenty minutes Penny was relaxing into her second glass of champagne, as Kent or Sussex, or whatever it was, slid by in a happy green-and-brown blur.

I was facing the wrong way, of course. Penny always liked to see where she was going. But I didn't really mind. I've always thought—and pay attention here, because this is about the only profound thought I've ever had—that life is like facing the wrong way on the train. Because, you see, the present, the bit of countryside that's exactly equal to where you are, is over before you know it's there, and then all you have is the dwindling afterward of it. And though you can guess what sorts of things are going to come rushing over your shoulder, because you can see roughly what sort of terrain you're in, there's always the chance of something *really* unexpected or scary, like a tunnel, or a field with horses, or Leeds.

Oh. I always thought it would look better when I wrote it down. Perhaps I just can't do profound.

"Interesting young man, that Milo," Penny said, between sips. In the rush I'd forgotten about her dramatic appearance at the party. "He said that he would also be in Paris, which was an amusing coincidence. He seemed so sensitive, so . . . attentive."

"That's the way of the PR, Penny. He probably had you down as a potential client."

"Oh no, I really don't think his interest was professional. I really am rather afraid I may have made another of my tragic conquests."

I choked on a complimentary peanut.

"But Penny, you must realize that Milo . . . " And then I stopped. This was really too delicious. Milo was going to love it. "You must know that Milo is terribly, um, confused . . . shy . . . vulnerable."

"Yes, I sensed it. And you feel I would be simply *too much woman* for him in his present state? Of course, of course. Not that I would ever stray; it's been so long now. But there's no law against dreaming," she said wistfully, her fingers pulling at the hem of her skirt. "And I do so feel for the poor boy, torn between the fatal intensity of possession and the emptiness of loss."

Already the journey was living up to expectations.

Champagne for Penny was a time machine, and eventually Milo was left behind and we found ourselves back in the sixties. Exactly which bit of the sixties was hard to work out, and Penny never specified, as that would have given away too much. I suspect it was a largely imaginary place, a sixties of the mind, a distillation of different times, combining late fifties debutante innocence with the lollipop-colored, country-house drug scene of 1969.

First, of course, there were the years at the Royal Academy of Dramatic Arts. She seemed to have been worshiped by Albert Finney, adored by Richard Harris, and fondled by Peter O'Toole (or, as I'm sure I heard it, tooled by Peter O'Fondle). In between her white-gloved carousing she flitted from voice production, to mime, to fencing ("my saber cuts once reduced Roy Kinnear to tears, poor lamb"), to ballet, to makeup, and back to voice. Her long-dead tutors, Ernest Milton, Hugh Millar, and Edward Burnham, joined us in the carriage, still graceful, fruity, and fey.

She talked of nights in the Gay Hussar or the White Elephant, followed by dancing to Dudley Moore in the Basement. Satire at the Establishment always seemed to go with bizarre passes by comedians: Lenny Bruce offered to share his syringe, Frankie Howerd performed some act of dark obscenity ("Well, darling, I *was* in drag").

Most of all, there were the clothes.

"Darling, I was divine in my white piqué Mary Quant, topstitched in black, and over it a black piqué coat with a stand-away collar. . . . and Ossie Clark *gave* me a bias cream crepe with a keyhole neck . . . and I wore my ribbed yellow wool A-line Courrèges, with the sweetest little pair of silver-buckled Guccis."

I sat back in my seat, drifting in and out of Penny's monologue. Every now and then I'd snap into focus to hear her say something like ". . . and then I looked down and Princess Margaret's hand was on my knee . . ." or ". . . I'd never seen anything like it before or since; I swear it was *purple*. . . ."

Who knows how much of it was true? Penny had a way of believing in her own creations, and that gave them a reality, a truth, beyond any humdrum business of fact. But there's something more to it with Penny. It's as if things only ever exist when they've been externalized: talked about or paraded before you. Nothing happens on the inside with Penny. What she thinks, she says, or rather she only thinks them once she's said them. And for all her extravagant displays of affection and loathing, I'm sure she'd have no feelings at all if there weren't people around to observe them. I suppose that this is just another way of saying that she's a drama queen. But drama queen is too ordinary and plebeian a concept for Penny. Perhaps drama empress comes closer. And how she loves a drama! I promise, more than once, I've seen her place the back of her hand across her forehead and literally *swoon*, generally speaking onto the first-floor ottoman, which might have been designed for such things.

I dozed, and without even noticing the tunnel bit, I found we were in France. You can always tell by the sudden profusion of small, erratically driven vans on the roads. And then the Gare du Nord. I was sent off to find a trolley, while Penny, swaying gently on the platform, defended our cases from the predatory French porters.

There are two quite distinct sides to our trips. The bad bit is the marathon trudge around the fabric stands that fill the three huge hangars, big enough for airships, of the Première Vision exhibition. That consumes days two and three. It's no fun, but it's worth it, because it buys me, us, the good bit.

The good bit is Paris itself. I don't care how much cooler Milan and New York are; I don't care if the food is better in London or the weather nicer in Rome. For me Paris has always been my Emerald City, my Wonderland, my place of dreams. As a girl I used to think that if

I could just get high enough in the park swings, I'd be able to see the tip of the Eiffel Tower peeping over the monochrome, rain-dulled roofs of East Grinstead. I'd get Veronica to push. "Higher! Higher!" I'd shout. But she was never up to the job, and I resented her for it.

And Penny *is* different, in Paris. Of course, she's still a tyrant and a bully; she still imagines that the world exists to pay her homage, or at least to make her life easy; and she still reacts with outrage when her importance is not acknowledged. But in Paris Penny manages to exude a light that warms rather than dazzles. Somehow the hand thrust into the face of the waiter at L'Assiette charms his habitually pursed lips into obeisance. Somehow her attempts at the language, an extraordinary mixture of underworld argot, finishing school refinement, and simple error (I once translated her instructions to a taxi driver back to her, with just the merest touch of editorial license, as, "Hey, fuck ears, we would be enchanted if you could direct for us your carriage to the front portal of our castle. You have the scrotum of a bat"), is greeted with indulgent good humor by the snootiest of Parisians.

We always stayed at the Hôtel de Université, on the rue de l'Université in Saint-Germain. This may surprise you, but we shared a room: it was another part of the strange intimacy of our Paris times. The payoff, the compensation to me for Penny's gentle snoring, and to her, for my whatever it is that irritates her, is that we had the grandest room: a neo-classical cube of perfection. The Université could not have existed anywhere else in the world. It combined, in Penny's words (and for once they seemed the right ones), "the stately grace of Racine with the panache and verve of Molière." The service was attentive but restrained, and even the youngest of the doormen knew that Penny, and not I, was the one to flirt with.

Most of all, the Université was perfect for the shops. And when in Paris, boy, did Penny shop. You see, she never bought other people's clothes in London: it seemed to her too much like sleeping with the enemy. But in Paris, despite the fact that she chose the same designers that she shunned at home, it was somehow okay. And for once there was some logic to her logic.

And so, after leaving our cases in our room, we skipped, on that first afternoon, as on every first Parisian afternoon, from Prada, to Paule Ka, to Kashiyama (not that it's called Kashiyama anymore, but Penny could never remember its silly new name and would look help-lessly at me if I used it), to Sabbia Rosa, and then back to Prada again. Leather was on the menu, and we both found something suitable; she in a rich chocolaty brown, me in camel.

Because I'm in fashion, you probably think that buy-ing clothes is something of a busman's holiday for me. Working for fifty hours a week neck deep in the kinds of clothes that 99 percent of the population can only dream about must, you surmise, dull the appetite? Wrong, so wrong. I still feel the near erotic pleasure, the jud-dering, ecstatic, transforming joy, of clothes. I love the foreplay—the touching, smelling, breathing of beautiful fabrics—before the sweet consummation of trying on and the sublime climax of the purchase. I shiver still for satin-backed crepe: cool, like a diamond, to the tongue. How thrilling it was to find out that silk velvet smells ex-actly as it should, of earth and leaf mold.

It is still now as intense as the first time, that wonder-ful afternoon when Dad, for the only occasion in his sad life getting things exactly right, brought me home a per-

fect princess dress of polyester pink taffeta, studded
with rosebuds, with a satin sash and a net underskirt. It
was my sixth birthday. At the party, Veronica spilled
punch on the dress and I pulled her hair until she cried.
She was lucky I didn't drown her in the punch bowl.

The first evening we had dinner in a little bistro that
Penny claimed to have been coming to since her honey-
moon, when she and Hugh had spent a month living in
a brothel. Or that was Penny's story, and a very amusing
one it was, full of comic misunderstandings of a classic
French farcical kind. Hugh told me it was actually a perfectly respectable hotel that just happened to have a lot
of velvet about the place. But Penny never let truth get in
the way of a good story or, for that matter, a bad one.

The bistro was like a thousand others in Paris, although it claimed distinction by virtue of an assumed
connection with an ancient guild of carpenters, or
wheelwrights, or hairdressers—Penny could never get
the story straight, and it had a habit of changing depending on which of the waiters you asked, should you
have the curiosity to inquire. In honor of this association, there hung from the ceiling an intricately carved
something, a kind of gothic parrot cage. Again depending on the whim of the waiter, this could be a model of
the vaulting of Notre Dame, a medieval clock, or *une
machine pour le fabriquer les cigarettes*.

As usual, Penny asked me what I'd like and then ordered something else for me altogether. And as usual, it
was an unmentionable part of a pig, with a gizzard gar-
nish. Before our food arrived, but well into the second
glass of wine, Penny broke off from a rambling monologue on what we should look out for at Première Vision
the next day and gave me a long and searching look, her

eyes seeming both to widen and yet sharpen their focus. That look was one of her specialties and perhaps her single greatest business asset. No man, and few women, could sustain eye contact with her in basilisk mode for long. It was her complete self-confidence, of course, the total absence of those goading, middle-of-the-night doubts that riddle most of us, that gave her gaze its power.

"Katie darling, do tell me what's wrong." That was a bit of a shock. It seemed that Penny had had another of those rare, invariably cynical flashes of insight.

"Nothing. Why?"

"Katie my dear, I *know* you. I know how you are. I know your ways." None of those things, I must add, were true, or even nearly true. Penny knew Penny; Penny knew the fashion business; Penny well may have known how to dance the highland fling; but Penny did *not* know me. The trouble was that something *was* wrong. I simply couldn't stop thinking about Liam. His face was projected onto elaborate eighteenth-century facades; his voice whispered through elegant corridors; his smile glimmered at me from the silver highlights on the gray brown waters of the river.

"I haven't the faintest idea what you're talking about."

Penny blinked away my objection. "Darling, I'm here to help. I know what it is. It's Ludo, isn't it?"

Ludo? What did she mean? There was no way she could know about anything. Unless Liam had . . . no, that was impossible. She was speculating, trying to lure me out. Play, I thought, the innocent, which, after all, I was.

"Ludo's a sweetie. What could be the matter there?"

"Katie, you're being brave. But I know you must be in anguish on the inside."

I wouldn't have called it anguish. What the hell was she getting at?

"You must be a bit tipsy," I said without any malice.

"Darling," she said, ignoring me, "you must understand that men are different from us. They have stronger . . . passions. You cannot blame them as individuals; it's the species that's to blame. I saw it on the television: their genes make them do all kinds of horrid things. We must learn to tolerate, to turn and face away. Victorian hypocrisy has something to be said for it."

I was now completely baffled.

"What do you mean, stronger passions? What horrid things?" I asked. But as I spoke, I began to realize what the old witch was up to. She was suggesting that *Ludo* was having an affair, or at least indulging in what Hugh would call "a touch of oats, wild, the sowing of." And that rubbish about not blaming. If poor old Hugh ever did anything more than flirt, she'd be at him with the pinking shears quicker than you could say Lorena Bobbitt. And why would she intimate that her beloved son was acting the young buck to his prospective spouse? There could be only one answer: She had not yet renounced her goal of driving us apart, of saving the family silver from the counter jumper. I had no idea if this latest stratagem was devised in advance or improvised on the spot. Either way, I had no intention of allowing it to succeed.

"But Ludo hasn't got any passions, except for the sea eagles, and socialism, and curriculum reform, and things. They *are* a bit boring, but I don't *really* mind them."

"Of course, there are those . . . enthusiasms Ludo permits you to know about, and then there are those which are secret."

"Penny, enough. Ludo is the most transparent, least secretive person I've ever met. I'm sure you as a mother like to think of him as a roguish blade, irresistible to women, but that's just not the way he is. *I* love him, but that's because of what he . . ."

"Has?"

"No, Penny, because of what he *is* on the inside."

I felt a bit stupid because of that "on the inside" stuff, but I knew I had won the moral high ground: not, generally, a terrain I'm particularly familiar with, but a rather satisfying place to find oneself. In any case, Penny was silenced, although that might have had more to do with the arrival of her sole, and my snout, than my redoubtable defense of her son's honor, and our love.

I wish I could make Première Vision itself sound more interesting or glamorous. Of course, it's very heaven if you're a fabric junkie. Every important, and most unimportant, European manufacturer is there. How many? I don't know; a thousand, maybe? Two thousand? And that's an awful lot of luscious silk velvet, fine wool crepe, and oh-so-wearable viscose. So it draws the world's designers. They come here eager for inspiration, desperate to find that look, the same and yet different from the others, strange and yet familiar, unusual enough to be a must-have, practical enough to become a must-wear.

And they come also to eye each other furtively, to chart slyly the course woven by competitors, to kiss and to smile and to joke insincerely; to cut, occasionally, an old foe, or a new friend; to drink champagne on the terrace bar; to sneer, to snoop, to gossip, and to weep.

As soon as you negotiate your way through the surely

exaggeratedly Gallic security (Penny never seems to mind the intimate body searches, offering herself up like those fish you hear about that go to special parts of the sea to be nibbled clean by other, smaller fishes), you find yourself in the first of the three colossal, hangarlike halls. Colossal and yet, because of the oppressively low roof, with its sinister girders and gantries, strangely claustrophobic.

Gliding from stand to stand, her fine head high, her step majestic, Penny was in her element. Penny Moss may be only a little company, but with Penny in the ring, it punched above its weight. Junior assistants would be imperiously thrust aside and factory managers summoned from dark corners, from which they would emerge, brushing away crumbs and smiling meekly.

My job was to see to it that Penny made no major mistakes, ensuring that her (now irregular) flashes of brilliance were not undermined by (the increasingly common) gaffes. Who, after all, could forget the Year of Lemon and Purple? The tactic, as you can probably guess, was to make Penny think that everything was her idea anyway. Flicking through the samples, she'd find something that caught her eye, and she'd make a noise, indicating pleasure or revulsion. I would join in with subtle harmonies or really quite delicate dissonance. Either way, the right decision would emerge. There may, at some deep level, have been a knowledge that I was contributing to, perhaps even determining, our choices. But at the level of consciousness, or at least insofar as that consciousness found itself transformed into words, the job was all Penny and my role merely that of factotum, sandwich girl, and drudge.

I was on my best behavior and in my worst mood. Penny's clumsy attempt to prize Ludo from my arms had, if you'll pardon a moment of melodrama, frozen my heart. And in Paris, of all places, where we were supposed to be friends, sisters, almost, with our shared room, and our suppers together, and the world to be won. I know that revenge is a dish best served cold, but that shouldn't necessarily limit your range: I planned whole buffets.

But then I'd done that before, and my plans always ended up like Miss Havisham's wedding cake. I always *mean* to be vindictive, but when it comes down to it I tend to forget what I was supposed to be angry about, or I just lose interest, so I settle for a good long bitching session with Veronica. Anyway, Penny was a special case. I'd worked too hard to get where I was to risk losing it. Penny being a cow was always part of the deal.

So, over the course of the day, I let slip my plans for punishment beatings, sabotage, slander, and fraud. But by some weird alchemical process, as these silly thoughts fell away, they left behind a strange residue. That residue solidified into the form of an Irish driver of vans. It certainly wasn't that I decided to use Liam as revenge against Penny. Penny couldn't possibly be hurt by *that*. The opposite, in fact. It would be to offer her my head on a plate. It was more a moral thing. Being treated badly by Penny made it okay to do something harmlessly wicked myself.

Toward the end of the day, as Penny was having a grappa with Signor Solbiati, a sad figure in crumpled linen, happy to escape into nostalgia with an old acquaintance, I noticed a familiar, elegant frame sliding toward me, followed by a less familiar, less elegant shadow.

"So Milo," I said, "what did you make of Penny in

the all-too-solid flesh?" I was expecting viaducts of archness, but I was to be disappointed.

"She was something of a hit. Added much to the gaiety of what was becoming a rather tiresome party. After all your griping, I had no idea she was going to be such a scream."

"So"—I laughed—"she was right, then."

"Right about what?"

"You do fancy her."

His reply was more thoughtful than bitchy: "Well, perhaps if she were forty years younger and a boy. Let's go for an ice cream. This, by the way, is Claude, Claude Malheurbe."

I looked blankly at the middle-aged man by his side. He was profoundly unattractive, with one of those faces that looks as if it's been put on upside down. He was wearing a black silk shirt, unbuttoned to show his pale chest, tight black trousers, and a pair of disastrous black pixie boots. His hair was long and smelled strongly of mousse.

"*Claude Malheurbe,*" repeated Milo with emphasis.

"*Bonjour, Claude,*" I said, none the wiser.

"*Deconstruction* Malheurbe," hissed Milo.

Of course. What was it—five years ago? that fashion got hold of some wacky French ideas and decided to make explicit the hitherto hidden fact that clothes are made rather than whatever the alternative was supposed to be. It did this by showing seams and generally having things inside out or upside down. Malheurbe was behind it all with his book *The Hermeneutics of Cloth,* the fashion world's favorite unread book. The previously unknown *philosophe* was courted by couturiers and was whisked from his provincial lycée to burn briefly as a media star. In those days he was much more beret and Gauloises, which was why I didn't guess immediately.

His second book, *Visceral Couture,* which advocated wearing clothes on the *inside* of the body as a way of exposing the last fallacy of "biologism," that the internal organs escape the endless play of signification, had mysteriously proved less popular than the first, and he disappeared from the fashion firmament.

There, you see. *My* three years in fashion college were *not* wasted.

"What are you doing here, Milo?"

"All rather secret. Really can't tell you. It's not as if you're known for your discretion. I assume that's why they call you flabby lips."

Malheurbe sneered, or leered, or sleered, showing one brown tooth.

"Fine. Really couldn't care less, anyway," I said. Milo knew I meant it and panicked.

"Oh, all right then, no need for the Gestapo treatment, I'll tell you. You know how XXX"—Milo mentioned here a terribly familiar chain that I really cannot tell you the name of, however flabby my lips—"are going down the pan? Well, I've been asked to help. I'm here to let it be known, subtly, that I'm working for them."

"But I thought Swank did their PR?"

"Yes, they do."

"So what are *you* doing?"

"Well, you see, I'm here to give the impression that *I'm* doing it."

"But you're not doing it?

"No."

"I don't get it."

"Look. It's quite simple. What kind of image has XXX got?"

"Worthy, dull, cheap."

"Exactly. And what kind of image has Smack! PR got?"

"Pretty cool, I suppose. Exclusive. Young. A bit druggy, a bit clubby."

"On the *head,* darling, thank you. So, you see, as soon as word gets around that XXX has signed up Smack!, the whole world, by which I mean the whole world that matters, *our* world, is going to think that they're revamping their image, dragging in new, younger people, all that jazz. And you know what that means for City confidence and share prices."

"But you're not actually *doing* their PR!"

"No."

"Why not?"

"Because the kind of PR I'd do would scare off the grannies once and for all. This way, those in the know think XXX is cool, and the rest just carry on buying their knickers. Inspired, really."

"Doesn't Swank mind? It doesn't make them look too good, does it?"

"It was Swank's idea."

"What's in it for them?"

"They get a load of industry kudos for thinking up the scheme and hiring me. There's awards in that kind of work. It's exactly the kind of thing PR pros love. One day PR shall talk only unto PR."

So here was Milo, paid by a PR firm to pretend to be doing the PR for a company whose PR was really being done by the firm who paid Milo to pretend to do their PR. Unfortunately for XXX, as I found out later, Milo told *everyone* who'd listen that he was only pretending to do their PR. This, of course, was good PR for him, but bad PR for XXX. I think.

By this point we'd queued for ice cream, and *I'd* shelled out a hundred francs for three tiny Häagen-Dazs—Milo's meanness in small things was legendary, an understandable if unattractive relic of his days of penury. We went to eat them in a bleak little garden, enclosed on all sides by glass walls and staring Japanese midget women.

I was a little unsettled by Penny's success with Milo, so I threw him a couple of examples of Penny's comical linguistic misunderstandings and consequent confusion, mainly concerning the admittedly rather bemusing system of signs in the building. Milo liked to squirrel away the Penny stories I gave him, which he could then, in other contexts, attach to whichever designer he felt the need to bitch about.

At the mention of "linguistic" and, even more so, "signs," Claude hurriedly swallowed the last of his ice cream (omitting, however, to wipe away a chocolaty smear from his upper lip) and started to speak, his eyes fixed on a point somewhere in the air above my head, as if he were addressing a lecture theater.

"Ah yes, I can here explain for you your mother"— MOTHER!—"and her fear of the sign."

He drew out the word *sigheeeeeen* in a vaguely fetishistic way.

"It is not just here. The whole world is now a text, a written text: everywhere there are words."

Although I tried to listen out of politeness, Malheurbe's voice soon took on the quality of birdsong: not unmelodious, but basically just noise. Occasionally it would float back into focus:

"We are unconsciously, passively, enmeshed in writing, in decoding and decrypting."

Only to fade out again. Quickly bored, I looked over his shoulder and saw Penny reemerge from her grappa with Signor Solbiati. From her excessively regal gait, it looked as if it may have been *some* grappi (or whatever the plural is) rather than *a* grappa. And with that ability that people have for seeing you when you least want to be seen, she spotted our little group, waved, and advanced toward us.

"For preliterate societies this natural impulse to comprehend the environment takes the form of a deeper engagement with the natural world. So, every physical feature has a meaning, every rock, every tree, every animal spore, a significance, a narrative, a myth."

Before Penny could get to the glass corridor, she had to negotiate a huge art installation. There was a new one every season, and this time it was a monstrous construction called *L'Esprit de Tissu,* consisting of a wigwam-shaped chrome frame draped with millions of tatty lengths of yarn.

"With civilization man loses the ability to read nature."

Rather than walk around the obstruction (which, to be fair, would have taken a good five minutes), Penny opted, in a very Penny way, to go through it.

"It was only with the arrival of the Romantics and the invention of the sublime that nature could again be comprehended, albeit as something 'incomprehensible.' "

I suppose the side she was facing may well have looked, to her grappa-fuddled mind, not unlike an easily navigated bead curtain, and the installation had a certain airiness that invited an internal exploration. With barely a pause Penny thrust her way into the interior.

"You see, when you call nature 'sublime' you have substituted a single, although admittedly complex, signifier for the multiplicity of meanings that primitive man saw in nature."

I could see Penny's outline through the gauzy curtains of yarn. She'd become disoriented inside the wigwam and was feeling her way along the various internal planes and angles.

"And then even the sublime goes away—who other than I now talks of the sublime?—and all we have is the simple good thing, the new 'nature,' which is completely benign, that thing which people with no style, no élan, walk through on a Sunday afternoon, with his ugly wife, with his ugly children and his ugly dog. I'm sorry, but I hate these peoples."

As her efforts to fight her way out became increasingly frantic, I noticed with alarm that the wigwam itself began to wobble. I was not the only one: nervous officials were moving toward L'Esprit de Tissu; among them were a couple of gendarmes excited by the possibility of being able to shoot an art terrorist in the act of desecrating a national monument.

"But as the natural world has become lost to language, so our social world, and the built environment, has become, as I said, all writing. And so what happens when a person finds himself in a country where he does not speak the language (this has never, of course, happened to me: I speak all the languages)?"

The gendarmes and PV flunkies reached the wigwam but seemed reluctant to break in, despite the now precarious state of the structure, which was being vigorously shaken by the one-woman earthquake within: who, after all, could know how heavily armed the terrorist might be? A fair crowd had gathered: sober-suited sales executives and flamboyant fashion junkies united in their lust for blood and the faint but not forlorn hope that *L'Esprit de Tissu* might implode.

"For example, your mother? I'll tell you. She is again in the position of the civilized person who cannot read nature and so feels again the giddy fear, the vertigo, terror, loss, panic. I think you will find this explains your mother. Now we go for sex, please, yes?"

With the mention of sex I tore my attention away from the engrossing spectacle beyond. I looked around. Milo had disappeared, the serpent. He'd probably been looking for the chance to dump the philosopher on somebody all day.

"Sex?" I said a little more loudly than I intended, resulting in a couple of turned heads. I had been caught off guard, but Parisian propositions were hardly novel, and I had a coping strategy to hand. "I'm sorry," I said, "I'm a little busy right now. Why don't I meet you tonight?"

I named a café in Montmartre, a place to which I'd never been nor had any intention of ever going. It's my standard way of dealing with that sort of pass. It always works. And when you don't turn up, they either think something poetic and tragic might have happened to you and hold you in a special place in their hearts all their lives, or they curse you for ten minutes and then forget all about it.

Penny burst forth from the wigwam. Her hair, which had been tightly and precisely coiled into a chignon, had broken free and hung raggedly across her face, with a stray clump pointing to ten o'clock. Somehow her neat knee-length skirt had revolved 180 degrees, and the split pointed accusingly at her navel. The audience broke into spontaneous applause and hissed the gendarmes as they laid rough hands upon her.

"Write down, please," demanded Malheurbe. I scribbled something on the piece of paper he shoved at me, and he scuttled off, clearly thinking that what was said about English girls was all true. The spell was broken, and I ran toward Penny. By the time I reached the crowd, I saw that I had been beaten to it. Milo, in perfect, mellifluous French, was gently soothing the gendarmes and flirting with the PV officials. Penny looked upon her savior with eyes of Magdalenic devotion and would, I'm sure, have washed his feet, dried them with her hair, and anointed them with fragrant oils, had the necessary equipment and sufficient privacy been available.

And that's about it, really, incidentwise. No charges were made against Penny, and she fortunately missed the satirical endpiece on the French early evening news. The next day was like the one before, except with more cloth, less philosophy, and a dramatic reduction in Penny-centered art installation–oriented mishaps. On Saturday morning we flicked off the safety catch and gave Paris another burst of semiautomatic shopping, and then it was Eurostar and home. And yes, I thought lots more about Liam. And yes, the idea of sleeping with him, just once or maybe twice, if it was nice, had grown in my mind, nurtured by boredom and Penny's haphazard malice. But no, at that stage, constancy, faithfulness, devotion, and love had the better, just, of abandonment, concupiscence (my favorite word since A levels, O dishy Mr. Carapace, dreamy stand-in teacher of English and inciter of teenage lust!), and revenge.

One thing more. In the station, and on the train back, I had the strangest feeling that I was being watched, perhaps followed. Nothing tangible, just that I sensed a shadow lurking at the edges of things. It was probably a metaphor.

CHAPTER 6

How Can I Deny, She's Mine, I'm Hers?

It was nice getting back on Sunday. Ludo capered around me like a puppy: if I'd let him, I'm sure he'd have licked my face. He'd even bought flowers; clueless flowers, but flowers. We had dinner upstairs at Odette's, surrounded by the magical golden mirrors that make you look beautiful, even when you're not. He was buzzing with ideas and jokes and little impersonations that lasted two seconds but caught someone completely. It was my favorite Ludo: serious and silly, letting his mind wander down strange and sometimes dark paths, but always coming back again into the light with some pretty bauble. And when Ludo was like this, I found that I changed, too. I wanted to play his word games and think about important things and shake my mind clear from the clutter and trivia and bitchiness.

We made love that night for the first time in weeks. It was one of the best ever. I've said that Ludo didn't have the sexiness gene, but that isn't fair (you may have noticed that I'm not always). It was more that I'd just got out of the habit of finding Ludo sexy. It had something to do with the fact that he thought sex was fundamentally amusing. And yes, we all know that funny men are sexy, but that doesn't mean that sex should be funny. Ludo had a way of saying just the wrong sort of funny thing at particularly . . . intense moments, and by breaking the tension, the moment would be lost. The worst thing he did was to turn the body (usually mine) into a comedy prop, tickling, blowing, nurdling, sucking, not from desire or to achieve any kind of focused sexual pleasure, but just to see what sorts of silly noises it would make.

Well, that night it was different. No blowing raspberries on my tummy this time, just a long, deep kiss at the top of the stairs, the kind of kiss that makes you lose where one face ends and the other begins, and without the kiss ever stopping we were in bed, and he was inside me, motionless but for a barely perceptible pulsing, and then building slowly, by tiny increments. I decided to fake a little orgasm—see, I told you I wasn't all bad—but after a couple of preliminary moans I found the real thing was sneaking up on me, and I sobbed and bit his shoulder in surprise, and then he came, laughing and joyous.

I was late for work on Monday morning. For once Penny had arrived before me. She was in tears. Sukie, a new girl with a bit more brains than the rest, had called me back as I ran up the stairs.

"You'd better watch it, Katie, Penny's had a setback."

"What kind of setback? It's not bloody Harvey Nicks again, is it? They're getting to be more trouble than they're worth."

"No, it's not Harvey Nicks. It's that Young British Designer Award thing. Somebody nominated Penny, and then one of the judges phoned up to see how old she was. When they found out she wasn't under thirty, they chucked her out."

"Oh, God. I wonder who nominated her? Probably did it herself."

Sukie gasped and giggled. Penny still had the status of a deity, and a potentially cruel one at that, among the shop girls. Blasphemy always shocked and excited them. I wasn't quite sure what to make of Sukie. She was certainly bright, and she knew how to show enthusiasm at the right moments. She looked like a pretty Richard III, dark and a little hunched, with unreadable eyes. She was Cheltenham Ladies College and claimed to be "filling in," although between what she never said. On balance I didn't trust her.

When I got to the office I found it full of people. Hugh was there, standing helplessly in the traditional English way. Tony, the sample machinist, was weeping in sympathy with Penny, mouthing the last word of each of her phrases. Mandy stood by, her mouth tense, pursed, and ready to spring.

"They called me mature. *Mature!*"

"Mature," mouthed Tony.

"How could they, the beasts?"

"Beasts," echoed Tony.

"You know, Penny my love," said Hugh, "maybe they have a point. Sixt—er, fifty is, well, you know, a touch, um, as they said, mature, for a, you know, *young* designer." I'd never seen Hugh so dithery. Distant, detached, divorced, yes, but dithery, no.

"Well," Penny said petulantly, irritated by such a lack of loyalty, "Sarah Bernhardt played Juliet at the age of sixty, with a wooden leg, and only one buttock."

"*One buttock?*" I asked, joining in.

"Yes, one buttock. But of course, that was in the days before bicycles."

This raised all kinds of interesting, if ghastly, questions. How did she lose a buttock? Or was she born with only one? And which buttock? The same side as the wooden leg? Were they lost in the same gruesome accident, one involving some unfathomable piece of farming equipment, with flails and blades? Or had Penny misunderstood? Perhaps Sarah whatever had lost a billhook or some butter.

"Isn't that somewhere in Voltaire?" Hugh suggested.

"Oh yes, she played all the great roles."

"No, I mean there's a story somewhere involving a siege at a harem—"

"Sarah Bernhardt," interrupted Penny, in a tone that suggested firmly that this particular conversation was at an end, "was not *that* sort of actress. Any more than I was."

After half an hour the storm showed little sign of abating. Penny's emotional stamina was legendary. Hugh performed an expert tactical retreat, leaving the soothing of Penny to those of us on the mollification payroll. We tried the line that Penny Moss was clearly far too established a company for the petty little awards, which were intended for struggling newcomers, and that they'd no more consider us than Gucci, Max Mara, or Yves Saint Laurent. There was some reduction in the flow, and sensing that hyperbole might yield the best results, I wheeled out the "But Penny, you're the last of the greats. Balenciaga, Dior, Chanel, gone, all gone. It's just you now, Penny. You owe it to the world to carry on."

"Yes, I suppose you're right," she said, but the life had gone from her face, and she looked close to her true age.

The phone rang. It was Sukie.

"There's a Milo Mayerbeer here to see Penny."

"Milo," I said aloud, "what does he want?"

Penny stopped sniffing. "Milo? Is that Milo. Oh, I suggested he pop in to chat about our profile. It was the least I could do after he helped with my little difficulty with that malevolent art object. Ask him to come up in five minutes."

Suddenly the face was alive again. Tiny muscles went into action, carving beauty out of the soft dough. Nose and eyes were dabbed dry, makeup was speedily applied. When Milo appeared at the top of the stairs, she was once more the perfect drag queen of his dreams.

Milo's advice was simple: a little less discretion about our famous customers; a little more work with the fashion editors; perhaps a touch more daring in the collection. I'd been saying the same thing to Penny for months, but it took Milo's dark eyes and full lips, along with a bill for a thousand pounds (not mentioned during the course of this preliminary chat), to drive the message home.

That afternoon Penny started on the collection for next winter. This involved sifting through her scribbled notes, her drawings, and her photographs, playing with the swatches from Première Vision. Somehow out of the confusion ideas would begin to form. An evening dress would be suggested by a single, sinuous line from a sketchbook. A perfect wedding outfit would emerge, hat first, from the clutter; jackets and skirts would form like a vampire, refleshed from a mound of bone ash, by a drop of virgin's blood.

And I watched and made my suggestions, deft hints, and criticisms. I fetched things, and made tea, and soothed and calmed and flattered. This was what I loved. You see, I told a bit of a white lie at the beginning when I said that I didn't really want to be a designer. Of course I did. That's why I went to fashion college. That's why I took the job in the shop. That's why I seduced Ludo. That's why I put up with the prima donna–ing of Penny. But everybody who works in fashion wants to be a designer, to achieve the holy grail of being "creative." It's pathetic, and I didn't want to appear pathetic. Not to you. Not then.

I'm conscious that I've made Penny into a bit of a grotesque. And she *is* a bit of a grotesque. But you have to remember that that's not all she is. She had it. I hate to say it, but it's true. I'm not talking now just about the bruising, battle-hardened self-belief. She had *that* in spades, but it's never quite enough. No, she had the other thing as well: the little homunculus inside her that told her what people wanted to wear, that whispered to her the secret of making women feel that yes, *this* was the suit to buy, that *this* was the dress that would make everything all right, that *these* were the clothes that would win the desire of men, earn the admiration or envy of women, that would secure the promotion at work.

You know the feeling. You've looked in the cramped little mirror in the changing room, and you're not sure, so you step in your stocking feet out into the shop to stand in front of the big mirror. You stroke the fabric over your hips; you twist each way to try to catch your bottom unawares. And the joy begins to well up inside you, as if you're three sips into a martini. The hours of chasing that feeling, of dissatisfaction, despair, are forgotten. The assistant coos and sighs, and for once you know she means it, and you even think about thanking her by buying the bag that goes with it (but you don't).

Penny had a kind of formula, which she tried to hammer into me when I began designing with her. "Darling," she'd say, "does it make her look rich, thin, or beddable? All three together and you've got a husband somewhere crying over his credit card bill."

So Penny could do it. Not as consistently as before, but her strike rate was still pretty high. And I was learning how. There would come a time when it would be *my* scribbles and notes that would take on life and move through the streets of London, and I would have a little Katie Castle of my own to do the things I do.

So Monday passed, and Tuesday passed. I hadn't quite forgotten about Thursday, but the thought of it was a toy to play with and not a real thing at all. It helped to occupy spare minutes, those lovely still moments when nothing happens. I quite enjoyed the thought that I'd been reckless and enjoyed even more the knowledge that I didn't actually have to do anything about it.

It was Wednesday. Ludo telephoned at five-thirty, just as I was thinking of going home.

"I'm in the supermarket. What do you want me to get?"

"Get for what?"

The line went funny. I heard something about Guinness.

What was he talking about? Guinness? I'm cold. Did he know about Liam?

"The line's bad. What did you say?"

"To go with the beef and Guinness pie?"

Hang on, deep breaths. Beef and Guinness pie was Ludo's dinner party special. And then it all came back.

I'd arranged a dinner party weeks ago. Liam and Paris had put it out of my head. Fuck. It was the last thing I wanted. Especially given the guests.

"Oh, vegetables or a salad or something. I don't really care."

"That's helpful, thanks. What shall I get to drink?"

"To go with beef and Guinness pie? What else but Guinness?"

"But you hate Guinness!"

"It's chic at the moment," I lied.

Midweek dinner parties are an obscenity, at least when they're yours. No time to get the house properly sorted. No time for dressing to look nice. Just a frantic tidy round and a smear of Mac. And I must have been insane to arrange this one just after Première Vision. Thank God Ludo likes to cook. He's not bad, either, as long as he sticks to hale-and-hearty and doesn't venture anything too elaborate or exotic. I always say he cooks like a cannibal: one big pot with some unfortunate beast half-in and half-out and a big spoon to stir. And he always says that tidying for me is like a martial art: a couple of savage kicks and thrusts and the room cowers in submission.

It being midweek, it was mainly second-division friends. Oh, and Ludo's. Ludo only really had two close friends: the aforementioned Tom, who was a fellow teacher; and Daniel, whom he'd known since his school days. Tom was a self-confessed roughneck from some depressed town in the Midlands: Birmingham or Nottingham, or somewhere else with factories. He was quite amusing, in a style that combined crudity with odd touches of surrealism. All of my friends hated and feared him, which made him occasionally useful.

Daniel was much more presentable. He worked for an auction house, albeit in a fairly lowly capacity, which made his shabby-genteel look acceptable. Just. Both of them were single: Tom was too mean to get a girlfriend, and Daniel was too nice.

By fluke or fate, there was a faintly Irish feel to the evening. As well as the Guinness, I'd invited a fashion writer whose name, as it appeared in print, was generally some variation on the theme of Blarãnuggh Œroughnãgh. It was, however, pronounced Blahna, and that's what I intend to call her. She was plump and rather vague, in a misty-eyed, Celtic Dawn manner. Whether this was a ploy or simple native stupidity, I could never work out. She worked for a more or less respectable Sunday newspaper, and although you'd have thought her position would give her a certain weight of punch in my world, the general feeling was that she'd plateaued. She certainly never quite made that inner circle of clittorati, whose whims and fancies end up as instructions passed to pattern cutters or fed into machines. I should stress that despite her name, Blahna was no more Irish than I was: her parents, stolid Stevenage midbourgeois, had picked out the name from the *Oxford Book of Pretentious Names No Sane Person Would Give Their Child*.

Blahna's husband, some kind of commercial lawyer called Luke, was very dry. One might almost say arid. Think Gobi Desert. Think Namibia. He had an irritating way of seeing through you that made it almost impossible not to stammer when you talked to him, and he wore rimless spectacles, which gave him the air of a concentration camp doctor. How he put up with Blahna of the Celtic Dawn I'll never know. The dinner party had been arranged mainly for their benefit, as we owed them one from two years ago.

Kookai and Kleavage were coming, because they were simply everywhere, and if you didn't want them to come to something, you actually had to single them out and tell them that they were *not welcome,* which was usually more trouble than it was worth. Anyway, they might bring along some new Milo stories.

Finally, there was the ever faithful Veronica. Veronica was my oldest friend. She'd been with me since our infant school in East Grinstead. She idolized me. She'd always copied what I wore. She used to try to speak and walk like me. We were sometimes mistaken for twins, not because of any physical resemblance (yuk)—no, Veronica most definitely belongs on the *wrong* side of plain—but because she was like an actress playing me, and sometimes her performance was uncanny.

Of course, everybody was late. Daniel and Tom had been drinking in the only local pub that hasn't metamorphosed into a restaurant. Ludo had seen off a bottle of wine in the kitchen, which at least meant he didn't feel the need to go into frantic catch-up mode. The boys brought carrier bags full of cans and bottles of beer. The girls brought flowers. Luke and Blahna didn't bring anything, which is something to do with hitting a certain point on the income spectrum.

The "posh crisps and chitchat" bit of the evening was a touch lame. I just couldn't be bothered catalyzing. The truth was that I didn't really care about these people. They weren't part of the plan, or at best they were tangential. The fashiony ones, Blahna, Kookai, and Kleavage, had little to offer in the way of influence or information, and the others weren't amusing enough to make up for their lack of relevance.

Veronica was different. Not better. In many ways much worse. But different. You see, she was a friend. I have this theory that friendship has nothing to do with liking people. There are lots of people you might like but would never count as friends. And (I admit this side of the argument is a bit more controversial) there are people you would have to count as friends whom you don't really like. So there has to be something else to it, and I think it's—and don't dare laugh—destiny. By a friend, I mean someone whose life has become so wrapped up in yours that it doesn't matter what you do, they'll just always be there. That was Veronica.

The only potential interest in the evening involved a loosely drawn up plan I had for matchmaking Daniel and Kookai. Or Tom and Kleavage. Or the other way round. Either way, it was a challenge. Not so much in the boy-to-girl direction. Whatever else you want to say about them, or not say, Kookai and Kleavage are both easy on the eye—they work in PR, after all. I was much more concerned about retuning K & K to the T & D frequency. But of course, I'd forgotten about the Big Change. And what's the Big Change? Why, the shift from there being lots of boys in hot pursuit of not very many girls to there being lots of girls searching feverishly for the increasingly scarce presentable man. And by presentable, I don't mean good-looking, clever, witty, or wise. I mean not weird, psychotic, deformed, or bankrupt. Related to this in some kind of complex way that I've never been able to work out (slide rules and log tables may be used, but *not* calculators) is the fact that deep down every girl, however humdrum, puddeny, slack-mouthed, spotty, snaggle-toothed, frizzy-haired, cross-eyed, knock-kneed or rankly fishy, now thinks she *deserves* a Jude Law.

It was only when we sat down to eat that I realized that while *I* had to fight down waves of extreme irritation, Kookai and Kleavage were transfixed by the boys' usual semi-stream-of-consciousness larking. Although Ludo had done most of the work on the main course, I still found myself in and out of the kitchen, and whenever I came back there would be a new subject bouncing around: bricolage, jelly tots as jewelry, the mystic significance of misshapen chocolates. At one point Tom announced that he was going to invade India.

"The whole subcontinent must be trembling," said Luke, never one to miss out on an opportunity for sarcasm.

"No, you see, that's just it. No invasion of India has ever failed."

"Rubbish—what about the Japanese!" said Daniel.

"They never made it past Burma, so they never technically invaded India. But my point is that either I'll succeed and become emperor or be worshiped as a god or whatever, or I'll blow it, and make it into the record books as the first person to fail to conquer India."

"I'm not really happy about you invading India," said Kookai, furrowing her pretty brow. Perhaps she really did think that Tom was about to leap from a landing craft onto the beach at Bombay. "Can't you invade somewhere else? What about Denmark or Paraguay?"

"No glory. But if you ask nicely, I'll think about it."

The next time I returned with a bottle of wine, the relative sizes of genitals among the great apes had come up (doesn't it always?). Daniel was in the lead this time:

". . . it's all to do with mating strategies. Gorillas operate in families, with one big male who has sole access to the females. So they don't need much in the way of . . . you know, wedding tackle—there's no competition. Chimps, on the other hand, live in big, promiscuous groups, where more or less everyone gets a go whenever a female comes in season. So the chimp with the biggest and best equipment wins—he basically flushes out the rivals."

Kleavage gave him a steely, blush-inducing look. "And what about you boys? Are you more like the chimp or the gorilla? Or are some of you one and some the other?"

"W-well," stammered Daniel, who'd begun his observation in a spirit of scientific inquiry, without expecting so brazen a turn, "that's very interesting, because humans are midway between chimps and gorillas in, er, um . . . in . . . size. That suggests that our natural mating behavior has elements of both. Perhaps family groups with a bit of infidelity on the side."

"What a load of balls," I said, going for a cheap laugh, but also rescuing Daniel from a blush so deep that even his palms were red.

Okay, so I suppose some of it was fun, but it really wasn't *fashion*. And even if it had been, I suspect that with each sip of my bittersweet Guinness I would still have drifted further away—not into some mythic Celtic Dawn, but into the arms of an altogether real slice of Celtic brawn. Sorry.

Veronica joined me in the kitchen.

"Ludo's lovely, isn't he."

"He has his moments."

"Have you set a date yet?"

It was the question I most hated. There was no smart or clever way out of it, no reply that didn't make me sound like a sap.

"Not an actual day, no. More a rough season."

"Oh, that's nice. Roughly when?"

"Roughly soon."

"I bet you've designed your dress. Is it beautiful?"

"Oh, look, Tom's acting out a gorilla and Daniel's being a chimp: let's go back in."

As ever, the beef and Guinness pie had gone down a storm with the boys and at best was barely nibbled at by the girls: teased, flattered, pushed around, and then neglected. At about eleven I made some remarks about an early start the next day, what with collections to design and shops to run. Blahna belatedly tried to get some steers about next winter, but I fobbed her off, yawning, with generalities about tartan being the new brown, or tweed the new velvet. I may even have said something profound about hemlines going down in a recession. She made a pencil note in a little black book, her tongue sticking sharply from the corner of her mouth. We were kissing both sides that year, and leaving took forever, but eventually, mercifully, even Veronica had gone, with a last lovelorn glance over her shoulder.

"You okay, my sweet thing?" asked Ludo as I loaded the dishwasher.

"Mmm. Seemed to go quite well, didn't it?"

"Yes. You know, I think that Sarenna might actually like Daniel. Or was it Tom? Or did Ayesha fancy Tom? No, she liked Daniel. I don't know. Someone liked somebody."

Ayesha? Sarenna? Who . . . ? Ah. Kookai and Kleavage. I'd almost forgotten.

Normally, of course, *I* would have known exactly who'd fallen for whom. That's what I'm here for. I can read the signs. Again, it's all to do with focus. The way that girls have of closing in like an owl on a mouse, excluding everything, senses trained on the victim. But to read the signs I need my own focus, and that was else-where.

"I've something to tell you," he said. "I didn't want to bring it up while the others were around."

Suddenly my focus was back right here in our kitchen. It could only mean one thing.

It was the date.

He'd fixed on the date!

Ever since it had become clear that we were going to get married, the date had remained, despite my best ef-forts, an infuriatingly vague "next year sometime" af-fair. Well, this was it. It was going to be July 29, or August 3, or June 15, or some *real* date, a day when real people were going to be born and to die, and we were going to be married. I leaped, yes, literally leapt, into the air, squealing like a schoolgirl.

"When when when?" I begged, jumping up and down. "I love you love you love you."

Ludo gave me a gorgeous shy smile, not a snake-oil salesman's showstopper, but a wonderfully human, gen-tle, loving smile; smile of my man.

"I didn't realize you cared so much about it. It's com-ing out next month."

My squeals died like a cockroach under a boot.

"I'm sorry? What's coming out next month?"

"The magazine. The magazine with my poem. The *London Poetry Review*."

And then I realized what he was talking about. In-spired by the "me me me" woman across the square, the one who put her head in the oven like a cake, he'd taken to writing poems. I half remembered him sending things off. And the mild despair as they returned. Perhaps he had said something about a piece being accepted.

"Do you want to see the poem they're using?"

"Why not?"

Was he blind or stupid? How could he not see that I was hurt? But no, fired with what he thought was my enthusiasm for his stupid poem, he scuttled off and then came back waving a sheet of A4.

"I didn't show it to you before I sent it in. There's a particularly good bit of sprung rhythm in the sixth line. . . ." Dully, I took the paper he proffered. Within two lines, say, eight seconds, I was crying. This is why:

SLEEP

All elegance awake, my love grows large
In sleep: her mouth gapes, and grunts escape
Her scum-encrusted lips. Her big hips barge
Their way through dreams with hairy-haunched, ape-
Like indifference. As old dogs leap
For phantom hares from fireside shagpile
So she pursues her chocolates asleep,
Then smiles a drowsy praline-sated smile.
Impenetrable thermal vest and pants
Encase her in true, tyrannic chastity—
A skin as tough as rhino hide 'twixt me
And her. I dream of knickers made in France
Of delicate dark lace. But now my love bestirs
And how can I deny, she's mine, I'm hers?

I mean, what would you have said or done? I tore it into little pieces and threw them in the bin. I then took the pieces back out of the bin and stamped them into the wooden floor of the kitchen.

"Katie, what's wrong?" said Ludo, plaintively. "Is it because it's in such a conventional verse form? There's been a move back toward traditional forms, as long as they're handled imaginatively. That's why I've used sprung rhythm and asymmetric caesuras. Or is it just that you think the Petrarchan sonnet is superior to the Shakespearean? For me the Petrarchan doesn't work in English, there just aren't enough rhymes in English as opposed to Italian, and so it always sounds forced."

"For Christ's sake, Ludo, can't you see, you've told the world that I'm fat and ugly, and look like an old dog or a rhino, or something? What will people think? You're a bastard, a total bastard, and I hate you."

"But darling, who do you know who's even heard of the *London Poetry Review*? It's an obscure journal with a readership of four hundred people, and you can be sure that none of them have any connection with the world of fashion. But anyway, my love, it's a *poem*. It's an artificial construct that's got nothing to do with the world. It's an artifact made of words. It's not real. It's not about you. It could be about anyone. Or no one."

"Ludo," I said.

"Yes?"

"Will you please take your Shakespearean sonnet, your asymmetric caesuras, and your gorilla-sized . . . whatever and stick them up your fucking arse in any kind of rhythm you like, sprung or otherwise."

And then I went to bed, having made it quite clear, I think, that I did not expect to be joined there by Ludo.

CHAPTER 7

The Deed of Darkness

Well, that's the background. I've laid it all before you: the vague feeling of dissatisfaction, which fed, in turn, the desire for a last little fling before I curled up like a cat into contented, uneventful, safe domesticity; the general irritation with Penny, which gave me a doubtless spurious sense of moral justification for any minor act of betrayal; the arrival into my life of opportunity in the beguiling form of Liam; the immediate, bitter spur of that poem.

None of those would have been enough on its own to make me do what I did. I often wonder what would have happened if I'd wriggled out of going to the depot that day, or if Liam hadn't been there, or if the bloody *London Review of Stupid Poetry* hadn't accepted Ludo's crappy poem, or if Penny hadn't been a cow. I'm not saying that I'd be a candidate for beatification, with old ladies in Peru claiming that I'd cured their warts or irregular periods, and pilgrims going to East Grinstead to bathe in the miraculous waters that sprang from my dad's rock garden, but I'm sure I wouldn't have got into so much trouble.

I didn't sleep well that night. For what felt like hours,

I lay and listened, with that supernatural acuity you get when you're *really* pissed off, to the music of the night: car alarms calling to each other; the heavy rumble of the late night train that Ludo says carries nuclear waste through the heart of London; the eerie sound, like babies being roasted alive, of cats fucking in the back garden; the astonishingly clear tone of a man having a pee next door. My mind was racing. Images triggered by the nighttime noises mingled with scenes from the past few days, forming a dizzying, nauseating montage. I tried to calm myself by thinking about lovely shoes by Manolo Blahnik, and Gina, and Jimmy Choo, shoes I would one day own in rack upon rack, like Imelda Marcos. But the shoes kept getting run over by nuclear trains, or worn by roasted babies, or screwed by rampant cats, or peed on by old men.

Finally, searching for an oasis of calm in all the horror, I settled on Liam. His face, like his voice, both soothed and excited me; his narrow hips, his predatory walk, his hands, long fingered but work-hardened, just plain excited me. And without any act of will on my part, I found myself doing something I'd never done before. I fantasized about a man, a man of flesh and blood who existed in the real world of people and things. Of course, I'd had endless, intense erotic fantasies before, at least one per day, often dozens, but the beauty of a fantasy is that it never needs to be, and in fact should never be, tethered to reality. At school, faceless, perfect boys would come to me as I worked in class and kiss me and caress me as I pressed my thighs together under the desk. One teacher, Miss Plenty, knew, I'm sure, what I was doing, but she only smiled a faint smile and looked through me with her pale gray eyes. The same boys came to me still. Often, when Penny thought I was concentrating on some particularly thorny production problem, hunched over a pattern or a book of swatches, I would be trembling, with my nails cutting deep into my palms and my cheeks flushed.

I'd never even, with one exception, moved from these exquisite, pure, ethereal forms to pop stars or actors. The exception was David Bowie, who used to enter like a ghost into the spindly, pimply frame of Conor O'Neil as we snogged at the Methodist youth club disco, with Veronica looking on.

But now here I was summoning *his* presence, touching *my* breasts with *his* hand through *my* hand, writhing and undulating to rhythms I gave him. At last the night noises were banished, and I finally fell asleep with my hand still clasped moistly between my thighs.

Well, at least it sent me off with a smile on my face.

And then it was morning. On came the radio alarm, tuned, irritatingly, to Radio 3. I pinged it back to 4 and rolled over to elbow Ludo into the kitchen. It took me a second or two of elbowing air, pillow, and duvet before I realized what was happening. Morning tea with Ludo was always one of our best times, talking over the day to come, laughing at all the silly things in the world. Well, not today. I was too annoyed to go for a snuggle on the couch, where, I guessed, he'd spent the night.

Dressing was a bit of a dilemma. If I met Liam, I'd be going out straight from work, so my outfit had to do for both. The girls at work are like Eskimos with snow: they can spot nuances invisible to the untrained eye. If I laid it on too thick, they'd know I was going out. And they'd know it wasn't with the girls.

In the end I opted for La Perla underwear (obvious, I know, but sometimes obvious is just right), a vintage YSL dinner jacket, Chloe indigo jeans, and some funky fuchsia mules. I grabbed my Bill Amberg case, a lovely present from Milo, who does the PR, or rather did, before he was eased out for purloining too many goodies for his intimates, and went for a coffee on the corner. I sat in the window for twenty minutes, smoking three whole Silk Cuts, my heart hardening with each shallow draw.

I hadn't written it down, but I remembered the name of the pub. I hadn't yet quite decided to go, but I had decided that I definitely wouldn't *not* go. If you see what I mean. The idea of Kilburn was a bigger obstacle than infidelity. I'd only ever been to Kilburn once, and that was by mistake. It was truly horrid. Brixton may be a bit hairy, but at least it's cool, and there are places in Brixton where you might actually want to go. But Kilburn just seemed to be a seedy high street, with shops for poor people, selling cheap batteries and East European cooking implements, and wherever you looked there were drunks lying down on the pavement, and women with no tights, and dirty little children holding on to the pram, and old people with nowhere to go because all they had was their state pensions, and ugly men with dogs, staring at you and hating you and wanting to kill you. Well, that's what I thought in the seven minutes it took me to get a taxi the hell outta there.

At midday Ludo called to apologize.

"I'm sorry. I think I understand why you were upset. I can see it was insensitive."

"Forget it," I said, spitting out the words like a curse.

"Oh, God," said Ludo, dismayed, "you've done that hardening-your-heart thing, haven't you?"

"I have, actually, yes. If you'd been in the café this morning, you'd have heard it, like pack ice forming."

"Please don't do that. Look, I'm going to do my guppy face for you now. You know that always makes you laugh. Are you ready? Here it comes."

There was a pause of four or five seconds.

"You're not laughing, are you?"

"No."

"Right. That's it. I'm going to walk like an ape. That *always* works."

I was determined not to laugh. If I laughed, I'd feel a love surge, and I wouldn't be able to do the bad thing; and I wanted to do the bad thing.

"Look, just please stop it. I'm not in the mood. Give me a couple of days and I'll be okay about it."

"I can't wait a couple of days. I feel sick. You know I'd give anything for that poem to have been rejected."

"No, you wouldn't. *I* would. How would you like it if I told everyone that you couldn't get it up?"

"That's not fair. How many times has that happened? Twice?"

"Four times, actually, but you're missing the point. The point is that if you'd sat down with the greatest minds in history, Albert Einstein and Madame Curie, Isaac Newton and Vivienne Westwood, and whoever else you want, you couldn't have come up with anything more insulting."

"Look, I've said I'm sorry, I've tried to explain that it's not even about you. I don't know what else I can do. Let's go out and get drunk tonight and it'll all be all right."

"Sorry, I'm out with the girls tonight."

"Which girls?" he asked dully, and without suspicion.

"*The* girls, silly." I knew he wouldn't inquire further.

"Oh. You *were* joking when you put Vivienne Westwood in with Isaac Newton, weren't you?"

"Really, Ludo! And I thought irony was supposed to be a male thing."

It was five to six. Penny was long gone. The studio was emptying fast. The girls in the shop were poised, like herons over a fish pond, waiting to shut the door and cash up. I was on the phone to Veronica.

"If you had a boyfriend, Veronica, would you ever think of seeing another man?"

"Katie!" she shouted. "No! Never! When I give myself to a man, it will be completely, or I'll never—"

"Yes, very sweet. But it's easy for you. It's easy to be good when you haven't got the choice."

"Look, what's this about, Katie? You're not thinking of . . . doing something, are you?"

"Of course not, stupid. I was just thinking in general, you know, in the round."

"But Katie, you don't do anything in general. You always do things in specific."

"Veronica, if I wanted to be psychoanalyzed, I'd have gone to . . ." But I couldn't think of anyone I'd have gone to, so I settled for, "a psychoanalyst. And who gave you the right," I carried on nastily, "to tear my character to ribbons? What do you know about anything? You sit there with all your files, and things, and what good do you do? All you can do is criticize and carp, and be sarcastic." Veronica was a receptionist in an alternative pain clinic, full of acupuncturists, and herbalists, and cranial osteopaths, and other loonies. The nearest I came to complementary medicine was feeling better when somebody told me I looked nice.

"I'm sorry, Katie. I know you wouldn't do anything cruel to Ludo. I know how much you love him. But you *have* treated boys badly in the past."

"Name one."

"Malcolm Gidlow."

"*Malcolm Gidlow!* He was a joke. You can hardly blame me for *that*."

"Stephen Solanki."

"He went away to university, and you can't expect me to have hung around waiting for his holidays." I checked the clock on the wall. "Look, I'm sorry, I have to go. Talk soon, bye."

I put the phone down. Damned if I was going to be lectured at by Veronica, of all people. A few more quick calls to make. First, directory inquiries to get the number of the Black Lamb. Straightforward enough. And then phone the pub to find out exactly how to get there.

"Hello," says a voice.

"Is that the Black Lamb?"

"No, er, yes, it is. I mean I'm not, but it is."

"Exactly where are you, please?"

"I'm just on the phone, the one by the lounge bar."

"Look, I haven't got time to play games. Where is the Black Lamb?"

"Ah now, well, where you are coming from?"

"The tube station."

"Well, just walk down the High Road on the left hand side. There's some shops and what-have-you, and then you get to us. It'll take four minutes from the station."

That would do.

The one thing you can say in favor of Kilburn is that it's on the Jubilee line, the one with the fewest smelly people. Funny it should go to a dump like Kilburn. It took twenty minutes from Bond Street. It was an interlude of intense excitement. I kept saying to myself that nothing would happen, that I'd stay for one drink and then make some excuse. But my body had ideas of its own, and I realized that I was smiling only when a woman opposite, in a covetable fake ocelot, smiled back.

And when I left the station Kilburn seemed, despite the dark and the drizzle, momentarily less disgusting than I remembered. There were trees here, and a block of expensive private apartments, and a road with the quaint name of Shoot-up Hill. And then I passed under the brooding, dripping bridges: one, two, three, all within a hundred yards of the station. Each had its sinister population of hunched, shabby pigeons. So many bridges: it was as if all the world wanted to pass over the Kilburn High Road, hurrying to and from the places in the world that mattered, the places where nice people lived and money was made.

I had entered Kilburn proper. I'd forgotten about the kebab houses with their grisly torsos turning on the spit; I'd forgotten about the funny little food shops where Africans and Asians buy their okra and yams and the brown thing that looks like an old lady's arthritic knee joint (or is *that* a yam?). Didn't they know there was a gleaming Marks & Spencer not ten minutes away by car? I'd forgotten about the curious "Irish" bakeries, full of white bread and sticky buns gone fluffy and yesterday's cakes half price.

Most of all, I'd forgotten about the sickly sweet smell of the Halal butchers. I was early, and for some reason I stopped and looked through one window at the strips and hunks and flanks of meat. There was a stack of what looked like firewood against the wall opposite the counter. I couldn't work it out. And then I saw the sign: SPEND £10 ON MEAT AND GET A COW LEG FREE. I started to laugh hysterically. I looked again at the wood. It had feet, hoof things. It was legs. What in God's name do you do with a cow's leg? What if you don't want the leg? I thought. Do you *have* to take it? I was suddenly caught in the iron teeth of a fantasy, in which I bought some meat from this shop and the butcher chased me down the street, waving the hideous limb above his head, shouting, "Lady, lady, your cow leg, your cow leg!" I hurried on.

I passed a couple of pubs. They looked like gone-to-seed funeral parlors. And then the Black Lamb. From the outside it had a certain presence, with turrets and cupolas and intricate brickwork. Despite these not especially maritime features, the overall effect was faintly shiplike. A sign proudly proclaimed that the place had been "Rebuilt in 1898." I wondered what natural, or man-made, disaster had necessitated the rebuilding—fire? meteorite strike? hygiene inspection?

There were three entrances, which was two too many from my point of view. Which was the correct one? I was vaguely aware of some kind of etiquette to do with different bits of pubs: the lounge, the public bar, the snug, and for all I knew, the mizzenmast, and the hold.

And what was I to do when I got into the godforsaken place? Of course, I'd been to a few pubs when I was still a student, but that was always in the middle of a huge gang, and even then I was gravitating to bars and clubs and other places beyond the ken of the petty criminals, day laborers, spent prostitutes, and football hooligans that I took to make up the majority of the public house clientele. Did I go straight up to the bar and order a shot of the hard stuff, firing off a phlegm bullet into a handy spittoon? Did I wander around, peering into dark corners, staring out the local hags and hardcases, until I found my man? Or did I go and sit quietly at the nearest table and pray that nobody bothered me?

*   *   *

Now I'm sorry about this, but I'm going to have to leave me there, poised to enter the secret kingdom for a moment or two, while I indulge in a quick digression on the subject of pubs, and in particular the issue of the relative merits of pubs and other venues for social gatherings. I know this may seem strange, given that I have just conceded my ignorance on the subject, but I had endless heated debates (not infrequently descending to playful little bites and gouges on my part and sulks on his) with Ludo, who was a Friend of the Pub. His point was that in pubs, as opposed to either cafés, wine bars, or clubs, people (by which he usually meant men) talked about "ideas."

"It's the one place," he'd say, "where, whatever your class or educational background, you talk about *concepts*."

"I thought the point was to get drunk?"

"Drink is an alibi," he'd say.

At all other social gatherings, people (by which he meant women, gay men, and straight men who spent more on trousers than on books and records) talked about people. I asked him for some examples of the wonderful ideas discussed in his last visit to the pub. He pondered for a moment and then, counting them off on his fingers until he came to the inconvenient eleventh, which was left to hang like a lone sock on the line, he came out with:

1. Tony Blair: the New Margaret Thatcher, the New Harold Wilson, or the New Benito Mussolini?
2. (in two parts)
    (i)   Why is pease pudding called pease pudding when it clearly has no peas in it?
    (ii) What *has* it got in it?

3. Why all modern art is conservative, with big *and* small c's [neither abstraction nor Britart playfulness can adequately address social ishoos. Ooo, I must tell the girls!].

4. Why fascism is camp and camp fascist [something, apparently, to do with a love of display].

5. The purpose and origins of male nipples.

6. Hemingway v. Chandler as prose stylist.

7. Were the Wombles the great underappreciated arthouse glamrock band of the seventies?

8. Flat back four vs. wing-back system [don't ask me, but something, apparently, to do with football].

9. What was the little bloke in Boney-M *for*?

10. The relative merits of Psion organizer and Palm-Pilot [the latter, it seems, is not a euphemism for masturbation, but an electronic diary].

11. Is love still possible in the postmodern world?

I was obviously supposed to be impressed.

"But why is it better to talk about football and art than about people?" I asked, not unreasonably.

"Because what that usually means is talking about yourself. It's all just narcissism. We have a duty to go out and understand the universe, not just the world inside our heads."

"And pease pudding is the key to the universe?"

"No . . . yes. Can't you see that wanting to know what goes into making yellow gloop, wanting to know how you make complex things out of simple elements, is the beginning of alchemy, which leads to chemistry, which leads to . . . everything. But the point is that the powers-that-be"—a phrase he used without embarrassment or irony—"want you, us, to go on gossiping about who's sleeping with who, and what they were wearing before they did it, because it means we're not scrutinizing *them.* And the way we scrutinize them is to find out how the world is made. When you do that, you can show how most of what they say is lies."

"It seems to me that when you say you talk about ideas, what you mean half the time is that you talk about *things,* which are surely the *opposite* of ideas," I said. I was getting annoyed at his implied—no *explicit*—criticism of everything I liked best. "All you've said is just to cover up the fact that you like stuff better than people, because you're a social inadequate with just two friends."

Just so you know, I said the last bit with a big smile and gave him a kiss at the end, which had the result of ending the argument on my terms and leaving everyone content.

But back to the middle door of the Black Lamb. I took the plunge. It was locked. I could see people inside. They looked around, faces blank and uninquisitive as I pushed at the door, rattling some loose system of chains and bolts. A man jabbed his thumb toward another of the doors.

As I entered, my eyes lost the ability to focus, so thick was the fog bank of fag smoke and beer vapor. I had no idea which way to turn, where to go. I wanted to cry. Close to panic, I decided to leave. Suddenly Ludo seemed like the most perfect man in the world, and I felt an idiot for ever considering so rash a venture.

And then I felt a touch on my shoulder, and a mouth was at my ear, close enough for me to feel the warm breath.

"Give you a hand there, Katie?" he said for the second time. "Not going already, are you?"

"I couldn't see you. I thought it might be the wrong place. Can we sit down?" I was talking too quickly.

Liam was dressed simply in a white shirt and a soft moleskin suit. I noted with amusement that a thickish golden hoop was threaded through each ear. I couldn't believe that I was meeting a man with earrings. So very David Essex, circa 1974. It gave him a gypsical or piratical air. But although in theory I loathed them, I also found myself a little intrigued. Uncannily, when I weighed up my feelings, I found that the revulsion and attraction of the earrings exactly canceled each other out, leaving me precisely where I began.

Liam found a table.

"So it's a Guinness, then," he said, the gentlest touch of satire in his voice. He obviously expected me to opt for something more appropriate. He probably thought real ladies drank nothing but Malibu, or crème de menthe, or Advocat.

"Yeah, pint, please." I'd been rehearsing the phrase over and over in my head.

As Liam fought his way to the bar, I began to take in my surroundings. The place was amazing. The dark green walls and oxblood ceiling were covered in gilded moldings. The walls bore elaborate reliefs, showing what I took to be Poseidon with a train of nymphs and zephyrs and dryads and other pretty mythological girlies. The ceiling had even more complex, but abstract, designs that mixed hallucinogenically with the swirling clouds of smoke. I wondered for a moment if the gilding might just be deposits of nicotine, caught on the peaks like snow on the Alps in summer. The overall effect was part classical, part gothic, all weird.

A huge blackened oak bar ran the length of the main room. Rows of optics ascended glimmering behind it, the contents ranging from pale amber to burnt umber. A panda in a clear plastic bag, a prize, I guessed, for some forlorn raffle, hung like a sacrificial offering to the god of whiskey.

The people, though odd and emphatically not of my world, could not hope to match the strangeness of the building. Most of them were men. The older ones wore suits and frayed polyester shirts. The younger ones wore the standard casual uniform of T-shirts and jeans and trainers. They had thick necks and short hair and rough hands, but they seemed strangely gentle, like broken circus lions.

The few women were again divided into old and young. The old were stout in heavy tweed coats, clutching string bags and cackling. All the young girls had hair bleached a shade too blond. There was something tragic about their desperation to look pretty and enjoy themselves. Perhaps the sadness was greatest in those who came closest to achieving the look they had seen in the magazine or on the TV. It showed that even effort, and ingenuity, and decent raw material were never enough. For a few seconds I was aware of how little would have to have been different in the world for me to be one of them: a matter of a few miles east or west, or some other tiny variation in events long ago. But then I shuddered and dismissed the thought. I was glad I wasn't one of them. And here was Liam.

He put down the Guinness in front of me. It really was rather a beautiful thing, with its profound black depths, still faintly agitated, as if star clusters and galaxies were being formed at its heart, and its head the color and texture of clotted cream. I put it to my lips and shuddered. It was just as disgusting as I remembered.

"Delicious," I said.

Liam narrowed his eyes at me. "Not quite your sort of place, is it, Katie?"

"No, not quite."

"Do you want to go somewhere else? There's a new bar just down the road full of people like you."

"And what do you mean by 'people like me'?" I wasn't sure if he was teasing me or just stating a fact.

"Now Katie, you know exactly what I mean. I mean, if you had a big sieve, and you put all that crowd and all this crowd in it, and you as well, and gave it a good shake, there'd be this lot left in the sieve, and then the other lot'd fall through, and you with them."

How very homely a metaphor, I thought. I had a sudden image of Liam in a pinafore. Or, come to think of it, perhaps it was more ghoulish than gastronomic, like some painting by Hieronymus Bosch, with a huge devil sieving out the damned from the saved. I switched to an image of Liam with horns and a trident. It suited him rather better.

"And where would you be? Caught in the sieve with the lumps, or through with the flour?"

"I'd follow you anywhere," he said, smiling.

I wasn't sure exactly when the music had started, but I knew that it was terrible. Country-and-western standards, with an abysmal electric piano and drum machine backing, wafted in from another room, interrupted by sporadic applause and the odd whistle. I suppose Milo might have found some charm in it in a "so crap it's cool" kind of way.

"I thought you said the music here was good. I was expecting something a bit more traditional. You mentioned fiddles. All I can hear is a cowboy riding a synthesizer."

"Ah, you mean you're after the uileann pipes, and the pennywhistle, and a beard in a woolly jumper singing about the troubles and the great rebellion of '98?"

"Well, yes, actually. Beats 'Stand by Your Man,' " I sang, echoing the last verse from next door.

"It's what the people want. Reminds them of the dance halls back home. If you hang around, you might hear a bit of the fusty auld stuff later."

The pub was filling up, and soon the place took on a new character, humming, vibrant, drunk. We chatted, moving gradually away from the shallow end of fashion to the deeper waters of personal history. I found that I was enjoying myself. Liam had an easy way about him and a manner that made the simplest of his statements seem engaging. Best of all, he had the feminine trick of appearing to find *you* interesting, and *your* jokes funny, and *your* observations profound. Pease pudding, male nipples, and the flat back four made a brief appearance, purely for humorous effect. The fizzing excitement I had felt earlier left me, but its place was taken by something close to real pleasure.

Somehow I managed to finish the Guinness. Time for another drink. I decided to ask for a glass of white wine. Liam had the good grace not to smirk. The request seemed to cause a mild panic behind the bar. Heads were shaken. A boy scuttled off and came back with a two-liter screw-top, which he tipped into a sherry glass. Drinking it was a bigger ordeal than the Guinness, and I thought the best way to minimize the horror was to throw it back in one.

Liam said, "Bravo! Another?"

"Gin and tonic, I think, this time."

It came without ice or lemon but was still an improvement.

Blissfully, the music stopped, followed by a final ragged round of applause. A fat man in a sweat-drenched pink T-shirt appeared and sat at the table.

"Liam, how's about helpin' out wit' a tune after we've had a point. Ah, I see ye've a lady wit' yer. Chance fer yer to show her what yer can do wit' yer throat."

"I'll maybe see, Pat. But I don't want to leave her alone here with all these wild beasts and animals."

"Oh, go on. I'd like it. Where's the loo?"

The ladies, when I got there, almost sobered me, it was so rank. It looked and smelled as though it had never been cleaned. One lavatory was choked with paper and sanitary towels and worse. The other had no seat. There was a Durex machine next to the filthy sink. Someone had written on it in black felt-tip: "For a refund, insert baby." I thought that was quite funny.

When I came back, Pat was sitting alone at the table, which filled me, as you can imagine, with joy. I looked around and saw Liam across the room, engaged in some kind of transaction with Frankenstein's monster, who'd managed to trade his bolt for a fiberglass toupee.

"Liam'll just be a minute," said Pat, sounding no more comfortable than I felt. He sat with one hand on top of his closely cropped head. His eyes feverishly searched the floor for a conversational gambit somebody might have dropped there. Inspiration dawned.

"D'yer know deaf people?" he asked, his voice modulating curiously, as if he were coming through on a badly tuned shortwave radio.

"I know *of* them," I responded.

"Ah!" he said, unsure of what to make of my reply. He built up his courage again.

"*I* don't think they're really deaf at all," he said positively, tapping the sticky tabletop with his finger.

"Not deaf?" I said, praying that Liam would hurry back.

"I mean," he went on, his voice rising to something just a notch or two below a bellow, "*how would you know? How would you really know?* All you have to do is say 'Pardon?' when someone speaks to yez and yev convinced them yer a deaf man. And then it's easy street for the rest of yer life."

Liam came back to rescue us both.

"Okay, Pat, I'll join you. As long as Marty has a scratch at his fiddle."

"Who was that scary man you were talking to?" I asked.

"Just big Jonah. Scary's right."

"Why, what does he do?"

"He scares people."

"You mean protection?" I said, rather proud of the terminology.

"Oh yes. And debt collecting. He's famous for his catchphrase. You see, he's something of a philosopher, and when he has to work, he first says to the guy 'Are ye familiar with the works of Friedrich Nietzsche?'"—this basso profundo, in what I took to be a Glasgow accent—"And then he takes out his hammer. Time for a tune. Come on through, Katie."

The next room was almost as big as the main bar. People had crammed in to see the band, and there were no seats left. Liam found me a good place and then climbed up to join three other people on a little stage in the corner. Pat abandoned his keyboard and slung on a huge great piano accordion. A wiry old fellow with a face like a collapsed lung stood poised with a fiddle, and another with colossal sideburns, perhaps just a whisker short of a muttonchop, had a banjo. Liam picked up a guitar.

"Hello, London," he said rock star fashion, and winked at me through the crowd. "You'll of heard this before about a million times. But tonight I'm singing it with a bit more feeling than usual." The crowd shouted and laughed. Had they heard the patter before, as well as the song?

If it was familiar, even clichéd, to the exiled Irish of Kilburn and Cricklewood, the song Liam sang was entirely new to me. The music I was used to was the sound track to a thousand clothes shops, a muted form of whatever was happening in the club scene. Music to pose by. Music to fill the spaces in between thought. This was something very different. It had a yearning and a sadness, and it squeezed me in its big rough hands.

O Peggy Gordon, you are my darling,
Come sit you down upon my knee,
And tell to me the very reason
Why I am slighted so by thee.

Liam's was not a beautiful voice, nor for that matter a powerful one. But it inhabited the music perfectly, breathing sincerity and pain.

I'm so in love, I can't deny it,
My heart lies smothered in my breast;
It's not for you to let the world know it,
A troubled mind can know no rest.

As he sang he kept his eyes on me. He was so clearly singing to one particular person that people in the crowd started to look round.

I did put my head to a cask of brandy,
It was my fancy I do declare;
For when I'm drinking I'm always thinking
Of when Peggy Gordon was here.

The banjo man had produced a pennywhistle from somewhere, and its delicate notes dipped and skipped around the words like a girl-child playing among the feet of adults.

I wish I was away in Inglo,
Far across the briny sea,
Sailing o'er the deepest ocean,
Where womankind never bother me.

I wish I was in some lonely valley,
Where womankind could not be found,
And the pretty small birds would change their voices,
And every moment a different sound.

As soon as Liam began to reprieve the first verse, I knew something genuinely awful was going to happen. It was an extraordinarily, transparently naff thing to do, but it didn't stop him. Nor did it prevent the thrill I felt creeping up my spine to the back of my neck, or the warm feeling in my pelvis.

O Katie Castle, you are my darling,
Come sit you down upon my knee,
And tell to me the very reason
Why I am slighted so by thee.

The crowd whooped and cheered, and Liam climbed down, to have his back slapped and his hair ruffled by

old-timers in strange hats and middle-aged women in
the terminal stage of sexual excitation. He fought his
way over to me.

"I'm sorry about that changing-the-name thing, Katie.
It must have seemed like an awfully daft thing to do.
Ye'd have thought I'd have picked up a bit of cool
from all my years of carting stuff around for the likes of
you."

"You know what?" I said. "I liked it. I think it's time
I bought a drink."

And then . . . well, you know how it is. I reached
that stage of being drunk when you love the world
and when that love for the world finds a focus in the
person you happen to be with. We slid together on the
torn leatherette of the bench, but I don't think we
touched at all, which added greatly to the intensity of
the experience.

I knew I was on good form. Liam was no bimbo, and
in between the flirting and silly stuff, we talked about serious things: Northern Ireland, of course, but also the
nature of identity and being a stranger in another culture. I even produced some of the Deconstruction Malheurbe stuff, about signs, which rather bemused Liam.

The point came, as it was bound to do, when Liam
made his move. I was expecting an extended meander
around the subject, but when it came it was thrillingly
direct.

"I've borrowed a key for a place near here. A place we
can go to."

"I can't stay the night."

"I understand. Shall we go?"

As we made our way to the door, an old man I recognized as the fiddle player staggered toward us. He put an
arm around our shoulders, which, given his diminutive

stature, took some stretching on his part and stooping on ours. Clumps of wiry white hair were unevenly distributed about his face and head. He seemed to be toothless.

"Liam, now, Liam . . ." he said, swaying slightly. A blast of whiskey breath hit me, damp and deathly.

"Ah, Marty darlin', that was a great clatter on the fiddle you gave us tonight," said Liam, trying to work himself free from the old man's surprisingly firm grip.

Marty ignored his compliment and fixed him with a bleary but steady gaze.

"The *child*," he said, looking to me, coughing with emotion, "ah, the child. You'll not blackguard the child? Liam, you'll not blackguard the *child*?" He coughed again, and I felt a spray of TB spores hit my face. Nauseated, I yanked myself away and ran gasping into the street. Liam followed a moment later.

"Sorry about that, Katie. Poor auld Marty's not the man he was. He gets notions; he has flights of fancy."

"It's all right. I haven't been called a child for a year or two. And I don't think I've heard blackguard used as a verb before. In fact, I don't think I've heard it used as an anything before. Anyway, will you?"

"Will I what?"

"Blackguard me, silly."

He smiled one of his specials and, for the first time, put his arm around me. He led me off the High Road, and we were soon lost in the side-street labyrinth of once stolidly bourgeois, now shabby and decrepit, red-brick houses.

Now, you probably think that I was acting like a slut, drinking in a dive with a man I hardly knew and then just going off with him like that. And of course, you'd be right. But it was, as I've said, my last chance, my last bit of nonsense, the final fling. And who would deny a girl her final fling?

We arrived. It was a house like all the others. A broken-backed path of checkered tiles led up to a door of flaky green. Pushing through the high tide of unopened junk mail, we found ourselves in a hallway so narrow that you felt the need to turn sideways. The scum-colored carpet was pockmarked with cigarette burns. We carefully navigated the dismembered corpse of a bike and what looked suspiciously like a whorl of cat poo. There was a smell of old damp cardboard. I suddenly felt a lot less drunk.

"What a dump."

"Yeah, I'm sorry about this, Katie. If I'd known what it was like, I'd never have brought you here."

We squeezed up the stairs, where carpet gave way to blistered lino. Two flights later Liam was fitting a key warily into a lock. I expected something hideous, and I was relieved that it was only *quite* bad. Three rooms: a living room/kitchen, a bathroom, and a bedroom. It seemed to be clean, if spartan. There was a mattress with a black duvet on the floor in the bedroom. The walls were covered in an almost pretty wallpaper patterned with cherries and blackberries and other fruits of the forest; but whoever had decorated had not known to match up the pattern between rolls, which gave a very strange, genetic engineering effect, where cherries grew out of elderberries, or red currants, or thin air.

I flopped down on the duvet, trying not to think about who or what might have shared it in the recent past.

"Would you like a coffee?" said Liam.

"Yes, if you can find any."

I looked at my watch for the first time that evening. It was only ten o'clock. So much seemed to have happened in just a couple of hours. I'd had my adventure, I thought. I'd explored a world I never knew existed, and I could now slip safely back into my own. It would make (suitably sanitized and censored) an amusing dinner party story. I might even tell Milo the whole thing. He'd love the "don't blackguard the child" bit. I was giggling at this when Liam came in with the coffee.

"There's no milk."

"Doesn't matter. Is there a phone? I'd like to call a taxi."

"Sure, I'll call you one after the coffee. I know a number."

He sat next to me on the mattress. I put my head on his shoulder. He circled me with his arm and gently kissed the top of my head. I slid back and brought my lips up to meet his. As with all first kisses, there was a moment or two of adjustment, as a fact-finding mission is sent to establish the precise whereabouts of lips, teeth, and tongue.

The beauty of the kiss, the reason for its allure, for its strangeness, is that it is at the same time the most innocent and the filthiest form of human contact: the first thing a mother does to her baby, the one thing a prostitute will never do. No subsequent erotic experience ever matches the intensity of the first kiss, so perfect because it sketches for you vast horizons, limitless spaces, endless possibilities. Whatever failures and flops follow, the kiss is never held responsible. The kiss never promises satisfaction, so it can never disappoint.

But neither, especially when a man and a woman are alone in a bedroom for the first time, is a kiss ever just a kiss. My top came away in his hands. And then I was naked. He broke off the kiss just long enough to breathe, "Katie, you are so beautiful, so perfect."

I put my arms around the knotted muscles of his shoulders and kissed his neck and face.

But then from somewhere deep inside a voice spoke, and it said, No. It wasn't a rational thing, it wasn't that I thought I was going to get caught and exposed. And it certainly wasn't a moral voice. It was just some primeval instinct thingy, a warning, the voice that told the ape-man that a saber-toothed tiger was just outside the circle of light cast by the campfire.

"Look, Liam, I'm sorry, I just can't go on with this. I've messed you about. I'm an idiot. You're a lovely man, but I really can't do it."

"Ah, Katie darlin', that's all right," he said tenderly. "I understand. It's my fault. I shouldn't have bothered you. I really am an auld bollix."

Then, looking down, he said half-smilingly, half in genuine frustration, "But what the fuck am I supposed to do with this damn thing."

I followed his eye. And there it was. The most colossal erection I had ever seen. I'm sorry, I don't want to be crude, but it was simply one of the wonders of the world. The combination of that stupendous, glistening willy and his helpless, boyish frustration, was irresistible. I lost myself in giggles, and he joined in. I opened my arms.

"Poor boy," I said as he came to me, "you'd better put it here."

And so we spent an hour there in that room with its mattress on the floor, and the black duvet, and the mis-aligned pattern. We did everything. Yes, even *that*.

*   *   *

The minicab driver was from the Ivory Coast. He'd been a political prisoner. He was an accountant by trade. I listened to him talking sweetly about his family, and sadly about having to drive for a living (he was in truth a terrible driver, staying, as far as I could make out, in third gear all the way), rather than using his qualifications. I gave him a big tip. On impulse I asked him, as I handed him the money, if he'd driven girls from that address before.

"Oh yes, miss, many times," he replied.

CHAPTER 8

A Short Chapter,
Punctuated by a Colon

I came in as quietly as I could, hoping Ludo would have gone to bed, but he was in his study, marking books.

"Hi, babe," he called. "Have a good time with the girls?"

"Nothing special. I *stink* of smoke. I'm just going to dive in the shower."

After the shower I slipped between my clean white sheets and thanked the Lord for Primrose Hill. The hour had been a good hour, but now it was gone forever, and I was happy.

Ludo soon came to bed. He curled around me from behind in the familiar way, cupping my breast in his hand. He nuzzled my ear and began to roll down my knickers. And the astonishing thing is that I was actually quite turned on. But not even I was brazen enough to do it with two different men in the same evening. And besides, I was a bit . . . sore. I felt a wave of affection for my boy and put him off as gently as I could.

When I opened my eyes the next morning, I felt a great surge of energy. There was no sign of sun through the heavy October clouds, but I felt as if I'd just thrown back the curtains on a new world. I crept out of bed, which was hard because I wanted to leap, and went to make coffee. I brought it in to Ludo on a tray with some cornflakes and the paper and kissed him awake. His hair was doing its usual mad morning corkscrew thing, but I thought he looked lovely.

I decided to forgive him for the poem.

"Full of beans this morning," he said drowsily. "Haven't got a hangover?"

It was funny, I really ought to have had—more than a glass of wine usually leaves me putrid the next day. But then I suppose I sort of *did* have a hangover. I've been told that when you're on morphine you are still vaguely aware of the fact that you're in pain, but you just don't mind. That's how I felt.

"Just glad to be alive," I said in a Sunday-school way.

My good mood continued all the way in to work and beyond. Even the Northern Line was having one of its rare Dr.-Jekyll-rather-than-Mr.-Hyde days. In place of the usual mix of ashen-faced, jowly drones and maniacal starers, the carriage seemed to be filled with color and life and excitement, as if the Rio carnival had taken to commuting in to London.

That morning was the most fertile I'd ever had. I did something dramatic in all the different bits of my job: design, production, PR, selling. I even managed to change the cartridge in the printer, which usually entails getting in a specialist, while six of us girlies stand around gasping at the cleverness of boys, as if he'd just brought the gift of fire to our previously dark and cold Neanderthal cave.

Penny swanned in at eleven-thirty with an amusing

tale about being joined in the Jacuzzi at her health club by "a Middle Eastern gentleman" who proceeded to remove his trunks.

"He just sat back with his arms and legs open, and his do-dah waving about in the current, like a conger eel. I didn't know what to do with my face."

Mandy, who was up from the studio to complain about the new temporary sample machinist (who she claimed was "breathing funny on purpose to get on my nerves"), chipped in with a similar story, which seemed to be set in some Caribbean all-inclusive resort.

"And you know what I did," she said, her face puckered in contempt, "when he slid round to my bit? I peed in the water, that's what I did, and got out. Let them stew in *your* juice, is what I say."

"But doesn't the water turn red?" said Penny, intrigued.

"Biggest myth going. And I should know, I've *been* in every municipal pool in south London."

"What a creature," said Penny after Mandy had gone, and then we both fell into silence and thought about Mandy's methodical passage through the pools of the metropolis.

Milo phoned in the afternoon to chat about his birthday. He was having a party in his newly "restyled" flat, the look of which was perhaps the third most discussed topic in the fashion PR world that season, after cocaine and the size of you-know-who's arse. He was having trouble color matching the canapés with the curtains but didn't want to give too much away. My guess was that there was a lot of piebald going on, which suggested ponyskin everything.

"The problem is black—there just aren't enough

black things you can eat, once you've gone past caviar and olives."

"What about squid in its own, or a friend's, ink?"

"Nice thought, but doesn't work as a nibble."

"What about the funny black bit you get in fresh tuna? Couldn't you use that as a sort of sushi?"

It soon transpired that there was more to Milo's concern than met the eye. Trouble was brewing between Pippin and the Persian Boy.

"Pip is just unbearable. He's shagging anything that moves, just to get at me. Not that I care. *And* he's been spreading that rumor about Xerxes. He hates him. That's why I didn't invite him for Saturday. I love a scene, but not when I'm *in* it. But I collided with him at the Met Bar the other day, emerging from a cubicle with some kind of thug, and he'd just assumed he was coming. Must have thought he was so special that he didn't even need an invite. And I couldn't then tell him not to come. Would have been horrid. He'd have *stabbed* me. Carries a Stanley knife, you know. Does it to impress the football hooligans he likes to pick up."

• "Slashed."

"I beg your pardon?"

"I understand you slash people with Stanley knives, rather than stab them. Ludo's always confiscating them at school."

"Quite. Anyway, if there's a fight, you will break it up, won't you? After all, that's why I asked you along. Are you bringing dear old Ludo?"

"How could I not?"

"Mmyeh. Pity. Well, perhaps he could "confiscate" Pippin's knife, and earn his . . . *passage*?"

*   *   *

A good day had become perfect. Milo had asked *my* advice about his party. Just getting invited made my nipples harden, although I would never have spoken nicely to him again if I hadn't made the cut, but now here I was being confided in, even given a clue about the famous redesign.

The party promised to be utterly, absolutely, the best ever. He was squeezing the fifty most important people he knew into his chic Camden apartment. The roll call was impressive: all the fashion editors; one-third of the holy trinity of Japanese designers; a tall, thin American actress, famous for being able to do a perfect English accent without swallowing her own tongue; two rival TV fashion pundits; and Vanessa Eastleigh's pet poodle, Casper, sent in place of his owner, who would have loved to be there if the party hadn't clashed with her colonic irrigation. After Milo had rung off, I laughed about *that* with Penny, whose reaction was unexpected.

"Who does she go to?" she asked sharply.

"I've no idea. Some crystal-wielding weirdo, I expect. You know what she's like."

"Yes, I'm afraid I do, which is why I'm concerned. I hope she doesn't go to *my* man in Harley Street. I wouldn't like to get the equipment after *her*. She doesn't wear knickers."

"Penny! Don't tell me you've been going to colonic irrigation. It's sooo eighties."

"You shouldn't sneer at what you don't understand. I find it frees up my creativity. The first time *was* a bit nerve-racking, though. I held my breath all the way through. And the whole thing's recorded, you know. I think it's mainly for their own protection, but they'll sell you a copy of the video for thirty pounds, if you want it, as a souvenir."

"A video of what, exactly?" I asked, astonished. "I don't understand."

"Well, they put this miniature camera on the end of the hose."

"Yuck! And ouch!"

"No, no, it's not painful: they put Vaseline on the lens, which has the advantage of making you look younger on the film." So spoke the actress.

A thought occurred to me.

"Penny?"

"Yes, Katie?"

"You didn't, you know, *buy* one, did you?"

"No! Well . . . yes, in a way. But not a copy. I insisted on the original. I didn't want it falling into the *wrong* hands. Look, here it is," she said, pulling a parcel from her desk drawer. "I'd like you to put it out in a bin liner, but mark it 'Toxic Waste: Incinerate.' "

I put it on my desk, already planning how I would tell the story to Milo.

The rest of the week dragged a little. My eyes were fixed on the party, and I spent long hours mulling over what to wear. The options fell into three distinct groups. I could go classic, or I could go way-out and funky, or I could try some hybrid, halfway house. For once the middle way looked like the trickiest to pull off: wild-child and Prada-girl are both no-brainers, but looking startling and chic at the same time required a pen and paper and a good two hours with a sympathetic mirror.

Things had settled down with Ludo. He was relieved that the poem storm had blown over, and I was pleased my fling was safely flung—so far, at least—so we were both on our best behavior. I'd left it properly vague with

Liam. There was some talk of having to do it again, but Liam understood the rules, didn't he?

He called on Thursday.

"Hi, Katie."

"Oh, hello," I said quietly, quickly checking the office to make sure no one was within earshot.

"You don't sound too pleased to hear from me."

"No, it's not that. It's just rather difficult at work—you know why."

"Sure, sure. Look, I was just wondering if you're busy on Saturday. I thought maybe we could grab a bite to eat or something." Of course, van drivers, even fashion van drivers, would hardly be invited to a Milo party.

"No, I'm sorry, I'm doing something."

"Oh, okay. Maybe another time. How are you fixed up for next week?"

"Next week's quite tricky, actually."

It was looking annoyingly as if I might have to tell him straight.

"Look, Liam, I think you're a great guy, but—"

"Yeah, I get it—wham, bam, thank you, and good-bye, Li-am," he cut in quickly.

"Well, yes, actually, I'm afraid so. Sorry."

Whoever first thought of being cruel to be kind should have got an award.

"Don't bother. No hard feelings. See you around."

Could have been worse. Could have been much worse.

CHAPTER 9

Zenith

"Look, you can leave after half an hour, I really don't care. But if we don't turn up together, people will ask, and that's a waste of good networking time."

Ludo was in his usual pre–fash bash bad mood.

"I just don't get it. I don't like them, they don't like me, but I always have to go. I'd a million times rather sit in the pub with Tom and Daniel. You don't understand what I have to go through at these things. My insides boil, and I sweat, and I can't breathe . . ."

"My God, I thought fashion was full of drama queens. That's the campest thing I've heard since Jasper Conran last pitched his tent."

That threw him slightly, and he entered meekly into the sullen acceptance phase of the evening, which is manageable, if boring. There was one final small skirmish, over transport:

"It's a ten-minute walk, for chrissake," he grumbled, "why do we need a taxi?"

I took off my shoe, a Sergio Rossi of infinite beauty, and waved its lethal heel at him, like a chichi battle-ax from the days of chivalry.

"This," I said ambiguously, "is potentially lethal footwear. These boots," I added a touch inaccurately, as my gauzy slipper was as far from a boot as Milo's party was from a hike in the fells, "were *not* made for walking."

The invitation said eight, we arrived at nine, which was still probably twenty minutes too early. It's so hard to get it right these days. A Vietnamese serving boy opened the door. Milo had brought in caterers, who were doing *everything* at cost in exchange for the good publicity.

What I found inside made me gasp. I always knew that I would gasp, and I knew that I was *expected* to gasp. Gasping was clearly the appropriate physical response, and nothing else would do. The idle or the mute could have come with recorded gasps performed by resting actors to be played on crossing the threshold. A sigh of wonderment, a smile, a round of applause, a groveling prostration, all might signify some degree of appreciation, but the restyle was engineered with one piece missing, and that piece was gasp shaped.

What I did not anticipate was that my gasp would be one of horror: the restyling of Milo's famous apartment was a *fiasco*. I was half-right about the ponyskin, which covered the sofa, an armchair, and a chrome-framed recliner. That was part of the problem. In the past week ponyskin had done the thing that every fad does, yet which still manages to catch people out: it had become crap. It had peaked sometime late on Wednesday night, when Jude Law had worn his ponyskin tie to the premiere of a film in which the delectable and hitherto impeccably Merchant Ivory Stephanie Phylum-Crater had performed fellatio on a yellow mongrel dog called Nobby, thereby breaking the last taboo—that English actresses of good breeding only ever perform with pedigrees. Since then ponyskin had fallen faster than a first-time snowboarder.

But there was more to it than the understandable misfortune of backing the wrong pony. Everything, quite simply everything, in the flat was flayed from the carcass of a dead beast. The flooring was of a curiously textured leather, which may have been trying to create the impression of crocodile but made me think of intestines. The walls were clad in a similar shaded, but untextured, leather. Fur rugs, whether rabbit, or cat, or llama, I couldn't tell, were scattered on the floor and seating. It was like being at the same time on the inside and the outside of some mythological creature: for some reason my mind came up with the name camelopard, although that couldn't be right, because I knew that was only an old name for the giraffe. Anyway, it was disgusting. And it was only a season ago that Smack! had attracted headlines in the fashion press for dropping clients who used fur.

Some of the detailing *was* impressive: Mies van der Rohe chairs, placed with slide-rule casualness; sixties sci-fi lighting arcing overhead in elegant swoops; kinky padded doors, suggestive of sinful zones beyond. But the irony was too convoluted and layered to be effective, and one was left with a simple, old-fashioned impression of neuralgic bad taste.

There were only ten or so people there, mainly clumped around Milo and the Persian Boy. Milo was in silver, which I had thought was very last year, but I must have got it wrong, because Milo, at least in the realm of fashion, never did. Perhaps it was the shade of silver. Xerxes looked as absurd and as beautiful as ever in a tight black girlie top with puffy silk chiffon sleeves dotted with dark stars. Kookai and Kleavage were there, in a semiprofessional capacity, making the room look busy in the early stages before the real guests came.

One of the TV fashion pundits had arrived as well, trying not to look annoyed at being an early bird. I guessed a researcher was going to pay for that. She really was as shockingly ugly in the flesh as Milo had said. Telly is *so* kind to short, fat blondes. And as for her look, she gave the impression of simultaneously having tried too hard and not bothered enough.

I noticed Canvey Island in an adjacent cluster. She was telling the story about the maggot-feet man. No one was listening.

"What do you think of it?" asked Milo. I sensed that his usual armor plating of smugness had thinned to gossamer. He desperately needed reassurance. Somewhere inside, he must have known that it had gone tragically wrong, but to admit it would crush him. He needed the fire walker's self-belief.

"It's simply stupendous," I said. "It makes me want to cry, it's so wonderful."

Obviously my voice on its own would not have been sufficient to allay Milo's doubts, but added to the general chorus of sycophantic approval, and finding a natural homeland in Milo's own towering vanity, it served its purpose, and Milo welcomed me with a convincing show of affection. This time no discommoding tongues or sly nips. I joined the little group and injected some much needed energy into a system clearly approaching entropy (funny what you remember from GCSE physics). Ludo filed off in search of the drinks tray, although his quest for a beer would be fruitless, as for reasons known only to a few initiates, fashion parties have served only sea breezes and champagne since 1995.

As usual, Milo's choice of music was abysmal: a plinky-plonky jazz track that sounded like something from a Bulgarian avant-garde animation from the 1960s. You'd think there'd be a lot of cross-fertilization between the music and fashion worlds, but there really isn't much interchange. Not at *my* sort of level, anyway, the level where you have to spend *money*. In fact, music and fashion have two completely different archetypes of cool, neither of which is prepared to acknowledge the other. Ludo, who has a friend who works for some pointless little record label, says it's like two almost identical warblers singing away in a bush, but they just won't mate, because one has a brown stripe over its eye and the other olive, or one has a song that goes "pee po pee" and the other goes "po pee po." *I* think it's because you just can't know about everything. And remember most people *in* and *of* fashion are pretty dim, and if they let their attention stray for a moment, then they'd be out of sync forevermore. Ditto, other way round, music.

"So, Katie, tell us some filth, you know you want to," said Milo after a while.

I'd come prepared.

"What do you want, politics, show business, or the law?"

"Katie Castle, if you had a cock, you'd be mine," said Milo excitedly. I wondered if his latest cocaine fast had been broken already. "Let's raise the tone; give us some politics."

So I told them about the opposition front-bencher, who'd been buying his mistress—and when I say mistress, I mean breast enhancement, bum tattoo, collagen implants, high-pitched giggle, the works—one of our silk shantung slip dresses, when who should walk in but his wife, a city fund manager and long-standing customer of ours.

Milo exploded: "But that's impossible, he's notorious! He's mauver than mauve! He's been seen rampaging through every gay pickup in London *and* Brighton. He has his own bush on the Heath. It's common knowledge that the Tory Party fixed him up with a suitable wife who had . . . other concerns, and who didn't mind."

"Yes, that's what he wanted the world to think, but it turns out that it was all just a cover for his rampant heterosexuality, and now he's been outed as straight."

"What did his wife say?" asked someone.

"Oh, nothing at all; just turned to ice. But she won't be doing a Mary Archer. No standing by *her* man. Look in the *Mail* tomorrow."

After my little coup, things went joyously. All the new arrivals found me at the hub, acting almost as co-host with Milo, and I felt the shares in katiecastle.com rise on the back of it. The Persian Boy objected to my usurpation in the only way he could, by hissing through his clenched teeth and flashing Zoroastrian fire from his lovely eyes. But I didn't mind. I was no longer peripheral. Almost everyone knew who I was before the party (except for two Australian lesbian concept artists, whose latest installation, a set of obscene pink udders purchased from a bemused abattoir, supposedly depicting society's worship of the mother, protruded from the wall in Milo's otherwise aseptic kitchen), but now I was viewed with more calculation. Suddenly I was a person who might be able to do them harm; someone who should be courted. The caterers eased around the party with noiseless efficiency. Drinks would appear at exactly the right moment, and canapés, should one have been of a mind to eat, arrived just as a hand was freed to select one.

The actress came, along with an unexpected prize mullet, who may have been her manager. I heard her say something about Jude Law weeping outside, having been turned away by the concierge on the grounds of over-familiarity. *I* had no time for such luxuries as bantering with the famous: my job was working on the influential. I worked the fashion editors like a pro, coaxing smiles from the nicotine-tanned faces with twelve-bore flattery, scattering hints about well-known customers who could be name-dropped in articles and suggesting features on the clothes worn by e-businesswomen. Broadsheets, mushy middlebrow tabloids, and glossy monthlies all fell before my onslaught, and I felt like a much, much prettier, and only slightly less ruthless, version of one of my favorite A-level characters, Tamburlaine.

And you must bear in mind that this wasn't all pure self-aggrandizement. Success for a fashion company depends on lots of different factors, and making good clothes is only one of them, and far from the most important. Have you ever wondered why certain names always crop up in the fashion pages? Why some collections steal all the limelight? You've looked at the clothes and thought, well, quite nice, or foul, or plain silly, but you've never quite worked out why *them* and not someone else. Well, I'm afraid it's because the designer or the PR put in the time at parties like this one. They charmed the leathery editors; they scammed and they schemed.

And please don't think that this is some kind of exposé, a KATIE CASTLE TELLS THE AWFUL TRUTH ABOUT FASH-

ION. Because as far as I can see, there's no other way you could do it. There are so many clothes clamoring for attention, there just has to be a way of filtering it into interesting and uninteresting. And the way that happens is by being there with a tactical Silk Cut when the dwarfish fashion supremo at the *Daily Beast* finds that the nicotine-impregnated chewing gum, patch, and suppository have done nothing to quell her craving, and baubles of quicksilver sweat stand glistening amid the faultlines around her mouth, and her lips are peeling back from her red gums in a rictus of horror.

I love it.

A steady stream of guests had been arriving, and it seemed that pretty well everyone was here. The Japanese designer came in with an angry face, looking for a battleship to crash into, but Milo soon had him giggling a strange high-pitched giggle at some tale of courtesans and couturiers. Yes, the party was perfectly shaped: there was a definite feeling that it was one group, with one purpose, yet there was sufficient bitchiness and animosity amid and between the various little subsets to provide endless interest.

Much of this interest was focused on Pippin, who had turned up smashed, coked, and stinking of rent boy, determined to do his "last dark days of Sebastian Flyte" impression. He staggered from group to group, bursting into the middle of conversations, which he then hijacked for his own monomaniacal purpose: the badmouthing of Milo and Xerxes. In the end, even Milo's coolness was tested too far. He beckoned two of the burlier caterers, dipped into his wallet, whispered some instructions, and turned away.

The caterers, one obviously supplementing his student

loan, the other faintly sinister in a butcher's boy kind of way, pocketed what looked like diamond-sharp new fifties and, with very little roughness, guided Pippin to the door. His passivity may have been born of a conviction that the two were after a little entertainment. Only at the last moment did he seem to realize that he was getting the bum's rush in quite a different sense, calling over his shoulder in a gesture so theatrical that it simply had to be deliberate and, if so, represented Pippin's triumph, the zenith of his career as drama queen:

"I'll get you, you bitch! You'll pay for this."

Already the party was guaranteed immortality.

Amid all the fun, I noticed that a rather elegant figure had taken the opportunity of the open door to enter. It was a full three seconds before I realized that it was Ludo's bolshie friend Tom. He was dressed head to toe in charcoal gray Paul Smith, which may have been unimaginative, but it certainly worked wonders for him. His hair had been cut rather nicely, too, and I guessed that an elderly Italian in N19, or wherever Tom lived, had missed out on his £5 this month. But that didn't tell me what he was doing here. I supposed Ludo must have invited him to play crutch, which could get me in serious trouble with Milo. Plenty of perfectly estimable fashion people had failed to make it onto the guest list, and good space being taken up by yet another *schoolteacher* with no fashion or showbiz cred at all (despite his ever-so-proficient makeover) was precisely the kind of inefficiency that Milo found unacceptable.

"What a lovely surprise," I said as Tom spied me and came over. He looked disconcertingly confident, contrasting with the half-sheepish half-surly way that Ludo always appeared at these events.

"Hello," he said, declining, as ever, to kiss. He had the typical working-class aversion to polite physical contact.

"I suppose you're after Ludo. I haven't seen him for a while."

"Er . . . no. Actually, I've found who I was looking for."

And at that Kookai appeared. Tom's face melted into a huge smile. I realized that I'd never seen his teeth before. They looked as though they might have been fixed in the very recent past. Kookai stood on her tippy toes, threw back her head, kissed him on the lips, and then slipped down to nestle at his side.

I worked hard at controlling my body's urge to go into shock mode, checking that my jaw hadn't dropped, my eyes popped, or my bladder emptied. Think sardonic, think cool, think collected, I told myself. I decided to raise an eyebrow.

"So, you two an item, then?"

"No, I always just go up and snog women at parties," Tom said unnecessarily.

"Tom, be nice now. After all, it was lovely Katie who brought us together." Was it my imagination, or was I being patronized by Kookai? Surely not.

I decided to go and look for Ludo, not something I'd ever felt like doing at a party before. I assumed he'd be slumped in a corner somewhere, mumbling to himself about how hideous fashion people are, so I was amazed to find him amid the steam ovens, chrome juicers, and other equipment that would never be used, in the burnished bronze of Milo's high-tech kitchen.

More astonishingly, Ludo was at the center of rather a fun little group. I recognized a couple of pretty fashion journalists (too young yet to have acquired the leathery hide, the crooked back, and the evil countenance of the editors), both called Jane; a famously moody East European photographer, dressed in snow-wash denims and an ill-gotten biker jacket; and Galatea Gisbourne, the too, too trendy designer who'd come up with the *concept* for Milo's flat. Apart from her extraordinary looks, with her blue-black hair and white face and bee-stung lips, which guaranteed her a place in any article on up-and-coming designers, Galatea was known principally for her elaborate and highly amusing speech impediment, a kind of lisp that made her pronounce "s" as "sh," a sound accompanied by a bubbling and hissing of spittle around her back teeth. Unkind people were always trying to get her to say "sshcrambled eggssh," or "sshpinach," or "Sshasshkatchewan."

As well as these familiar figures, another, darker, stood with his back to me. Something about his shape gave me a vague feeling of unease. It was a feeling that escalated into near panic when I heard him speak. I heard only one word clearly above the background party hubbub, but it was enough: the word was *"siii-hens."*

In reply to whatever the dark figure was saying, Galatea replied excitedly, "Yesssh, who would deny the sshignificanssh of sshigns?" but I was reeling too much to enjoy it. I started to back out of the kitchen, when Ludo caught sight of me.

"Katie, come and say hello. It's amazing, I'm actually enjoying one of your parties. I didn't realize that you lot knew philosophers."

I thought quickly. I'd done nothing wrong. In fact, the opposite. I'd nothing to be ashamed about. So what if I gave this bozo the runaround? Served him right for that lazy pass he made at me. Fuck him! I'll brazen it out.

Malheurbe turned and looked at me.

"You! Katie! I cannot believe my good fortune. I have been wanting to see you, to apologize."

"What? You two know each other?" said Ludo, looking puzzled and amused.

"No," I said, but Malheurbe was already talking.

"I did this lady a miserable ungallantry. She arranged to meet me for an assignation in Paris. Her arrangements were very professional, which we do not expect from the English in this situation. But I had a terrible indisposition, and I could not meet her. I felt so sorry when I thought of her standing still waiting for the man who does not come."

Suddenly everyone was staring at me. The journos sensed something amusing was on the cards. Ludo's expression had moved from puzzlement to a sort of armed neutrality, like Switzerland.

"What's he talking about, Katie?" he asked coolly.

I'd been hugely thrown by Malheurbe's apology. I didn't know if he really hadn't turned up or if this was all some carefully planned revenge. Try blanket denial.

"This man is clearly some kind of loony. I've no idea what he's talking about."

"But Katie, my dear," said the French Fuck smoothly, "I understand you are angry. But if you knew how deep are my feelings, you would forgive. Look, you see, I have kept the note of love you gave me when we met."

Jesus, the directions. Christ, the kisses.

He held out his hand. And there it was, the fold of faint-lined A4, with my handwriting and my little pyramid of three kisses. Everyone knew that was my signature.

The mood among the onlookers changed from excitement to embarrassment, and they began to edge away.

I turned to Ludo.

"Look, darling, let me explain. This . . . man was with Milo at Première Vision. He made the most appalling pass at me, and I arranged to meet him just to get rid of him. You can ask Milo if you don't believe me."

Malheurbe interrupted: "I am sorry, I did not realize that there is an association between you two people."

"She's going to be my wife."

"Ah, let me commend you on the liberality and openness of your relationship. Again, this is not a sophistication we expect from the English."

Ludo hit him, hard, in the mouth.

The Janes gave a little synchronized gasp. I'd never seen him doing anything violent before. He was so gentle. I briefly considered feeling turned on by the spectacle, but I just felt sick. The photographer took out a small but expensive-looking camera and took a picture of the crumpled and bloody philosopher.

Ludo turned away and strode back into the main room. I ran after him. The party had continued, unaware of the drama in the kitchen. Nobody seemed to notice as we twisted and writhed our way to the door. I caught him just before he reached the lift in the hall.

"Ludo, please. You can't believe that rubbish. It's funny, it's so mad."

He looked at me gravely for several seconds.

"I believe you," he said, but without smiling.

"Please come back in to the party. I'll stay by your side all night, I promise. And you'll never guess what, Tom's come, and he's with Kookai!"

Now he smiled, but not with his eyes.

"Yes, I knew about them. I thought I'd mentioned it. But I can't go back in. I acted like an arse. And I'm really quite upset about the whole thing. You know, Katie, you really shouldn't behave like such a . . . slag. It's no wonder people get the wrong idea. I trust you, I think, but it still makes me look like a fool. Why don't you just go to the party and have some fun. I'm going to wander around for a bit. Maybe get some ice for my hand."

I looked down. His index finger was purple, and there was a deep cut, which must have come from Malheurbe's tooth. I took it in my hands and kissed it better. He winced and pulled away.

"Just leave it for now, Katie. I'm suddenly very tired."

I gave a little wave as the doors closed. He smiled back sadly, looking defeated.

But could I face the party after all the fuss? Well, the whole point of Katie Castle is that she goes back into parties when her fiancé has just punched a French philosopher to the ground for claiming to have had an affair with her. Isn't it?

So back I went. Frankly, the kitchen spat was small fry compared with the Pippin incident and barely seemed to have registered on the party Geiger counter. Malheurbe smirked at me, which made it plain that revenge had been his motive. At least he had a bloody lip to remember me by.

I drifted around for a while, but my heart had gone out of it. I noticed that Tom and Kookai were having fun. Kookai was telling a surprisingly amusing story at her own expense about having to "bus surf" her way into work when she first started in PR. Penniless, she'd get on a bus going her way, and when the conductor got around to asking for her fare (which always takes a few minutes), she'd search desperately through her bag, finally bursting into tears. Explaining that she'd lost her purse, she'd offer to get off the bus at the next stop. About half the time they'd smilingly let her ride all the way. If she did have to get off, she'd just do the same on the next bus. "You know, it really made getting into work quite an adventure," she said, winningly, "but it once took me four buses, and I was cried out for a week afterward."

Sly minx, I thought. Not nearly so dumb. Here she was subtly playing on our perceptions of her as a bimbo, but making us all love her for it. Perhaps there's a PR genius in there after all.

As I was thinking about leaving, Milo cornered me.

"So how do you think it went?"

"Couldn't have been better. Flat looked fab, everyone came, catering worked a treat, two major fistfights, blood on the kitchen floor. What more could you want?"

"Yes, I heard about Ludo and that buffoon Malheurbe. No long-term damage, I hope?"

"What, to Malheurbe? Nah, just a bust lip."

"Pity. But I was thinking more about you and Ludo."

"No, he's a sweetie."

"Pity."

"*Milo!*"

"Only joking."

"I should think so. You know you'd have nothing to do with me if it weren't for Penny Moss; and if it weren't for Ludo, then I'd still be . . . well, a God knows what. Without Ludo I'd never have made it past the Vietnamese child." At the mention of the Vietnamese, Milo emitted a groan of animal lust. It looked as though Milo would be playing United Nations after the party fizzled, what with his Persian and Vietnamese boys and the unwholesome Czech, or Latvian, or Pole, or whatever-he-was photographer, who seemed to be hanging around in the hope of something.

Milo paused whatever secret video he was playing in his mind.

"Katie, really! You're not trying to say that that if you went back to being a little fashion wannabe, with no money, and no influence, and no prospects, I'd drop you, are you, darling? Heaven forfend!"

"Like a ton of hot shit," I said, surprising myself with my crudity and vehemence. It had meant to come out a touch more lightly.

CHAPTER 10

In which Katie Doesn't Cry

I got in about three, exhausted and just a bit depressed. Overall the party had been a success, but somehow I couldn't derive much satisfaction from it. I knew that I should have followed Ludo, played kissy-kissy-make-up-now-best-friends-please. But I'd wanted to consolidate my gains, drive home my advantage. Instead, toward the end I had drifted aimlessly, watching as the coke-heads got jitterier and jitterier. I've always preferred the honest blur of alcohol to the false clarity of coke, but I never really minded other people doing it. Made them laugh more at your jokes. But like everything, repetition grates, and the scraping and cutting and sniffing and false laughter came to seem boring, and pointless, and ill-mannered.

As soon as I opened the door, I sensed that something was wrong. The flat felt cold and empty. Ludo wasn't there. I checked all the rooms in case he'd fallen asleep in a closet or something, but I knew I wouldn't find him. I wasn't particularly worried. Ludo wasn't the kind of boy who'd get into a fight with broken bottles and bicycle chains. I assumed he'd gone round to Daniel's. I slept lightly and dreamed of dragons.

When Ludo still wasn't there the next morning, I did begin to become concerned. I thought I'd better talk to Penny to see if she knew where he was, but as I was about to call I saw that there were a couple of messages on the answering machine. I used to love getting messages. I always felt a little shudder of excitement; after all, it might be something that would change your life.

The first message was from Veronica, which I deleted after listening to the first drawn-out, soppy, "Hell-oo, Katie." It was bound to be boring or depressing: a new rejection or a food-related crisis.

The second was from Penny. The machine's irritating Stephen Hawking voice told me it was from "one thirty-seven" in the morning.

"Katie, this is Penny. Ludo is here, but not for much longer. Something has happened, and I want to see you in the office tomorrow. I suggest you get there at eleven o'clock. You *will* be there, and you *won't* be late. I know it's a Sunday."

What on earth was this about? There must be an emergency at work. I'd occasionally gone in on a Sunday when things were frantic, but it was unknown for Penny to forgo her morning with the color supplements. A thought struck: surely it couldn't be that idiot Malheurbe, could it? Had Ludo taken that nonsense to heart after all? He did brood on things. Had he run to Mummy in his hour of need? No, no. Ludo being there was a red herring. It was probably the landlords, or Liberty's, or a new buyer who could only make Sundays, or another of the factories had gone under and we were going to have to switch production to Latvia, or something.

It was one of those rare sunny early November mornings that seem so wondrous because of the inevitable grayness before and after. I reached the shop at five to eleven and rang the bell. I was amazed when it was answered by Hugh. He unlocked the door and stood aside as I entered. He didn't offer to kiss me.

"Hugh," I said, "this is all very mysterious. What's going on? I'm not used to adventures on a Sunday." I tried to keep my voice just on this side of flirtation.

"Better leave that for Penny," he said, refusing to look me in the eyes, which was very un-Hugh. I was afraid now. Everything was wrong. Penny-work-Sunday-Hugh-Ludo, it was a horrid combination. I followed Hugh silently up the stairs. I had a brief but powerful hallucination that I was going up the steps to the gallows. The tumbrels tumbreled, and hags knitted, and culottes were in very short supply.

More surprises lay in store for me up in the office. Rather than just the expected Penny, I saw that she was with *Cavafy,* of all people. Why on earth did Penny want him to be there? It was the first time I'd ever seen the little Greek outside the factory. It was deeply disorienting. He looked at me strangely for a moment, his face angled away. I didn't know if it was sadness or hostility, but the old kindness had gone.

Hugh joined them on the far side of Penny's desk, which was pulled away from the wall and arranged for interrogation.

"The Committee of Public Safety," I mumbled. Hugh seemed to read my mind and smiled, then coughed to hide the smile. Penny didn't know or care what I might be thinking.

"Now, Katie," she began in her most businesslike manner, "I've no intention of beating about the brush."

"Bush," said Hugh quietly, taking his life in his hands. On this occasion Penny chose to ignore him.

"You've been found out. It was only a matter of time. I never thought you were suitable for Ludo. I feel no personal animosity. I'm sure you just couldn't help yourself."

What, who did she mean? Christ, what to do? Try bluster.

"How many times do I have to tell people that that fucking Frenchman was a criminal fantasist. I gave him the note to get rid of him. He's an ugly, boring, pointless little nobody. Who cares about deconstructive fashion now? I wouldn't dream of doing anything with *him.*"

"Well, Katie," continued Penny, "that may or *may not* have been the case. Ludo told me the facts, and we might have been prepared to give you the benefit of the doubt. But that isn't why we've called you here. You'll have noticed that Cavafy has been kind enough to come along. In fact, he's why we're here. He came to me yesterday with a story, you see; a story he'd been told by Angel."

Enlightenment arrived, dazzling, terrifying. This was nothing to do with Malheurbe. A rush of nausea hit me. It happens a lot to bulimics. But still, I had to fight.

"For God's sake, Penny, you know Angel has always had a crush on me. Whatever he says is tainted."

"My boy, he don't lie," Cavafy said quietly, but with intensity crackling along the edges of the words like static electricity.

"Let's get to the point, Katie," returned Penny. "Did you know that Liam Callaghan and young Angel were friends?"

"No, not friends," interrupted Cavafy pedantically. "Just acquaintances, who have sometimes drinks together."

"As you please, Cavafy. And what do you think boys

talk about when they have their little drinks? Boys like Liam Callaghan? Cut flowers? The stock market? Or maybe, just perhaps, girls?" Penny was actually rather good at sarcasm. "Put yourself in Liam's shoes, Katie dear. Try to imagine being a boy. A boy who's just been to bed with someone as pretty and clever and well placed as you. Wouldn't *you* have a sly little boast about it, mmm? *I* would."

So, there it was. Liam had blabbed. Perhaps he knew that Angel was sweet on me, perhaps he didn't. Either way, good little Angel went running straight to his dear daddy. And dear Daddy happened to be Penny's old friend.

Cavafy spoke.

"Katie, you know I always like you. You know I want you for my boy, because he like you so much, too. But when I hear about this with that driver, I was angry. So, you too good for my Angel, but not too good for this Irish person? It's not right, I say to myself. Not right for Penny, not right for her Ludo. Who is also good boy. Now maybe I am sorry that I came to Penny with this story. But I thought it was better from a friend."

"Thank you, Cavafy," said Penny. "As ever, you have the instincts of a gentleman."

No doubt you are wondering at my relative passivity through all this. My natural instinct was to rail at the lot of them. Who did they think they were to sit in judgment over me? It was absurd. But I felt drugged and drained of energy. My legs and arms were heavy and my mind numb. It wasn't guilt. It was just that I'd done the math. I had the heavy brigade ranged against me, and all I had for defense was the small child's "I didn't do it" when her face is covered in the same chocolate that's smeared on the walls and the carpet and the curtains.

But no one's ever said I was a quitter. Fight on, however feeble the weapons.

"Look, Penny, Cavafy, I'm not saying Angel's made this up. I'm fond of Angel, and I'm sorry it never worked out for us. It's Liam. Liam made a pass at me the last time I was at the depot. He sort of lunged, and I slapped him down. Men hate that, and so he's made this all up to get back at me, or to boost his ego, or just to cause trouble. I don't know."

"Good try, Katie, but it won't wash, it really won't wash." Penny knew she had the upper hand, and she was smooth and unruffled. "Your French paramour proved that this is part of a pattern. And anyway, I've spoken to Liam. He's distraught." I bet he is, I thought. "Did you know he's married? That he has two children?"

She paused, waiting for the information to sink in. I was frozen. Blindingly obvious, of course. Why else the borrowed flat? Why else the curious evasions? So maybe it was just a bit of stupid male bragging on Liam's part and not an attempt to get even. How much had Penny made him wriggle? I wondered. Had she wheedled or had she bullied? She could do good cop, bad cop all by herself.

"He has much more to lose than you. According to *his* story, you told him you were desperate for a 'quick fling'—really, how sordid—before 'settling down' with Ludo. He says it was *you* who lured *him*. And frankly, I believe him." And then she added in an aside to Hugh, "He's one of the best drivers we've ever had."

The swine. Why had I trusted him? But still I couldn't work up a useful head of righteous indignation. I was sinking. I had to consciously and laboriously move my lips and tongue to speak. And all I could do was bleat:

"This is just madness, this whole thing. Where's Ludo? I want Ludo."

"By now Ludo will have gone away. I thought it was best to send him out of town for a while. There's some *project* looking after eagles. . . ."

"Guarding their eggs," added Hugh.

"Eggs? But who'd want to eat eagle eggs? Anyway, I've sent him to Mull, or Muck, or somewhere. We all agreed it was the *healthiest* thing."

I wasn't going to cry.

"What happens next?"

"Well, obviously you'll have to move out of the flat."

"But you can't do that! It's where I live. I've nowhere else to go."

Penny ignored my words, not even bothering with a "Well, you should have thought of that." She just plowed straight on:

"And we really don't think it's appropriate that you carry on working *here,* either. I'm sure that you can see that that would be impossible." With one sharp nail she pushed something toward me. "In this envelope you'll find a month's wages, which I think is quite generous, and a reference, which, all things considered, is also rather generous. Sukie, by the way, is taking over."

"Bitch," I said, but without any real force. I suppose I was thinking about Sukie as much as Penny.

"Come on now, Katie," said Hugh, tearing his eyes away from the pattern in the carpet. "You know the rules. You took a chance and you lost. Can't blame Penny for this. You know, I've always thought you were a splendid girl, and I wish you well for the future, but you must see we . . . they have to let you go. Penny and Ludo."

That was it. If I'd lost Hugh, then I'd lost everything.

And now I *had* lost everything. Bang! flat; bang! lover; bang! job; bang! everything.

"We've put your things in there," said Penny, pointing to a cardboard box under my desk, which I now noticed was clear. I could see my red fluffy pencil case, a gift from Veronica, sticking out the top. I'd kept it as another reminder of how far I'd come.

"When am I supposed to move out of the flat?" I asked. This was my public admission of defeat.

"I've arranged for a taxi to collect everything while you've been here."

"But that's outrageous. Surely you can't do that. And what things? How can I fit all I own into a taxi?"

"Katie, you weren't planning on taking any furnishings, were you? I understand that Ludo bought everything. And how well I remember you arriving in a taxi. As you came, so shall you go."

"*You just can't do this.*" It was my final stand, and all I had left emotionally went into it, just as all my material possessions were in the taxi.

"Oh, but Katie, we can. You've been living a dream. You thought you had become one of us, one of the people who matter. Well, you hadn't, not really. We just let you pretend for a while. And now it's time to wake up."

I then had one of my light-headed insights, which you are quite entitled to view as a fantasy, if you prefer. Hugh, Cavafy, Penny—these were no longer real people, but before my eyes they were transformed into representative figures, or symbols. Hugh was a former city type, a stockbroker, or trader, or bond dealer (I've never really understood the difference); Cavafy was a factory owner; Penny, an entrepreneur, of sorts. It was capitalism in all its glory—Finance, Commerce, the Means of Production, all ranged against me. I was being officially crushed by the system! Okay, so Hugh wasn't exactly a hotshot, and Cavafy's factory barely brought in enough to pay the mortgage on the semi in Hitchin, and Penny's entrepreneurial skills were qualified by incipient dementia, but then being rubbish at the job never stopped the Scarecrow, Tin Man, and Cowardly Lion. I thought, I must tell Ludo about this, he'll love it, but of course I was never going to see him again.

"What am I supposed to do?"

"Katie, you're a clever girl, you'll think of something."

Then Penny and Hugh and Cavafy made those faint "Meeting over" noises, little sighs, an "ah," and a restrained smacking of lips. Hugh gallantly picked up my box and walked with me down the stairs. When we were safely down one flight, he turned and said, "I thought one month was a bit *tight,* so I've made it up to three. Keep it to yourself. Penny'll go through the roof if she ever finds out."

The tears now were rolling down my face, but I only count it as crying if you sob, and I definitely would not be sobbing.

When we reached the street, Hugh felt for his wallet and gave me twenty pounds, saying, "And you'd better get a taxi back to the flat as well."

I can't remember if I said thanks. I certainly didn't mean to.

The cab took me back through the depressing Sunday streets. The day had clouded over, and the sky seemed low enough to bump your head on. A phrase came to me from somewhere: the pathetic fallacy. I must have said it aloud, because the taxi driver said, "Sorry?" but I just shook my head.

By the time we reached Camden, my inertia and unhealthy detachment had begun to peel away, and some of the old fire was glimmering. At least seven superb re-torts came to me, and I writhed and gnashed at having submitted so meekly. If only I'd seen it coming, I could have fought them into the ground. I may not have saved my life, but I would have left them in need of a stiff drink. Instead, they had, I felt, pitied me. Never again.

The taxi pulled up outside the flat, nose to nose with another. I didn't tip the driver: I was going to need every penny I had.

"You waiting for me?" I asked the second driver.

"You Miss Castle?"

"Mm."

"Then I'm waiting for you."

"Is your meter running?"

"Not your problem, love. Young feller sorted it."

I looked in the back. It was filled almost to the roof with cases and black bin liners. There was just enough room for me and my box.

But first I wanted to check round the flat, partly to see if there was anything of mine they had forgotten. My key turned in the Yale, but the door wouldn't open. I shoved it with my shoulder. Still nothing. Then I saw that there was a new lock in addition to the old. Coolly I appreciated Penny's thriftiness. Why go to the expense of changing the lock when you could keep me out *and* gain additional security by adding another? My heart hardened a little more as another layer of crystal was de-posited on the inside.

Back down the drive I stooped, on impulse, and picked up a stone. Without much thinking about it, I turned and flung it at the window, like a teenage thug. Sadly, I missed both the window and the house, and it bounced off the plaster two doors down. If only I'd paid more attention in PE.

I climbed in the taxi and saw that an envelope was taped to the bulging beer belly of one of the black bags. I recognized Ludo's writing. Before I could open it, the driver slid his window across and asked where to. At some deep level of my being, I'd always known what I was going to say when that question came, as it inevitably would. Known, but dreaded to admit it consciously to myself.

"Tollington Road."

"That Finsbury Park? Off Stroud Green?"

"Mm."

Veronica.

We set off, and I read the note. This is what it said:

Katie

Mum phoned when I got back last night. She told me about you and that Callaghan person. If it hadn't been for the French thing, I would never have believed her. But then if it hadn't been for Callaghan, I would never have believed the French thing.

Why did you do it, Katie? I loved you so much, and we could have been so happy. Was it because I wasn't cool enough, or was it a sex thing? All I can think about is you with them. I banged my head against the wall to try to drive out the images, but it didn't work. That's why I can't ever see you again. I've got to try to forget about you or I'll go mad.

I'm sorry about the flat. Penny insisted. You know it belongs to her. I said that I thought the lock thing was unnecessary, but she said she didn't want you ever to set foot in the place again. The most amazing thing about all this is that she actually managed to be right about something. I suppose it's the law of averages.

I'm not going to be here when you get back. I'm flying out to the west of Scotland to work on a conservation project. It's something I've been involved in for a couple of years, but you probably haven't noticed. It was Penny's idea that I go, but it was still a good one. I don't know how long I'll be there for. If they want me, I might never come back.

I don't blame you, and I don't hate you. Part of me will always love you. I'm just so, so sad. I hope you have a nice life.

L

I tried very hard to laugh at the self-pity and the pomposity. But it didn't work. And I'm going to have to end this chapter here, because I promised that I wouldn't cry in it, and now I'm about to.

CHAPTER 11

The House of Mirth

So I blubbed. There were tears of self-pity; there were tears of frustration; there were tears of anger. There were no tears of remorse. It lasted eleven minutes, just long enough to get to the Holloway Road (it's a Sunday, remember). It was useful and it was good. Without the cry I would have remained in shock, paralyzed and unable to act.

With the return of clarity, two jobs pressed. I thought I'd better make sure Veronica was in, although where *she* might go to on a Sunday afternoon, I've no idea, unless it was to mooch around in the park on her own, sniffing and snuffling. At least I still had my mobile. I rang. A strange voice, young, male, gormless.

"Yeah, hi?"

"Hello, is Veronica there, please?"

"Nah, she's er . . . you know . . . out."

"Can you tell me when she'll be back?"

"Dunno."

Curse! Veronica was the last person in London without a mobile—concerns about brain tumors, biorhythms, and miscarriage (fat chance) put her off, she claimed.

"Look, this is very important," I said sternly. "Are you going to be in for the next twenty minutes?"

"Yeah, probably. Why d'yer wanna know?"

"My name's Katie Castle. I'm an old friend of Veronica's and I'm coming to stay. She must have forgotten. You'll have to let me in."

Boy sounded like a cretin. I tried to remember who Veronica lived with. It was a big, sprawling, studenty house full of misfits and inadequates like Veronica. I'd only been there twice before, both also in emergencies (lost keys; first big row with Ludo over mess, which required elementary-level brinkmanship). Last time I was there the rooms were occupied by, as well as Veronica, an irritating pixie who edited a magazine about trampolining; a somber German, here to learn how to brood in English; a civil servant, anxious to talk about VAT; and a pretty, but malicious, jewelry designer, who specialized, apparently, in stealing people's boyfriends. I've no idea what any of them were called. The cretin must be new.

Okay, so accommodation sorted. Now for that cunt—I'm sorry, but occasionally there really is no alternative, so I say again—that cunt Liam. I had only his mobile number, the one he used for business. I'd programmed it into my Nokia under "clothing removal," which had amused me at the time, but not now.

First I had to think carefully about what to say. There were a number of possible approaches. I could rant and rave, which would make me feel better and would make him uncomfortable for the length of the phone call, but which was unlikely to reap much in the way of an objective improvement in my condition. I could be cold and malicious, threatening to use my contacts to destroy his business unless he recanted (with the intention of destroying his business anyway). I could employ some hybrid of these two, ranting at him before cooling it and showing him the steel. I could use reason and point out to him the strong ethical reasons for recanting and saving my skin. I could kill him. I drew up a mental table to help me work it out:

	ADVANTAGES	DISADVANTAGES	MARKS (out of ten)
1. Rant and Rave	Get it off my chest; give him a hard time	Makes me look like a loony; gives him the satisfaction of knowing he's had an effect on me	6
2. Cold Assassin	Maximum long-term impact on Liam	No immediate psychological release	7
3. Hybrid of 1 & 2	Quite tricky to pull off	Still potential for looking mad	8
4. Reasoned Argument	None	No psychological release; no damage to Liam	1
5. Kill Liam	Maximum psychological release	Likely to serve 10–15 years of life sentence	5

Although the points system suggested the hybrid approach, I was still undecided when I pressed dial, but we were getting close to Veronica's, and I wanted it out of the way by the time I arrived. After four nervous rings I was diverted to Liam's voice mail. He had recorded a new message. This is what it said:

"Hello, this is Liam Callaghan. I'm away for the next two weeks and I won't be able to take on any new jobs until I get back. If that is Katie Castle, please, please stop harassing me and my family. I have had to inform the police about your activities."

Fuck.

Fuck.

Fuck.

That was really it. Really, absolutely, and totally it. Now the whole world was going to think of me as a classic bunny boiler. I had underestimated Liam. He had worked it all out, and I half admired him for it. Faced with the possibility of losing business through some kind of seedy association with mine and Ludo's breakup, he had cunningly portrayed me as a psycho. Everybody used Liam. Everybody who used him left messages on his phone. The news would spread faster than Ebola in a Congo village. A weird noise came out of my throat, and it took me a couple of seconds to work out that it was a laugh.

"You all right back there, love?" asked the taxi driver.

"Fine," I said, gasping for air. We were in Tollington Road. "It's number 116, just here on the left."

I asked the taxi driver to hang on while I went to ring. After a minute a youth with long hair and bare feet came to the door. I took this to be the cretin. He was actually reasonably good-looking in a scruffy, *What's Eating Gilbert Grape* kind of way. He pushed the hair out of his eyes and said, "Oh, hi. You Katie?"

"Yeah."

"Malan," he said.

"I beg your pardon?"

"Er . . . I'm Alan, I mean."

"Look, Alan, or Malan, or whoever you are," I said in a strict, but flirty way, "I've got a couple of bags. Could you give me a hand?"

He looked down at his feet, and you could sense him

weighing up the options—schlep back upstairs for some shoes? Or slap out on the path with nothing but his verrucas between him and the slug trails? Barefoot, he followed.

It took five minutes of heaving to transfer all my worldlies from the taxi to the hall. I think the driver realized that this was not the best day of my life, and he very sweetly helped out.

The youth looked at my sad heap of bin liners, my two cheap, pre-Ludo cardboard suitcases, and some more recent Louis Vuitton.

"Where d'yer want this stuff? I mean, are you, like, moving in?"

"I'll be in Veronica's room, for a while."

It took six journeys, two for me and four for Malan, to get me settled in Veronica's room. It had not changed over the past two years. Still bead curtains hanging around aimlessly. Still the stumps of a thousand scented candles. Still the racks of self-help books: *Eat Yourself to a Better Job; Feng Shui on a Plate; Ditch the Guru: How to Wean Yourself off Self-Help Books*. Still the ethnic rugs, handwoven from yak pelts. Still the old acoustic typewriter, on which she'd hammer out those interminable, unread letters about her inner torment. I emptied out one of my bin liners and started to fill it with some of her rubbish. I didn't know how long I would be staying, but some order and discipline would have to be imposed if it was going to be tolerable.

My next job was to elbow some room in her hopelessly inadequate hold-your-breath-and-walk-in wardrobe for my clothes. A number of Veronica's voracious jumpers joined the rubbish in the bin liner. And only then, semi-settled, the horror of homelessness and crumpled clothes temporarily, at least, receding, did I lie back on Veronica's bed and light a cigarette.

As ever, it brought a clarity and objectivity to my thought. I replayed the morning. I then rewound further and played everything from the ill-omened meeting with Liam in the Loading Bay of Doom. I saw all of my mistakes and miscalculations, my errors of judgment, and my bad luck. And there I saw the key moment, the hinge on which my history turned. It was my handling of Liam when he'd called to ask me on a second date. What I should have done was to come across as clingy and desperate. He then would have felt for me little but pity and contempt, and I would have been in the clear. My aloofness and disdain could only have had two results: made his yearning for me all the sharper, or triggered the revenge response.

For some reason, the full audit of my catastrophe calmed me. I had managed, through logic and reason, to erect a dam between the horror and me. I could see it boiling and bubbling like lava behind the wall, but for now it was safely contained.

I was just lighting my third Silk Cut (two stubs bobbed in the half cup of cold coffee left by Veronica beside her bed) when the door was thrown back and Veronica burst in.

"Katie, how lovely," she said, her eyes watering with the smoke. "But what are you doing here? What are all these bags and things?" And then more urgently: "Katie, what's happened?"

"I've left Ludo."

"Oh, Katie," she said, sympathy adding to the chemically induced tears, "please, please tell me what's happened."

"I suppose you'll find out sooner or later. Some man,

a driver, made up a story about me. Ludo believed it, and he's thrown me out. Or rather Penny has. Veronica, I've nowhere to go, no one to turn to except you. Can I please stay here until I find somewhere else?"

"Katie, of course you can," she said, and flung her heavy arms around me. "It'll be fun. We'll have to share the bed, though, just like when we were little." *I* had no recollection whatsoever of having spent time in the same bed as Veronica, however little we may have been. I hadn't fully thought through the sleeping arrangements. Still, in a time of crisis one must make sacrifices. "But," Veronica continued, "I'll have to run it past the house council tonight. It should be a formality. And I have to tell you, Katie, and I know it's only the stress that has made you do it, but this is a strictly nonsmoking household. If you want to smoke, you'll have to go outside, onto the patio."

"Patio! Yuck. I didn't realize that people had patios anymore. I thought it was all decking. But of course I shall respect your rules. Thank you so much, Veronica, I shall never forget this. I've already unpacked a few things. . . ."

And so we spent quite a pleasant afternoon, considering my life was ruined. For once Veronica's close attendance was exactly what I needed. She comforted and praised, and lamented, and cursed in all the right places. I needed some unconditional love, and Veronica had plenty and nowhere else to put it. She made me coffee with hot milk and later brought me a bacon sandwich, despite her fervent vegetarianism. I hadn't eaten all day, and I inhaled it in three big gasps.

Late in the afternoon she said, "You've come on the right day: we always have Sunday dinner together—it's a house thing. I'm doing a buckwheat pilaf. Let's go and meet the gang, they should be around by now. You know most of them: Colin's still here, you know, the VAT person; so is Roxanne, the jewelry girl. And little Tracy, with her trampoline, and leotard, and things. But Otto has gone."

"Replaced by Malan."

"Who?"

"You know, zombie boy, 'I'mmmalan.' "

"Oh yes, Katie, you're so funny. No, he goes out with Roxanne, but he spends most of his time here because he hasn't anywhere else to go. A bit like you, really." Before I had time to lash out, Veronica carried on, "No, no, Roddy's moved into Otto's room."

I sensed that a change had occurred. Veronica had gone all dreamy and was squirming on her bottom in a repellently animal way.

"Roddy, I see. And what does Roddy do?"

"Roddy's an actor," she said reverently.

"And would I be wrong to say that just maybe perhaps Veronica has a tiny weenie soft spot for this handsome actor?"

"Silly!" said Veronica, blushing and giggling and looking away.

"Well, let's go and meet them, then, before this beanbag swallows me whole."

Veronica's house was on three floors, and her bedroom was at the top. The house certainly had potential, with its huge rooms and high ceilings and big windows and wide stairs. But the faraway owner, old Mrs. Alzheimer, who'd inherited the place in 1906, was mindful now only of her colostomy bag and Stannah stair lift, and was never going to put anything into it, so it was left on its knees, begging for a lick of paint, and some new carpets and furniture, and perhaps for a UN helicopter airlift out of Finsbury Park.

The living room had two 1970s sofas, slashed at some period by a sword-wielding samurai, exposing their discolored viscera to the buttocks of an uncaring world. The rough floorboards were randomly covered or exposed by a network of old mats and rugs, assembled from charity shops, car boot sales, and prison workshops. There was also a weird-looking orthopedic rocking chair, designed, Veronica told me, to help correct curvature of the spine. About a third of the room was taken up with a dining table fashioned from roughly hewn planks, in the crevices between which lurked earwigs, and wood lice, and other writhing things.

The sofas were occupied by Tracy, Malan, Roxanne, and Colin. They turned and stared as I came in. I had the impression that the gormless one had been trying to tell them about the new arrival, in which case they were probably expecting a bearded Ethiopian carrying a blunderbuss and a camel harness.

"Oh, it's you, Katie," Roxanne said neutrally.

"Hi, everyone," said Veronica. "If nobody objects or anything, Katie's going to stay for a couple of days until she sorts out her life. Is that okay?"

There was a noncommittal murmur, which could just about be interpreted as consent.

"Is . . . em . . . Roddy around?" Veronica said wistfully. "We should check with him as well." Roxanne and Tracy performed a synchronized eye roll.

"He's fiddling with his taxi. Be in soon," said Colin. His face still had the same blue tinge that I remembered. He looked like the ghost of a Victorian child, blown up to man size and dressed in cheap casuals. Deeply creepy.

Veronica beamed at me. "He drives an old black cab instead of a car. He's soooo eccentric."

I sat in the rocking chair. Big mistake. The top half grabbed me and twisted one way, while the bottom half twisted the other, as if I were a dishcloth and it were wringing me out. At the same time it punched me in the kidneys and felt up my skirt. Every nerve begged me to leap out, but as the alternative was squeezing in next to Colin, I stayed where I was.

About half an hour of desultory conversation followed, ebbing over and around the buzzing from the black-and-white telly in the corner. Carefully dissecting the house mood, I found that Roxanne and Tracy were clearly on the hostile side of neutral, counterbalanced by Malan and Colin.

I gave them a carefully edited version of the week's events: I'd had enough of victimhood, so I milked it for a few laughs, while trying to retain their sympathy. My line was roughly: There but for the grace of God go you, so don't even think about calling me a slag, but yes, I was a *bit* naughty.

I thought it best to make polite inquiries about their lives, but just as Colin was about to tell me of a particularly interesting VAT case involving bird food, Roddy came in. He was startlingly handsome, tall, broad, with wavy strawberry-blond hair. He was wearing old and oily clothes, but you could see that they had once cost a country gentleman a lot of money.

"Well well well, we've a visitor. I don't think we've met. I'm Roddy."

"Katie Castle," I said, struggling to get out of the torture chair.

"No, for God's sake, don't get up. After a while you'll find you adapt to it, and the pain dies down. But then for the rest of your life your arse precedes you round corners by a full three seconds."

Veronica made her gulping laugh. "Ughh ughh ughh, stop it, Roddy."

Perhaps it was adversity, but I felt a real surge of pity for Veronica. Poor, poor thing, I thought, what chance do you stand with your tearstained hair, and your hourglass legs, and your uncared-for cheese-grater skin? Why couldn't you have picked on Colin? He'd have you. Be like making love to a cold fried egg.

From then on the evening rather improved. Roddy had a way of infecting others with his energy and good humor. The girls all clearly adored him, and the boys were disarmed by what appeared to be his self-deprecating humor, which mainly concerned theatrical mishaps. I say "appeared" because when you thought about the stories a little more carefully, he always seemed to come out of them well. "Look," they all said, "others in the acting profession may be pompous and self-important, but I am different: *I* can laugh at myself." This pose was premised, of course, on the understanding that we all thought he was marvelous, and within that safe haven he could caper and fool as much as he liked. How long would it survive a challenge? I wondered.

An opportunity to find out came when I asked him if he'd been in anything I might have seen. We were sitting round the dinner table, each struggling in his or her own way with the pilaf—a struggle not helped by the absence of wine. Roddy strained manfully to swallow the coarse vegetative matter, then mumbled the names of plays and theaters entirely unfamiliar to me, but which smacked strongly of rooms over pubs. But I was a guest here, so I smiled sweetly and tried to look quietly impressed.

"Any telly?" I asked.

"Yes, actually. You may have seen my Crunchie?" I had to concentrate hard not to laugh.

"Your Crunchie?"

"Yes, you know," he said, talking a little too quickly, "that 'Friday feeling' campaign. I was in an office, and I bite the Crunchie and turn into a Claymation thing, you know, like Wallace and Gromit, and I surf out of there on a wave of chocolate. You must have seen it? They modeled the clay figure on me very closely. It got an award."

"I love Crunchies," said Veronica. If Roddy had been in an advert for pig slurry, she'd have loved that, too.

"And of course, I'm a bit of a regular on *Casualty,*" Roddy continued after tossing Veronica a quick smile of acknowledgment.

"Wow," I said. "I haven't watched it for a while. What are you, a doctor or one of the gay male nurses, or perhaps you're one of the nasty administrators telling them to cut back on bandages and plasters and things?"

"Well, no, none of those. I've played lots of different characters. I'm on the rota for patients, you know, for big road crashes, and that sort of thing." Some of his ebullience had drained away. I was sorry, I really hadn't meant to expose him. I tried being silly.

"Oh, I see, you're a serial victim: appendix one week, scrotum caught on barbed-wire fence the next. Must be a bit depressing always dying on stage."

Harmless though it was, Tracy gasped and Veronica swooned. I'd gone too far—how could I mention the young god's scrotum in a way so lacking in proper reverence? But Roddy gallantly came to my rescue, cheerfully detailing more TV failures: the *Teletubbies* audition where he'd fluffed his lines, the coffee advert where he'd choked and fired a fine spray of coffee and mucus out of his nose into Joanna Lumley's face. It was all very endearing, and I made a point of being endeared.

Bed, which I had been dreading, turned out to be quite easy. Veronica and I giggled as we slipped into our nightdresses. The sheets were clean, and the smell of candles wasn't too overpowering. Veronica snuggled up to me, gave me a kiss on the cheek, turned over, and was snoring gently within five minutes. I had every intention of lying awake, tormenting myself with images from the day, but the candles, and the snoring, and the susurrus from the passing cars lulled me, and I slept, thus ending the worst day of my life. So far.

CHAPTER 12

The Second Time as Farce

What an odd week that was. I know I should have been grieving for the life that I had lost, but somehow I never quite got round to it. Perhaps I was still in post-traumatic stress mode, still too numb and shocked to face the horrid reality. Objectively, my world had crumbled, but some combination of that numbness and the old faith in my own ability to rise through quickness of thought and ruthlessness of action insulated me from the fact. Things just didn't seem too bad.

I awoke on the Monday morning to the sound of Veronica heavily entering her tights. She reminded me of a kind of animal that I couldn't remember the name of. Something large, and slow, and harmless, but also deeply strange.

"Oh, you're awake," she said cheerily. "I have to go to work. I've left some keys out for you—just treat this as your home."

"Tapir," I said blearily.

"Pardon?"

"I said thank you."

I quickly showered and coffeed and then set to work. I had some serious calling to do. I thought it was at least worth one more try to see if Penny had calmed down and realized that she couldn't get by without me. A familiar but subtly changed voice answered. It was Sukie.

"Can I speak to Penny?"

"Is that Katie?"

"You know it is. Just please put me through."

"She's very busy. I'm screening her calls."

"Not from me."

"*Particularly* from you."

"Look, Sukie, I know that Penny has given you my job . . . temporarily, but we both know you haven't the experience or the balls for it. In two weeks Penny will realize that she can't manage, and then I'll be back. If I were you, I really wouldn't antagonize me." I didn't want to sound like a bitch, but I had to take a hard line. I expected meek submission. This was a girl, after all, who a mere three days before had to do *whatever* I told her to, whether it was making my coffee, calling my hairdresser, or polishing buttons.

What I got was laughter.

"Katie, you poor, poor thing. Don't you understand what's happened? You've been purged. You don't exist anymore. Penny won't speak to you because she can't even pick up the frequency of your thin, common little voice. Katie, you don't register. And Penny's said that she's always wanted someone more like me to help represent the company. Someone with more . . . panache . . . elegance."

She meant, of course, money, class.

"Listen to me, you humpy-backed dwarf, either you put me through right now or—" Click.

Be cool, be calm, I told myself; it's immature to rage impotently when someone hangs up. I spent two minutes raging impotently, pulling leaves off the weeping fig by the phone. The cretin appeared briefly at the top of the stairs in his T-shirt and boxers. He looked baffled for a moment, then retreated.

On the off chance, I tried Ludo at the flat—I didn't entirely swallow the eagle egg. No answer. I tried his school. I was put through to the deputy head, a limp-voiced moaner with, I pictured, a polyester tie and terminal dandruff and cum-stained trousers and receding gums. No, they didn't know where he was. He'd resigned, no notice, nothing. They were furious. Children's education put at risk, blah blah blah. It was my turn to slam the phone down.

Rethink. Job gone. Boy gone. First thing to do: Get new job. Second: Get new boy. Number two could wait. The job, surely, must be easy. Good production managers are few and far between. I had three solid years behind me. I had contacts everywhere—and Hugh had been silly enough to put my red contacts book in the box with my things (or was that perhaps another deliberate act of generosity?).

I called four companies, all around the same size as Penny Moss. In each I spoke to someone at about my level. Three of them were friends of mine, not that we liked each other much. All were charm personified. None was prepared to put me through to the boss. I said that I was looking for production work. There wasn't any going. Each suggested I send in my CV.

Over the next two days, I telephoned everybody else I knew in the business. I no longer thought in terms of production manager: production assistant would do. I didn't care, I could check skirts, and write dockets, and order buttons, and count shoulder pads until new opportunities arose. But always the same polite rebuff and always the same sense that a circle had closed, leaving me on the outside.

I wasn't sure what this all meant. It could be that just at this moment there really wasn't anything out there. It happens, sometimes. It could mean, being a little less wide-eyed and innocent, that my peers would hardly welcome a rival such as me on board. Or, switching to full-blown paranoia mode, perhaps some combination of Liam's stinky message and Penny's malicious stirring had left me as a pariah, an untouchable, the last spangly boob tube on the sale rack.

But still I didn't panic. One step back, two steps forward, I kept telling myself. If it came to it, I could do shop work again. It would be a new challenge. I decided to send letters applying for production work and also offering to work in the shops. How could anyone resist? I had done it all before: I was well-known and respected. I was a player.

The evenings added to the sense of strangeness. My ship had been wrecked, but I'd been washed up immediately onto an island, and although the island might be a long way from civilization, it had on it all I needed for immediate survival. The house often did things together, like go to the pub or one of the cheap local restaurants, and I entered into their innocent world quite easily. These weren't people I'd normally invest my energy in, but then these weren't normal times. I drank quite a lot and flirted with Roddy. The pixie trampolinist turned out to be perfectly pleasant, if horribly limited in conversation. Once you strayed from the fairly restrictive subject of vertical oscillation, on which she was happy to chirrup endlessly, her discourse seemed to be limited to random squeaks and a curious, but inoffensive, purring noise. The cretin was easily won over and

was soon induced to dote. He was a freelance Web page
designer, which was why he was always hanging around
the house during the day. The doting accounted for my
one failure: Roxanne maintained her hostility with a
commendable dedication to duty. However, using what
I assume Tom meant when he said that I did by instinct
what Machiavelli and Clausewitz had struggled to set
down as theory, I soon had her bypassed, isolated, cut
off, and beleaguered. Colin the VAT man would go into
a preejaculatory shudder every time I remembered his
name.

Veronica and I became closer than we'd ever been. We
took to cuddling up together in bed each night (and
no, don't even think about it—this isn't *that* kind of
story), talking over the day. Usually *my* day—who, after
all, wants to hear about old ladies with sore thyroids
signing up for arnica and hypnotherapy? Gradually my
things, specifically shoes and clothes, took over her
room, driving out the mobiles and candles and too-long-
cherished soft toys. It was an object lesson in Darwinism.

On one afternoon a few rays of nervous late autumn
sunshine broke through, and I wandered down to the
park—a characterless affair with ducks and trees and
other undistinguished parky things. Half-lost, I stum-
bled across some playing fields. Blotchy, pink-faced
youths were running around with sticks. It looked like
hockey reinvented by a criminal psychopath. A bell rang
and I made a connection: this must be hurley. Was there
no escaping from the Irish? I could feel that I was in danger of jabbering. Keen to find work though I might be,
the job of park madlady was not one I coveted, and I
hurried home.

*   *   *

So, the week passed and Saturday morning appeared. I felt I'd earned a treat. My finances were a fiasco—I owed nearly three thousand pounds on my credit card, and I was eight hundred pounds overdrawn at the bank—but I had the envelope from Hugh with the best part of five grand in it. You might think that the sensible thing would be to pay off the credit card, but that would have left me depressed and listless, and I knew that I needed to be on my best form over the coming weeks. The only thing, the hard-nosed, sane, and practical thing, was to buy at least one whole new outfit, from shoes to earrings and back again. I'd phoned a couple of nonfashion friends (yes, I did have some—well, two, Carol and Ursula, who'd both taken the family route and had children and dogs and houses, and dull husbands in the City, and time to kill) and arranged to meet them for lunch at Joe's Café in Fenwicks.

I was out of the door by nine, my heart singing with expectancy. To be properly effective, this had to be done by the book. This wasn't alternative shopping, it was mainstream bags-with-names, attentive assistants, pain-free, epidural shopping. I soon latched on to the Bond Street fashion jugular, hitting Donna Karan's black mausoleum, the inevitable Joseph, Liberty (for the sake of one particular adorable, middle-aged, tank-topped assistant I always return to when my fash batteries are low), and the Versace bordello.

I met the girls already drunk and giddy with shopping. We had a fun time, laughing so much that a very pretty waiter had to come over and tell us, charmingly, to please, please consider the other diners. Carol and Ursula were both convinced I'd find something soon, and I allowed myself to be lulled by their confidence.

We drank two bottles of wine and ate a small salad among us.

I got back to Veronica's at about three. The post had come, and I found nine letters in creamy thick envelopes waiting for me. Among them, I was convinced, would lie the key to my future, the answer to everything, the silver bullet. Excitedly, I scooped them up and ran to Veronica's room. The house seemed to be empty. I tore open the first. It was a rejection, but one so enchantingly worded that I actually felt *more* positive, rather than less, about my prospects.

Three rejections later, my mood had changed. Each on its own was as encouraging as a "no" could be. Taken together, they felt like a kick in the guts. I quickly opened the others. Nothing. Nothing. Nothing. Nothing. Nothing.

There's a film effect that everyone was using a couple of years ago, where the foreground rushes toward you while at the same time the background recedes. Something like that happened to me now, and I felt like a little girl in the middle of a huge room, unsupported, alone. Insignificant things became incredibly clear: a raisin on the carpet, strands of my blond commingled with Veronica's brown on her hairbrush; a fragile exoskeleton of ash from a cigarette; a spent asthma inhaler.

I wasn't aware that I'd made any kind of noise, but I must have sobbed, or wailed, or screamed, because the door opened and Roddy appeared. His big handsome head carefully re-formed itself from curiosity to sympathy.

"Katie, what is it?" he said, coming into the room. Then he looked at the nest of letters around me. "Ah, I see. Fuck 'em, Katie. They're not worth your tears."

Only with those words did I realize that I was crying. Roddy came and sat next to me on the low bed.

"Where is everyone?" I asked.

"They've all gone for one of their walks. I had to cram for an audition." He paused and stroked my hair. "We'll get there, Katie," he said softly. "One day, you and me." It was his first admission that *he* hadn't got there, wherever "there" was, yet, and I felt, through my own pain, a welling of sympathy for him. If only I'd had more experience of actors; perhaps then I'd have realized that vulnerability was just another role.

I gave a little laugh, which ended up as another bout of choking sobs. Roddy "there-thered" me and put his arm around my shoulder. I felt a pricking of déjà vu, which should have been a warning. I also started to feel the, for once unwelcome, electric shimmer of incipient arousal. Roddy's skin smelled so clean, despite the gentle roughing of golden stubble on his cheeks. Even when he was lying around the house, there was something calculated in his careless elegance.

Despite the intimacy of our position, perched there on Veronica's bed, I was genuinely surprised when I felt the pressure of his hand on my breast. He slid his fingers between the buttons on my blouse and began to flick them loose. Although I had been turned on, and pleased that I had attracted him, something about the rapidity and professionalism of Roddy's maneuver left me cold. Here I was, for once in my life genuinely vulnerable and in need of innocent comfort, and I was being taken advantage of. I felt like a Victorian parlor maid being groped by the young master. I was about to tell him to stop when something made me look up. And there, standing silently by the door, was Veronica.

There was a look on Veronica's face that I'd never

seen before. Not the tears, or sadness, or resignation, or shock, or defeat that I might have expected. No. Cold fury. It was a face *I* would have been proud of.

By now Roddy had noticed Veronica, and his hand left my blouse with a conjurer's speed, but Veronica had seen.

"Get out, please, Roddy. I want to speak with Katie." Roddy, head bowed, obeyed wordlessly.

"Veronica, I know how this looks, but just let me explain."

"Shut up, Katie. I've been listening to you for twenty years, and now it's my turn to say something. I believed you when you said that you hadn't done anything with that French person, or the van driver. *They* all said you were poison. I defended you. Nobody else did. All these years, Katie, I've put up with the selfishness, and the conceit, and little catty insults that you think I don't get. I've watched you climb over the backs of people to get ahead. I've seen you lie and steal and manipulate and connive. But all along I thought that you were a good person underneath. All because of one act of kindness years ago, when you rescued me from—"

"Yes, yes, yes, the clay bin."

"Well, Katie, I think I've repaid that debt. And you know, I'm actually quite pleased that I caught you with Roddy. Now I know what you're really like, the true Katie Castle. You're a bitch, and a slut. Roxanne said you were trying to seduce Alan. . . ."

"Alan? Give me some credit. I'm a fashion designer, not a social worker. I wouldn't touch that moron without surgical gloves."

"I believe you. Because he wasn't good enough for you, was he?"

"Too right."

"But Roddy was, is. And so you decided to go for him, even though you . . . even though you knew that I . . . that I . . ."

And finally she broke down and cried, screwing her fists into her eyes like a little girl.

What could I say? I tried again to explain my way out of this quagmire.

"Veronica, please, please listen. I was upset because I got rejected by everyone I wrote to. I was here on my own, and Roddy came in to comfort me. And then he started to touch me. I'd only just worked out what he was up to when you came in. It was his fault—I didn't encourage him, I promise."

"Stop it stop it stop it!" screamed Veronica. "Why do you have to contaminate everything? Why do you have to drag everyone down into the filth with you? I know it was you and not Roddy. It's always you. I just want you to get out now. Get out forever. I never want to see you again, ever ever ever. I hate you hate you hate you."

The door opened and Roxanne and Tracy came in, hurling Medusa looks at me.

"Look what you've done," spat Roxanne. "We let you stay here, and you've repaid us with nothing but spite. You vamped Alan, and he wouldn't have you, so you tried it on with Roddy. Nobody wants you, nobody likes you, nobody cares if you die in the street. Just go away and leave us alone."

It was funny, genuinely funny: I was being rejected by the leper colony. Oh, how I wanted to lay into this collection of retards. But I couldn't. Not yet. For the second time I was forced to ask an implacable foe, "But what am I supposed to do? I've got nowhere else to go."

"You can go to hell," said Tracy. "I'll call you a cab."

"No," said Veronica, looking over the stockade of arms that encircled her, "you can go home, Katie, you can go home." And with that she threw back her head and laughed like a lunatic.

CHAPTER 13

Katie Looks Back in Languor

Home, home, home: only Veronica could know how that very sound was like a bell tolling for the death of my soul. By home, she meant not any place in which I might happen to reside during the course of my London life, but that maelstrom of tedium, the place that is to boredom what New York is to salt beef, and Siberia to salt mines: East Grinstead.

So I suppose the time has come for me to tell you a bit more about the early life of Katie Castle, describing for you the fetid compost heap from which I sprang with such revulsion, and joy. This isn't pleasant for me, so I'll ask for as much sympathy and understanding as you can manage.

East Grinstead. How could anything good happen in a place with a name like that? East Grinstead was home for the first eighteen years of my life, although "life" hardly seems the right word.

Where to begin? My parents seems logical. You've probably guessed that I was an only child. I came late to my parents, and they loved me beyond reason. It had cost them years of humdrum toil to create a little refuge of order out of the chaos of the universe in a house they called Daisybank, but which was really 139 Achilles Mount. And into that mundane Eden came I, Adam and Eve and the serpent rolled into one. All of their hopes and dreams rested with me, but in such a meek and help-less way that it felt more like an irritant than a burden. I was the princess and they were my pea. It took consid-erable ingenuity to find ways of hurting them.

That must sound very cruel, and I'm going to have to get a lot crueler before I've finished. But what you have to remember is that what follows is a view of my parents through the eyes of a selfish, bored, clever, thin-skinned teenage girl, whose life was ruled not by hate, as it might sound, but by embarrassment, which so often looks and smells and tastes like hate. And underneath, often, I admit, a long, long way underneath, love moved.

Mum, poor Mum. I'll tell you the three most annoy-ing things about Mum:

1. As she walked down the street she would speak the names of the shops: "Woolworth's, Smedley's the Family Butcher, W. H. Smith's," and on until the street stopped or I hit her. After years of nagging and cringing, I finally got her to stop saying the names out loud, but you could still see her lips forming the hated syllables.
2. She used to write to manufacturers of washing pow-ders, household cleaners, and processed foods, thanking them for their products.
3. She agreed with everything anyone ever said to her.

Unkind, I know. And which of us could stand up to that cold-eyed, penetrating teenage gaze? My mum had nothing but goodness and sadness in her soul, and by the time I was sixteen I spent my evenings imagining ways in which she would disappear from my world. Hezbollah kidnapping, alien abduction, arrest and imprisonment for cocaine smuggling: none came to my rescue.

My mum wore aprons all the time. She had her hair done once a fortnight at the local salon. With impossible optimism she would ask for Kevin, the head stylist, but she always got the newest trainee, Anita, or Shelley, or Rubella. The trainee would commit some act of gross indecency upon her head, which would be washed away in silent grief that same evening.

My mum, at least, had the traditional woman's gift of invisibility. She was the most ignorable person I ever met. Perhaps it was just that her clothes bore uncanny resemblances to the curtain or upholstery fabric of her surroundings, but she seemed to be able to melt into backgrounds, like a chameleon on a bad hair day. And her voice was like piped music, an unobtrusive, endless sound wave, maddening only when a peek flickered briefly into consciousness.

If only Dad had been so hard to notice. He worked as an actuary for the local council. If you asked him what he did, he'd say, wheezing at his own joke, "I'm one of the four accountants of the apocalypse." He was small and bald, with a classic three-strand comb-over that really belonged in a jar of formaldehyde in the Black Museum at Scotland Yard. And yes, he wore tank tops, and cardigans, and carpet slippers, and trousers coarsely woven of fluff, mold, mildew and the heavy air from an old tomb.

The most interesting thing about Dad was that he pronounced "Castle" to rhyme with "hassle" and not, well, "metatarsal" (it's a bone, I think). This was something to do with the fact that his father, my granddad Castle, was vaguely northern. My only memory of him—in fact my only memory of any of my grandparents—is of his heels, which were protected by special doughnut-shaped pads because of his bedsores. He was dying of cancer in Dewsbury, or Doncaster, or Halifax, or wherever it was. After he died I was convinced it was the bad heels that killed him.

Once a year Dad would get drunk at the office party. One time (I was fourteen and at my most vulnerable), he came in bleary and boozy. He went straight to the bathroom and threw up in the loo. Mum tutted, good-humoredly. I wept inwardly. I was dying for a pee, and when Dad finally flushed the loo and staggered out, I dived quickly in, avoiding his ghastly, bloodshot eyes. I was about to pull up my knickers when I happened to glance down. I saw something glittering beneath the amber water in the bowl. I peered more closely. It was some kind of contraption made of plastic and metal. Intrigued, I fished it out with the loo brush.

Oh, God.

It was teeth.

There, on the end of the brush, was a gruesome, intricate dental appliance, the like of which I'd never seen or dreamed of. It had several distinct and isolated teeth, separated by cantileverings of wire and smooth arches of glaucous pink plastic. As soon as I realized what I'd harpooned, I screamed and leapt back, hurling the thing into the bath. At the same moment my dad burst into the bathroom. He covered his mouth with his hand and half wailed, half groaned, "Whu ith it, whu ith it?" Numbed by shock, I pointed to the bath. Dad pounced, and before I could stop him, he fitted the monstrous device into his mouth, jigsawing together the real and the false teeth.

That's the kind of thing I had to endure.

I began to be embarrassed about my parents when I was eleven, which is quite late these days, but once I'd begun, there was really no end to it.

St. Simon Stylites Junior School had been fun, or at least easy. It was there that I met Veronica—Veronica Tottle, as she was then, is now, and ever shall be, world without end, amen. She was upside down in the clay bin (which was, literally, a big plastic bin with modeling clay in it—all classrooms used to have them when I was a kid, although they may have gone the way of slide rules and log tables and free milk), so all I could see were her fuzzy green knickers, her blotchy pink-and-white legs, her sad, graying socks, and her scuffed red sandals. She was blocking my route to the clay, so I pulled her out of the bin by the ankles. I think she'd been stuck in there for several minutes, too shy to scream for help. She'd been crying quietly to herself, and her tears mixed with the brown clots of clay adhering to her face. She wiped her eyes with her sleeve, gave me a kiss on the cheek, and ran away.

Even in those days she was a fat little thing, with greasy hair and eyes of no special color. My act of charity left her in bondage to me, a bondage that was to last until . . . well, that you know. Poor Veronica worked hard to fight her way out of the bottom third of the class, without ever quite making it. She was never naughty, never late. If she was blamed for something she hadn't done, she would never complain, but simply lower her colorless eyes and accept her punishment. It made her profoundly useful to me.

I was naughty nearly all of the time. But because I was

clever and, more important, pretty, I was seldom pun-
ished. I was only ever spanked once at school. Sister
Henrietta (usually called Hairy Henry, because of the
mole) had read to us the story of Perseus and the winged
horse Pegasus. Hairy Henry drew an outline of Pegasus
on a giant sheet of cartridge paper and stuck it on the
wall. We all had to cut out feather-shaped pieces of
paper, curl them between the scissor blades, and stick
them on the wings. For some reason I couldn't get my
feathers to curl, so I stabbed Veronica in the arm, drawing a tiny spot of blood. Henry then loomed out of nowhere, a look of hellfire on her horrid hairy face. She
lifted up my skirt and smacked the backs of my legs.
That made Veronica howl:

"Sister, don't, please, it was an accident, it was my
fault," she implored.

Henry then looked even more enraged. "Why didn't
you say so before you contrary monster?" she said, and
then smacked Veronica on the backs of the legs as well.

Life at Pontius Pilate High School followed the same
pattern. I was popular and successful, despite the ever-
present threat of people finding out how gruesome
my parents were. Veronica limped along behind: she
was the one the boys tormented and the smart girls ignored. If ever a plastic bag came blowing down the
street, you'd know it would head for Veronica and wrap
itself around a foot and stay there, immune to any shak-
ing, scraping, or pulling. Exotic birds would migrate to
East Grinstead solely to pooh on her shoulder. *She'd* always get the doughnut without the jam.

My main concession to her was to allow her to occasionally carry the can for my misdemeanors. Cigarettes
would find their way into her bag during spot inspec-
tions. There was the notorious incident with the Durex.

I was the fifth girl in the year to have sex. The third if you discount those whose partners were blood relations. I was twelve when I had my first boyfriend, a harmless, gangling, floppy-haired youth called Tony. On our first date we sat on a bench in the park and shared a packet of pickled onion–flavor Monster Munch and a Yorkie bar. On the second date he took me fishing. He'd never been fishing before, and the episode was a disaster. He couldn't sort out the rod and line and things and ended up hugely losing his cool and throwing the whole lot out into the reservoir. But then he somehow pulled it round by making a joke about a hand appearing and catching it, like the Lady of the Lake in the film *Excalibur*. I let him kiss me on the shingly bank (and no, that is *not* a euphemism), and he gave me my bus fare home. For the third date he took me to the cinema, and for the first time I tasted human tongue and found it good.

But Tony was a touch lame and lacked any kind of killer instinct, and I soon moved on to Mick Tordoff. Mick was the best Ping-Pong player in the school. The boys used to play winner-stays-on in the common room at break, and Mick was unbeatable. Tony played him once, all disjointed arms and legs and his hair in his face. It was 20–6 to Mick, when Tony stepped on the ball. With the quiet efficiency of a Mafia assassin, Mick walked around the table and punched him in the face. Mick's groping technique was as proficient as his table tennis and his thuggery: he could undo a bra with his eyelashes.

Yet it was not Mick, or any English boy, who had the prize. That fell, on my fifteenth birthday, to an Italian called Guido. I met Guido on a school skiing trip. My parents couldn't really afford it or the expensive outfits I insisted on taking with me. But I was damned if I was going to look uncool on the slopes. I've no idea how old Guido was—neither of us could count past three in the other's language. He turned up on the last night disco. He wore his labels discreetly, but his Armani and Gucci trumped the C&A, Mister Byrite, and Levi's (slight seconds) casuals of the boys from Pontius Pilate. I took him up to my room an hour into the disco. The teachers were too busy getting drunk on grappa to notice. There were four bunk beds crammed into the room, which made Guido laugh.

"No babies?" he said. What did he mean? Did I have any? Did I want any? Perhaps it wasn't a question, but reassurance. I shook my head. I didn't know what to do next, but I knew this was it.

"I careful."

We lay down on one of the bunks—not mine, Veronica's. I felt as if I had been programmed and had no will of my own. I liked it. He kissed me. Then he took hold of my hand and put it on his cock, which was sticking out through his zip. It was long and thin, and I thought to myself, Thank God, it won't hurt as much. Somehow I was naked except for my bra, which was pulled up over my breasts. He was still fully clothed. He spat on his hand and rubbed it gently into my lips. And then, with his cock still just sticking out through his pants, he entered me. And it really didn't hurt very much. Nor was it particularly pleasant, but what can you expect for the first time? He came in four diminishing squirts over my belly and the duvet. I've done it, I've done it, I've done it, I've done it, I thought. And with an Italian.

I closed my eyes and luxuriated in how shocked and disgusted and disappointed my parents would be. The knowledge of what I had done turned me on much more than the act itself, and I wanted to do it again. And only then did I become aware of the fact that I was alone. Guido had gone. I never saw him again. I wiped myself clean with a Bugs Bunny sweatshirt I found on the bed, went back down to the disco, and danced the night away with the boys and girls of Pontius Pilate High School.

With all this talk of skiing and sex and Italians, I'm making my life sound far too colorful. In fact nearly everything in East Grinstead was brown, as if the world were made of run-together Plasticine. The houses, the streets, the trees, the birds, all brown. In this dun world there was nothing for teenagers to do except try to find somewhere to have sex. Even the drugs were comical household materials: glue, boot polish, lighter fuel, Domestos.

All I wanted to do was escape, and as long as I could remember, I knew the way. It had to be fashion. Somehow I was always aware that everyone in East Grinstead looked terrible. Not just that they all had bad hair and bad teeth and bodies like something you'd find in the hold of a Russian factory ship. I knew when skirts were the wrong length and trousers the wrong shape. I hated the lumpy bodies squeezed into scratchy suits. I hated the mechanically extruded polyester slacks with the seam down the front that you could have in any color as long as it was, yes, you've guessed it, brown. That seam always offended me: both functionless and ugly. Some actual person who had a nameplate on his door telling the world he was a DESIGNER sat down one day and decided that he would put that seam there, drawing attention to the awfulness of the fabric, the ineptitude of the cut, and the flabbiness of the thigh to which it invariably clung.

The only real glamour in my life came from the maga-

zines I pestered my mum and dad into buying for me.
When I reached the age of fashion consciousness (in my
case, ten), I wouldn't let Mum get the *Women's Journal*
anymore, but forced her instead to progress through
Options, Elle, Vogue, American *Vogue,* and finally French
Vogue (where I've stayed ever since). It was the only
order for French *Vogue* ever placed at our local news
agents, and the first time I went with Mum to collect it,
Mr. Forster, the drab little man who stood behind the
counter, called back to his wife, "Come and look, Netty,
it's them that ordered the foreign magazine." My mum
said she'd never live down the humiliation. But once in
Vogue, I was out of East Grinstead. *Vogue* was a Wonderland, and I was Alice.

Mum and Dad humored me. They thought it was a
phase. My dad's ambition was that I should become a
chartered accountant, a profession that for him held the
same allure that head designer at Dior had for me.
GCSEs were a breeze, and A levels were straightforward
enough, except for my habit of becoming whichever
character took my fancy in the set texts we were doing.
When it was *Vile Bodies* I was one of the Bright Young
People, and everything became "too, too sick-making"
or, occasionally, "too, too bogus." Lady Macbeth was
fun for a while, but I suppose it was lucky that there was
no one called Duncan in the sixth form, or I might have
had somebody stab him. Critics might have said that my
Phlebas the Phoenician (a fortnight dead) took things a
little too far, but how else is one to find out the limits of
one's world?

Perhaps the highlight of my school career came when
Miss Cruikshank mentioned the importance of the nov-
els of Fanny Burney in the history of women's fiction.
My reply was instant, as was the fame that followed.

"Fanny Burney, miss?" I said, putting on my best wide-eyed-and-innocent look. "Surely that is a medical condition and not an author."

Miss Cruikshank looked cross for a second or two, then smiled indulgently, which was all the consent needed by the five girls and two boys in the class to burst into gasping laughter. Veronica beamed proudly, for all the world as if *she'd* come out with the joke.

So you see, I was really quite clever, and you know you can trust me when I tell you I was, because I've told you all the horrid stuff as well, like stabbing Veronica. Almost everything that I wanted to do, I could do, with the exception of burning East Grinstead to the ground and banishing its inhabitants to hell, or Slough.

When the exams came around, it became clear to me what had to be done. I got straight Ds. Anything better would have meant economics and accountancy at Somewhere Earnest. Three Ds was all I needed for the small fashion college in London I'd set my heart on, so three Ds was exactly what I got. This brilliantly ruled out any pressure Dad might have tried to exert in the direction of accountancy. I think it may have broken his heart, but I had other things on my mind.

Veronica, of course, had followed me doggedly in my fantasies; she was the Nurse to my Juliet, the Grace Poole to my first Mrs. Rochester. By this stage she had grown from an ugly duckling into a glorious goose. She did have a boyfriend, or boy*fiend,* as I called him. A Trevor, inevitably. He used to drive her off into the country, where he'd park in a lay-by and try to fight his way through her all-too-solid defensive wall (complete with moat). The *really* amusing thing is that he'd charge her "taxi fare" for driving her home. When she told me this, I naturally enough told her to dump him. Nobody, surely, could be *that* desperate. Veronica, however, incapable of seeing the world as it is, and grateful, no doubt, for the grubby affections of Trevor, pleaded on his behalf:

"But Katie, he phoned around to all the local cab companies and asked them what they charged, and then he matched the lowest fare. That shows a true generosity of spirit, doesn't it?"

Poor Veronica could not, of course, follow me to fashion college. For her it was something to do with geography at Bangor. The annoying thing is that she ended up with better grades than I did. And although I told everybody at school about my plan, I don't think they really believed me. Except Veronica herself. But the truth is that I couldn't have cared less what the honest folk of East Grinstead thought about me. To me they were already shadows, scarcely perceptible against the glorious bright light of London, toward which I was moving.

Dad wanted to drive me up into town, but I wouldn't let him in case we were seen. So they waved me off at the station, two sad, gray people, dwindling from tiny to invisible.

After my expectations, London life itself proved, as I guess it always proves, a disappointment. I was no longer a peacock among pigeons, but now just another pigeon, insignificant in the flock. I hated the fact that most of the other students were more fashionably dressed than me—they had, after all, the advantage of not coming from East Grinstead. Suddenly *I* was a kind of *Veronica*. That didn't last long. Within a week I had made the appropriate adjustments. But I didn't have the money to shine. It was a valuable lesson.

When it came to my course, valuable lessons were few and far between. I can honestly say that nothing, not one solitary fact, technique, or principle I learned in the lectures, tutorials, and workshops of the college, was of any use to me when first I tried to get a job, and later worked, in the fashion world. True, I found out that Madeline Vionnet was "the Euclid of fashion"; that Fortuny was "the Magician of Venice," and that Elsa Schiaparelli invented shocking pink. I learned how to make hats out of objects found in a Dumpster. I learned how to incorporate decorative motifs from Aztec, Polynesian, and Celtic art into my designs. I learned how to talk about fashion as one of the high arts, how to sneer at mundane concepts like wearability; how to mock the High Street and its shoppers.

Some things I picked up *were* useful, but that knowledge was generally accessed outside the classroom. I learned how to drink my coffee and smoke my cigarettes. I learned how to flirt with gay men and straight women. I learned how to get into clubs without paying. I learned how to live on fifty pounds a week. It was all huge fun, breathless, trivial, superficial, empty, transient fun, but fun.

And then it was over. Two interviews were all it took for me to discover that I had a practically useless degree. The options were stark. Back to Dad for a loan to study accountancy; or a trashy job and cheap digs, and wait for the opportunity that I knew, in my childish innocence, would come.

So I worked for three months in Whistles, for six months in the Paul Smith sales shop, for a week in Selfridges. For most of that time I was going out with a Danish architecture student called Cnut. He was very serious in manner, but very silly in dress, favoring frock coats and cravats. Mysteriously, I found him quite cool at the time. I chucked him over a joke. It was his birthday, and on his card I wrote "to Cnut" (along with some love stuff you don't want to hear about), but with the "C" backward.

"Katie, this is incorrect," he said, pointing to the errant letter.

"What, you mean you can't turn back the c, Cnut?"

That was supposed to be my present to him. It took me ages to think it up. He looked at me for a good fifteen seconds without saying anything, then finally said:

"I understand. That is supposed to be a joke, yes?"

"Yes. It's for you. Do you like it?"

"In my country it is not considered to be polite to make fun of the names."

And that was that.

I wasn't at all at a low ebb through all of this. And it's okay being poor when you're twenty-two. I don't think it stops being okay until you reach twenty-four. No, that's a little harsh. Twenty-four is still just on the right side of the border. But twenty-five and poor is unforgivable, in any woman of ingenuity unencumbered by ethics or facial deformity.

I went back just once to see Mum and Dad. They were less irritating than I remembered, but more pitiable, which is much, much worse. Dad was retired, and I was all they had to think about. It had been two years since I'd seen them, but I was still woven into the texture of their daily lives. Despite the fact that my screaming-at-them days were over, they knew better than to ask me any detailed questions about my life.

"How's things in, you know . . . fashion?" asked Dad, nodding toward the corner of the room, as if that were where fashion lived. Mum mouthed "fashion."

"Just fine."

In true bereaved parent style, they'd kept my room exactly as I'd left it at eighteen, with my retro David Bowie and Roxy Music posters, and my animals, Stinky the Penguin, Freddy Teddy, and the Blue Thing, which wasn't any species known to science and so couldn't have a human name, either. My books were still there, dusted daily, but now yellowing: a row of Judy Blumes, *Rebecca, Wide Sargasso Sea, Fat Is a Feminist Issue* (no, it's not). It was all too sad to bear. So I slipped away before tea, saying I had to be back in town for a catwalk show, knowing that it was something they'd understand.

Well, that's more or less where I was the day I walked past Penny Moss and saw the HELP WANTED sign. And if it doesn't tell you why the thought of going back home to Mum and Dad filled me with the same feelings of joy and expectancy as female circumcision and flaying alive, well, then I give up.

PART TWO

The Three
Metamorphoses
of
the Spirit

CHAPTER 14

Katie's Dead-Dog Bounce

"One more night, on the couch."

I'd wrung that single concession out of Veronica, reluctantly accepted by the others.

"But I don't want to see you tonight, and you're gone by the time I get home tomorrow." I was clearly bringing the best out of my dear old friend. I considered saying something about vipers nurtured in bosoms, but that would have been too, too Veronica. Anyway, which the viper, who's the bosom? as someone was liable to ask.

But what could I do with this final evening? We weren't going to sit around together watching *Antiques Roadshow,* that was for sure. I couldn't face any of my other friends. I couldn't face fashion chitchat and bitching with Milo, assuming he hadn't already erased me from history. Yes, of course, my face had already been retouched out of the politburo snapshots. I wasn't too proud to beg for charity from somewhere, but I just couldn't think of anyone to beg from.

But all along I suppose I must have known what I was going to do. Calculation and rational thought hadn't helped one little bit. It was time to get my hormones in on the act, and to follow instinct.

So twenty minutes later I was in yet another taxi. It was to be my last for a long, long time. I'd passed through the cluster of lepers and out of the front door without a further word, my head held high, my heart in tumult. I walked in the gloom down to the Seven Sisters Road, with the life I would lead in East Grinstead projected onto the buildings around me, like the old films in *Cinema Paradiso*. There I was, on a high gable, welcomed tearfully by Mum and Dad: she ringing her hands in joyful anguish, he holding a brown teapot nestling in a knitted cozy. And there, thrown against the dirty brick wall of the church, I was starting work checking claims down at the housing benefit office, dressed smartly in a blue polyester suit with a white blouse and a bow at the neck. There, on the slate roofs, I was dancing around my plastic handbag at the Please Fuck Me, It's Friday disco, trying to catch the eye of a fitter (whatever that is), or plumber, or housebreaker, with "loev" and "haet" inked onto his knuckles by East Grinstead's famous dyslexic tattooist. And there, cast up onto the very heavens for all the world to see, I was standing without tights in the cold, looking for love, smiling at strangers.

No. None of those things were going to happen. If the worst came to the worst, I might have to go home for a while to recharge my batteries and plot a new course. I wouldn't be there long enough for the tendrils to grow around me, for the devils to pull me down, like Faust, into that hell. Would I?

But first there was the little matter of revenge. "Every Sunday, except in Lent," he'd said. Well, it was Sunday, and it wasn't Lent. I had at least learned that from Sister Henrietta. A black cab appeared, and I journeyed west, passing perilously close to the places I had come to love.

I said revenge, but that isn't quite right. Nor does the

instinct/hormone thing quite catch it. I don't really know
what I was doing going back to see Liam. I'd *more or
less* abandoned the idea of actually stabbing him to
death, although I hadn't ruled out the possibility of seeing if my six months of boxercise classes a couple of
years earlier had left me with the ability to land a good
punch in the throat. But it was more that I just wanted
him to confront what he'd done to me; to see how he'd
messed up my life; to say sorry. A proverb kept coming
into my head: A dog always returneth to its own vomit.
Not pretty, but it held a truth.

I got the cabbie to drop me at the tube station: it was
still quite early, and I thought I'd kill time by having a
drink at each of the pubs I'd seen on that other, fatal,
trip to Kilburn. And if a pub crawl seems to you like a
faintly eccentric thing to do in my circumstances, then
you'd be absolutely right. Could it be that I was deliberately seeking degradation, debasing myself so that I
could go through some weird cathartic rebirth thingy?
Or was I nervous and wanted to get sloshed?

The first pub I came to was called the North Star.
From the outside it looked quite nice, almost like one
of the girl-friendly, foody pubs of Primrose Hill. Clean
bright plaster, neat paintwork. Only the bustle of waiters and the swish of clean blond hair seemed to be missing. I stepped through the door marked PUBLIC BAR and
immediately realized how far I had to go before I would
come to understand the parallel universe of the pub.

The Black Lamb had been full of poor and desperate
people, but they were there to have some species of fun.
They were looking for a good time, elusive and transi-
tory though it might be. But this was very different. As I
stepped through the door I was confronted by a wall of
hostile faces: sullen, cruel, male. This wasn't a place for

fun. This was a place to drink, to drink until everything kind and human and frail had been dissolved away, and then to drink some more.

I thought about walking straight back out again, but something about the very grimness of the place chimed with my mood. And anyway, after Penny and the lepers, I wasn't going to be driven out of anywhere ever again. I marched boldly up to the bar, feeling for the first time in ages that here was a challenge I was actually up to, a problem I could solve. From sheer bloody-minded bravado I ordered a Dubonnet and lemonade, something I hadn't drunk since I was seventeen. I was with Veronica and one or two other girls from school on a big night out after some mock exams. When we sat down with our proud array of Cinzanos, snowballs, and the other drinks beloved of sweet-toothed teenage girls, Veronica whispered in my ear, "I don't think you pronounce the 't.' " I didn't speak to her for the rest of the evening. Back in the North Star, the barman, big and white and moist, like something carved out of a massive block of genetically enhanced lard, looked at me for a good two seconds, half turned away, spun slowly back toward me, and then turned finally away again. He rocked himself over to a far corner of the bar and returned with the thin magenta liquid.

"Ice," I said, meeting his eyes, which were bloodshot and malevolent. I guessed that he was a collector of child porn and Nazi military regalia.

He pointed to a bucket on the bar, then grunted, "Two pounds."

I gulped down the Dubonnet at the bar, dribbling a little from the corner of my mouth, and walked out. Bizarrely, the experience gave me courage: surely there could not be a worse pub anywhere in the world? And

I had survived, drunk a Dubonnet and lemonade and walked away.

Just over the road from the North Star I saw something that appeared a little more promising. Powers Bar was obviously designed to look like one of those quaint little pubs you see in Irish postcards, perhaps with a donkey parked outside. The front of the place was quite small. It was painted a bright blue. I stepped through the door and into a world of warmth and noise. The music was student/Indie stuff, which I didn't really expect in Kilburn. It was obviously where the local bohemians and nonlaboring youth drank, and it had a vaguely alternative, arty feel. The walls were pleasantly hung with irony: a huge buffalo-head thing loomed out of the gloom. There were real fires, which were welcome—it was clear and cold out, and I wasn't wearing enough clothes. Even more welcome, there were women: not ancient, drunken hags, but young women in moderately fashionable gear. They weren't like me, but I felt we wouldn't need a translator to talk. I thought it was even worth risking a glass of wine. A pretty young Australian served me and poured out a proper big glass of Chilean Sauvignon Blanc.

Although the bar was crowded, I still managed to find a corner to sit in, not far away from one of the fires. The next table was full of overweight middle-aged men in ponytails and/or goatees, talking loudly about music videos. One seemed to be a director, another worked for a record company. A third, spindlier than the others, was wearing those black oblong spectacles that scream out to all the world "Look, I'm a music journalist. Ha!"

"Gotta throw at least one fifty at it," said the director, straining at his leathers. "You know as well as I do the shittier the band, the better the video."

I made a bet with myself that they'd speak to me within five minutes. I must have been giving off scary signals, because during the time it took me to drain two glasses they did nothing more than venture the odd furtive glance. I had the impression that they may even have caught my mood, and their conversation had died by the time I left.

"Still think shit's a bit hard," said the journo.

Crossing over the road again, I came to McGovern's, which looked like an Albanian bingo hall. I strode in without a thought. It was so full of closely packed men that I at first thought it must be a gay bar. But no: not a decent haircut among them, and they looked as though they'd all just raided a tweed warehouse and run away dressed in whatever came to hand, however ill fitting. But there was an atmosphere of jollity among them: backs were being slapped, grins exchanged. Laughter rolled back and forth along the bar. Nobody seemed bothered about my presence, and I squeezed through the crush and ordered a Guinness. Turning away from the bar with what felt like an enormous quantity of drink, I saw an old man on a bench by a wall smile at me. He looked familiar. Of course, it was the fiddler. I couldn't remember his name. He beckoned me, indicating a space by his side. Although the thought of his wheezing, death-bed breath nauseated me, I could think of no way of escaping, so I went over to him.

"It's Katie, isn't it?" He sounded surprisingly sober.

"Yes. You remembered. And you were right: he black-guarded me."

"The dirty, dirty swine. If I was thirty years younger, I'd see to him myself. But what are you doing over here, child? I'd heard something of your trouble, and I didn't think we'd be seeing you again."

"I can't really explain it. I just had to see Liam. Hit him, or something."

"What good would that do? Why don't you just go back to your own part of town, your own people?"

"Easier said than done. I haven't really got a part of town anymore. And my own people? Don't make me laugh. Will Liam be in the Black Lamb tonight?"

"Well, yes, he may be. But what's the profit of any of this? Go home, child, go home."

"You're a sweet man, but I haven't got anything else to lose now."

"Nobody's so low they can't sink lower. I myself have had times when I thought now, surely to God this is the bottom. Surely now I've hit rock. But then you find it's just a crust, and down you go again."

"Thanks, that's helped cheer me up." I said it with a smile, because I didn't feel that bad. I think the Dubonnet, the wine, and the Guinness were doing their thing. "And now? Are you at the bottom yet?"

"Ah!" he said, also smiling. "Well, you know in those films with submarines, when they get the hell blown out of them by the boys up above? And they have to take her down, and some fella goes around and changes all the light bulbs to red ones, and then a pipe bursts and some other fella hits it with a spanner until it stops? Well, I'm a bit like that: red in the eye and a bit leaky."

With that he stood up, pointed toward the gents, and, with a wink that might have charmed a Kerry milkmaid back in 1932, waddled off. I finished my Guinness and left. It was time to go to work. I crossed again over the Kilburn High Road. No pausing this time outside the Black Lamb. I walked straight into its gothic/baroque arms.

It was fairly quiet. I looked around for Liam but

couldn't see him. I ordered a large G'n'T at the bar. There was no one I recognized from my first visit. I felt relieved and disappointed. I could still feel the tingle of adrenaline. Or was it some other hormone? As I sat down, a thought came to me. Perhaps after all I wasn't here for revenge. Could it be, could it just possibly be, that I was here for a shag? No no no. Too simple, and too horrid. I was here to achieve closure, to scrape the poison out of the wound. Oh, God knows.

I sat at the same table. The positive blip in my mood was gone, and I slumped into a brooding depression. The little fiddler man was right. It was mad to have come here. Mad and sad. Mad and sad and stupid. There was nothing Liam could do now, anyway, to help me. I was already old news. What is fashion for, after all, if not moving on? And I'd been left behind. I looked around at the exuberant decoration. The nymphs and dryads had become mocking devils. The birds etched into the glass were vultures. The walls ran with blood and gore. I ordered another G'n'T.

I was struck again by how my life seemed to be repeating itself. People think that fashion goes in circles, but that's wrong, as Penny showed with her safari suit fiasco at the vodka party. It's more a sort of a spiral, and so things come back round again, but displaced. And the loops of the spiral get smaller and smaller, so things come around again ever more quickly, giving that disorienting impression of simultaneous novelty and tired recapitulation. That's how my life felt, the eternal recurrence, everything the same and yet different; my world spiraling down uncontrollably.

"You look like you need a friend." The voice jolted me out of my reverie. It was grave, and deep, and scary, like the sound of old bones being ground up in a monstrous mortar. My head had sunk almost to the dank tabletop. I looked up and saw a huge slab of a man, like a lost lump of Stonehenge. Like many of the other older drinkers, he was wearing a suit, but his was dark and well cut and looked as if it might have been made for him. It was certainly hard to imagine anything off the peg fitting his massive shoulders. I recognized him as the Frankenstein that Liam had been talking to.

"I know you. Jonah. Big Jonah. Should be Giant Jonah. Or Big Boner. Ought to alliterate."

"Your face is familiar, I don't think I've had the pleasure," he replied with the strange courtesy of a diplomat feeling his way into a new language. Although he was built like a monolith, there was nothing particularly threatening about Jonah. I suppose it's that old chestnut about really hard men not having to prove it. Especially not to eight-stone girls in an obvious state of distress. (Okay, *okay,* eight and a half.) That, or I was so drunk that I'd have petted a tiger. "Wait," he went on, "I know, you're Katie, aren't you? Katie . . . Katie . . . Castle."

"Yup. Got it in one."

He smiled. His teeth were strong and yellow. "Three things I never forget: a name, a face, a debt. Mind if I have a wee sit and a chat?" I shook my head, which could have meant either yes or no. He took it as a yes.

"Liam told me about . . . well, he mentioned you."

"I've come here to talk to him. There are things I . . . want to say."

"Maybe that's not such a good idea." That refrain was getting boring.

"How the hell would you know?" Careful, Katie. Remember the man's a brutal villain. Jonah ran a big hand over the back of his close-cropped, graying head.

"Are ye at all familiar with the works of Friedrich Nietzsche?" he said after a pause.

"Are you going to hit me with your hammer?" I asked, doing a Betty Boop. He looked disappointed.

"The hammer's a useful tool. With a hammer you can build things and you can break them. But I only use a hammer when a person has proved himself incapable of following a simple syllogism."

"What's a shyllogimsum?" Dammit! Thought I was playing it pretty cool. But I'd had one Dubonnet too many for a tricky new word like that.

"It's an argument with two premises and a conclusion like—"

"Yeah, I know," I cut in, anxious for a chance to reestablish my credentials, "all men are bastards, Liam Callaghan is a man, therefore Liam Callaghan is a bastard. Fuck philosophy—philosophy sure fucked me."

Jonah smiled his faintly (but only faintly) sinister smile. "I was saying, Nietzsche . . ."

"Big mustache."

"Aye, big mustache."

"Bit of a fascist?"

"Aye, well, maybe a *bit* of a fascist. But he was no anti-Semite. He thought the Jews were the nearest thing to a master race in Europe. But I'm maybe thinking I should tell ye about the three metamorphoses of the spirit. It might bring you a parcel of inner peace, or at least some understanding of where you are."

"Sounds like fun." I was running out of energy again, and sarcasm was all I had left.

"Well, maybe not fun, but the man was a great one for joy. Anyway, you see, the spirit has to pass through three stages. First of all the spirit has to become like a camel—"

"Camel? Ugly, smelly, spits at people. Thanks. Just what I need."

"Like a *camel,* and has to feed upon the acorns and grass of knowledge, and to suffer, and to bear great weights, and travel stony paths into the desert."

"Well, you've sold it to me. Where do I sign up?"

"It looks to me like you already have."

"Couldn't I be something prettier, a gazelle, or antelope, or something?" I was beginning to enjoy the conversation, in an odd, surreal sort of way.

"Has to be a camel. But as I've said, there are three stages. In the second metamorphosis you must become a lion, and struggle to wrest freedom from the great dragon."

"Sounds a bit more like it. I suppose the dragon stands for something?"

"Aye: 'Thou shalt!' And the lion answers. 'I will.' In that 'I will,' the lion renounces all existing values. It creates for itself new freedoms, new values."

"I could do with some of those. And what about the third stage. Elephant? Rhinoceros? Tapeworm?"

"Well, no, not exactly." Jonah, it turned out, was not one for quips and repartee. "In the third metamorphosis of the spirit the lion becomes a child."

"Bummer! Should have guessed. It's always a child, isn't it. Becoming one, I mean. So what does the child have to do? Renounce all values by dribbling and pooing his pants?"

"The child is innocence and forgetfulness, a new beginning, a sport, a self-propelling wheel, a first motion, a sacred Yes."

If it hadn't been for a yes, I thought to myself, a yes perhaps more profane than sacred, I would never have found myself in such a fucking godforsaken mess. The charm of pub Nietzsche had faded, and I was beginning to get bored.

"Look," I said, "do you really think I'm going to be impressed by all that? Fashion's dripping with the same old hippie-dippie, up-yer-own-arse Buddhist/Taoist bullshit. Haven't you ever seen *Ab Fab*? You've really got to work on your chat-up technique."

Jonah shook his head like an actor miming sorrow. "You know, you people disappoint me. You're just not prepared to put in a wee bit of work, just a little time and thought. All you want is the quick escape, the easy way out." He reached into his pocket and pulled out a handful of white pills, each, I saw, embossed with a leaping dolphin. "This is all you want now. Philosophy in an easy-to-swallow capsule. I took these off some lads outside earlier on. I don't like my drinking disturbed by that kind of thing. I explained to them the error of their ways." He stroked his jacket, and I thought I saw the outline of a useful carpenter's tool for a moment dimpling the dark wool.

"I'm sorry if I've bothered you," he said, putting the Ecstasy tablets back in his pocket and standing up to leave. "Liam'll be in sooner or later, if you must see him, but it's my honest opinion that you should go."

I felt guilty about wounding his pride. And that guilt proved to be the straw that broke this camel's back. One fat tear ran down my cheek. I stared at the ceiling to keep the others in, and I prayed that no one was looking. Jonah sat down again.

"Look, it's me that should be sorry," I said. "I'm sure you were only trying to help. It's just that everything's gone wrong since I met Liam. I've lost my job, I've lost my house, I've lost my boyfriend, I've lost my future.

I've got to go and live in East Grinstead. My whole life is ruined."

"Yes, well, you see, Katie, this is the barren place I was talking about, and you've got some hard times to get through. But maybe I can help you. Look, I've got a flat not far from here . . . well, you know about that. I've been letting it out on a short-term basis. If you're desperate for somewhere to stay, I can let you have it for a fair rent."

I was stunned. I couldn't decide if it was kind or cruel. Ludo once told me that the ancient Greeks had the same word for poison and cure (don't ask me what it was). This felt a bit like that. Obviously a chance to stay in London was welcome, but in *that* flat? Anyway, there were practical difficulties. The proposition at least had the effect of stemming my tears.

"That's very kind of you, but I haven't a penny. I couldn't afford the rent or the deposit. Not without a job. "

"Well, as for the deposit, I've never needed to ask for one. I've generally found that tenants are happy to be able to pay me for any damage." I imagined they probably were, when confronted with the hammer, and the "Introduction to Nietzsche" tutorial.

"Again, that's awfully nice of you, but it doesn't exactly help me if I haven't got a job."

"Come on now, I find it hard to believe that a clever wee girl like you can't find a way to earn a shilling. You're rag trade, aren't you?"

"I suppose you could say that." How Penny would have recoiled from the description!

"I've a connection or two there. I'm owed the odd favor." I speculated about what this might mean. I didn't suppose Jonah's contacts were with Harvey Nicks. Per-

haps some sweatshop owner had arranged for the de-
livery of a horse's head. I wondered how much he'd
charge me to slip one into Penny's bed. Probably take
her all morning to realize it wasn't Hugh with a hangover. But I was thinking seriously about the proposition.
It was a desperate course, but what were my options? If
there were any other way of staying in London, I'd have
taken it.

"Have a minute to think it over," said Jonah. "I'm
just going to the . . ." He hesitated, obviously unsure
which word to use in front of a girl like me. "The . . .
the, you know."

When he'd gone I saw something lying on the seat
next to me. Something small and white. It was one of the
Es. It must have escaped as he'd crammed the pills back
into his pocket.

Now this may sound a bit silly, as well as so very old-
fashioned, but I've always rather liked Ecstasy. Not that
I've taken it much—maybe three or four times, and the
last had been at least two years before. It just wasn't
the sort of thing done in my circle, where cocaine was
the indulgence of choice (after, depending on sex, Prada,
and the love of underage boys). But there is something
so good-natured and noncompetitive about E that it
completely won me over. I scratched and fought all day
at work, and I didn't want to do more of the same in my
leisure hours. Cocaine makes everyone from shop girls
to supermodels feel and act like big-shot City traders,
pumped up with machismo, and testosterone, and unnecessary braces. It makes people horrid and noisy.
They feel great, but everybody not similarly tooled up
hates them. E, on the other hand, just makes you nice.
Boring and crap at dancing, perhaps, but nice. And
happy. And seeing the little white pill there, I had an im-

pulse. I *wanted* the easy way out. And, I thought, maybe it'll help me say what I want to say to Liam. Without thinking further about the consequences, I took the E between my thumb and forefinger, popped it in my mouth, and swallowed it down with a gulp of gin and tonic.

There's always the little moment of disappointment with illicit drugs, when nothing happens. The teenage dreams of instant gratification or sudden brilliant visions featuring Abyssinian maids and dulcimers and caves of ice and secret pleasure domes never come true. I looked around. Everything was the same. But you know you have to just roll with it and carry on doing whatever you're doing, until you suddenly find that you're flying.

Jonah came back.

"Still no sign of Liam," he said. "He may not be in tonight at all. Perhaps you'd better leave." He smiled what I think was meant to be a kindly, paternal sort of smile. I could have sworn there was a faint rumbling as the tectonic plates of his face shifted. If I'd been in California, I'd have screamed. I didn't believe him.

"But I'm having such a lovely time here with you, anyway. Nietzsche and things. And I'm still thinking about the offer. You didn't say how much the rent was."

He mentioned a sum. It was less than I was paying for a hovel when I was a student. Kilburn was up-and-coming. It had the Jubilee line and . . . and . . . Irish bakers and Halal butchers. What was there to lose?

I was going to say yes when I began to feel queer. I'd forgotten about the E. But this didn't feel quite right. My toes had gone numb. Perhaps it was just pins and needles from sitting still. Or maybe the drink.

"Just going to the loo," I said, and stood up a little

unsteadily. I put a hand out and flapped at air for a second, until Jonah caught me.

"I think maybe you've had enough to drink for tonight."

"I'm fine, I'm fine," I said. "Just need to pee."

The room was doing strange things. It had become a huge concertina, played by a drunk. Somehow I made it to the ladies'. I splashed some water on my face. The sink was full of fag ends and toilet paper. I stared at myself in the cracked mirror. I looked truly dreadful. My hair was matted with sweat. My makeup was all wrong. I tried to fix it, but I couldn't work the zip on my bag. I took a few deep, urine flavored, breaths and thought I felt a little better. I found my hairbrush and pushed it through my hair. Have to go home, I thought. Get Liam another time. Probably won't come. Money for a taxi. Borrow from Veronica.

I opened the door and there he was, at the center of a group of young men and women. They seemed to have just burst in that moment. They were laughing at some story he was telling them. I saw Jonah going toward them. Then he saw me, and the tectonic plates shifted again, to what might have been concern. What was happening to my legs? My legs weren't there. I looked down. I could see them, but they weren't there. And then I couldn't see them, either. All I could see was carpet, swirls of red and gold. I could feel it against my cheek, dusty and hot. Someone was pressing my face down into the carpet. Pushing me under it, to where everything was black and silent.

CHAPTER 15

Nadir

"Katie? Can you hear me?"

"Mmnngh."

"Katie, do you know where you are?" The voice was sharp and strict. I'd nodded off in the classroom again. It must be double physics.

"Mmnngh."

"Katie, your father's here."

I opened my eyes. Everything was very bright, so I shut them again.

"Katie, try to wake up. Do you know where you are?"

"Saphics."

"Katie, you're in St. Mary's Hospital."

I opened my eyes again. There was a black nurse. Machines. My throat was sore and my head hurt. What had she said? My dad was here? It was my wisdom teeth. No, that was years ago, and the pain was much worse. They'd bashed them out with baseball bats or blasted them with TNT. Then another face loomed over. A big face. Easter Island. Not Daddy. And I remembered. Remembered some things. Images. The carpet. Jonah came close and whispered in my ear.

"Hello."

"Am I all right?"

"Yes," said the nurse over Jonah's shoulder. "You've been very lucky. You're a silly girl. Thank God your father was there to look after you."

"What happened?"

"Have you heard of ketamine?" said the nurse.

"No."

"It's a tranquilizer used for horses. Some dealers sell it as Ecstasy." The nurse bustled off, humming and tutting at the same time, which was some trick.

Jonah leaned closer. "I brought you in last night after you collapsed. I've told them I'm your father. It was the only way they'd let me stay with you. I need your help here, Katie. Play along with this and you can stay in the flat for six months without paying anything. And there's other things I can do for you."

I looked at him without quite comprehending. I made my mind work over what had happened. I'd taken the pill. So it wasn't Ecstasy. I was stupid. I couldn't really blame Jonah, but he was obviously terrified that I would say that I had got the drugs from him. I could use this.

"The police are going to want to talk to you. They won't charge you, because you haven't even taken a banned substance. And even if you had, they'd only caution you—no record or anything. But if you tell them I gave you the stuff, then that's me done for supplying, even though you nicked it off me."

"Rent-free for a year."

Jonah smiled, looking relieved. He'd probably expected hysteria. "That's a hard bargain you drive. Nine months. And I'll see about that job."

"Nine months, then." Nine months in which to rebuild my life. I could do it. I knew I could do it. One thing preyed on my mind. Something I read about. Something that happens when you faint.

"Jonah?"

"Yes, child?"

"Back in the pub, when I passed out. You know, in front of . . . everybody."

"Yes, go on."

"Did I, you know . . . did I *do* anything?"

"I'm not with you."

"I didn't . . . wet myself, or anything, did I?"

"Not that anyone would notice. Not . . . anyone else."

Oh, God.

"Thanks."

So I spent a night in intensive care and another night on a mixed ward with the wretched of the earth. Wherever I looked there were colostomy bags and varicose veins and arthritic hips. A telly was always flickering in the corner of the ward, but the sound was never loud enough to hear what was going on. I could tell the nurses didn't like me, but the doctors lingered. I wasn't very ill. It seems that ketamine poisoning isn't at all serious, as long as you don't die.

The police came, a him and a her. He was baby faced and chinless, and she had the little feet and tired eyes of a ballerina. They were much less strict than the nurses. I gave them a detailed description of the two boys who pressed the pill on me. One was a virtual midget, with "eyes that burned right through you." The other was a gormless beanpole, with four studs in his nose, protruding goofy teeth, and an elaborate limp. I got the policeman to go through a variety of silly walks until he hit upon the correct one, in which the right foot undertook a little epicycle at the midpoint between backswing and follow-through. And yes, I thought I'd recognize them if I saw them again. And yes, I'd be happy to point them out in a lineup.

They wouldn't be pressing any charges against me. I'd suffered enough.

I'd given Jonah Veronica's address, and he promised to send someone to collect my things. He said he'd have the place looking spick-and-span by the time I got there. I was still unsure about his generosity. Could he really be so scared of what I'd tell the police? I suppose drug dealing, if that's how they'd see it, would mean a couple of years inside. Or was it the philosophy? But taking pity on me didn't sound much like the lion renouncing all values. Nor did guilt. Not very Nietzschean at all, I thought. Perhaps he fancied me. Was he setting me up in a love nest? That, at least, I could understand. But it didn't seem to ring true. There was something other-worldly, almost monkish, about Jonah. I suppose the truth is that you never really quite get to the bottom of why people do things, except in books.

On Wednesday morning a handsome young registrar, with a mop of curly hair that made me think of my poor lost Ludo, said I was fit to go. He gave me a lecture about drugs and made me promise to call a special help line if I was tempted again. As he walked away, he glanced back over his shoulder and smiled. I thought he was going to ask me out, but his courage failed him, and he fiddled instead with his stethoscope.

Jonah had said to phone him when I was ready to leave.

"I'll send an associate of mine to collect you," he said when I called.

I liked the sinister sound of "associate." As I stepped out of the horrid hospital nightie and into my civilian clothes, I speculated on who it might be. I was expecting some underworld heavy, a grandnephew of the Krays, perhaps, or a Yardie hit man. I was disappointed and not a little embarrassed to find a less formidable figure stumbling down the ward toward me. It was the funny little man from the pub, the one who thought deaf people weren't really deaf. Amazingly, I could remember his name: Pat.

"Hello there, miss," he said, looking intently at the pattern in the hospital lino. "I've come for yez."

We drove back to Kilburn in his ancient Ford Escort van. Pat's lank brown hair was smoothed down neatly except for one tuft that stuck out at right angles above his left ear. He was wearing a blue anorak, buttoned tightly at the neck but otherwise open. On one side the nylon had melted, leaving the charred white filling exposed. The coat smelled strongly of meat, as though he'd recently handled carcasses. I tried to open the window, but there was just a jagged chromium stump where the handle-turny thing should have been. As he drove he peered through the filthy windscreen, a look of intense concentration on his face.

"So you work for Jonah, then?"

"I do a bit of work for him now and then, now and then."

"He's been very kind to *me*," I said, fishing for more information.

"Oh sure, he's a great one for all sorts of kindness. Unless you're a Hegelian. He has a fearful hatred for Hegelians, the whole lot of 'em. I've heard him say it many a time. I'd go so far as to say he's prejudiced. I've never been to Hegelia meself."

Was that a joke? Before I had time to work it out, he began to blather at high speed about how the Pyramids in Egypt and "them other places, like Africa and such-like," were built by aliens. That at least filled the rest of the journey.

I'd never been to Kilburn in the daytime. The High Road was solid with traffic; the pavements teemed with life. It had the feel of a Cairo or Calcutta (I *imagine*: I haven't been to them, either), not because of the racial mix or the obvious poverty, but more because of the straining effort, the energy, the propelling urge to make, buy, sell, live. Stalls spilled out of shopfronts. House-wives haggled. Children wailed for sweets. A window had a sign saying, EVERYTHING ONE POUND. For a mo-ment I thought that it meant that you could have liter-ally everything, the whole stock of toilet rolls and bin liners and cigarette lighters and cheese graters and fine crystal decanters and imitation Barbie dolls, all for a pound.

We arrived. Pat leapt around to my side to open the door.

"Can't get out from in," he said, and I think I under-stood.

The hallway was as smelly and cluttered as I remem-bered. However, I was convinced that a different bike lay in pieces on the carpet. Oh, and the cat poo was gone. The flat was something else.

"Fixed it up a bit for yez," Pat said shyly. There was a strong smell of paint, and all the walls gleamed white. I looked around. The mattress now had a base and a plain headboard. My clothes had been put into a big black wardrobe and a chest of drawers, both new addi-tions to the room. The kitchen was spotless and had one or two additions: a toaster caught my eye. There was a new table in the living room, with four chairs, each by a different father. There was a tiny vase of daisies on the table.

"Got yez some flowers," said Pat, pointing.

Suddenly I felt very tired and weepy. I suppose I was still weak from my brush with ketamine. I gave Pat's hand a squeeze, which made him blush and wriggle.

"I'll be going, then," he said. "Jonah'll be in to see yez tomorrow."

"Thank you. Thank you very much," I replied, and he fled.

It was eleven o'clock. I lay down on the bed and tried to think. After all the disasters and fiascos of the past few weeks, I seemed to have hit some kind of a ledge. I could now either start the climb back up the near vertical cliff face, or I could slip and fall the rest of the way to the rocks below. But for now I needed to sleep. I looked for the handholds and footholds, but I was too tired. Tired, so tired.

I woke up hungry at three. I'd seen a supermarket on the High Road, and the word *readymeal* flashed in neon before my eyes. I looked in my purse. I had fifteen pounds. An hour later and half a bottle of wine and an individual fisherman's pie to the good (although this particular fisherman seemed inordinately fond of potatoes and flour and rather scornful of fish), I settled down on the small couch in the living room.

Jonah had been good over the flat. I could do something with it. I'd enjoy that. I'd never really had a place all to myself. And Kilburn wasn't *that* bad. Compared to the alternative, East Grinstead, it was the Garden of Eden. So *living* was solved. But *working* was still a problem. And money. I had little faith in Jonah's contacts. I suspected the closest he had been to the fashion industry was sewing the arrows on prison uniforms. My best bet still seemed to be retail. But it was dispiriting to think how low I would have to stoop before I escaped the bad smell I had left behind me. That could mean chain stores. I shuddered.

Then a thought struck me. Milo was always complaining about the brain-dead bimbos he had working for him. Kookai and Kleavage were, believe it or not, the pick of the bunch. Perhaps it was time for a change of direction. Wasn't I made for fashion PR? Could I shmooze and smarm with the best of 'em? Didn't I have a contact book full of names? Okay, so I'd have to begin by licking envelopes and making coffee. I could do that. But surely it wouldn't be long before I would be . . . would be . . . going to parties and all the other things that Milo did.

Up until now I'd been avoiding phoning Milo. He was such a Nazi and hated the weak and the poor and the jobless. I'd wanted to reestablish links when things had normalized; but now I knew things were never going to normalize. It had to be done.

There was a phone in the room. It was live. I called Smack!.

"Smack! PR, how can I help you?"

It was Justine, the famous Smack! phone girl. She could make her voice deep and husky or little-girl vulnerable as the situation demanded. She was masterly. Any man hearing her say "Smack!" would immediately feel impelled to sign up with Milo, just for the chance to meet her. But how, in the flesh, she disappointed. You could hear the sound of faces falling from two blocks away: a noise like frogs being stepped on in the dark.

"Justine, hi, it's Katie."

"Katie?"

"Katie Castle."

"Katie!" she enthused, suddenly my oldest friend. "Where have you *beeeeeeen*?"

"Oh, you know . . . busy. Look, can I speak to Milo? It's quite important."

"God. You haven't heard, have you?"

"Heard what? What's happened?"

"Look, I'd better put you through to Ayesha." Ayesha? Kookai or Kleavage? Think, think, think. Yes, Kookai.

"Hello, Katie?"

"Ayesha, what's going on? Justine sounded very mysterious."

"Oh, Katie, it's awful. It's Milo. He's been . . . stabbed."

"My God! What do you mean? Who by?"

"It was Pippin. You remember the party?"

"Yes, of course. Who could forget? But we didn't take him seriously. I thought he was just being camp. How did it happen?"

"Pippin got into his flat. He must have had a key. He scared off Xerxes with a fire extinguisher and then he tied Milo up. There was some sort of device. . . ."

"What do you mean device? Electrical?"

"A . . . *stimulator* of some sort, I think he said. Not quite sure . . . Oh, Katie, I'm not really supposed to say, it's all top secret. I promised."

"For heaven's sake, Ayesha, I'm family."

"Well, Pippin stabbed him with this thing, in, you know, the behind."

"Christ. How Edward the Second."

"Pardon?"

"Never mind."

"It's terribly serious. He's ruptured a spleen. They had

to amputate. But that's okay, because apparently you can get by perfectly well on one."

"So he's alive?"

"Yes, and he's out of danger now, but still too ill for visitors. He's in St. Mary's, the private bit. The Lindo Wing, I think it's called. He's been there since Sunday."

I didn't mention the eerie coincidence to Kookai.

"What about Pippin?"

"He's on the run. No one's seen him. He's just disappeared."

"How was Milo . . . discovered? Did he call for help?"

"No, his cleaning lady found him unconscious the next morning. The battery was still running. It must have been awful."

There was a pause as I constructed the scene in my head and reined in the wild horses of laughter.

"So what's happening to Smack!?"

"Well, it's weird. Sarenna . . . she's sort of taken over. She said that Milo had okayed it, but I don't quite see how. Anyway, things are more or less going on as before, but with less Milo and more Sarenna."

"Look, Ayesha, I'll be brutally frank. The reason I phoned was that I've had a few problems workwise lately. . . ."

"Yes, you poor darling. We'd heard about those. I was so shocked."

"Well, yes. Anyway, I was phoning to see if Milo . . . if you, had anything. You know, a *place*. I could do anything, I mean *anything*."

"Oh God! Katie, you know we all think you're amazing. Nobody in the world, and I mean the *whole wide* world, knows more than you do about fash and things, but it's just that Sarenna took someone on just yesterday, a new trainee, and I don't think there's much else for anyone to do."

Bit of a body blow, that. I tried to sound breezy.

"Oh well, it was just a thought. Anyone I know?"

"Well, yes, actually. It's an old friend of yours. You'll be so excited. It's Veronica Tottle."

CHAPTER 16

Katie Goes Native

It was the supreme test. I could laugh at Milo's misfortune, but could I also laugh at my own? I passed, but only just. It was funny, there were no two ways about it. Milo in ER, Veronica in PR. But where did it leave poor, poor Katie Castle? The laughter saved me from self-pity.

I decided to go see Milo. The Lindo Wing was an unimpressive redbrick structure, but it at least had a certain well-intentioned earnestness about it: if it had worn a jacket, it would have had leather patches on the elbows. Inside it was not at all like a hospital, but rather had the feel of a country solicitor's office, with scratched wood paneling and glazed partitions. I asked for Milo at reception.

"You family?" said a man through a hatch. He was wearing a bus conductor's cap several sizes too small for his head.

"Yes, I'm his sister . . . Callista."

"Sign in. Third floor."

So much for the no visitors.

I had to look into several rooms before I found Milo. In one an old man was ponderously climbing down from his bed. His hospital shortie-nightie had bunched over his haunches, and I got an eyeful of wrinkly buttock. In other rooms faces stared blankly back at me or smiled expectantly before I sorried away.

I found him lying facedown, his head at the bottom of the bed, watching a telly in the corner. The sheet was held suspended over his middle third by some kind of frame. The room was dark and stuffy: heavy curtains covered the windows, which were grimy and closed. The room gave the impression of being untended. There were no flowers, which made me pleased that I'd remembered.

"Look at the state of Judy today," said Milo in a strange monotone. He appeared unable to tear his eyes away from the screen. "She looks like she's been attacked by a bear. You don't suppose Richard beats her, do you?" His face was a powdery white but for the black rings around his blacker eyes. As he spoke his breath hit me in waves, heavy, drugged, cadaverous.

"I'd guess it's more the other way round. I brought you some flowers. Just peonies, I'm afraid. Best the Edgware Road could do. How's your gizzards?"

"Terrible state. My bottom looks like potted meat. I suppose you heard the story?"

"I got a version from Ayesha, but she seemed a bit confused about your spleens. Still, I got the basics."

"Nobody's come to visit, you know," said Milo, still looking at the screen.

"Isn't that because you were too ill to see people?"

"Everyone was supposed to ignore that: you did. The nurse said there've only been two phone calls. One was my mother, which counts as a minus, so the real score is zero."

I'd met Milo's mother once at a charity lunch, so I knew what he meant.

"Perhaps people just haven't heard about it yet."

At that Milo laughed and, in laughing, winced.

"Not heard yet? *Everyone* has heard. Those two cosmonauts marooned on *Mir*, they've heard. Yak herdsmen in Mongolia can talk of little else. This is my greatest ever PR coup. Superb word of mouth; magnificent brand recognition."

Such bitterness, howsoever wrapped in his characteristically baroque exaggeration, was alien to Milo. Bitter undermines bitchy, which needs detachment and superiority and casual malice. Bitterness is the preserve of those who have failed. I sat on the edge of the bed and stroked his head.

"What about Xerxes?"

"Disappeared. Have to count the spoons when I get home. Little shit. At least Pippin cared enough to . . . do what he did."

"Poor Milo. I've had some problems as well, you know."

"He's mad, of course. I always knew it. But I like to think it was love that drove him mad."

"Ludo's left me."

"If he'd hung around, I might have taken him back."

"And Penny's kicked me out of the company. I'm single, homeless, and unemployed."

"Sorry, what were you saying? Makes you think about friendship, all this. All those people I invited to the party. I would have called most of them friends. But it's all an illusion. It's our business, Katie, it's all about pretending: pretending things matter when they don't, pretending things are rare when they're common, or common when they're rare. We don't make anything real, anything that people can use. We work in lies; we sell lies."

"You sound like Ludo."

"What were you saying about Ludo? I heard he's dumped you. Shouldn't worry too much. Another day, another sucker."

I stopped stroking and went and sat on a chair.

"Milo, listen to me, please, and for God's sake, stop watching the telly. I need help. I need help really badly. Everything's gone wrong for me. I need a job. I need to get my life back."

Finally Milo's eyes turned to meet mine.

"So, you too. You didn't come here to see me. You came to see what you could get. Well, I can't give you anything. I'm out of the business, out of PR, out of fashion. Forever. If that's all you wanted, you can go now."

Another door had slammed in my face. It was worth the effort, but I now slightly regretted the overpriced peonies.

"I'm not going to leave with a quarrel. I came to see how you were; true, I also needed some help, but I'd have come anyway. I hope your bottom gets better soon. By the way, *I* did make things. I made clothes, not lies. And I'll make them again."

The bell rang at seven-thirty the next morning, and I buzzed Jonah in.

"How are you feeling today?" he asked, doing his best to sound considerate.

"Raring to go. The world is my oyster, or winkle, or whatever."

"That's the spirit. You'll go all the way yet."

"You mean your three transformations nonsense?"

"I mean the three transformations. Anyway, I'm a

man of my word, and I've arranged for you to meet another associate of mine." This time I restricted my imagination.

"Your rag trade connection?"

"That's right. Mr. Ayyub. Well, strictly speaking, my associate is *old* Mr. Ayyub, Shirkuh, but you'll be seeing Kamil, his nephew. He's in charge of the day-to-day . . . action."

I had nothing to lose by going to see what was on offer.

We drove in Jonah's ancient but strangely impressive car, which I think may have been a Ford Zephyr, from Kilburn into deepest Willesden. The inside of the car seemed to be lined entirely with sheepskin. Four fir tree car fresheners dangled from strategic points, and books were crammed into every crevice.

We really were now traveling into the heart of darkness, as far as I was concerned. I was vaguely aware of the fact that it, Willesden, existed somewhere in London, but I would have had no idea where to start looking on a map. We drove along a narrow high street and turned off into a world of warehouses and industrial estates. What did they make there? Sandals with enormous spikes in the soles for aerating your lawn? Novelty toilet seats? Crossbows? Car fresheners? The world would never know.

Jonah was very quiet, and I wondered if he was regretting his "generosity." It may just have been that he wasn't one for small talk. I filled time by looking at some of the books. They were all paperbacks, battered and broken spined. Like, I thought to myself, one of Jonah's "customers," late for a payment. The first to catch my eye was *The Gay Science,* which seemed to answer my love nest speculations. But it turned out to be the inevitable Nietzsche. Many of the titles had a fine ring to them: *The Birth of Tragedy; Thus Spake Zarathustra; Human, All Too Human; Twilight of the Idols*. As well as Nietzsche, there were tracts by people I'd never even heard of: Schopenhauer, Feuerbach, Schelling, Fichte.

"Help yourself, Katie," said Jonah, mistaking my idle perusal for interest. "I've formed a little reading group. We meet up once a week and discuss a key text. We're doing *Beyond Good and Evil* this week, and then next *The World as Will and Representation*—just the first part, of course, not all the irrelevant rubbish in the second volume."

"Thanks, but I'm afraid that I'm a bit busy at the moment, what with . . . well, you know." The idea of being locked in a room with Jonah, half a dozen other loonies, and a tome as thick as two short PR girls, hardly appealed. I decided on a quick change of subject.

"So how do you know the Ayyubs?"

"I've taken care of some of their, ah, security and, er, debt recovery situations."

Oh.

We finally found the right industrial estate, and Jonah pulled up outside a long, low, flat-roofed, cheaply built unit. A gaudily painted sign told me we had arrived at Ayyub's Parisian Fashions, who, the sign proudly proclaimed, operated out of Paris (*naturellement*), New York, Kabul, and Willesden. A faint, familiar sound of whirring and clacking reached me through a small window.

We got out of the car, but before we reached the door it was thrown open, and a small man with a huge mustache, wearing a leather jacket, and beige slacks, and Cuban heels, sprang toward us.

"Jonah Mister Whale!" he gushed, undertaking a couple of rather dainty-looking boxing maneuvers, entirely ignored by the impassive Jonah. "And this is the lady, Miss Castle, you said."

"Katie, meet Kamil. I've a bit of business to attend to elsewhere. I'll be back in an hour." I had to fight an impulse to beg him to stay.

"Come into the office. May I call you Katie, okay?"

"Of course."

The office was the size of a child's bedroom, and it appeared as if a child with a reform-school future ahead of him had been hard at work creating havoc. Wherever you looked there were piles of paper, eviscerated box files, elastic bands, mold-bearing coffee cups, fast-food cartons, and other rubbish. One corner of the office was taken up by a hand-cranked fax machine that might have been cutting-edge technology during the Boer War. What messages it must have received: "Unsinkable Liner Hit by Iceberg"; "The Lights Are Going Out All Over Europe"; "England Celebrates World Cup Victory." A broken venetian blind fell at an acute angle across the dirty window, throwing weird striations over the ghastly scene.

A thin girl, who looked as if she were killing time before the next methadone prescription, gazed wanly at me and murmured weakly, "Hi."

"Welcome to my kingdom," Kamil said ingratiatingly. "This is my PA, Vicky, called Vic for short. Take a pew."

He spoke a weird combination of classic Estuary English, with every "l" converted subtly into a "w" and no glottal left unstopped, with the occasional slurring into American, and a subtle undertone of all-purpose Middle Eastern.

"So, you've come for our job as head of production lady. It's a very hard job and long hours, but the money is good, say, starting at twelve grand a year, and there is no reason not to go higher if you're doin' it good."

"Wait a moment, are you offering me the job?"

"Yeah, 'course. What else you doin' here?"

"I thought there would be an interview, you know, questions, finding out about my experience."

"Look, good enough for Jonah Mr. Whale, good enough for Kamil Ayyub, I think. So what you say?"

As we spoke, Vicky looked blankly from face to face.

"I was paid a lot more in my last job."

"Look, Katie, if some things hadn't gone bad for you, you'd not be here knocking on my door. Twelve fifty's a good wage for here."

"What about fifteen?"

"No way can do. Maybe go up to thirteen. Any more and good-bye, no matter Mister big man Jonah Whale."

Well, thirteen thousand was crap money, but it wasn't any less than I'd get working in a shop. And I didn't have to worry about rent, so it was all play money. And at least I could keep my hand in, production-wise. But I wanted to know a bit more about Ayyub's Parisian Fashions, of Paris, New York, Kabul, and Willesden.

"What kind of clothes do you make?"

"All kinds, very fashionable."

"Who do you supply?"

"We got one shop in Kilburn, you must have seen? One of your jobs is go there and sometimes be manager. Kick ass, stop them chewing gum, and all that shit. And then we sell to many other shops, across whole of north-west London: Queens Park, Kensal Rise, you name it. And then some big players . . ." He mentioned here some vaguely familiar names, like half-forgotten battles. One was a mail-order company, another a make I'd thought had disappeared with the Boomtown Rats. "We produce stuff for them. But the markup is shit, 'scuse French. Best money is with our own lines."

"What's your turnover?"

Kamil looked hurt. "What is it now? Tax man, is it? You can leave the numbers game to me."

"Can I have a look around?"

"Sure, look, see everything."

The office led on to what Kamil called the showroom.

"Here all the top buyers come. . . ."

"From all over northwest London."

"Yeah, sure."

The room looked like a store cupboard for all the crap that wasn't up to the high standards set in the main office. My eye was particularly caught by the one piece of furniture: a red plastic stacking chair, with a fertility-threatening gash in the seat. This was obviously where the top buyers relaxed as Kate, Cindy, and Naomi paraded before them.

Beyond the showroom we entered the sweatshop, or "main production facilities," as Kamil put it. The room was crammed with machinists: there must have been twenty in a shed the size of a middle-of-the-range conservatory. Anxious brown faces looked up as we came in, but none paused for a moment in their labor. Somehow four industrial steam irons and a cutting table had also been squeezed into the space. The sweatshop managed to be both stifling and chilly, and you simultaneously wanted to fan your face and pull on a cardie.

"Have to watch 'em like the hawk. All very lazy. Be havin' chin wags and coffee left, right, and center on my money if I let 'em."

We went back into the office. Vicky was standing motionless before the fax machine. For a moment I thought that her reverential silence might signify that she was a member of some weird fax-worshiping new age cult, but then Kamil threw his arm around her shoulder, saying:

"Vic, baby doll. I show you once, I show you thirty million times how to use. Put in numbers here like any telephone, then press blue button like so, and off she goes into the sky, voilà. Ah, okay, maybe not work now, but later, when it warm up." Then, disengaging and turning to me, he said, "Now Katie, we got a big order in. Lots to be getting on with. You start tomorrow?"

I still wasn't quite sure what I was supposed to do, but what the hell.

"Okay. Let's try each other out for a month."

Kamil smiled and opened his arms. I think he may have expected me to step forward for an embrace. Er, thanks, but no thanks.

So another new and very different period of my life began. The parallel universe thing could have been made up specially for me; some things were the same. I was, after all, working in fashion . . . well, in *garments*. But then everything else was different. Here I was, in a *sweatshop*, working for a company that made the kinds of clothes people rummaged for in grubby little markets, the kinds of polyester abortions people in *East Grinstead* might wear on a visit to the chip shop or liquor store. Pretty Primrose Hill had been transformed around me into Kilburn, which was, well, not pretty. Ludo once jokingly said I reminded him of Quetzalcoatl, the Aztec god of death, or war, or whatever. Apparently, you have to appease him by cutting out hearts and other gory bits, or else he, he . . . well, I can't remember, but I had the feeling I hadn't offered up enough hot, still-beating, bloody organs to the bad-tempered fellow. Hence Kilburn; hence Ayyub's Parisian Fashions.

But to set against all that, I at least had an easy commute. I could take the Jubilee line up to Willesden Green and walk for twenty minutes, or I could hop on a bus, which dropped me a little closer. Heading out of town on public transport at peak hours was curiously soothing. Nobody was in a rush, nobody pushed, nobody jostled. There was always a seat. The other passengers were mainly pensioners about their single-minded, unfathomable purposes.

On the first morning I decided to sort out the office. We filled three bin liners full of rubbish and realigned the furniture. Vicky proved willing enough, as long as you told her exactly what to do and monitored her progress closely. Kamil, as quick and furtive as a stoat, appeared and disappeared at irregular intervals, looking sometimes baffled, sometimes pleased at the rearrangement of his empire.

The big order turned out to be 150 blue knee-length skirts for a market trader. We were supplying them at five pounds each. The label suggested they were made from cotton and linen, but although the fabric may have originated in a plant, the plant in question was on Teesside, had forty chimneys, and pumped toxic effluent into the North Sea.

I looked in on the machinists. Again the fearful glances; again the terror of stopping. I tried to talk to the first woman I came to, middle-aged, with a thick black plait of hair reaching to her waist. She looked at me and shook her head. A voice piped up from the back.

"It's no good, she don't speak English. None of 'em do, much."

I looked to see who had spoken. It was a young girl, perhaps sixteen. Asian, like the others. I went over to her.

"Hello, I'm Katie Castle. I've just started to work here."

"Yeah, we know."

"Can you ask the girls to stop for a minute? I want to speak to them."

The young girl looked worried. "If we stop, we don't get paid."

"What do you mean?"

"We only get paid for what we do. If we stop, it's hard to earn enough to live."

Piecework. I should have guessed. So much for the minimum wage.

"Look, it's only going to be for a minute. Can you speak to them in their language?"

"Which one: Gujarati? Hindi? Urdu?"

"Oh God. Can you translate them all?"

"Yeah, enough."

"Look, please just tell them not to worry. I just want to wander around and see how they're doing. It's not a test or anything. And sorry, what's your name?" I felt helpless.

"Latifa. Yeah, I'll tell them. There's a couple more speak some English."

I moved up and down the rows of machines. Some of the women looked up and smiled, some managed to say hello. Some kept their heads bowed.

I retreated back to the office and mulled.

The next day, Friday, I started to go through the books. It was clear that Ayyub's Parisian Fashions was not a multimillion-pound operation. The profits were there, but they were meager. Here and there odd payments came in that didn't appear to relate to anything else. It was those payments that seemed to be keeping the company going.

That weekend I worked hard at making the Kilburn flat look nice. I hadn't even had the chance to unpack all my things. Jonah called on Saturday afternoon and offered to take me out to dinner, but I declined, which I think was a relief to him. Instead he brought me round a portable telly, which was thoughtful, even if the reception was so bad that it was hard to tell what you were watching. Still, its fuzzy blue light made me feel a little less lonely.

Although the flat looked okay, with pretty fabrics draped over that which ought to be hidden, and fresh flowers, and simple curtains, by eight o'clock I still felt desolate. Never had I been so isolated, never so weak, never so lost. There was nobody I could call, nobody I could chatter inanely with. It was really rather poignant: I had all these hilarious stories about the events of the past weeks (I'd already perfected my Jonah impersonation, and my Kamil voice wasn't far behind), but they were transformed from comedy to tragedy by the fact that I had no one to tell them to.

As I sorted through the last of my possessions, I came across a ragged plastic bag that I couldn't quite place. The handles were knotted together, and I had to tear the plastic to see inside. The first breath of air from the bag told me what it was. The air was slightly stale and musty; not clean, but not at all offensive. In fact, it smelled to me more sweet than Coco Chanel, more rich and blissful than fresh coffee, and sadder than honeysuckle on a grave.

I tore a bigger gash into the bag and emptied its contents onto the bed. Out spilled Ludo's dirty socks and underpants, his mixture of threadbare, pre-me M&S, and the designer stuff I bought for him, but which he hardly ever wore, claiming they were "for best," a best that seemed never to come. I don't know how the bag of dirty clothes came to be caught up with my things, but having Ludo so tangibly with me was more than I could bear. The tears I cried in the immediate aftermath of the disaster were bitter little tears, tears that I know brought me no credit or sympathy but gave some small physical relief. Now, with Ludo's dirty things all around me, I cried again. My mind was suffused with images of Ludo: Ludo smiling, Ludo talking and joking, Ludo making love, trying so hard to do it right. I swept armfuls of the pants and socks to myself and squeezed them tightly. I rubbed my face into them and breathed deep their pure essence of Ludo. I screamed and wept, and wailed, and ululated. God knows what the neighbors thought.

I slept that night with Ludo's things in bed with me. In the morning I found a nice new bag for them, which I then kept in the bottom of the wardrobe, to be used only in the direst of emotional emergencies.

The next week I began to get a clearer idea of what my job was all about. I was there to choose which designs we ripped off, to get the patterns done as cheaply as possible, and to crack the whip while the girls churned them out. Simple and yuckie. Kamil did the selling, which mainly involved getting drunk with burly, tattooed market traders or poor-looking Asian retailers with black circles round their eyes. These sessions would occasionally end back in the office in bitter tears as Kamil wept about being a bad Muslim and a disgrace to his family, both of which accusations had the ring of truth.

I spent Wednesday at the Kilburn shop, which was a five-minute walk from the flat. Most things in the shop cost less than a coffee and sandwich in Bond Street, and most of the stock looked highly flammable. Animal prints on nylon; pink Lycra tube dresses; shorty shorts and microtops conspiring to reveal exactly that which should never be seen. Dolce & Gabbana redone by a blind madman with no taste and a hatred of humanity and a toothache. I was amazed we sold anything at all, but there was a steady stream of teenagers, and mad people, and the poor. The two shop girls, Stacey and Charity, were borderline gormless, as well as over-weight, lazy, and unhelpful. It was quite nice having the chance to shout at an underling. By the end of the day I had them acting and looking a bit more like people who might be quite interested in selling you some clothes, rather than two rottweilers half-doped by the burglar's poisoned sausages. I even managed to win them round by choosing a couple of outfits for them from the stock, although Stacey may have been less pleased about my recommendation of a good deodorizing soap.

Over the week I had the machinists into the office one at a time, with Latifa to translate where necessary. They were browbeaten and submissive, but between them they had a lot of experience. I looked at the quality of their work. Sure, the fabrics were awful, and the de-signs, a mixture of badly copied H&M and monstrosi-ties engendered by the sleep of reason, were at best dull, at worst plain horrid. But, surprisingly, some of the workmanship was good, amazingly so given the speed at which they labored. The fastest of them could hope to earn perhaps three pounds an hour, but the average was more like two fifty.

I can't say I was particularly shocked. And you wouldn't swallow it if I came out as a champion of the poor and downtrodden. I knew what the fashion world was like. To compete with cheap imports, people like

Kamil had to pay poverty wages. And I knew that there were worse places than Ayyub's. At least here there was a toilet and a place to prepare food. The problem was that the margins were so tight at this end of the market. And turning out cheap tat hardly fulfilled the potential of the workforce.

Nor will I pretend that I bonded with the women, but I did soon begin to see them as individuals, rather than as an undifferentiated mass. I learned that Vimla, a handsome and serene woman in her mid-thirties and one of the most skilled seamstresses, had a three-month-old baby, and it broke her heart to be away from him; I learned that Roshni was ill with some unpleasant and painful gynecological condition but couldn't afford to take time off, as Kamil would not give them sick pay. I learned of the long-running feud between Pratima and Bina, the origins of which even they had forgotten. I also became aware of the division between the Muslims and Hindus, although that division was undermined by individual friendships. There were also more subtle and elusive tensions, which I initially put down to caste, although for all I knew they could just as easily have been based in geography or support for rival football teams. As well as Urdu, Hindi, and Gujarati, some of the girls spoke Bengali, Telugu, or Punjabi, and I soon abandoned my early intention to learn how to say hello and good-bye in each, convincing myself the women would find it patronizing.

Most of our dealings were through Latifa, who was a clever little thing, not sixteen, as she looked, but twenty. She wasn't particularly good on the machines, but she was quick-witted and lively. I found it hard to believe that she couldn't do better. I asked her what she was doing working in a place like this.

"My dad wanted me to marry a man in Bangladesh. He was all right, but I already had a boyfriend here. My mum didn't want me to go, so Dad kicked us both out. She's old and I've got to look after her."

"Shouldn't you go to college or something?"

"Yeah, well, I'm saving up."

When Kamil next showed his face, I asked to speak to him.

"You're not paying these girls the minimum wage, are you."

"Oh, shit, Katie, excuse French, you're not going to break my balls, are you? This business is on a knife edge. It's a cutthroat market out there. If our costs go up, who's gonna buy jack diddly anything off us? And these ladies, half got no papers, half illegal. They are all happy to have a good job. Why do you want to make their life ruined?"

I had a counterargument, but I didn't want to use it yet. I had to find out more about the business. I let him think he'd won me round with the brilliance of his rhetoric.

Most days I'd sit on a box in the scuzzy yard to eat my lunchtime sandwich; unless it was raining pretty hard, it beat watching Kamil pick his teeth or listening to Vicky sniff. I was usually left alone with my thoughts and my lettuce-and-tomato with lo-cal dressing, but one day Latifa came out and sat next to me.

"I saw you out here, and I thought you looked a bit sad."

"Do I? I thought I was more enigmatic than that." I was surprised that Latifa had come to join me like this on her own initiative. Pleased, too: I didn't get the chance to talk much, apart from buttons and bows.

"You normally hide it pretty well. What made you come here to work for Kamil? I mean you don't seem like the type."

"Long story."

"Well, we've got the full twenty minutes Kamil lets us have to eat our chapatis," she said with pleasing sarcasm. I noticed that she carried an apple and a Diet Coke.

"I used to have a good job. . . ."

"You mean there's somewhere better than this?" Latifa could be very deadpan when she wanted to be.

"Different."

"Better?"

"Better."

"What happened?"

"I sort of messed up."

"On the job?"

"More a personal thing."

"Shagging?"

"Latifa," I spluttered, laughing. "I didn't think you knew words like that!"

"Well, what do you think we talk about at the machines—good places to buy curry powder?"

"Look, Latifa, you don't have to keep trying to prove to me how you're not all from another planet. For God's sake, I live in the most cosmopolitan city in the world. I know we're all the same underneath."

"Try telling that to Pratima and Bina. It's not that we're all the same. It's that we're all different."

"Latifa, I know."

"But you have this look on your face sometimes."

"What look?"

"A 'Who are these people and what am I doing here?' kind of look."

I knew the kind of look she meant.

"And sometimes something worse—a kind of a sneer."

"Oh, Latifa, it's not a sneer. But the thing is, I've always been a bit of a cow. It's what people used to like about me. I'd say bitchy things and generally take the piss. I'm not suddenly Mother Theresa because I've come to Willesden. I still think cross-eyed people are inherently funny, and people who can't pwonounce r's, and people who come out of the loo with their sari tucked into their tights. It's just that now it's got nowhere to go, because I haven't got any friends left to share it with."

Latifa was laughing. "It wasn't me, was it?"

"What, with the sari? You don't even wear one. No, it was Roshni."

And we then spent ten minutes having a general, all-round, low-intensity bitch. It was like plunging my face into a cool mountain stream. Latifa then put on an almost serious face and said:

"How long before you move on? I mean, you're only slumming here, aren't you?"

I looked closely into her eyes, which were steady. She really was a self-possessed young woman.

"I won't lie to you, Latifa. I don't want to spend my life making crap clothes for Kamil. But I don't want any of you to do that. And we won't have to."

"Why, have you got a plan?" she said with a delicate, needling irony.

I smiled. "Well, yes, I have, actually."

And I did. Sort of.

After a couple of weeks I asked to speak to Kamil again. I'd spent the time thinking carefully, scheming, calculating. It helped to fill the long, empty hours; helped to block out the sound of traffic on the Kilburn High Road; helped keep my mind off Ludo and the lost world.

Things had gone quiet, and Kamil was beginning to mumble about laying off some of the girls. I knew that I wasn't going to get anywhere by appealing to his better side.

"Kamil," I began, "I think this business has potential."

"Yeah, yeah. I'm thinking of myself expanding to cover Golders Green and maybe even Wembley. Big potential."

"Good idea, but that's not quite what I mean. Every good businessman knows that it's all about people. People are your number one asset. You've managed to recruit some excellent staff. You're a good judge of character."

"Yeah sure, school of real life, plus North London Polytechnic business studies, you bet."

"And I think that with your know-how, and some of my ideas, and the skills of your girls, we can do some amazing things, some new things."

Kamil was listening carefully. "I think you are up to something, Katie Castle," he said craftily. "I know what you are like. You are a naughty girl."

I decided it was time to get to the point.

"Kamil, I've looked at the books, and basically we're flogging our guts out just to stay solvent. There's no money to be made at the bottom end of the market: we just can't compete with the Far East, or even places like Poland and Lithuania. And we can hardly say that we live in a more beautiful world because the unemployed teenage mothers of Kilburn and Willesden Green wear our microskirts and boob tubes." Kamil mimed hurt, shocked, and outraged in quick succession, but I plowed on before he had the chance to interrupt. "Our only hope is to move upmarket. It's the only way to increase our margins. And to tell you the truth, I'm wasted here at the moment. I've got the experience, and I've got the contacts. All we have to do is to draw up some basic, classic designs—I can do that in a couple of weeks— then invest in some decent fabric, and we can undercut every middle-market manufacturer in the country."

"How can you undercut? You said good margins."

"Because everything's in-house—design, production, distribution. It's never been done in this sector before. We'll be pioneers." (Okay, so not strictly true, but I was giving Kamil the big sell, and he owed me a liberty or two.) "I can guarantee you that by the spring I'll have our clothes in thirty good shops across the U.K., and half a dozen more in Ireland and the rest of Europe. That's just the first year. Who knows what we can do in the long term."

I took a deep breath—it was a long speech, and it had worn me out.

"How much?" Kamil wasn't such a fool: he realized that my plan would need some up-front investment.

"Not much, to begin with. All I need is a couple of dozen yards of good cloth to make the samples. We can drive around to the shops, so we don't even have to fit out a decent showroom. We don't have to buy cloth in any real quantity until we get the orders in."

"How much then, up front?"

"If things go well, I'll need ten thousand for the cloth."

"Ten thousand! You make big joke, ha ha ha. Where

can I get ten thousand pounds from? Father Christmas doesn't visit Kurdish houses."

"Kamil, it's a one-off. After that, the whole thing will be self-financing. And I've seen that you have . . . payments that come in sometimes. Big payments."

"Ah, that's my special dealings. They don't concern your business. Look, I'll see what I can do. What about five thousand? I maybe can by wheeling and dealing get five thousand."

"Well, it would be a start. But there's something else. If we're going to shift up a gear, we're going to have to change the way we pay the girls. Piecework is fine if all that matters is quantity, but now we need quality, and quality means time. We're going to have to pay by the hour. It means the minimum wage."

Kamil was laughing.

"Katie, Katie, you sly fox. Soon you'll be flying red flags and singing 'Internationale.' But I think maybe I like your idea. Like I said, I've been thinking about going up-market myself. It's why I find you. I says to Mister Jonah Whale: 'Get me a girl with the experience of *Vogue* and suchlike.' We'll see if you get good orders for the high-margin clothes. If you get the orders, then we'll pay minimum wage." Then he added, half to himself: "Ha, always makes me laugh, that 'minimum wage.' Really mean big maximum wages. Makes me laugh, ha ha."

"And I've thought of a name."

"Name for what?"

"For the collection. KC."

"KC, KC, what is this KC?" Kamil said suspiciously. "I know what for this stands—"

"For Kamil's Couture," I put in quickly.

"Oh, KC, Kamil's Couture, eh? Gotta nice ringing to it."

"One last, final thing."

"Ah God, more last things. More money I bet."

"I'll need a production assistant. Latifa is perfect."

"And Latifa?"

I had just called her into the office and told her about her new role. She was excited but tried to play it cool. Kamil was out, "wheeling and dealing" for cheap teabags and toilet rolls down at the cash-and-carry. Vicky was outside having a fag break.

"Yeah?"

"How much do you know about Kamil and his family?"

"Well, I know they're big in the Kurdish community. They're meant to have a load of money."

"And Kamil, does he get up to anything, um, *funny?*"

"How do you mean?"

"I just wondered if you or the others knew if he had any other income, any other *activities.*"

"Oh yeah. Maybe I shouldn't gossip, but one of the girls, Roxana, who speaks a bit of English, heard him talking to one of the market traders."

"What about?"

"Women."

"Women?" I smiled.

Latifa giggled. "I don't mean his girlfriends. I don't think he's got one. I mean he has girls, you know, for sale."

"*Prostitutes!*" I gasped.

"Yeah, he's got loads of 'em in houses all over. Roxana heard him say they were 'high-class ones, not scrubbers, white, black, brown, you name it.' "

Well, it sort of fitted. It explained the occasional cash injections. It was a pity. I really thought my business plan might be a runner. It would have been fun trying, at least. But I couldn't work for a pimp. Almost anything—work in a shoe shop, even East Grinstead—would be better than that. It wasn't really a moral thing, more that it was just so tacky. I decided to resign as soon as he showed his face.

A little later Vicky reappeared, snuffling and shuffling. I was really annoyed and came straight out with, "So I suppose you knew about the prostitutes?"

Vicky started, then put a shushing finger to her lips. "Nah, not prossies," she whispered. "Not Kamil."

"One of the girls has told me all about it, there's no point pretending." I assumed Vicky was implicated in some way. Perhaps it was how she earned enough for the methadone.

"You just don't get it, do yah? You see, the prostitution thing is a one of them thingies, a smoke screen." My face betrayed my incredulity. "Nah," she went on, "you've got it all wrong. It's drugs."

"Drugs! Oh, well, that's *all right,* then. What do you mean, drugs?"

"Well. You see, the prostitution thing is to hide the fact that he's importing drugs from Turkey, where his lot are from. But nothing bad, you know, just the usual shit, heroin and stuff. The police think he's just a pimp, and they don't bother him. It's brilliant, really."

"Yeah, sheer genius."

So it was drugs, not prostitution. Better or worse? A close call, but given that it was heroin and not just a few spliffs' worth of blow, worse on balance, I supposed. Either way I was furious with Jonah for getting me into this.

Eventually Kamil returned, peering over a pack of seventy-two economy toilet rolls.

"Piss off and have another fag break, will you, Vicky—it's been almost half an hour since the last one," I snapped. She was too indolent to tut.

"Katie, not like you use bad foul language like piss. What's up?"

"What is it, Kamil, drugs or whores, or both? Either way, I'm out."

"Katie, Katie, what the ladies saying? You've been had on. You don't understand."

"One of the machinists told me about the prostitution, and Vicky said it was just a front for drug running. I don't want anything to do with them, or you, or anything."

I picked up my bag and coat. Kamil put out an arm to stop me. All the humiliation and bitterness and pain and frustration of my fall from grace exploded into one, perfect punch, landing exquisitely on the point of Kamil's jaw. He fell down like a sack of shit, 'scuse French. Unfortunately, he was slumped in front of the door, and as I tried to drag it open, he began to plead.

"Katie, let me tell you about it. Tell you about my people. Not any drugs, not any whores. My people are Kurds. Turkey shits on the Kurds, Iraq shit on the Kurds, Iran shit on the Kurds. And then the U.S.A. shits on the Kurds. Everyone shit on the Kurds. Only the PPK stands up for the Kurds. I work for the PPK. I get them help. Guns, medicines, radios. I just pretend with the drugs and the girls. Please. It's true. For this some money comes in and some money goes out. We are freedom fighters!"

This last bold assertion was rendered less than stirring by the fact that it was uttered in a high-pitched squeal, as the door I was still wrenching pinched into the flimsy muscle on his skinny thigh. I sat down. Was it any less plausible than the prostitution and drugs? Yes, slightly less plausible. Was it—international terrorism—any better? Well, I supposed it was. I was dimly aware of the plight of the Kurds. It did seem that there had been a pretty general excremental evacuation in their direction, as Kamil had claimed. I wanted to believe it. It meant I could carry on with my scheme with something like a good conscience. And after all, what else did I have?

CHAPTER 17

Tea with the Ayyubs, A Gaudy Bullfinch, and Other Festivities

"On Sunday I see my uncle Shirkuh. He'll maybe help us with pump-priming finance, you bet."

Another week had passed, and I'd drawn up a business plan. Realistically, we had to hit the retailers with our samples by the end of January. That gave me a couple of months to design the collection and make up the samples. Tight, but not impossible. I'd decided to forget London. There was too much blood on that carpet. Anyway, most of the Penny Moss wholesale customers, and therefore my connections, were scattered around the south of England, with a few northern outposts, a shop in Dublin, another in Cork, and three or four in Europe.

I phoned half a dozen of my best contacts: buyers with whom I'd worked up a good relationship, usually on the basis of a shared exasperation with Penny. They had all heard vague rumors about me "moving on," but the whole truth seemed to have been kept within the M25 whisper zone. I told them what amounted to the truth, that I had been doing much of the Penny Moss design work for the past couple of years and had now gone into partnership with an established U.K. manufacturer.

Each of the buyers was more than willing to have a look at a collection that promised Penny Moss quality but undercut by a third in price.

"That's great," I said, not really listening.

"Only one small problem."

"Mmm, what's that?" I was thinking about buttons. Nice buttons can make a huge difference. Amazing how often a decent suit is let down by—

"My uncle Shirkuh, he's a bad man. He thinks it's a big joke ha ha to make fun of me. And, well, he says bad things about me."

"What kinds of things?" I was getting interested, but not very.

"He's an old lying bastard, and here I make no excuse for French. He says I don't like girls, that's why I'm not married, despite being forty-two years. He says I like boys."

"Oh, do you?"

" 'Course I don't like boys, crazy lady. I like girls so much that's why I don't get married, too busy playing field, eh, Vic?"

Vicky, who had been hard at work reading her horoscope, looked up and said, "Yeah." She caught my eye and smiled.

"So," Kamil carried on, "I got the small problem I said. Thing is, I shut his fat mouth, and he'll give us the pump priming, if I turn up with a top foxy chick, who's my girl, maybe fiancée or something like that."

I laughed out loud. "I get it. You want me to pretend to be your girlfriend, to persuade Uncle Shirkuh you aren't a queer, so he gives us the money for the cloth?"

"Yeah, like that."

"Can't you take Vicky?"

"Well, no offense, Vic, but she ain't the sharpest tool

in the pack. Better if you come, and then you can help explain how the margins are bigger, and the new shops, and everything."

The idea was so preposterous, it couldn't help but appeal to my sense of the absurd. Anyway, he'd called me a top foxy chick, so I owed him a favor.

"Okay, I'll do it."

Later, when Vicky and I were alone, I asked her if she'd had a thing going with Kamil.

"Well," she said, "he took me out a few times, and I was pleased, because I wanted to try out the IUD I'd had fitted. But he didn't do anything, for ages. And then when he finally asked me back for a coffee, all he kept asking was if I'd like it, you know, up the bum. And I said not likely and told him where to get off, and that was it, really."

So the next Sunday afternoon I was riding in Kamil's maroon Jaguar up to Wood Green to meet the fabled and fearsome Shirkuh, for what Kamil reverentially called "high tea." Kamil was nervous and seemed to be rehearsing sentences as he drove, of which I caught scraps: ". . . low end is low margins, complete crap," "go international," "fly business class," "four, maybe five kids."

The senior Ayyub's residence was an unimposing semidetached, in a quiet street. Kamil knocked on the door, which was answered by a young girl with big, sad brown eyes. She turned over her shoulder and screamed, "Mam, it's Kamil and a lady." She then ran back into the house. We followed.

The house smelled strongly, and pleasantly, of spices, but my immediate feeling was of slight panic, as I sank into the deepest shagpile carpet I'd ever come across.

"Take off your shoes, please," whispered Kamil, but

I'd expected that. I was wearing my longest skirt and a very sensible jacket. No point offending the old tyrant. We stepped into the living room. It was alive with writhing children. It was impossible to count, but there may have been seven, not counting the ones lost forever in the shagpile. There were also two grave, but pretty, teenage girls and a smiling middle-aged woman in what I took to be Kurdish dress.

"Hello, hello, welcome," she said to me warmly, ignoring Kamil.

"Auntie, this is Katie. Katie, this is my auntie."

We shook hands.

"Where is Uncle?" Kamil asked.

"He's having one of his bad days. It could be his thyroid or it could be his gall," replied Auntie, and then added something else quickly in Kurdish (or Klingon, for all I knew). "But please sit down," she said to me. "You will take tea?"

There followed a mildly amusing half hour as Auntie tried to find out more about me. In order to get at the truth, she fed me with pastries so toxically sweet, there was probably an international treaty limiting their proliferation. There was doubtless an old Kurdish proverb, translated as "Son, be a dentist, your hands will never be still or your purse empty."

"And your father is an actuary? How good," about summed up the conversation. But Auntie was really, like her pastries, very sweet, and I liked her. Even the children were, squirming aside, polite and helpful, acting as tiny servants to bring more sweetmeats and frightful tea. The two teenage girls stared at me, taking in details of hair, and clothes, and toenails, as I sank deeper and deeper into the softest of soft furnishings.

Kamil was fidgeting.

"Best see Uncle. I will go first, and call you in five or ten minutes, after I soften him up."

A few moments later I heard a voice cry out, "Don't show me the monkey, I want the organ grinder! Show me the organ grinder!" Kamil then called down for me. Prompted by Auntie, one of the little girls took me by the hand and showed me up to Uncle's room.

The door was open. There, on the bed, swathed in folds of white cotton, which might have been some ethnic garment, or simply the bed linen, lay a very fat man, completely bald, smiling. His age was hard to judge, but I'd have guessed he was about seventy. Either by design or accident, the sheets were parted over his midriff, revealing a brown belly that seemed to possess a malevolent power entirely independent of its owner. It looked as if it might move, amoeba-like, to engulf you, quite of its own volition. Shirkuh looked every inch the sybarite, a depraved emperor living only for the gratification of his appetites. "Another quail, boy," I imagined him saying. "No, no, not to eat, not to eat, mmm, yessss, ughhhhh, aaahhhhhhh, aaaahhhhhhh, aaaaaahhhhhhhhh! That's better. Now I'll eat it."

"So, young lady, you want me to pump and to prime?" The voice was thin, humorous, and engaging. "I'm most terribly sorry about the bed. I have a weak back, and my gall is, galling, ha ha hee hee."

I changed my mind about the sybarite and apologized, internally, over the quail.

"Yes, after a fashion. Kamil's sent you the business plan?"

"He has indeed. And very impressive, too. Tell me more about your experience, and about your contacts in the business of fabric importation." Patting the bed, he added, "Sit down, my dear, sit down."

There ensued a long and detailed discussion of the plan. Shirkuh had an excellent grasp of the opportunities and potential pitfalls. He knew the rag trade inside out. Kamil's little operation was only one of his interests. It seemed he had businesses all over London, as well as engaging in mysterious-sounding import and export activities. Poor Kamil, afraid to interrupt, sat quietly on the floor, his legs crossed.

We must have been at it for about an hour, when Shirkuh said: "Kamil, my dear boy, please go and get your uncle an aspirin and some water. It will take you several minutes."

When he was gone, Shirkuh said to me, "I suppose Kamil was fantasizing when he suggested that you and he were betrothed?"

There seemed little point in lying.

"Yes. He thought it would help with the proposal."

"Mmm, mmm. I appreciate your frankness. I must also ask you, has he talked about his involvement in various activities? Illegal, or disreputable activities?"

"Well, yes. But I know the prostitution and drugs were invented to hide his gunrunning for the PPK."

Shirkuh laughed, wheezed, and coughed.

"PPK! PPK! And a clever woman like you believed it?"

"I liked the idea of it better than the other . . . possibilities."

"Dear Miss Castle, Kamil is not involved in anything other than running a small and not very successful business manufacturing and supplying cheap garments, worn largely by women living on social security or poverty wages."

I saw it. The gunrunning was a cover for the drugs, which were a cover for the prostitutes, which were a

cover for the sad fact that Kamil was a failed fashion ty-
coon living on handouts from his fat uncle. I felt a bijou
wave of affection for the little man and a surge of desire
to make our plan work.

"Kamil's not a bad boy," Shirkuh went on, his voice
losing some of its humor and taking on a more tender
tone, "but he was always embarrassed about being in
the rag trade. His cousin, my son, was killed fighting for
the freedom of our people against the Turkish army.
Kamil feels it should have been him. Feels the family
looks down on him for not dying like a man. But I can
tell you that I would give anything for my son to be alive
and well now, working, for all I care, as a cleaner in a
public toilet, than to be dead, and not even a grave
where I could weep." His eyes glistened, but he smiled.
"Kamil, come in, don't be hovering there. Give me my
aspirin."

As Kamil leaned over the old man, Shirkuh took his
head in his hands and kissed it. "You have done well,
my nephew. You have chosen a good partner. I like your
plan, and I think it will earn us all some good money. I
am proud."

Deep down I think I'd assumed that something would
go wrong, that the plan would never be allowed to ripen
and bear fruit. Someone would be eaten by a crocodile,
or struck by a golden ball blown off a pawnbroker's, or
an earthquake would swallow Tokyo, leading to global
economic meltdown. But now, amazingly, it was all sys-
tems go. For the next month I worked harder than I'd
ever worked before, harder than I thought it was possible to work.

On Monday I phoned around the half-dozen fabric
agents I knew. I was looking for relatively small amounts

of cloth, and it was easy enough to find stray rolls that nobody else wanted. I'd always got on quite well with the agents: down-to-earth middle-aged men, for the most part, more than happy to give me a good deal in exchange for a quick flirt, especially as I was after the odds and sods that often went unclaimed. In a week I had what I needed; not exactly what I wanted, but just enough to make the samples.

Nor was the basic designing too difficult. I had sketches and ideas galore, and after another week of pencil chewing, head scratching, magazine thumbing, and general, all-purpose pondering, I had half a dozen Penny Moss pastiches, which I knew the buyers would go for. I tried to make things just a touch funkier and younger than the Penny Moss stuff, but nothing that could frighten the horse-faced women of Wiltshire, and Hereford, and Rutland. I'd discarded anything that required serious tailoring, concentrating on sexy, fifties retro dresses. Keeping a cap on costs meant we had to stick primarily to fresh cottons and printed viscose. The colors were mainly sugar almond and pretty pastel, pointing sometimes at Marilyn Monroe, sometimes at Courtney Love. I was proudest of a halter-neck jersey wrap dress, in a wild chocolate-and-aquamarine print. Very Diane von Furstenberg. Probably too crazy to sell that well, but I needed one small indulgence or it all would have been too soul destroying.

But I always knew the tough bit would begin when the fabric and designs had been settled. Every fashion student learns pattern cutting. And then forgets it. It's difficult, boring, time-consuming, and plebe-y. A bit like life drawing for art students. Anything other than a casual disdain for pattern cutting amounts to admitting that you'll never be a real designer, with other people to do *that* for you. And of course, it's the one really useful skill that fashion college teaches, or could teach if the silly students had any brains. Good pattern cutters never go hungry or end up working in McDonald's like most of the people I went to college with.

Stupidly, like the others, I bunked off from pattern cutting, learning just enough to scrape through the exams. I then went through all my memory files and wiped out whatever feeble scraps of knowledge might have adhered, just in case they got in the way of anything more important. The result was that I now had to relearn painfully all the horrid little tricks of the trade (*never* put a center back seam through a bias dress; don't confuse your model with your customer). I felt like a stroke victim having to learn again how to talk, and go to the lavatory, and eat without dribbling mush down her chin. Yet it felt good. I was making real things with my hands, cutting, with each snip of the scissors, into the woven fabric of the world.

Latifa loved it all. Suddenly, from nowhere, she had a job she didn't hate, a job that paid her enough not to have to fret about the bus fare to work. She threw herself into every task I gave her and watched everything I did, so she could learn the ways of production. The awkward thing about dragging someone up from the ranks is the possibility of resentment from those not so graced, as I knew all too well. But none of the machinists seemed to mind, and Latifa acted as the perfect link between the office and the shop floor. She made a point of getting the best of the machinists to run their eyes over the designs to help advise over what was possible and what merely fanciful.

It was Latifa's idea to have the catwalk show for the girls.

"I don't think we can," I said at first. "We haven't got enough of the collection ready. You know we're only just doing the toiles." (Toiles are mock-ups in calico to give the designer an idea how things are going.)

"Couldn't we roughly make some up in the proper fabric, just four or five pieces? It'll give a much better idea what they'll look like."

"I *suppose* we could, but it seems mad having a show when we're still only halfway there."

Although I could see the problems, I quite liked the idea, and I was open to further persuasion.

"It'll be a laugh," said Latifa, gaining confidence from the absence of a blanket refusal. "And more important, it's the way to get the best out of the girls. It'll make them all feel part of the plan. Working here with your nose in the machine all day, you never get the chance to understand the big picture; you never even really see the whole garment you've just made. My dad was a right bolshie, and he used to go on about how people are alienated from the product of their labor, and that makes them hate their work. Not that he knew much about labor: he was on the dole most of the time. Well, anyway, this is a way of de-alienating the workers."

I was impressed with her argument; perhaps it could really help to pull the team together. And boy, did we need that.

"Okay, then," I said decisively. "But you'll have to be the model."

"Katie!" she said, clearly delighted. "I can't do that! I can't do the walk, you know, the *bum* thing!"

"I'll show you."

"I'll do it if you do it, too."

"Deal."

So four days later all twenty machinists, chattering

and giggling with expectancy, plus Kamil and Vicky, crammed into the showroom. Several of the women had brought in food, and spicy samosas, onion bhajis, and vegetable pakoras were passed around, to be washed down with sweet tea and cans of full-fat Coke. I noticed that some of the women had put on eye makeup and lipstick, which I hadn't seen before. Latifa brought in a ghetto blaster, and the urgent, breathless sound of Bhangra, a high-energy cross of Eastern and Western dance music, filled the air. Kamil went around joking with the girls, squeezing arms and patting knees in a slightly forced attempt at familiarity, but even that couldn't spoil the sense of fun.

"Like Versace in bloody Paris, damn right it is, eh?" he said to Pratima and Bina, who were standing together, carefully ignoring each other at point-blank range. Their eyes met for a second before they had to cover their mouths with their hands to hide their laughter. "Yeah, Versace, or maybe Christian Dior," he continued, pouting a little.

Latifa and I were watching through a crack in the door.

"Out you go, girl," I said, patting her bottom.

And out she went, dancing and skipping to the Bhangra beat, in the first of the print dresses. The women outside gasped and laughed and clapped. There were playful taunts and jokes in all of the factory languages. They were more respectful when I went out but still smiled and clapped in time to the music. I was careful about using only the longer dresses (particularly on Latifa) so as not to offend their sensibilities, but I think the holiday atmosphere would have excused almost anything short of full-blown nudity. It helped, of course, that we were all girls together, apart from Kamil, the palace eunuch.

So we took it in turns, helping each other in and out of the clothes and swigging from an illicit bottle of gin. Nothing was quite finished, and there were plenty of dangling threads and pinned hems, but that hardly mattered, and any defects were lost in the swirl and music and laughter. I let Latifa finish with a very rough approximation to the Diane von Furstenberg number (it was taking a long time to get it to fall in the right way, but you could tell that it was going to be something special), and even Vicky roused herself sufficiently to say, "Wow!"

At the end I made a little speech thanking them all for their efforts. I had to single out Vimla and Pratima for special praise, as they'd done most of the skilled work, but the others didn't seem to mind and clapped them enthusiastically, which made them both blush and look down at their feet. I could see that they were moved.

It seemed very quiet in the flat when I got home that night.

You're probably wondering about what I did when I wasn't working. In one way I can answer that by simply saying that I was never not working. Every waking second at least a part of my brain was worrying at a problem, eating silently into it, like bacteria on a tooth: the best way to stitch that panel or join that collar; the areas to skimp, the details to get right.

I did see Carol and Ursula one evening, but I couldn't talk to them about my life, and they didn't even seem that interested. What did they care of Kilburn? They wanted the old Katie, light, and bitchy, and silly; they wanted tales about famous designers, and models, and actresses. I

began one story about a beautiful actress, generally per-
ceived as sincere and "real," who was trying on dresses
in her suite at Claridge's. "It's no good," she squealed
(Milo, of course, swore he was there, and it wasn't
impossible), "I can't choose, I can't choose! I just look
so pretty in *all* of them." But then I saw their eyes,
and I realized I had told them the story before. For the
first time ever, our parting "must do this again soon"
sounded insincere.

Jonah took me out to the pub two or three times. Not,
I should stress, the Black Lamb, but to a quiet place in
St. John's Wood that made me think of Primrose Hill,
long ago and far away. He talked gently about philosophy and the way to find a meaning in life. He seemed
pleased about the developments at Ayyub's. It struck
him as all very camelish. He asked me if, now I was
"more stable, and a bit less, you know, crackers," I
wanted to talk things through with Liam. I thought
about it for a moment, but the answer was no. He had
saved his marriage at my expense, which, if one looked
at it with cool detachment, was an understandable thing
to do, even if he was a fucking lying rat. On balance I
really felt very little animosity.

Every couple of weeks I'd have a Ludo evening. I'd
take out the bag with the socks and pants, open a bottle
of wine, and take them both to bed, where I would weep
myself to sleep. Indulgent, I know, but cheaper and less
fattening than pizza.

So, summing up, my life had settled into a pattern of
intense and actually quite satisfying work, essentially
unrelieved by any kind of social activity at all (assuming
you discount my affair with the laundry bag). And it
was okay. Until I looked up and found that it was
Christmas.

*   *   *

I had always tried to be cynical about Christmas: the tawdry commercialism, the false emotions, the terrible telly. But somehow it always got me in the end. As soon as the Oxford Street lights went on, I would feel a little (say, two-espresso) thrill of elation. Christmas was always fun at work. The shops were busy, which kept the girls happy, and Penny insisted on decorations in the office and the studio, which somehow took the edge off the usual bitching and backbiting. If we'd had a good season, and often even if we hadn't, Penny would take everyone out for a posh dinner at San Lorenzo or Le Caprice. Hugh was always at his best at the Christmas dinner, flirting methodically with everyone from whichever new callow teenager we had in the shop to Dorothy, the seventy-five-year-old cleaner. Penny would make a speech, which, after beginning well with hearty thanks and congratulations to all present, would usually drift off into one of the familiar anecdotes involving proposals by show business luminaries of yesteryear.

It had to be different at Ayyub's. There wasn't the money for much in the way of festivity, even if there hadn't been religious sensitivities to take into account. I talked to Kamil about a bonus for the machinists, but he replied:

"Katie, you want us to go upmarket, I agree. You decide we must pay our ladies top rates for the job minimum wage, I agree. You want a production assistant, I agree. You say we must allow the ladies to be sick, I agree." (That last, incidentally, with astounding bad grace.) "But now you want a special payment for doing nothing, to mark a festival we don't celebrate. That, Katie, is going damn shit too far, too far."

The best I could do was persuade him to close an hour

early on Christmas Eve. As I was packing up, Latifa and two of the machinists came into the office.

"We've got you something," Latifa said shyly. "Something for Christmas. It was Vimla's idea. It isn't much." She pushed Vimla forward. "Here—" Vimla gave me a box, tied neatly with a pink ribbon.

"Can I open it now?"

Presents were, of course, what I always liked best about Christmas. Before our first together, Ludo had asked me what I wanted. I'd replied casually, "Oh, nothing, really, just a book or something cheap," and the idiot took it at face value. Now I can dissemble with the best of them, but even Ludo must have seen that the look on my face when I unwrapped *The Rise and Fall of the Great Powers* was not ecstatic joy. That was a lesson I made sure he learned.

But a gift from the girls? I was hugely touched, but also fearful.

"Yeah," said Latifa.

I unwrapped the box carefully, keen that they should see that I treated their gift with the proper reverence. I saw it. I gasped. My worst fears were confirmed. It was a hideous gewgaw, a knickknack. Of all things, an ornament. It was a little porcelain bird, a goldfinch, or bullfinch, or some finch. It served no purpose, it had no function. It was ugly and ill made. It could have been a metaphor for all of the things I had come to London to escape.

Yet even as my aesthetic sense recoiled, I felt my heart swell with emotion. These women, who hardly knew me and for whom I had done very little, had contributed out of their meager earnings to buy me this. I turned upon their expectant faces my best smile, and like the orgasms I used to fake for Ludo, the smile became real. I kissed the three of them, Latifa, Vimla, and Rahima. I then rushed into the machine room to throw a net of tearful thanks over the others.

It was the bullfinch that decided me on home. The idea of going back to East Grinstead had hovered in the back of my mind for a week. I hadn't spent a Christmas with Mum and Dad since I first came to London. But the idea of spending it alone by the telly with an individual Christmas pudding was hard to face. Both Jonah and Kamil had made separate offers, and each had been rejected as politely as I could.

So I went back to Kilburn that afternoon, packed a bag, took the tube to Victoria, and trundled through the suburbs of south London on the train to East Grinstead. For a moment, as we left behind the rows of terraced houses, I thought it had begun to snow, but it was only sleet against the window, and that soon turned to a heavy, black rain.

There were no cabs at the station, and I was drenched and freezing when I reached 139 Achilles Mount, aka Daisybank. Dad answered the door. He looked blankly at me for a couple of seconds. He was probably expecting carol singers, or vandals, or Jehovah's Witnesses, or anyone except for his own daughter.

"Katie," he said finally. "You'd better come in. Your mum'll be pleased."

I took off my coat and hung it in the hall. Mum appeared in the kitchen doorway. Dad put his hand on my shoulder, then wrapped his arms around me. Mum hovered, and I disengaged from Dad and squeezed her.

"How long are you here for?" she asked.

"Christmas. A few days. If that's okay?"

"It's lucky we got you a present," said Dad.

"For me? But how did you know?"

"Oh well, we always get you one, just in case."

And that year I got eight presents from my parents, one for each year I had been away, each retrieved from the back of the wardrobe, still in its wrapping. Each must have been agonized over, so close did they come to being right.

"How's that young chap of yours?" asked Dad on Christmas afternoon as Mum watched on quietly from the corner of the settee. "Seemed like a very nice, well-brought-up sort of fellow. Helped me fix the broken . . . the broken . . . whatever it was out in the shed."

It was a question I'd been dreading. They'd met Ludo once. I was worried about bringing him home to meet them, but Ludo insisted. I thought it would be a catastrophe, but in fact they all got along quite well. Dad took Ludo out to help him mend the whatever-it-was in his shed—Ludo was always good with machines and gadgets—and they came back laughing and joking like old friends. At the time, I held it as a black mark against Ludo. The old Katie, the mad Katie, as I now thought of her, didn't want a boyfriend who liked the ways of East Grinstead. She wanted a fellow Metropolitan sneerer. But now, looking back on Ludo's easy, down-to-earth charm and good manners, I saw it as yet another reason to love and to mourn him.

"I messed up, Dad."

"Oh. I'm sorry."

"You never know, Katie," said Mum, "he might come back."

"Yeah," I said to comfort them, "he might come back."

"Because you know your father once made a big mistake, and *he* thought he'd lost everything. But I forgave him, and I'm glad I did."

My dad turned and smiled at her and took her hand. What had been his sin? I wondered. Surely not another woman? But what else could it be? What else is it ever? Suddenly I saw Mum and Dad as real people caught up in the same passions and temptations as I was. I know it's not an original insight: *Ooh, look, the older generation are human, too!* But it hit me with the force of revelation, and Mum and Dad paradoxically came at the same time into a sharper and yet a softer focus: I saw them with greater clarity and yet more sympathy.

I won't pretend that I stopped finding my parents irritating. I suppose you *never* stop finding your parents irritating. But somehow the irritation coexisted with the love that I found I had neatly wrapped and stored away inside myself, at the back of some interior wardrobe. So my dad's way of suddenly continuing a sentence that he may have begun years before, to someone else entirely, or my mum's inability to watch the simplest film without repeatedly asking what was happening, or who was married to whom, or why that man had shot the other man, or stabbed him through the heart with his sword, or gone off in a hot-air balloon in the first place, still made me want to weep with exasperation, but they didn't make me want to run away, and they didn't make me ashamed.

CHAPTER 18

Strange Meetings

As the end of January approached, most of the samples were ready. The catwalk show had helped us to define more closely what we wanted to do. I was pleased with the results: one or two things hadn't quite worked and were discarded, and some ideas, although pretty, proved too time-consuming and costly to make. But on the whole our capsule collection was good. Not outstanding—headlines would not be made, no actress would wear KC at a premiere—but I was proud of what we'd done, and I was sure that it would sell.

Latifa had been brilliant, growing in confidence and stature by the hour, and the selected machinists had risen to the challenge of transforming quantity into quality, which Jonah described with a sad shake of the head as "very Hegelian." Even Kamil startled us by showing that he was not altogether useless at absolutely everything. I found that he was quite good at sourcing buttons and fripperies. More surprisingly, he actually had a respectable eye for line, and more than once I took his advice on the shape of a skirt or pair of trousers.

Things were going so well that I decided to treat myself to an afternoon at the sales: I felt my shoe situation was not all that it could be. The twin absences of a social life and rent meant that my finances were off the critical list, if still in intensive care.

And so it was that I was patrolling along South Molton Street when a voice called to me, a voice as soft and unsettling as a moth landing on a child's face.

"It *is* you, Katie, isn't it? It's been such a long, long time."

I turned around. Juliet. Mad, bad Juliet, Penny's half sister. Ludo used to go white at the very mention of her name. I'd sat next to her once at some family do, a wedding or funeral. She'd spent the whole meal murmuring appalling secrets into my ear about the other guests. Tales of incest, and theft, and murder. Penny hated her, and for once her excessive emotion was justified.

"Juliet, how nice."

"How lucky to have bumped into you. Why don't you let me buy you lunch? You look so thin." It was like being confronted by the weaving head of a cobra. I was mesmerized, paralyzed, and I could not think.

"That'd be lovely."

As ever, Juliet was dressed with the impossible precision and elegance of the utterly self-absorbed. She was wearing a high-buttoned Catherine Walker suit obviously chosen to match her emeralds. She was still beautiful in a repellent, Snow Queen kind of way, with huge dark eyes and cheekbones too sharp to be English, too delicate to be Slavic. Her skin had, with age, taken on the fascinating but creepy translucency of a fetus. Sitting opposite her a few minutes later in the Connaught, I was reminded of a slow-moving creature of the night I'd once seen in a documentary, a kind of lemur, called an aye-aye, which could turn its head almost all the way round and picked white grubs out of crevices with one enormously elongated finger. Like it, she radiated a timeless evil, somehow beyond the petty malice that infects most of us.

"So," she began after ordering a bottle of champagne and engaging in some initial rudimentary pleasantries, "you know how I have always felt you were a kindred spirit. And now I hear that my dear, dear sister has thrust you also from the bosom of the family. I know what it is like to be isolated, and rejected."

Her eyes lied eloquently of the indignities and cruelty inflicted upon her. Juliet had, according to Ludo, spent much of her youth in a lunatic asylum. She had emerged exquisite but damaged: a famous, fatal, beauty. She married a property developer who was intent only on a trophy wife and proceeded to cuckold him with his best friend, his brother, and his father. She left the marriage a wealthy woman, but a pariah.

"Well, you *could* say that I had it coming. You've heard about the circumstances."

She took my hand in her long, dry fingers. "My darling, do you not see that that is their way, to make you feel that it is all your fault? First they break you, and then they demand that you thank them for breaking you. You must not turn against yourself."

"Oh well, I'm not, really. Actually I've got something—"

"You must not turn your hatred on yourself," she stressed again, "but you must turn it against them. Yes, against them. And what you need is a weapon."

"A weapon? What sort of weapon?"

I knew that everything that Juliet ever said had a purpose. Time and experience had stripped away everything unnecessary or inefficient, leaving her as perfect as an arrowhead. She was not a maker of idle chat.

"Katie, what do you want from life?" Before I had a chance to reply in some general terms, she added, "Would you like to work again in some capacity, in some *higher* capacity, for Penny Moss?"

"That's not very likely, is it? Given, given . . . everything."

"I suppose when I spoke of a weapon, I meant a lever of some kind, a tool with which to . . . bargain."

"For heaven's sake, Juliet, what *are* you getting at?"

"Has my dear sister ever told you about her first work for the cinema?"

I tried to remember. Had she been one of the girls chasing John, Paul, George, and (bafflingly) Ringo in *Hard Day's Night*? Was her face caught for a moment, reflected in a mirror in that film where Mick Jagger fucks with James Fox's head? Was it some Visconti masterpiece? I thought I remembered Penny claiming all of these.

"She may have; I don't remember."

"I think it rather unlikely. You see, it was not the sort of film she would like the world to know about. You must remember that things were very difficult for Penny back in the sixties, after she emerged from RADA. The problem was that although she had certain . . . assets, she really was quite a *terrible* actress. And so the usual progression from regional repertory to West End wasn't on for her. Yes, those were difficult years. Which made her error of judgment perfectly understandable."

"What error of judgment?"

"*Albert and Clittoria*, I believe it was called."

I laughed incredulously. "Wait a minute, are you trying to tell me that Penny made a *porn* film?"

"Yes. Quite an advanced one, for its time. Very few of us know about it. I went with . . . well, that doesn't matter, but I went to see it at a specialist cinema club in Greek Street."

"But how did you know it was showing?"

"Oh, I didn't, but . . . my *friend* at the time wanted to take me to experience something *novel,* and then there she was . . . performing. I confronted her about it afterward, and she had to admit it. She swore me to secrecy, and I have kept the secret till this day."

Waiting for the right moment to detonate it, I thought.

"Look, Juliet, I really don't know why you're telling me this."

"Come on, Katie, you disappoint me. I mentioned before the weapon, the lever. A copy of *Albert and Clittoria* must still exist somewhere. These things don't just disappear. If you were to find it, then Penny would, I'm sure, grant you almost anything you were to ask."

The cunning old bitch, I thought. But I can't pretend I wasn't interested. Here was a ladder that could take me back to where I belonged. But blackmail was so ugly. Could I really stoop that low? Low enough to brush hands with the serpent Juliet? It was food for thought.

"Oh look, the bill," she said. "You must let *me*."

"Jonah?"

It was two days later, and Jonah had come round to fix the leaking skylight in the kitchen.

"Yeth?" He had a mouthful of screws.

"Have you ever had anything to do with . . . films?"

"What thort of . . ."

"Dirty films."

Jonah dropped his screwdriver and spat out the screws, *put put put.*

"For God's sake, Katie, you're not going to ask me to

get you into the porn industry, are you? I can't do that, it wouldn't be right. Okay, so the money's good while you're still young, but it doesn't last. And there's AIDS. You can do better than that."

"No, no, no, you misunderstand me. I meant haven't you got any contacts in . . . distributing the videos. I assumed that people like you . . . I mean people involved in the what-do-you-call-it, underworld, did things . . . like . . . that."

Jonah still looked wary. "I may know a man who knows a man. Why?"

"It's nothing sinister, it's just that there's a particular film, a classic, I suppose you could say, that I'd like to get hold of, for sentimental reasons. . . ."

We were almost there. The first appointment was scheduled for a Monday, in Winchester. We'd taken on Pat as our driver, on the understanding that he get a new anorak, fumigate his van, and park it well out of the buyers' eyeshot. By five o'clock on Friday there was just one sample left unfinished, but it was an important one, my showcase halter-neck wrap dress. I asked Vimla to come in to do it on the Saturday, and she didn't seem to mind, as long as she could sort out some child care. Latifa also volunteered to come in, mainly because she liked hanging around with me, but there were always little jobs I could find for her about the place. I, on the other hand, once I had opened up the office, had nothing much to do, albeit in a calm-before-the-storm kind of way. Bliss.

At nine o'clock Latifa appeared at the door, rolling her eyes.

"Katie, trouble."

"What is it?"

"It's Vimla. She called me at home this morning. Her child minder's run off with a man who delivers hot face towels to curry restaurants. She's got no one to look after the baby."

Shit. Vimla was the best seamstress we had, one of the best, in fact, that I had ever seen. Even if I could persuade one of the other women to come in to finish the job, it wouldn't be the same quality.

"Couldn't you go and baby-sit for her for a couple of hours?"

Latifa looked worried. "Yeah, if you want, but I'm a bit scared of kids. I always drop them, or leave them behind in shops, or give them the wrong stuff to eat."

I had an impulse.

"I'll tell you what, Latifa, I've got nothing much to do today. Why don't I leave you in charge, and I'll look after Vimla's baby for the morning. It shouldn't take her more than a couple of hours to finish the job."

Was it some sly squeak from my ovaries? Curiosity? Boredom? I don't know, but it proved fateful. I phoned Vimla, who seemed content, if baffled, by the arrangement. Then, standing up quickly, I somehow managed to overtip a full cup of cold, neglected coffee over my outfit.

"Fuck fuck fuck," I swore quietly to myself. "I said I'd be straight round. Do you think I've got time to nip home and change?"

"It's a bit tight, Katie. But if you're only baby-sitting, why not just put on something from the factory?"

I had a quick look in the machine room. I didn't want to risk wearing one of the samples, so it was a choice of hideous skirts and terrible tops.

"What about these?" said Latifa, smiling and holding up two pieces of malevolent pink nylon tracksuit.

"My God, do we still make those? I thought they'd been humanely killed."

"Just a couple left over. Go on, it'd be funny seeing you in this."

And she was right. The idea of it tickled me, well, pink. I put it on and Latifa emitted a high-pitched squeal of laughter. I joined in.

"Just let me do this," she said, taking a handful of my hair and tying it into a topnot with a glittery hairband she'd found on one of the tables. She bit her lip with glee. "There, perfect!"

What the hell? It might be amusing to wander around Kilburn in disguise. After all, haven't I always been a bit of an actress?

Vimla lived in a big council block not far from me in Kilburn. Even on a bright, fresh morning like this, it was a grim place. I walked around it for twenty minutes trying to find out how to get in, but it seemed that wherever I turned I'd meet a slab of concrete, or a wall of glass, or find myself suddenly deep in the stinking, dripping, subterranean car park. So I phoned up to her on my mobile and asked her to meet me in the street.

Vimla's baby, a little girl called Seema, had a scrunched-up face and a disconcertingly full head of hair, which made her look a little like some scary trophy in a rain-forest clearing, designed to ward off evil spirits or strangers. She was fast asleep.

"I know you'll be careful with my baby," Vimla said hopefully. "Here is bottle, here is nappy. Feed please in two hours."

"She'll be fine with me, I'm used to kids," I lied.

What on earth was I playing at? Scratch the squeak from the ovaries: I must have been insane. As soon as

Vimla got on the bus, Seema woke up and started to wail. Thank God it was sunny. There was a park just off the High Road. It was quite nicely kept, with tennis courts and a toddlers' play area, as well as wilder bits harboring drunks and worse. I don't know why, but I'd grown fond of it, and I often spent a half hour there reading a book or a magazine or just watching the elaborate courtship of the pigeons.

Walking the pram in the weak sunlight calmed the baby. She looked up at me with her black eyes, and I wondered what she saw. A high-flying fashion designer, friends in all the right places, beautiful flat, handsome and devoted partner? A single mum, scrimping on milk to pay for the smack? Or just a blur because little babies don't know how to focus?

"Katie!"

I looked up. A group of men, some sitting on a wall, others lolling on the ground, had turned to face me. Hard faces, some florid but scraped clean, some pale and stubbled. Hair—dirty white, nicotine yellow, greasy brown—went in all directions, like a turbulent current playing over a dying coral reef. They were clutching the usual drunk's assortment of aviation-grade lager, British sherry, Thunderbird wine, and cheap cider.

"Katie!" the voice repeated. "Don't tell me you've been snatching babies again."

It was Jonah. He seemed to be at the epicenter of the group. But what was he doing with the drunks? He may not have been a regular in the *Tatler* diary, but I'd assumed he moved in a slightly higher society than this. And then I saw the books. The reading group.

"Well, we can't all be beyond good and evil," I said back pertly, which was one of those remarks that sound funny at the time but turn out not to mean anything when you replay them later. Nevertheless he laughed, and the others joined in, raggedly.

"Come on over and meet the boys. We're discussing the point at which it becomes illogical to continue asking 'Why?' "

Unsavory though the members of Jonah's academy were, I had nothing much else to do, and I thought he might be offended if I turned down his offer while continuing to push my burden around the park. Anyway, wouldn't we all like to know the point at which it becomes illogical to continue asking "Why?" A place was made for me and the pram in what now took on the form of a rough circle around Jonah. They may have been drinking and scruffy, but at least they didn't smell, which said something. In fact, I'd noticed how the drunks of Kilburn always began the day looking spick-and-span, as though a team of devoted wives had got them ready for the day ahead, straightening ties, brushing jackets, pecking cheeks with a fond "Have a nice day at the office." The splattering vomit, the spray of blood and mucus, the growing stain at the crotch, all followed much later.

"We've all been there," Jonah was saying, "when some young brat keeps asking 'Why?' 'Why can't I have that bike?' 'Because I can't afford it,' you say. 'Why can't you afford it?' 'Because I haven't got the money.' 'Why haven't you got the money?' 'Because I haven't a job.' 'Why haven't you a job?' 'Because I hit the foreman.' 'Why did you hit the foreman?' 'Because I was drunk.' 'Why was you drunk?' And on it goes."

There was a general murmur of comprehension and agreement. Someone said, "Ah, the young pup, he'd be feelin' the back of my hand." Another added, "The price of bikes an' all."

"Well," continued Jonah, "there's a time when this same young buck asks why is it wrong to lie, or to steal, or to kill. And what do you say?"

"The church says they're all wrong. There's a Commandment for each of 'em, sure to Jesus Christ all-fecken'-mighty."

"Well, you might say that, but that's hardly a *philosophical* answer, is it? It's wrong because some book says it's wrong. And the young fella, now he can still say 'Why?'—'Why does the book say it's wrong?'—and there's nothing *illogical* in it."

"Ah, but the book's only the Word of God, is it not?"

"Fine, so you say that the Bible is correct because it is the Word of God. But what if God had said something different? What if the Commandment had been Thou *shalt* kill?"

"Why would he say that?"

"Why shouldn't he?"

"Because that would be wrong."

"Well, here's a development. You're saying God says what is right *because* it's right, not that whatever God says *is* right."

There was a long pause, followed by a few ahs and ohs, which may or may not have signaled understanding.

"And if that's what you're saying, we still aren't at the bottom of it, and our young hooligan can still ask 'Why?,' can't he, without being illogical."

Again, a murmur of consent.

"And the truth of it is, you *never* get to the bottom, you *never* reach a solid foundation. Someone might say that what is right is what promotes the general happiness. . . ."

"I'm all for that, give us some o' that," proclaimed a voice.

"And that might be a *philosophical* answer, after a fashion, because it's putting forward a theory, but the young hothead can still ask why should we promote the general happiness. . . ."

"A curse on his head, down with him, down with him!"

"No, not down with him, not if you're still thinking *philosophically*. The point I'm trying to make is that if you keep asking 'Why?,' you'll always just come up against someone saying 'Because I say so,' and that's no kind of an answer. What it means is that it benefits certain people for you to believe it. It's all like, it's like . . ."

"Fashion," *I* said, becoming bored with listening.

"Aye, like fashion. Go on, Katie."

"Well, I'm only a girlie and everything, among you wise men, but I do think that fashion is like that. Some things are mysteriously felt to be better than other things: long skirts or short skirts . . ."

"I'm all for the short skirts meself," leered a brown tooth.

"Or black or gray, or white, and sometimes there are reasons given—black's so practical, white looks good with a tan—but ultimately it's just because someone says so, and they say so because they want you to buy things that you don't really need. Thank God."

"Good contribution, Katie. And this is where my man Nietzsche comes in. He's the only one to say that all the stuff about morality is just talk, just lies. And when you see that, you can be liberated. Suddenly you're free from the shackles. And that's when you can start to make your own laws, become your own legislator. So with fashion, instead of looking at the magazines and wearing what you're told to wear, you invent your own costume, create your own wardrobe—"

"God save us from tie-dye," I said in an aside to the baby.

"In fact, you know, I'm sure, Nietzsche talks about fashion somewhere. Would you just hold this a minute while I look it up?"

Jonah held out to me a can of Carlsberg Special Brew, also known as Kilburn Perrier. I took it from him without thinking, and he reached down into a plastic carrier bag full of books.

And then, for the second time that morning, a voice cried out, "Katie!"

I turned away from the group and beheld there on the path two women, both young, both glamorous, both pure and glowing like angels in the cold bright sunshine.

Kookai and Kleavage.

"Ayesha, Sarenna, what are you doing here?" I seemed to have lost control over the tone of my voice, and it came out as a mad screech.

Ayesha, Kookai, answered, pointing in the opposite direction to the Kilburn High Road. "I live just up there, in West Hampstead. This is the nearest park. We were having a stroll. But what about you?" Then, looking at the pram, "I didn't realize . . . how . . . who . . . oh God, sorry." Kleavage, Sarenna, pinched her.

"No, this isn't mine," I said desperately. "I'm just looking after it."

I'd made a broad gesture with my arm, and I noticed that the two girls were staring at my hand. Not at my hand. At the can of lager. Which was foaming over, spilling onto my wrist.

"And I'm just holding this for my friend."

Another overly expansive gesture in the direction of Jonah. More spilled beer. He was still fishing about in the plastic bag, surrounded by the bums, who were jabbering and cackling. The girls looked toward them and quickly away. Kleavage whispered something in Kookai's ear. Kookai then said, "I'm sorry, Katie, we'd love to stay and chat, but I've got to go and meet . . . er, we've got to be . . . I have to pick up my dry cleaning. But give me a call. Let's have lunch, or supper, or . . . breakfast. That's if you eat breakfast."

And then they were going. "But wait, how's Tom and everything, and what about Milo?" I called after them, but the baby had started to scream, and then Jonah shouted out, "Got it! Here it is, page two hundred and six," and then the girls were gone.

Thinking about it later, I decided that Kookai and Kleavage had probably left to spare *me* embarrassment, although then and there it seemed like the bitchiest clawing I'd ever had. But who could blame them? Look at me, I thought, here with a screaming baby, wearing— Oh, Christ, I'd forgotten—*a pink tracksuit,* flailing about at ten o'clock in the morning with a can of super-strength lager, best friends with a gang of drunken old derelicts. And what would they do, what would *I* do, in the circumstances? Tell every living soul in the fashion universe about the decline and final fall of Katie Castle.

CHAPTER 19

A Winged Victory

Veronica's letter came a week later. It had been a good week, although not good enough to take the sting out of Saturday's humiliation. That would have required a substantial lottery win, the discovery that due to a computer error I was really five years younger than I thought, and the arrival of an offer from Armani that I simply *could not* refuse. Winchester had gone well. The buyer, who ran the shop with her sister, liked what she saw and showed just the right amount of skepticism about how we could do it for the price. What made things particularly sweet was what she said about Penny Moss.

"They've lost it, Katie," she confided over a coffee. "The collection's completely schizophrenic: it's split between the frumpy and the plain weird. It's as though half has been designed by Beatrix Potter and half by Damien Hirst."

Ha! I knew exactly why. Penny had divided the collection down the middle with that silly bitch Sukie. It was insanity. Penny and I had always worked together. Her conservatism had tempered my flair, made it commercial, and my zip and zing had kept her classics contemporary.

"I felt obliged to order one or two things," the buyer continued satisfyingly, "just for old times' sake, but I already have them penciled in for the sale."

The same sort of thing happened on Wednesday in Bath, on Thursday in Bristol, and on Friday in Sevenoaks. Penny was taking a beating, and I was filling the hole.

I recognized the lavender envelope from my stay in the Veronica household. How had she found me? Directory inquiries, I supposed. Even Veronica could manage that. I expected gloating, or more vitriol, and considered binning the letter unopened. But that would have required a stronger character than mine.

Veronica's handwriting had the overfed, rounded look that always seems to go with dull, diligent girls with greasy hair. At least it wasn't hard to read. This is what she wrote:

Dear Katie

Little did I think that I would ever again take up the pen and aim it at you. I thought that our time of intimacy had ended forever on that fateful day when I came in and caught you wrapped up with Roddy like two snakes in a pit. Except that he was a poor rabbit, or gerbil, and you were the snake with your coils around him and your fangs out.

But now I have heard about your sad plight from Ayesha, and I think I can forgive you. I know the baby can't be yours, but the very fact that you are working as a child minder and drinking in the morning means that you must have really fallen apart. I pity you, and pity drives out hate. And then I have received other information, which changes things. That is why I am writing now. I also thought you might want to know about what's happened to the world since you dropped out of it.

After you left I cried—yes, I cried all night and all day. My whole life was turned upside down. I had thought that you were the best friend that anyone could ever have, but then I saw you for what you are and I had to go back and look at everything that had happened to me all over again. And I saw at each point that you had hurt me, or done me down, or ruined things for me. It was like when the Russians went around smashing up the statues of Lenin and Stalin and Trotsky after communism, well, maybe not Trotsky, but the others, anyway. It was painful, but it was healthy. It was cathartic. Suddenly I was free and I could do what I wanted.

And then, the day you left, there was a phone call from Ayesha. She wanted you, but I told her what had happened and that you'd disappeared. Then she told me about poor Milo (who I never liked anyway), and said that she was desperate for a person to help in the office. And I knew that it was my chance. I said I could do it. I'd always got on with Ayesha, and she said she'd see about giving me a try.

So there I was, a week later, working in PR! The pain clinic people were upset about the short notice, but I said to them look, this is the first time I've ever done anything just for me and I think they understood. One of the women there who can sense auras said mine was all black and horrible, and that I needed to learn how to cleanse it by forgiving, but I wasn't ready then.

Ayesha looked at me on the day I started and then went off and found some clothes from the office and said I should put them on. She said not to worry because they did that to all the new people. They were a bit tight, but they still looked quite nice. And then she said I should get my hair cut, which I did. She told me where to go, and it cost fifty pounds, which is twenty-five pounds more than I've ever spent before. But I felt fantastic afterward, and all the girls in the office said I looked great.

I'm just trying to tell you that what you did to me turned out to be a blessing in disguise. Suddenly I had a new life. I felt like I'd shed my old skin. I didn't want to eat cakes anymore, and Ayesha encouraged me to take up smoking to help me lose weight, and although I still didn't like it, it made me feel better about myself.

The work was very easy. To begin with I just did filing and making coffee, but then I helped by being nice to people on the phone. I couldn't believe I was getting paid for it! In fact, I can't believe *anyone* gets paid for it. But things still hadn't finished getting better. Because out of the blue who should turn up but Ludo! He was back on leave from looking after the poor eagles on his island, and his friend Tom, who is going out with Ayesha, told him that I was working at Smack! and that you had stayed with me. He wanted to know how you were. He took me out to lunch. He was very depressed, both about his eagles, one of which was poorly, and about you, and life and everything. He couldn't believe how I'd changed. And I *had* changed. I had become beautiful, or at least pretty, and not just on the inside, and I had new friends. We had a really nice time, and I think I cheered him up. I told him all about you and Roddy, which made him laugh in a sardonic way. Or it might have been a bitter way, you can't always tell. At the end he held my hand and said he'd like to go out for a drink one evening and I said okay, then what about tomorrow, and he said yes. I couldn't believe I was being so decisive.

The next evening we went out for dinner at Browns. He began by talking about you, but I changed the subject to him. I don't think he'd been given the chance to talk about himself much for the past few years, and it all came gushing out. We had quite a lot to drink, him more than me. After the meal we went to the pub. He said he hadn't enjoyed himself so much in ages, and then he sort of passed out. Somehow I managed to get him into a taxi and took him back to his flat in Primrose Hill. He half woke up when we got there and asked me to come in. I helped him up to his bed, and as I was putting him in he grabbed hold of me and started to try to kiss me. I initially resisted, but then I thought why not. He was very mushy. I hadn't had a proper kiss since New Year's Eve three years ago, and that was in the dark and I didn't even know who it was. I didn't mind that he was too drunk to do anything else. He made up for that the next morning. There was great pain in Ludo's heart. He is the best, the kindest, the simplest soul in the world. He had all this love and goodness and nowhere for it to go. You had poisoned him, and the poison was still in his bloodstream, and I thought it was my job to suck it out. Also, it was time I had a bit of attention and love, too. I won't say that sleeping with Ludo didn't have other attractions. Yes, it enabled me to triumph over you! Yes, I was rid forever of my sense of inferiority and shame. Yes, I thought, I have beaten the great Katie Castle in the game of love!! I felt like the Winged Victory of Samothrace, my arms out, my wings back, my mantle flying in the breeze. But with a head, of course.

What makes a woman loved? It is never the kindest, or most generous of spirit, or the cleverest, or the funniest, or even those who are the joy bringers. Nor is it even the most beautiful. It is always the ones like you, the cruelest, the most selfish. You make people love you. That's what you exist for. You do it ruthlessly. It's a game. Perhaps men are drawn to evil. Is that why I loved you?

It lasted for a couple of weeks. I suppose deep inside I knew he would return to his eagles. Even deeper inside I knew that I was only a substitute. No, not for the eagles, but for you. I played at being you, which was why Ludo slept with me. I imagined I was you as we made love. By making love to me, I know he was really making love to you. But by making love to him, I was, in a way, also making love to you. He was in me, he had been in you, so I was in you and you were in me. But it was all lies. I couldn't live with the pretense. Because yes, Katie, he still loves you. And that is why I wrote to him a week ago telling him about Roddy's confession. You see, Roddy told Tracy that he was as much to blame as you for the incident in the bedroom. In fact, he said that you had tried to stop it, which again, I think shows his nobility of soul, although it's a bit late now. I don't know what it means about the other occasions with the Frenchman and the driver, but at least it clears you (partially) of one of the offenses.

So, what I am telling you is that a) I forgive you, and b) my life is now much better, thanks to you, but no thanks to you, and c) that I think you should go to him, and live with him on his island, looking after the eagles and breathing the clean air of the sea and the mountains.

I said I'd tell you about what had happened to all the people you used to know. I *can* tell you because people in PR hear everything that's ever happened to anybody. The big story is, obviously, Milo. He was in hospital for two weeks. And I think while he was there he had some kind of a religious experience. When he came out he told everyone that he didn't want to carry on as he had before. He wanted greater "spirituality." And the next thing we heard was that he had the contract to do the PR for the Dalai Lama and had flown out to India, which must have been painful, given his bottom.

Poor Pippin was caught after a few days on the run. He was disguised as a Smithfield meat porter. Apparently he was handed in to the police after one of the other porters caught him doing something strange to one of the carcasses. I've no idea what, but I heard Sarenna say she'd never eat another sausage as long as she lived. It was decided that Pippin wasn't fit to plead, and now he's in an asylum for the criminally insane. They have a little theater there, and he's allowed to put on plays and concerts and things, which is nice.

After Milo, the biggest news concerns poor Penny. Just last Monday Penny was working late, which apparently had never happened before, and she went down to the basement to look for some Fairy Liquid to wash her cup, which also, everyone said, had never happened before—you see, it was an incredible train of events. And then because she didn't know where to look, she opened the wrong closet and guess what? You never could. Hugh was in there with Sukie! Of course, Penny flew off the handle and grabbed poor

Sukie by the hair and literally threw her out of the building. Apparently there were scraps of hair and scalp all over the stairs. Hugh's staying at his club, and heaven knows what will happen next, but by all accounts Penny is a broken woman.

Oh, I forgot to say about Tom. Ayesha's found a place for him at Smack! as well. He's incredibly good with figures, and they've put him in charge of accounting, and collecting money from clients, which they didn't use to bother with in the old days. Tom says that one day soon *everyone* will work in PR, and I see what he means.

Well, that is the news. Sorry if it went on a bit. And you mustn't think that I'm trying to rub your nose in the fact that you're so out of touch. I'm beyond all that now. And although I don't know if I can ever fully trust you again, I like to think that perhaps one day we can laugh about everything that has happened.

I have enclosed a card for Alcoholics Anonymous.

I genuinely and sincerely wish you luck,

                                                            Veronica

On reading this gush I gave serious consideration to, in order,
        hysterical laughter,
            bitter laughter,
                tender laughter,
                    bitter tears,
                        hysterical tears,
                            tender tears.

In the end I settled for what I hoped was a wry smile, although it may have looked to an unbiased observer

more like the shell-shocked expression of a raw recruit
to the trenches after a six-day barrage. Too many reve-
lations, too much to take in. Ludo and Veronica! Veronica and *anyone* had the smack of absurdity about it,
but Veronica and *my* ex-boyfriend beggared belief. But
then the suggestion that Ludo still loved me. What could
I make of that? Was that what I wanted? Of course it
was. And Penny finding Hugh in the closet with Sukie! I
felt sorry for the old fellow, who'd always treated me de-
cently. Sukie must have been insane. What was she trying to achieve?

After a second reading my wry smile became a little
more convincing. Veronica's unexpected metamorphosis
from pain clinic caterpillar into PR butterfly seemed to
find an echo in the way the letter clunkily changed gear
from earnest moralizing to casual gossip. But it really
did seem that Veronica had come of age. I felt no regret
about her assertion of independence after the years of
colonial rule, and if the only way to achieve that independence was by sleeping with Ludo, well, that was
something I owed her. And if Ludo had to be screwing
anyone, I would have settled for Veronica rather than
someone cleverer and prettier than me. But that didn't
mean that it wasn't painful, and sick making, and bite-
the-pillow tragic.

My speculations about Ludo were accompanied by
another train of thought, one rather more practical; a
harsh critic might say opportunistic. Penny was clearly
in trouble. From what I had picked up from the buyers,
it had been a terrible season for the business. The Sukie
experiment had been a disaster; and now the Hugh
thing. The incident in the park had brought home to me
the fact that I could never willingly let go of my old life
to forge a new one in the parallel universe of Kilburn

and Willesden. The shame and frustration of that meeting had burned deep into my soul. I still wanted my life back, and now I had a chance—faint, perhaps, but a chance—to reclaim it. Sukie had left at the worst possible time of the year. The London Designer Show was only a month away, and there would be so much to do. Penny would never be able to cope on her own.

On impulse I called Hugh's club in St. James's Square. He'd popped out for a constitutional, so I left a message to say that I'd come round in the afternoon.

"Is that really you, Katie, you naughty girl?" he said rising from his favorite oxblood leather armchair.

It was the second time I'd been to the club, which had only recently allowed women into its dreary, musty rooms lined with bad paintings of forgotten Victorian luminaries. Unsurprisingly, few women had taken up the opportunity, and the bar was populated exclusively by beblazered septuagenarians, some rakish, some raffish, some catatonic. Not a place for a big night out with the girls. But they still served a mean gin and tonic.

"Not for the first time, Hugh, kettles and pots come to mind." It was a little hard, but I knew he could take it. "But how are you? I heard about Sukie. What on earth were you playing at?"

Hugh shook his head slowly. He was still a handsome man, but I didn't suppose it was his beauty that attracted Sukie.

"I fucked up, Katie. No two ways about it. Trouble is, at my age you become very easy to flatter. To be honest, I'm not entirely sure I've ever turned down the chance of a dalliance, given a woman of anything like reasonable looks. Not in my nature. My way has been to try to keep myself out of the path of temptation. It's why I've always spent so much time here. That and steering clear of

Penny, when she's on the rampage. So when that young fox started giving me the eye, there wasn't much I could do about it. I *did* try. Fought her off for a couple of months. But the flesh is weak. That was the first time, in the closet."

"But Sukie, Hugh, what was she doing? I don't mean to be rude, but . . ."

"Yes, I know, old enough to be her father. Thanks for rubbing it in. The truth is, I may have slightly talked up my role in the company. Painted myself as some sort of kingmaker. Silly vanity. But she swallowed it. Probably thought I'd oust my own wife to put her on the throne. Like the Franks of the Fourth Crusade, setting up a harlot on the patriarch's chair in Constantinople."

"Quite," I said, bemused. "Where is she now?"

"God knows. Lost interest, obviously, when she saw how the ground lay. But she'll land on her feet. Her sort always do."

Her sort, my sort, said an honest voice within.

"What about you and Penny? Do you want to go back to her?"

"Of course I do. Can't get by without the old girl."

"Will she have you back?"

"I always thought she would, but it's been a terrible blow to her, all this. And I don't think the business is going too well at the moment. So, you see, everything's gone a bit belly-up since you left. I spoke to one of the girls in the shop. It seems Penny's not what she was. Lost a lot of her, you know, Penny stuff. The balls. Always took life by the scruff of the neck. That's why I loved her. Still do, of course. Have me back? God, I hope so. I *am* an arse. But listen, I haven't asked anything about you. Heard some rumor about you shooting up heroin in broad daylight, keeping your needles hidden under a live baby. Couldn't see it myself."

I told him the tale of the last few months, played mainly for laughs to help cheer him up.

"Sounds like you've rallied pretty well. Always knew you would. Can't keep a good trooper down. What's next on the agendum?"

"Bit like you, really. I want Penny to take me back. Do you think she will?"

"Too close to call, Katie, that one. No harm in trying. Always worth having the odd carrot and, oblique or, stick up your sleeve, I find, when dealing with Penny."

"I'll bear that in mind."

There was one other thing I wanted to discuss.

"Have you heard much from Ludo?"

"Despair of that boy of mine. Came down from his aerie a while ago. Mooched about for a bit, then went back. My guess is he's still carrying a torch for you. I would, if I were him."

"But there doesn't seem to be much I can do about it, with five hundred miles between us."

"Well, he is on a mountain, after all. You could always make like Mohammed."

CHAPTER 20

Ending in a Colon

I allocated Sunday as a planning day. There were so many pieces that I had to fit together. I actually considered doing some sort of huge color-coded chart. But that would have meant going out to buy felt-tip pens, and the weather was foul. It would also have meant that I'd have turned into Veronica. In place of felt-tips, I had filter-tips, nine out of my pack of ten by two in the afternoon, and coffee: three pots, drunk down to the cold dregs.

Just as a strategy was beginning to form out of the general fug, the bell went. It was Jonah.

"I've something for you," he said mysteriously, through the intercom.

I let him into the flat. He had a small brown paper parcel.

"You remember, Katie, asking me for something."

It took a second or two before I realized what he was talking about.

"My God, the film!"

I hadn't thought about it since I'd asked Jonah if he could find it. I'd assumed it would be impossible to get hold of.

"This, Katie," he said, holding up the parcel in his

huge hands, "has caused me more grief than you can imagine. I've had to involve myself with some bad people, some very bad people." He was even graver than usual. "That industry attracts the worst sort of . . . businessman. It's very rare to find a world without some kind of ethical framework, however warped, some code of honor, some system of values. But here . . . only nihilism, emptiness."

"But nothing's wrong?" I was worried by his seriousness.

"Well, I have the film, or rather a video. As I'm sure you know, everything made before the eighties is on film rather than video. My contact managed to track down a print of *Albert and Clittoria,* as far as I know the only one ever made. But to be usable it had to be transferred onto video, and the film hadn't been properly conserved. It literally fell to pieces during the process."

"Oh," I said, almost relieved, "so it didn't work? The video's a blank?"

Penny's indiscretion was no longer part of my plans. I suppose it never *really* had been.

"No, no, here it is. This is now the only copy in the world. The original has gone forever. But things have become . . . complicated. You see, the truth is that after handing over the copy, my . . . er, associate asked himself why *I* was prepared to go to such lengths to find one old forgotten porn film when there was so much new, explicit stuff available. I suppose we're lucky that he isn't philosophically trained, or he might have begun to ask questions before."

"So what did you tell him?" I wasn't quite sure where this was leading, but I feared it was no place good.

"Well, I told him something about what was going on. That was a mistake. He refused to believe that my interest was . . . humanitarian, in that I was helping you. He thought there was some kind of scam, and he wants the video back, after you have used it for your own purpose. I think he means to use it to blackmail the . . . person involved. And he's not a man to be taken lightly. You see, porn and drugs go together in this city like Marx and Engels."

"But surely, Jonah, you can handle him?"

I had always thought of Jonah as possessing superhuman powers; I couldn't imagine him being afraid of anyone.

"Katie, I am one man, and not a young one. This other is a whole organization. And the younger people in business today . . . they have no boundaries. And no philosophy. Katie, they are capable of killing people who stand in their way."

Shit. This *definitely* wasn't part of the plan. If there was any blackmailing going on, then it ought to be done by me. Except that I wouldn't have. I suddenly felt out of my depth. I'd always known that Jonah moved in a dark and dangerous world, but somehow it had never seemed real to me. And now I was like a schoolgirl who plays with a Ouija board without believing any of it and then accidentally summons a genuine ghoul.

"But this is terrible, Jonah, what can we do?"

"We've no choice; we have to return the tape. Actions, Katie have consequences. Surely you've learned that much?"

A little bit of long overdue good fortune had seemed to put my fate back in my own hands; I'd achieved a kind of order, forced the world back within the bounds of reason. But now with this new complication chaos had been unleashed again. I closed my eyes and moaned. When I opened them again I found I was looking at my bookshelf. And at one end of the shelf was something that wasn't a book.

I'd swear you could hear the ping from the street outside.

It was like coming home starving, convinced you've nothing in the fridge, and then when you look you find a forgotten, lifesaving Marks & Spencer chicken pie, just on the right side of the sell-by date.

"Has this pornographer of yours seen the video?"

"No, not personally. The transfer was done by some technician. Why?"

"Oh, I have an idea."

After another week of successful touring, I told Kamil that I needed Friday afternoon off to attend to some private business. He was happy—the orders were rolling in, the factory purred like a stroked cat: he looked at himself and found that he had become a successful entrepreneur.

Latifa told me shyly that he had asked her out.

"What did you say?"

"Told him I'd let him know."

"What's holding you back?"

"Well, he is a bit of a tit, isn't he?"

"Yeah, but he's okay underneath."

"And the girls would really take the piss. I don't know if I could live with the embarrassment."

"Latifa, never let embarrassment stop you getting something you really want. And the great thing about boys is that if there's anything about them you don't like, you just change it."

"Mean a lot of work with Kamil."

*   *   *

I treated myself to a taxi into town. Yes, my first since, well, you remember. And I thought about tactics. I recalled Hugh once talking about the difference between strategy and tactics. "Strategy's how you win the war," he'd said with Churchillian grandeur and authority apropos of some minor fashion world skirmish over the cost of acetate linings, "tactics is how you win the battle."

My strategy was in place, but I hadn't worked out quite how to fight this last great battle. However reduced, Penny was sure to be a formidable opponent. Her weapons were powerful, most of all that blunderbuss of an ego. In a clash of wills could I be sure that mine was the stronger? Only, perhaps, if I used the supreme performance-enhancing drug: anger, burning cold and white. I played yet again through the memories of the last few months: the humiliations and disasters. My mind returned once more to that hideous interrogation by Penny and Hugh and little Cavafy. I felt my jaw tighten with rage. Good, good, but I made it stop because I knew how unattractive it made me look. I played back further and found endless other slights, spots of intensity in the sweeping pattern of manipulation. That feeble attempt to put me off Ludo in Paris; another time when she'd dropped hints about some wasting disease that would confine Ludo to a hospice within a year. A suggestion that he might be gay. All attempts to prize us apart. And soon I was there, smack in the zone, ready to take whatever Penny could throw at me; take it and then hit back. I searched for the right sort of image to fix in my mind and hit on a samurai warrior, wielding a glistening sword with murderous precision while making those peculiar getting-into-a-hot-bath sounds so characteristic of a Japanese on the rampage.

Walking down the narrow lane to the shop, I was assailed by a swarm of ghosts: spectral voices, images, memories. But I was here on business, and I shooed them away. The window was a mess: too many competing ideas. Three mannequins had been squeezed in, making it look like a bad morning on the tube. The colors clashed, and the angles were all wrong. It gave me toothache.

I didn't recognize any of the girls in the shop. As I opened the door, two of them leapt up and sprang toward me like lionesses. Wrong, all wrong. They shouldn't have been sitting in the first place, and they certainly shouldn't have signaled their desperation for a sale. Surely Sukie hadn't put them on commission? Before they had time to maul me, I said:

"I've an appointment with Penny. I'll go straight up; she's expecting me."

The girls lost interest as soon as it became clear I wasn't a customer. I was confident they wouldn't ring upstairs to check.

The studio was strangely inert. It should have been buzzing at this time of year. Tony and Mandy were both there, but it was dispiriting to see them sitting quietly, rather than hissing at each other. Even the machines seemed to have lost their happy buzz, wheezing and coughing now like asthmatics. I caught Tony's eye, and his face lit up with pleasure. Before he had the chance to shout, I put my finger to my lips and pointed heavenward. I mouthed, "See you later," and moved on up.

At first, as I emerged at the top of the ladder-steep stairs, I thought the office was empty. Gone the clatter of keyboards, the tinkle of coffee cups; banished the chatter, the giggling. And then I saw her. Not that I recognized her at first, as she gazed out of the window at the narrow band of heavy air allowed her by the London

skyline. Surely this frail lady could not be the fearsome
Penny Moss, the Boudicca of fashion? Penny's hair was
a vibrant red, dyed, of course, but all the more feisty for
being the product of an act of will rather than an accident of nature. But this woman's hair was sapped of life.
It was not that the roots were showing, but rather that
the color had simply given up, surrendered to the un-
stoppable advance of entropy. And that ashen, lined
skin—where was the plump vigor, the famous HRT-
enhanced luminosity? This lady stooped over the desk,
but Penny was finishing school straight. Only six months
before, I'd seen grown Italians hesitate before deciding
which of us to leer at as we walked down the street. It
must be a trap, I told myself. I adopted a cold, commercial tone.

"Penny?"

She turned, and the gray eyes struggled to focus.

"Who's that? Who's there, standing in the shadows?"

"It's me, Penny, Katie."

The eyes narrowed, and I saw the effort as she
wrenched herself back from whatever place of cold refuge
her mind had found.

"Katie, Katie. Is that really you?" The voice was melancholy. I thought, perhaps, that there may have been
some regret, even affection, in the tone. But then it
sharpened. "What have you come back for? Here to
gloat? Or to beg for your old job back?"

It was that feeble show of spirit that broke my resolve:
it so illuminated the change. I would have needed everything in my arsenal to cope with a full-strength Penny,
and a display of self-pity would have irritated me into
crushing her. But here was Penny, mortally wounded,
toothless, and yet still game. Hate and fear drained out
of me, and I discarded plans A and B, which required the

various degrees of coercion at my command. My samurai sheathed his sword and trudged off.

"No, not gloating, not begging. Just here to talk. I take it that Sukie's gone for good?"

"Don't mention that name to me. Of course she's gone. My biggest mistake in thirty years, trusting her."

"What about Hugh?"

"Hugh?"

"Hugh . . . going."

"Oh, well, I don't really blame him, men being what they are. He's in the doghouse for a while, but I expect I'll let him back in, sooner or later. He couldn't survive on his own any more than . . . well, what *did* you want?"

A little bit of the spark had returned: the first twitching of a patient coming round from the anesthetic.

"I've had some ideas. I've been working with a small-scale manufacturer, and I think there may be some scope for synergy."

I cringed a little at the corporate babble and made a mental note never to use that word again.

"Things haven't been too good, you know, this season," said Penny. "Even before Sukie left."

I wasn't sure if she'd taken in what I'd said.

"But you've got lots going for you. The name, the history . . . and me again, if you want me."

I didn't know I was going to say that until it came out. Penny looked for the first time fully into my eyes.

"You hurt Ludo very deeply, you know."

"I know. But it all would have blown over if you . . . if we'd been allowed to talk it through."

A smile touched the corners of her mouth. "Yes, I'm sure you could have talked him into believing anything."

It was a crucial moment. I thought about calling back the samurai, who was sulking in a corner. And then I, too, smiled.

"You know I love him?"

Penny nodded, and the moment of tension passed.

"What about this . . . synergy thing?" she said. "Is that one of those new fabrics?"

"Well, you know we always wanted to expand, but could never quite work out how?"

And so I made my proposal. I'd work again as Penny's assistant. We'd keep the classic Penny Moss look, but then also do a younger, diffusion range, designed by me and made by Kamil. Perhaps use the Kilburn shop as a sale outlet. It meant we could double our turnover without any real risks. I'd already sold the idea to Kamil, and he was keen on some form of partnership.

Penny looked interested, but also very weary.

"Oh, I don't know, Katie. It's not just the problems with Sukie and Hugh. You remember Kuyper, and the lease?"

"How could I forget?"

"Well, all that's blown up. He's far worse than he used to be, now I'm alone. He's been threatening me. He comes in and he shouts and waves his fists around, and I really think he's going to hit me. But I don't mind that so much as the cost of going to the courts. I know we're in the right, but if he sues us for the money he says we owe, it would tip us into bankruptcy. And without Hugh or anyone else here to help, I just don't know what to do."

An image of a hammer slowly materialized in my mind.

"That, Penny, is one problem that I can solve for you.

I have a friend. His business is to . . . help negotiate in situations like this. He has the proper tools."

"Really, Katie? Would you do that for me after everything? Do you really think we could work together again? I fear I, we, may have treated you . . . a little unkindly, back . . . you know. But we were a good team, weren't we?"

"A very good team. Look, Penny, I'll be completely frank with you. I think my plan is a sound one, and everyone can benefit. But I also want my old life back. I want to come and work here with you again."

"Is that all you want?"

Still shrewd!

"I think you know that more than anything I want Ludo back."

"You know he came home to London for awhile? But then he returned to his island. I don't know why. I don't think he's very happy up there in Muck or Mull. I would love it if he were here. I could forgive, forget almost anything. I imagine you have learnt your lesson?"

"I've learnt lots of lessons."

And so, without the need to bully or cajole, or wheedle, or beg, I was back. And if Penny never quite fully recovered her old ferocity, she did find something unexpected in the months ahead: a sort of grace. My plan worked well enough. Penny Moss might never take over the world; we're not Armani, not Prada, not Gucci; but we make a little money, and the people who know have even begun to call us chic. Jonah visited Kuyper, and our lease was renegotiated shortly after, on very favorable terms. Penny allowed Hugh back, cowed and compliant, but still with a twinkle in his eye and a tendency to pat bottoms.

But what about the video *Albert and Clittoria*? And what about my lovely lost Ludo?

A month or so after rejoining Penny, I said to her, in an innocent, just-making-conversation kind of way, "Penny, do you remember your first ever film role?"

"Like it was yesterday. It was a gentle, humorous little erotic movie, directed incognito by a rather famous Italian director. I can't tell you his name because he swore the entire cast to secrecy. Sadly, it seems to rather have disappeared."

I was surprised by her openness.

"So you aren't, you know, embarrassed or ashamed about it?"

"Embarrassed? God, no. I had a body to dream about in those days. I'd give anything to see it again. Might even put a bit of lead in old Hugh's pencil."

"Penny, I don't quite know how to tell you this, but I've got a copy of it on video."

"Katie, you're joking. How on earth?"

"It really is too complicated a story to tell. I was just sounding you out. I was going to destroy it, and it's the only copy. I didn't expect you to be so enthusiastic about it. Here, you can have it, it's in my bag."

"Did you watch it?"

"No, actually. I thought it would be too yucky."

And that was the truth.

But what about the nasty pornographic drug-dealing gangster? Didn't he want the video for his own wicked purposes? I'll have to rewind a bit to explain what happened. Remember Penny's colonic irrigation video, shot with the Vaseline'd lens? Well, that video had been on my desk when my things were swept into the box in the course of my expulsion from Eden. I found it, of course, when I properly unpacked everything in the Kilburn flat.

I stuck it on a shelf and more or less forgot about it—until, that is, Jonah's visit.

And as you've probably guessed, I switched the tapes.

I gave the irrigation tape to Jonah a week later, and he returned it to the pornographer.

"My associate," Jonah said to me next time he saw me, "he was a wee bit surprised when he saw the tape."

"Really? I never watched it. I decided not to use it in the end."

"Yes, he was a bit surprised, but not disappointed. There was nothing to identify any particular individual on the tape, so it was of no use for extortion or the like. But the content made it attractive to those with . . . certain tastes. He's had it copied in the thousands. It's gone all over the world."

So Penny's bottom acquired a celluloid celebrity that the rest of her had never quite achieved. I didn't have the heart to tell her.

And Ludo?

CHAPTER 21

And Ludo

"Where do I find eagles?"

"Eagles? What sorts of eagles? What do you want with eagles, anyway?"

The man from the Royal Society for the Protection of Birds wasn't being very helpful.

"What sort have you got?"

"Well, breeding, we have golden eagles and white-tailed sea eagles."

"The ones with white tails. Scottish ones. They're on an island. And it isn't the eagles I want, it's the man who's looking after them. He's my fiancé." I thought I'd better keep it simple.

The man sounded at least partially mollified. He was obviously cheered by the unexpected news that bird enthusiasts could have fiancées.

"We have to be careful, you know. Egg collectors. So your fiancé is one of our wardens, on the white-tailed sea eagle reintroduction program? What's his name?"

Ten minutes later I had the name of the island and rough instructions on how to get there. I phoned rail inquiries and a ferry company. I then packed a small case with the nearest approximations I could manage to sensible clothing.

My first setback came at Euston with the news that all of the very few proper sleeper cabins were taken. That ended my *Orient Express* fantasy, and I was left with the prospect of twelve hours in what was claimed to be a "comfortable recliner," squashed in between, I imagined, an incontinent, drunken Glaswegian docker with a seismic snore and a sickly undertaker from Slough, heading north to recover from the nervous condition that had so exacerbated his epilepsy.

In fact the carriage was virtually empty, with just two old boys quietly playing cards down at the other end. This was the holiday train to the Highlands and Islands, and who wants to go there in February? I guessed that the posh berths were all taken by stray business types on expenses, unwilling to risk spending a whole night in Glasgow for fear of deep-fried Mars bars.

As ever, there came the little flutter of excitement as the journey began. My seat, if looked on as such and not as a bed, was comfortable enough to begin with, and I settled in. A gaily, if cheaply, liveried ticket inspector came along and stayed for a flirt. He made me think of Penny's Argentinean undergeneral, long ago and far away. He cheerie-byed and came back ten minutes later with an appropriately tartan blanket.

"Ye'll be needin' this, miss; gets more than a wee bit cold later on."

Remembering how well tartan hides stains, I thanked him and put it on the next seat.

I spent five minutes rummaging for my book before I realized that I didn't have one. Perfect. Months of working like a demon with barely a moment to dip into something trashy, and now, with hours of free time ahead of me, I had nothing to take my mind off the potential pit-falls of the day to come, the most important of my life. I stared at the black windows, but they showed me nothing but a worried face and what looked as though it might be a wrinkle. Miraculously, after a while the trundling rhythm of the train, combined with the hypnotism of the passing darkness, and aided perhaps by the large gin and tonic I'd bought in the station, lullabied me to sleep.

I awoke with a start to half-light. I was freezing cold. My mouth felt like a slug had crawled in there and died. And yes, *there* was the trail, dried now and flaky, down my chin. I'd dreamt, of course, of Ludo. Nothing that shaped up as a narrative, just random images and the knowledge that we were together again. It was horribly poignant.

It was four o'clock in the morning, and I knew I'd slept all I was going to. Looking down the carriage, I saw that the two guys were still playing cards. After a cleanup in the loo, I went and said hello. They invited me to join them, and over the next two hours I lost almost three pounds at poker, which was quite good, as I knew no more about the mysterious rules at the end than I had at the beginning. The men, through accents thicker than porridge, said they made the journey twice a week, traveling on to Calais on the Eurostar. There they bought sackfuls of illicit rolling tobacco, which they sold cheaply in the pubs of Glasgow. It seemed like a strange way to make a living, but then so, at times, did fashion.

Glasgow came and went, and with it the two guys. More passengers joined: day-trippers in cagoules and waterproof trousers, ready for the worst. As the light improved I became aware that we were in faraway country. Suddenly there were mountains, real mountains, and long lakes glimmering darkly, full of monsters. Perhaps it would have been pretty if the sun had shone, but under the furious sky it just looked moody and unwelcoming.

I thought about the abominable Malheurbe. What had he said? His words were mixed up in my head with images of Penny wrestling with Art. But it was something along the lines that only with the invention of the concept of the sublime had nature become comprehensible, and then only as the "incomprehensible." Mmmm. Ah. Well, if any landscape anywhere in the world was sublime, then this must be it. So, did I comprehend it as the "incomprehensible"? No, not really. It wasn't that I didn't understand nature: I just didn't care about it very much. Nature is never witty, or silly, or sexy, or flirtatious, or drunk, or camp, or clever, or gossipy. It can't chat you up, or tell you a funny story, or take you to a smart new restaurant. And nothing ever happens there, apart from rain. Often it smells of poo. Going to look at countryside always struck me as a bizarre thing to want to do, weirder even than other eccentric pastimes like opera or bowling. And you can test it. The next time someone tells you in that smug way they have that they're "going to the country," just ask them, "Why?" They never have a proper answer. So, I thought as Nature hammed it up outside, you're wasting your time with me.

At Fort William I had to change to a local train for Mallaig. The scenery, in its ill-mannered way, continued to shout for attention, and I continued to ignore it. At Mallaig there was a dash to the harbor for the boat. I'd imagined something like a slightly smaller cross-Channel ferry, but it looked more like a fishing boat seeing out its retirement. It was certainly in need of a lick of paint, and I hoped the plug was in.

The lady at the ticket office had looked surprised when I asked for a return to Ludo's island. "But there's nothing there," she said in the singsong Highland way, "unless you're a geologist or biologist. And I have to say that you don't look like either." I supposed that was a compliment. "There's only the youth hostel, you know? Oh, and the campsite. But at least the day's bonny," she added, looking through the window at the thousand shades of gray in the sky.

She told me more about the island as she wrote out the ticket. It was always the poorest of the Hebrides, she said, and perhaps the only place where the crofters got up a petition *begging* for eviction. But not even the sheep that replaced them could turn a profit for the laird. The island was eventually sold to an English mill owner, who transformed it into a hunting estate, importing deer and building an endearingly mad castle. But in time the ferocious midges, and the rain, and the gloom dulled the blood lust, and now the island belonged to the nation and was devoted to scientific research.

The name of the island, the ticket lady told me, was Gaelic for "Devil's Turnip." She started telling me a story about some Highland trickster who had a wager with the devil about which of them could throw a turnip the farthest out into the sea. As usual with these stories, the trickster's soul was at stake. I got as far as the devil hurling his turnip out to sea, and the turnip becoming the island ("And as you can see," the lady said, pointing to a map on the wall behind her, "it does look a wee bit like a turnip"), and the trickster eating *his* turnip, when, mercifully, I had to run for the boat.

The ferry was surprisingly crowded with young people, all sensibly backpacked, waxed, and waterproofed. These were the student geologists, geographers, and biologists, shepherded by nervous lecturers. Reassuringly, they mostly conformed to the stereotype, and I killed the first half hour by counting pustules.

It took about that long for the seasickness to get to work. The sea was choppy rather than rough, but the little boat rolled and pitched like a member of Jonah's academy after an all-day tutorial, refreshments supplied. I'd never been on such a small boat before, so I had no inkling of the true horrors of seasickness. I lay across three of the hard seats, and tried to wedge myself in with my knees against the row in front. I was nauseated from the souls of my feet to my scalp. My head throbbed and pulsed; my mouth was at the same time dry and yet flowing with saliva; my ears rang.

Eventually I could take it no longer. I dived through the small metal door to the deck, found a safe place on the side, and added my contribution to the aquatic food chain. I felt a little better, and wiping my eyes, I found that I was next to an anorak who'd just done the same. She turned out to be a bucktoothed girl called Smitty, from Luxembourg, studying marine biology.

"We have no coast, no sea, no islands, and so we have to use yours, which are some of the best in the European Community. I am the only marine biologist in Luxembourg, which is lonely."

I made some polite conversation about fish, which I think she appreciated.

After a couple of hours of churning we approached the island, big and black and lumpy. A high-pitched voice screamed out, "Dolphins!" and everyone on deck rushed to one side of the boat. I wobbled after them, in time to see nothing at all. And then the same cry went up from the other side of the boat. Again the surge, and again I missed the spectacle. I began to think the whole thing had been cooked up by the geographers to get back at me for being more attractive than them. One last time I followed the shout, and there, miraculously, I saw them: four dark backs breaking the surface. I expected to feel elated, but it just looked ominous.

There was no decent harbor on the island, so an even tinier boat had to come out to meet us. The transfer was predictably hairy, and I had to be rescued from near catastrophe by an enormous German, who rewarded himself with a quick, furtive squeeze of my breast. We landed in a small village, perhaps twenty houses, with a pub, a small shop, and one or two utility buildings. The castle, which was really a rather undistinguished country house with a couple of crenellations, stood outside the village on a small hill. Its outbuildings housed the youth hostel, and the students trudged off, a little subdued and wobbly after the crossing.

I headed for the pub. Not because I was desperate for a drink, but because it seemed like a good place to begin my search for Ludo. The pub was a newish bungalow, devoid of charm. But it was warm inside, and a fire was burning. I went to the ladies' and dried my hair on the small towel I'd brought. My coat was heavy with sea and rainwater, and my feet were sodden. How could I have thought that loafers would be up to the job? I changed into dry socks, but I'd stupidly forgotten a change of footwear.

With dry hair and feet, I felt more myself. I asked the landlord for a coffee, and when he suggested a little something in it I smiled acceptance. I asked about Ludo.

"Oh, aye, the young fellow up on the mountain. Yes, he's in here most nights. Nice lad."

"How can I find him?"

"Well, you could just wait here for a few hours, and he'll come down to you. You're not really dressed for the mountain, are you?"

"No, I can't wait, I have to go to him. How can I get there?"

"If ye must go, ye must go. You take the coast path for maybe a couple of miles along the shore. Then you take the path up the mountain. You can't miss it. The young fellow'll either be in his hide—you ken, a wee hut?—or just sitting out, watching over his eagles."

The barman's wife had appeared.

"Och"—yes, I'm sorry, but she really did throw in a quick "och"—"James, you're not sending this wee girl up on the mountain dressed like that?"

"I'm not sending her anywhere, Jessie. She's a mind to go."

Jessie shook her head and disappeared. She came back five minutes later with some clothes. There was a heavy waterproof jacket, some matching trousers, and a pair of gum boots.

"See if these fit," she said, and then, reading my expression, "May not be Carnaby Street, but they'll keep ye dry."

It was my first time in wellies since I was a little girl. This wasn't part of the plan. I'd hoped to look unbearably pretty for Ludo. Instead I looked like one of the less fashionable geographers. I thought about waiting in the warm until Ludo came to me, but somehow it just didn't seem right. Here I was, making the first extravagant romantic gesture of my life, traveling to the ends of the earth to find my lost love, so I might as well see it through.

I thanked the landlord and his wife and set off, my heart singing and expectant. The rain had slowed to a fine drizzle pattering cheerfully on the hood of my waterproof. The path by the sea was firm and easy. On one side the shore sloped away, grinding into shingle where it met the waves. On the other the land rose impressively barren and forbidding. There were no trees, just a low scuffing of tussocky grass and gorse in between the rocks and boulders.

The Wellies were a size too big, but I was grateful for them when, after an hour of ungainly flapping, I forked upward to the mountain. There was still a sort of path, but it was boggy and slimy. I was soon sweating despite the cold rain. Luckily the mountain was more of a big hill, and the path wound in manageably gentle curves up along its side. I wasn't sure quite what I was looking for. Would Ludo be right at the top? I kept thinking I was near the summit, but each time another ridge would rise out of the mist.

After a further hour of struggling, I began to despair. My feet were blistered from slithering around inside the boots. Rain and sweat ran down the back of my neck. I was spattered with smelly bog muck. My early enthusiasm had faded, leaving just the naked will to go on. Questions nagged away: What if he doesn't want me? The promise of meeting him had kept me moving upward, but could I ever make it back if he rejected me? Was there a handy cliff from which I could dramatically hurl myself? Or should I lie down in the mist and let the bog close over me? Just how terrible was my hair looking?

I sat down on a rock. I'd bought a packet of crisps and some chocolate for emergencies, and this felt like an emergency. The snack did all the right kinds of things to my blood sugar and serotonin levels, and I plowed on. Another ridge and I passed through the layer of mist. I could see the village below and the gray sea beyond. I turned slowly around. Other islands rose from the sea, some low and green, some high and jagged. Were they also root vegetables chucked by easily duped devils?

I was almost at the top of the mountain. I kept forcing my exhausted legs to keep moving and dragging air into my aching lungs, although I was now sure that Ludo wasn't here at all, that I'd come up the wrong mountain or landed on the wrong island altogether. Perhaps it was the parsnip or the celeriac I wanted and not the turnip.

Then, just as my will to go on was collapsing, I saw him, standing stark against the skyline, not thirty feet away. He looked thinner than I remembered. Cheekbones had appeared. His hair was wild and curly, which always used to annoy me back in London but here seemed the only way for hair to be. I approached, panting and giddy with emotion. I stood by his side. He did not turn to me at first, but I knew that he knew I was here. Had he seen me labor up the mountain? The view from here was superb, with dark cliffs falling away to the crashing sea.

"Do you see?" he whispered, pointing to the sky. His words were whipped away by the wind, but I knew him well enough to lip-read. "It's the courtship flight. The male brings the female a tidbit of food, some scrap of carrion, and they pass it back and forth in the air. It builds trust."

All I could see were two uninteresting black smudges against the solid folds of gray.

"How touching," I said, carefully moderating the irony. I had decided only at the last second to go for low-key. I had to fight the overpowering urge to throw my arms around him, to beg for forgiveness and love.

Ludo half turned and quarter smiled. "You've come a long way."

"Miles."

"What made you come?"

"Nothing much else on this weekend."

Again he smiled.

"I got a letter from Veronica," he said.

"She's nuttier than ever."

"She was nice about you."

"See what I mean?"

"There was something about a baby in the park, and drinking beer with tramps. She was worried about you."

"I'll tell you the story sometime, it'll make you laugh. But it's very long."

"Is there a short version?"

"Mmm. It wasn't my baby; it wasn't my beer; they weren't my tramps."

For the first time Ludo turned fully toward me. "What about the van driver chap?"

"It was nothing. He was nothing. But I'm sorry I fucked up."

"Everyone's allowed to fuck up. You suit wellies."

"You suit the wilderness. You must love it here."

"I always *thought* I would. The dream of escape, leaving civilization behind, all the deceit, the pretense."

I looked at him closely. "I'd never want to take you away from this, you know."

"Can I tell you something, Katie?"

"Mmm."

"Something so secret you must never tell it to anyone, ever."

"Go on."

"You swear?"

"I swear."

"I'm bored. Bored out of my skull."

"What?"

"Bored, bored, bored. I mean, eagles, and deer, and arctic skuas, and shearwaters, and seals, and dolphins. All very nice. For the first couple of months. But I haven't had a decent conversation since London. Tom's been e-mailing me about the bright lights. I miss it, all of it. I even miss the traffic. I can't sleep here, it's so quiet."

"Why don't you come home?"

He looked at me again, his brow wrinkled with some complex mixture of amusement and vexation and tenderness.

"I can't leave the eagles . . . yet. Not until the eggs are hatched. They need me."

"I can wait, if you want me to."

"I have to tell you about Veronica."

"You don't have to tell me anything."

"No, I want to. We spent the night together."

"Yes, I know."

"You know?"

"She told me."

"What did she say?"

"That you'd taken her out, got drunk, went to bed."

"But nothing really happened."

"Nothing?"

"No, not really. Just a cuddle. I got a bit emotional. Very shamefaced in the morning."

"So you didn't have a two-week affair?"

"A two-week affair? God, no."

"So why did you want to tell me about it?"

"Oh, just for the sake of completeness. I didn't want anything hidden. I hate secrets."

"I wouldn't have minded, too much, you know, if you had had an affair with Veronica. I think I probably owed you both that much."

"Owed us an affair?"

"Owed you forgiveness."

"You *have* changed, haven't you, Katie?" I wasn't sure if it was a question or a statement.

"Living means changing. Can't stop it. If you mean am I nicer, kinder, wiser, I don't know. Maybe, a bit. If you mean have I stopped being vain and self-centered, and driven, and bitchy, and in love with fashion, then no, not really."

"I'm not sure I'd have you any other way."

"I'm not sure you'd have a choice."

"But there's something else. Can't quite put my finger on it. . . ."

I laid my head on his shoulder and put my arm carefully around his waist. Together we watched the eagles, brought closer now and clear against the gray. Tossed about on the high wind, they seemed at the same time the playthings of great forces beyond their control and yet shrewd masters of their destiny, charming the wind with subtle feathers and cunning flesh.

And as we watched, some words came into my head, words from another time. Words about innocence and forgetfulness, about a new beginning . . . and a yes, a sacred Yes.

I must have murmured "Yes" out loud, because Ludo touched my cheek gently with his fingers and looked closely into my eyes and said (and this time I knew it was a question):

"Yes?"

And of course, what else could I say but another, and a final, "Yes."

CHAPTER 22

The Eternal Recurrence

"Latifa."

"Yeah?"

"What have we done?"

"Twelve here, nine at Beeching Place."

I wasn't really listening. I had other things on my mind.

"Oh, good. Twenty-two."

Latifa rolled her eyes.

We were sitting round the new conference table. Me, Latifa, Frankie (who was taking notes earnestly, trying to look like a real PA), Penny (who'd come in specially, as this was a corporate policy and not a design meeting, and she did, after all, still own the company), and Mandy and Vimla, who were there in a startlingly innovative move to represent the shop floor. Kamil would have been there, but he was in hospital having some gallstones removed, a shared complaint that had brought him closer to Uncle Shirkuh. Ludo paced around, looking restless. Of course, he had a hefty financial stake in things, but he was there mainly to make tea and give me a lift home afterward. We'd spent ten minutes talking about trivia, dwelling longest, after a ten-minute digression on the frayed cord for the steam iron, on the need for a new air-conditioning unit or at least a window that opened in the studio. It was Penny who, with an ironic smile, complete with the carefully arched eyebrows I'd seen her practice so many times in the mirror of her compact, brought us to order.

"Isn't it time we discussed the offer?"

Somehow I found Penny's newfangled sweet reasonableness more irritating than her old battle-ax mode.

The offer.

It had come more or less out of the blue. It must have been the Stephanie Phylum-Crater Oscar dress that did it. A side-draped Grecian column in jade satin georgette. Shockingly classical, was the general verdict; outrageous in its conservatism. And yeah, it was pretty cool.

And boy, did the Germans need some cool. Their clothes had become stuffy and dull and invisible. They still did catwalk shows, but no one ever reported them, not even the *Draper's Record*. They offered ten million, which would make Penny a very wealthy pensioner. I was tied in for three years, with Latifa as my assistant. I could wave good-bye to all the production bullshit and simply *design*. Just what I'd always wanted, wasn't it?

Well, yes. But I also wanted to run my own company, to make the decisions that mattered. In the past few months, as Penny had faded into the background, I had really felt as though it were all falling into place. I'd done most of the designing, with Latifa's increasingly shrewd judgment to back me up. Penny was allowed to nod things through to give her the illusion that she still mattered, but the truth is that she didn't. I'd also begun to revamp the business from the bottom up. The shops were being restyled by Galatea Gisbourne in a sheventiesh dishco pashtiche with revolving glitter balls and flashing underfoot lighting. I'd started to reshape our wholesale side, cutting out the deadwood and targeting young new retailers.

If we sold out to the Germans, then everything would change. I'd never inherit the company; I'd always be a wage slave, however pampered and stroked. Ludo's advice was useless. "You have to follow your heart," he'd said, meaning, I suppose, that I should say no to the offer, but my heart was torn.

"I talked to Veronica," I said, playing for time. "She thinks it'll be hard to sell it to the editors, not to mention the buyers. We've always made such a play about being homegrown. All that classic English rose stuff. There's bound to be a backlash when it comes out that the Germans are behind us."

Yes, Veronica was doing our PR. The full story would take too long to tell now, but let's just say that her simpleminded lack of guile was universally mistaken for high cunning, and she'd become about the most sought-after PR in London. Just having her on the team got you the coverage. I had to send Ludo round to beg, and I soon lost count of the precise number of layers of irony it all involved.

"But that will be *their* problem, won't it, Katie."

"Well, their problem and my problem. I *will* still be here."

"But we won't, will we?" Mandy cut in. She was chewing gum, or possibly tobacco, as well as dragging intermittently on a foul cigarette. Her anger seemed to be directed at me, although I was the only person standing between her and the big drop. Penny hadn't wanted Mandy and Vimla there at all. It wasn't the way *she* used to run things.

"I did try to get guarantees for the machinists," continued Penny, staring vaguely into space. "But you know they wanted the brand and the design team, not the production and manufacturing side. Mandy, Vimla, you're professionals, experts. Good machinists are rare. You'll all find something else."

"Back to the sweatshop," said Latifa, speaking for Vimla, who nodded vigorously at the interjection. It was going to be hard for the girls at Kamil's. Not to mention Kamil himself. They were never going to be part of the deal. They needed me. And in some curious way, I felt that I needed them, too.

And I could stop it all. The Germans wanted me as well as the brand. They might pay something just for the name Penny Moss, but not ten million. Not enough to make it all worthwhile. But why should I stop it? It would mean joining the fashion elite. I'd get so much personal coverage. The cameras would flash. The parties; if not fame, then something only just short of fame. Should I, *could* I say no, just for the sake of being in control? Just for the sake of the Willesden team? For Vimla, and Roshni with her erratic fallopians, and the still feuding Pratima and Bina, and all the other girls who'd saved my life; for Kamil, now proud and modest rather than ashamed and boastful?

Word had, of course, leaked out. I'd already noticed the change: the good table that materialized out of nowhere at Nobu; the look merely of condescension rather than cold hatred from the assistant at *Voyage;* the unexpected phone call from the the *Daily Beast*'s fashion editor. "So nice to chat, Katie dear," she'd said, and I could hear the leathery skin scrape and creak as she'd pulled it into a smile. "Why don't we do a feature together? And, you know, there's always room for a column, if you ever decide to immortalize your fashion wisdom."

It was a long way from East Grinstead, but still I couldn't decide.

Ludo caught my eye for a second and did his little frowny smile. I looked away and found myself lost for a moment, a long, long moment, in the memory of two nights ago. He was urgent and eager, with a hungry, vulpine light in those soft eyes. This was the biggest change. I suppose it was loss, and the fear of loss; pain and redemption; the abyss turned inside out to become a mountain. Anyway, it was nice. Very, very nice.

And then I saw that they were all looking at me. I must have missed something. My eyes were watering from Mandy's cigarette, and I had to blink four times quickly. As I looked back at them they began to fade and with them faded the memories of Willesden and Kilburn and I saw the lights of a thousand cameras flashing in constellations and galaxies and I was walking past the crowd and I half turned and bent back my head in the way I know looks so pretty and gave them my special smile and now I was saying to Penny, who was the only one I could still see clearly, and I didn't know exactly what I was saying yes to, but she knew, I said Yes, I will, yes.

"I'm sorry, Katie," said Penny with something of the old hauteur, "did you *say* something? You're mumbling, girl."

"Say? What did I say?" I had no very clear idea of what I'd said or what I was going to say next. What came out was: "I said, fuck the Germans."

"Fuck the Germans?"

"Fuck the Germans."

Ludo was smiling at me. "Fuck the Germans," he said softly.

And we did.

SLAVE TO LOVE

Alice Duclos walked down a street so grand it made her feel like a child lost in a cathedral. The buildings themselves seemed to peer disapprovingly at her, arching their eyebrows haughtily at the presence of such an unfamiliar creature. Wherever she looked there were shop windows bearing diamonds, rubies, emeralds. Other windows were draped with elegant, sinister furs, some, she saw with a shudder, still in possession of their foxy little faces and shining eyes. The poised and exquisite mannequins gazing out from the fashion boutiques made her feel drab, despite the new suit that had cost more than her total clothing budget for the preceding four years. Her mother, Kitty, had found the money somehow—not out of generosity, because that wasn't Kitty's way, but because of the shame she would have felt had Alice gone to work wearing her usual ill-matched collection of garments, loose where they should cling, pinching where they should drape.

The men and women in the street all seemed so tall, so important, so confident, shining with the radiance of the rich. They all knew precisely where they were going and what to do when they got there.

For the fiftieth time Alice cursed herself for allowing this to happen. Things had seemed so clear and straightforward at university. She knew what she wanted from life, and she knew how to achieve it. But then Kitty had become increasingly eccentric, impossible, ill. Alice's dream of research, of islands, of science, had melted away, leaving only the need, for the time being at least, to look after Kitty, and that meant a job, a real job in the real world with real money.

She stubbed her toe on an uneven paving stone. "Drat!" she said, as she saw that she had forgotten to put on her new shoes. She was wearing a favorite old pair—brown, comfy, about as fashionable as cellulite. She blushed slightly, and blushed more because of the embarrassment of blushing in a place like this, a place where people didn't blush. She put her head down, allowing her thick dark hair to fall over her face, and hurried on.

She didn't notice the stares of the men that she passed, didn't begin to discern the complexity of the response she was getting. First the quick glance, poised on the brink of dismissal. Then a longer look as they approached. And then, after they had passed, the pause, eyes wide in something like wonder, something like joy. She did not notice the carpenter, perched high on his scaffolding, who raised his fingers to his lips, preparing a purely conventional wolf whistle, only to leave them suspended there as though eating a slice of invisible cake.

She arrived. Seven steps up to a door high and wide enough to admit a knight on horseback. This was not just a new job for Alice; it was her first proper job, and the fear and excitement tingled like acid rain on her skin.

"Books," she said, to the cruel-looking woman at reception. "The Books Department. I've come . . . I have a job."

"How nice," said the woman, a Snow Queen in exile, forced to earn her living. "Second floor. There's a lift."

"I know," said Alice, and took the stairs.

Again she asked herself, as she trudged up a wide staircase designed, it seemed, for a Hollywood musical, what she was doing here. And for the first time another question rose into her consciousness, one linked to the first and yet more resonant: Who am I?

It was a question that was to be answered, at least in part, that very morning by Mr. Crumlish, whom Alice was destined never to call by his first name, Garnett.

Mr. Crumlish was then still part of the ill-defined stratum of middle managers within Books or, to use the full title, Books, Manuscripts, and Other Printed Matter. Books was the smallest department in Enderby's, the fifth-biggest auction house in London, which is quite as unimpressive as it sounds. The office building, an ornate Florentine palazzo, complete with dirty windows and spluttering drains and a grand statue of its founder, the buccaneering Mungo Enderby (1772–1861) in half-armor, was the one relic of the glory days, back in the 1920s, when Enderby's was briefly acknowledged as one of the Big Three. But then came the scandals: the famous fraud case, the fake Canaletto, the 1949 public indecency charge against Ashley Enderby. And so eventually the Americans had come, or rather the Americans who ran the business for the Japanese bank that bought, at bargain basement rates, 51 percent of Enderby's. Ashley Enderby had died without issue, alone in Marrakech, befuddled with intoxicants, and the family share had gone to the Brooksbanks, obscurely related by marriage. The Brooksbanks, whose interests were principally rural, were content for the Americans and Japanese to make decisions while they drew off what they could in the form of profit and prestige. Only one Brooksbank, Parry, was still involved in any practical sense in running the company, and he only in the way that the froth is technically still part of the beer. But he was, at least, a link of sorts with the past.

It fell to Mr. Crumlish to show Alice "the ropes," a phrase he used with such relish she assumed he felt it to be an expression of thrilling vulgarity.

"You see, if we leave aside dear dear Spammy over there"— at this point Crumlish toodled with his fingertips over to where Pamela, the office drudge, was arranging paper clips; in response Pam burst into gales of girlish laughter, which set off curious seismic events in the various pendulous and drooping zones of her body: a small tremor about her middle, a major quake in the jowls, a volcanic eruption of spittle at the lips, and a devastating bust tsunami—"everybody here is either a Toff or a Tart or a Swot. Oh. Are you allowed three *either*s? I can't remember. Anyway, *I*, of course, am a Toff. We don't know very much, but the gentry *do* like one of their own to deal with. Not perhaps when it comes to going on a *rummage;* then they seem to prefer it if you act like staff, and you think yourself lucky if cook gives you a chipped mug in the kitchen. But when they bring in one of their gewgaws for a valuation, they appreciate the rich and heady aroma of old money."

Alice was clearly supposed to be shocked by Mr. Crumlish's performance. But she noticed that the people in the office, the twenty or so men and women arranged in clumps about the room, paid him no attention, despite the arch and actorly projection of his voice. She assumed they had heard it all before, perhaps received the same initiation themselves.

"Ophelia," continued Mr. Crumlish, "is, as you can see, a Tart. Pretty, pretty, pretty."

With each *pretty,* Mr. Crumlish twitched the hem of his pin-striped suit jacket, flashing the vivid lilac lining.

Alice glanced quickly in the direction that Mr. Crumlish had flicked his thin wrist and saw a young woman of astonishing, languorous beauty playing idly with her long black hair. She seemed to have nothing else to do. Alice instantly felt shabby. Her own long hair was cheaply cut, underconditioned, and prone to acts of reckless rebellion; her shoes were scuffed; the new suit now seemed so wrong.

"The Tarts," continued Mr. Crumlish, breaking the spell that Ophelia's beauty had cast over Alice, "tend not to know very much either, but they *are* easy on the eye, and it's so much cheaper than getting the decorators in. Anyway, what else would they do with their History of Art degrees? The Swots, on the contrary, know everything; not everything about *everything,* but everything about *something.* Couldn't do without the Swots. *Could* do without the smell."

"The smell?" Alice was mystified.

"You know, the stale, composty, damp-tweed aroma, combined with the smell of a shirt worn for a *second* or even *third* day, mixed finally with the faint sweet tang of distressingly recent onanism. I present to you Mr. Cedric Clerihew." He pronounced Cedric *seed-rick,* which Alice hadn't heard before. She had no way of knowing if Crumlish was being amusing. Clerihew certainly wasn't going to put her right. He was a small round person and, like many small round people, his age was difficult to estimate, but certainly above twenty and below forty. He was very neatly dressed, almost like a boy receiving his first Holy Communion. He smiled and sweated toward Alice, but Crumlish swept her on and away before he had the chance to speak to her or reach out with his little hands, the fingers of which looked a knuckle shorter than the usual complement.

"Poor boy," said Crumlish, this time in a voice that only Alice could hear. "One day he might, by pure good fortune, stumble upon the right posterior, but until that happy time he licks in vain."

Alice giggled too loudly, hiding her wide mouth behind her hand. A couple of faces turned, Ophelia's among them. She performed what must have been a very deliberate up-and-down look of dismissal. Anyone who cared to glance toward Clerihew would have seen him staring intently at his desk, his face red, his mouth set hard. Mr. Crumlish, pleased with the response, moved Alice on through the large book-splattered room.

"But you, Alice, what are *you*? Not, obviously, one of the Tarts. I'm afraid your degree—what was it? Of course, *zoology* of all things—suggests that. Not to mention your commendable lack of vanity."

As was perhaps intended, Alice took the statement that she lacked vanity as a hint that she ought to rectify the deficit.

"Nor, despite your name, which, between the two of us I don't *entirely* believe, do you appear to be one of us—I mean a Toff. That only leaves the Swots. And, my dear Alice, you really are far too fragrant to be a Swot. I fear you may be sui generis, which is frightfully inconvenient for the . . . oh, what is the word? A putting-things-into-classes person?"

"A taxonomist. Was that a test, Mr. Crumlish?"

All this while they had been winding their way between the desks, each carrying its burden of computer and heavy reference books. In the far corner they finally came to two facing desks with a low partition between them. One was free and the other occupied by a young man who might have been handsome had the frown lines been etched a little less deeply.

"Oh," said Mr. Crumlish, "I've got it all wrong. There's a fourth category. As well as the Tarts and the Toffs and the Swots, we've recently acquired our first Oik. And look, he's to be your intimate desk chum. How affecting. Alice, meet Andrew Heathley. I suspect his *mates* call him Andy. Andrew, this is Alice Sui Generis. Be gentle with her."